THE WINGED DEMON

Swooping like a striking hawk, the winged devil plunged toward the beach and slew a bowman as he nocked an arrow. Conan, with a roar of rage, rushed to meet it, his cutlass flashing in the morning sun. He aimed a blow that should have cloven the creature's skull in twain. The blade snapped near the hilt, and only a small cut gaped in the creature's flesh. Then Conan knew that he had struck no ordinary skull, but one of strange and sinister destiny . . .

The grinning monster, ignoring Conan's hammerlike blows, closed in. Down came the taloned feet toward Conan's chest. With superhuman strength, the winged demon ripped the Cimmerian's leather jerkin, gashed his arms and tore an opening in his scalp, streaking his face with crimson. Half-blinded by his blood, Conan fought on . . .

CONAN
THE SWORDSMAN

CONAN
THE SWORDSMAN

BY L. SPRAGUE DE CAMP,
LIN CARTER, AND BJÖRN NYBERG

Illustrated by Tim Kirk

BANTAM BOOKS
TORONTO · NEW YORK · LONDON

CONAN THE SWORSDMAN
A Bantam Book/August 1978

ISBN 0-553-12018-2

Published simultaneously in the United States and Canada

PRINTED IN THE UNITED STATES OF AMERICA

ACKNOWLEDGMENTS

The story "People of the Summit" is a rewritten version of a story of the same title, by Björn Nyberg, in *The Mighty Swordsmen* (N.Y.: Lancer Books, 1970), copyright © 1970 by Hans Stefan Santesson.

The article "Hyborian Names" is expanded from the following articles by L. Sprague de Camp: "An Exegesis of Howard's Hyborian Tales" in *Amra*, II, 4, 5, & 6, copyright © 1959 by L. Sprague de Camp; "Addenda to the Exegesis" in *Amra*, II, 6, copyright © 1959 by George H. Scithers; "Exegetical Addenda" in *Amra*, II, 9, copyright © 1960 by G. H. Scithers; "Addenda to the Exegesis" in *Amra*, II, 40, copyright © 1966 by the Terminus, Owlswick, & Ft Mudge Electrick Street Railway Gazette; "Superaddendum to the Exegesis" in *Amra*, II, 45, copyright © 1967 by L. Sprague de Camp; "An Exegesis of Howard's Hyborian Tales" in *The Conan Reader* (Baltimore: Mirage Press, 1968), copyright © 1968 by L. Sprague de Camp; and "An Exegesis of Names Discarded by REH" in *Amra*, II, 51, copyright © 1969 by L. Sprague de Camp.

All the other materials in this volume are published here for the first time.

CONTENTS

THE CONAN SAGA

How would you like to go to a world where men are mighty, women are beautiful, problems are simple, and life is adventurous? Where gleaming cities raise their shining spires against the stars; sorcerers cast sinister spells from subterranean lairs; baleful spirits stalk crumbling ruins of hoary antiquity; primeval monsters crash through jungle thickets; and the fate of kingdoms is balanced on the bloody blades of broadswords brandished by heroes of preternatural might and valor? And where nobody so much as mentions the income tax or the school-dropout problem or atmospheric pollution?

This is the world of heroic fantasy; or, as some prefer to call it, swordplay-and-sorcery fiction. We apply the name "heroic fantasy" to stories laid in an imaginary, pre-industrial world—in the remote past, the remote future, another planet, or another dimension—where magic works, machinery has not been invented, and gods, demons, and other supernatural beings are real and portentous presences.

Fiction of this genre is pure entertainment. It is not intended to solve current social and economic problems; it has nothing to say about the faults of the foreign-aid program, or the woes of disadvantaged ethnics, or socialized medicine, or inflation. It is escape fiction of the purest kind, in which the reader escapes clear out of the real world. And why not? As J. R. R. Tolkien once said, a man in prison is not required to think of nothing but bars and cells and jailers.

The stories in this saga feature one of the most popular characters of heroic fantasy ever invented.

This is Conan the Cimmerian, the gigantic, invincible, swashbuckling prehistoric adventurer. Conan was conceived in 1932 by Robert Ervin Howard (1906–36) of Cross Plains, Texas. Robert E. Howard was a leading author of adventure fiction for the pulp magazines, which flourished in the 1920s and 1930s, dwindled away during the paper shortage of the Second World War, and were replaced in popular reading after that war by the paperbacked book.

Howard wrote not only fantasies but also science fiction, Western, sport, detective, historical, and oriental stories. After an early struggle to establish himself, he attained a fair degree of success, earning what was in the Depression days of the early 1930s a respectable income. He had a few close friends in west-central Texas—none of whom cared for his stories—and a growing circle of admiring correspondents, including leading fantasists of the time like H. P. Lovecraft, Clark Ashton Smith, and August Derleth. Although a big, powerful man like his heroes, Howard had his private demons, including an excessive devotion to and dependence upon his mother. In 1936, when his aged mother lay dying, he ended a promising literary career by suicide.

Howard's stories, although not without fault, are distinguished by strong plots, a sound, taut, economical, colorful, vivid style, a marvelous sense of pace and action, and most of all by a singular emotional intensity, which sweeps the reader along. As his pen pal Lovecraft wrote in a letter to E. Hoffmann Price, "the real secret is that he himself is in every one of [his stories]." Rudyard Kipling, Jack London, Harold Lamb, Talbot Mundy, Arthur D. Howden Smith, and Sax Rohmer all influenced him, but Howard achieved his own unique synthesis.

Like most of Howard's stories, the tales of the Conan saga are somber in tone, with a keen sense of the inevitable tragedy of life and the harshness of existence in the medieval and ancient worlds. There is only a rare gleam of humor. Nevertheless, Howard was by no means humorless. He wrote many boxing and Western stories full of broad, slapstick, frontier humor, often hilarious. Even at his pulpiest, Howard is always fun to read. The term "natural storyteller" applies to Howard as strongly as it does to any writer, ancient or modern.

Howard wrote several fantasy series, most of which appeared in the magazine *Weird Tales*, which began publication in 1923. Of these series, the most popular by far have been those about Conan the Cimmerian. They have been printed and reprinted, in this and in at least seven foreign countries, long after the death of the original author and the demise of the magazine in which they were first published.

Howard was the leading American pioneer in heroic fantasy. Fiction of this kind was introduced in the 1880s by the British artist, writer, reformer, decorator, poet, manufacturer, and printer William Morris. In the early twentieth century, it was further developed by Lord Dunsany and Eric R. Eddison and, later, by J. R. R. Tolkien (*The Lord of the Rings*) and T. H. White (*The Once and Future King*). Besides Robert E. Howard, leading American practitioners of the genre include Clark Ashton Smith, Catherine L. Moore, and Fritz Leiber.

With the end of the magazines *Unknown Worlds* in 1943 and *Weird Tales* in 1954, it looked for a while as if fantasy had become a casualty of the machine age. In the 1950s, publication in hard covers of Tolkien's three-volume novel *The Lord of the Rings* and the reprinting of the Conan stories began a modest revival. With the appearance both of the Tolkien and of the Howard stories in paperback came a tremendous upsurge of interest in fantasy. Millions of copies of both series have been sold, and other writers have composed fantastic tales obviously influenced by these two authors.

* * *

3

I became involved in this blooming of heroic fantasy in 1951, when I discovered a pile of unsold Howard manuscripts in the closet of a literary agent in New York. These included two unpublished Conan stories, one story originally written as a Conan story but actually published in a fan magazine with the hero's name changed, and several adventure stories with medieval and modern settings. By arrangement with the heirs of Robert E. Howard, I edited the rejected Conan stories and arranged for their publication. Later I rewrote four of the medieval and modern stories to turn them into Conan stories. I also collaborated with a Swedish fan, Björn Nyberg, on a novel, *The Return of Conan*.

A few years later, I was fortunate in being able to arrange for publication of the whole Conan saga in paperback, putting all the then-existing Conan stories in chronological order. More unpublished stories were discovered by Glenn Lord, agent for the Howard heirs. One was complete; the rest were fragments or synopses only. My colleagues Lin Carter, Björn Nyberg, and I have completed those unfinished Conan stories and, to fill the gaps in the saga, have written several Conan stories of our own, following the hints in Howard's letters and original stories. We have tried to copy Howard's style and type of plotting. How successful we have been in this endeavor, the reader must judge. Since the demand for Conan stories has become greater than Carter, Nyberg, and I could fill, other contemporary writers have also been enlisted to try their hands at Howard pastiches.

The first hint of the Conan stories came in a series of tales that Howard wrote in 1929, laid in the time of the supposed lost continent of Atlantis. His hero was a Stone Age Atlantean named Kull, who gets to the mainland, becomes a soldier in the civilized kingdom of Valusia, and rises to be king of that land. Howard wrote—or at least began—thirteen Kull stories but sold only three. One of these brought Kull by magical time travel to the historical era and involved him with another of Howard's heroes, the Pictish chieftain Bran Mak Morn of Roman times. Three Kull stories, left unfinished, were later completed by Lin Carter.

Since the Kull stories enjoyed only meager success, Howard put the idea aside. In 1931, however, Howard read a series of articles by a French writer on the Atlantis legend and was stimulated to try again his basic concept of a prehistoric adventure-fantasy world, this time in a more polished and carefully thought-out form. His hero would be named Conan, an old Celtic name borne by, among others, several dukes of medieval Brittany. Conan, Howard said, "simply grew up in my mind a few years ago when I was stopping in a little border town on the lower Rio Grande. . . . He simply stalked full grown out of oblivion and set me at work recording the saga of his adventures. . . . Some mechanism in my sub-consciousness took the dominant characteristics of various prize-fighters, gunmen, bootleggers, oil field bullies, gamblers, and honest workmen I have come in contact with, and combining them all, produced the amalgamation I call Conan the Cimmerian."

As a stage for Conan to stride across, Howard devised a Hyborian Age, about twelve thousand years ago, between the sinking of the Atlantis and the beginnings of recorded history. This period, Howard supposed, was one in which magic was rife and supernatural beings walked the earth. The records of this civilization were lost, save for myths and legends, as a result of barbarian invasions and natural catastrophes. Howard worked out a detailed fictional "history" of this Hyborian Age, covering several thousand years. In the midst of this time, Conan lived, loved, wandered, and battled his way to kingship.

Howard made it plain that this pseudo-history was invented for storytelling purposes and was not to be considered a serious theory of human prehistory. Howard had read widely in history and said he enjoyed writing historical fiction. It is sad that he did not survive to the 1950s, when such fiction was at the peak of its popularity.

Conan (Howard assumed) was a native of the bleak and barbarous northern land of Cimmeria. The Cimmerians he supposed to have been the ancestors of the historical Celts. Still further north lay the subarctic lands of Vanaheim, Asgard, and Hyperborea. Adventuring with a band of Æsir from Asgard on a raid into Hyperborea, Conan was captured and imprisoned. Escaping, he made his way southward to the land of Zamora, east of the Hyborian nations. These nations—Aquilonia, Nemedia, Corinthia, Ophir, and Koth—had arisen after the Hyborians, another group of northern barbarians, had conquered the sorcerous kingdom of Acheron and built up their own kingdoms on its ruins, three thousand years before Conan's time.

In Zamora, Corinthia, and Nemedia, Conan led a precarious life as a thief, more notable for strength and daring than for skill and subtlety. Becoming weary of this starveling existence, he enlisted in the armies of Turan. This kingdom lay east of Zamora, along the western shores of the great inland Sea of Vilayet, whose shrunken remnants we today call the Caspian. The Turanians were one of the nomadic peoples of Hyrkania, which began east of the sea and stretched for thousands of miles to far Khitai. Hyrkania corresponded to the steppes and deserts of Central Asia today.

As a soldier of Turan, Conan learned horsemanship and archery and rose to commissioned rank. Trouble with a superior caused him to desert. After some unsuccessful treasure hunting, he wandered westward, serving as a *condottiere* in Nemedia, Ophir, and Argos. Again, trouble with the law compelled him to flee, this time to sea. When his ship was captured by a pirate vessel of the black corsairs, commanded by the seductive Shemitish she-pirate Bêlit, he joined Bêlit in piratical raiding of the Black Coast.

After Bêlit's death, Conan resumed his career ashore as a mercenary soldier, first in the black countries, then in Shem and the Hyborian nations. He paid occasional visits to his Cimmerian homeland and spent a period as leader of an outlaw band, the *kozaki* of the steppes between Turan and Zamora. When the Turanian army broke up the band, Conan fought his way to leadership of a crew of pirates plying the Vilayet Sea.

Next, Conan became a soldier in the army of the small southeasterly Hyborian kingdom of Khauran and, later, leader of the desert-dwelling Zuagir nomads. His wanderings took him as far east as Vendhya (corresponding to modern India) and south to the deserts between the sinister land of Stygia and the equatorial jungles. He joined the pirates of the Barachan Isles, then became captain of one of the privateering ships of the Zingaran buccaneers.

When Conan's ship was sunk by Zingaran rivals, he served as a mercenary for Stygia. He sought and almost found his hoped-for fortune in the semicivilized black countries of Keshan and Punt. At last he traveled northward, to resume life as a mercenary soldier in Aquilonia, the mightiest of the Hyborian kingdoms. He served on the Pictish frontier, was involved in bloody affrays with the fierce savages of Pictland, and for his success was promoted to general and called back to the capital, Tarantia.

In Tarantia, the depraved and jealous King Numedides imprisoned Conan in a dungeon. But Conan escaped and adventured in the Pictish Wilderness with the primitive natives and with two bands of pirates. Eventually he found himself (at about forty years of age) leading a revolt against Numedides, whom he killed and whose throne he usurped.

Other stories follow Conan's adventures into middle and old age, but of those you can read elsewhere. This synopsis will give you the framework needed to place the stories in this volume in time and place.

So let us whet our steel, pull on our boots, and be off on a galloping charger or the heeling deck of a carack, to follow Conan through some of his many sorcerous and sanguinary adventures.

LEGIONS OF THE DEAD

Conan, born in the bleak, cloud-oppressed northern hills of Cimmeria, was known as a fighter around the council fires before he had seen fifteen snows. In that year, the Cimmerian tribesmen forgot their feuds and joined forces to repel the Gundermen who, pushing across the Aquilonian frontier, had built the frontier post of Venarium and begun to colonize the southern marches of Cimmeria. Conan was one of the howling, blood-mad horde that swept out of the northern hills, stormed over the stockade with sword and torch, and drove the Aquilonians back to their former border.

At the sack of Venarium, still short of his full growth, Conan already stood six feet tall and weighed 180 pounds. He had the alertness and stealth of the born woodsman, the iron-hardness of the mountain man, the Herculean physique of his blacksmith father, and a practical familiarity with knife, axe, and sword.

After the plunder of the Aquilonian outpost, Conan returns for a time to his tribe. Restless under the conflicting urges of his adolescence, his traditions, and his times, he becomes involved in a local feud and is not sorry to leave his village. He joins a band of Æsir in raiding the Vanir and the Hyperboreans. Some of the Hyperborean citadels, however, are under control of a caste of widely feared magicians, called Witchmen, and it is against one of these strongholds that Conan finds himself taking part in a foray.

9

1 • Blood on the Snow

A deer paused at the brink of the shallow stream and raised its head, sniffing the frosty air. Water dripped from its muzzle like beads of crystal. The lingering sun gleamed on its tawny hide and glistened on the tines of its branching antlers.

Whatever faint sound or scent had disturbed the animal was not repeated. Presently it bent to drink again from the frigid water, which rushed and bubbled amid crusts of broken ice.

On either side of the stream, steep banks of earth lay mantled in the new-fallen snow of early winter. Thickets of leafless bush grew close together under the somber boughs of the neighboring pines; and from the forest beyond, nothing could be heard but the ceaseless drip, drip of melting snow. The featureless leaden sky of the dying day scarcely seemed to clear the tops of the trees.

From the shelter of the woods, a slender javelin darted with deadly precision; and at the end of its arc, the long shaft caught the stag off guard and sank behind its shoulder. The stricken creature bolted for the far side of the creek; then staggered, coughed blood, and fell. For a moment or two it lay on its side, kicking and struggling. Then its eyes glazed, its head hung limply, and its heaving flanks grew still. Blood, mixed with froth and foam, dribbled from its sagging jaws to stain the virgin snow a brilliant crimson.

Two men emerged from the trees and studied the snowy landscape with searching eyes. The larger and older, plainly in command, was a giant of a man with massive shoulders and long, heavily muscled arms. The swell of his mighty chest and shoulders was visible beneath the cloak of fur that enveloped his stalwart figure and the coarse, baggy woolens he wore beneath the cloak. A broad belt of rawhide with a golden buckle held his garments around him, and a hood of wolf fur, forming part of the cloak, obscured his face.

Now pushing back the hood to peer about, he revealed a head of curling golden hair, slightly streaked with gray. A short, roughly trimmed beard of the same hue clothed his broad cheeks and heavy jaw. The color of his hair, his fair skin and ruddy cheeks, and his bold blue eyes marked him as one of the Æsir.

The youth beside him differed from him in many ways. Scarcely more than a boy, he was tall and brawny for his age—almost as tall as the full-grown Northman beside him—but lean and wiry rather than massive. He was dark and sullen, with straight, coarse black hair hacked off at the nape, and the skin of his somber visage was either naturally swarthy or heavily tanned. Under heavy black brows, his eyes were as blue as those of the giant at his elbow; but whereas the golden warrior's eyes sparkled with the joy of the hunt and zest for the kill, those of the dark youth glowered like the eyes of some wild and hungry predator. Unlike his bearded companion, the young man's beard was shaven clean, although a dark stubble shadowed his square jaw.

The bearded man was Njal, a *jarl* or chieftain of the Æsir and leader of a band of raiders known and feared on the wintry borders between Asgard and Hyperborea. The youth was Conan, a renegade from the rugged, cloud-haunted hills of Cimmeria to the south.

Satisfied that they were unobserved, the two emerged from cover, descended the bank, and waded the icy current to the place where their kill lay lifeless on the blood-spotted snow. Weighing almost as much as the two men together, the stag was too heavy and, with its branching antlers, too cumbersome to bear back to their camp. So, while the youth watched broodingly, the chieftain bent and, with a long knife, swiftly butchered the beast, peeling back the hide and separating the shoulders, haunches, and ribs from the rest of the carcass.

"Dig a hole, boy, and make it deep," grunted the man.

The youth cut into the frozen slope of the bank,

using the blade of the long-handled ax that had been strapped to his back. By the time that Njal had finished dressing the stag, Conan had hacked out a pit capacious enough to hide the offal. While the Northman cleaned the bloody quarters in the rushing stream, the youth buried all that was left of the carcass, and scraped the crimson snow into the pit along with the loosened soil. Then untying his fur cloak, the Cimmerian dragged it back and forth, obliterating the traces of his handiwork.

Njal wrapped the flesh of the deer in the freshly flayed hide of the beast and tied the mouth of the improvised sack with a thong brought along for the purpose. Conan cut a sapling with his ax and trimmed it down to a pole as long as a man, while the jarl cleansed his javelin by thrusting it into the sand in the bed of the stream. Njal tied the bag to the middle of the pole, which the two then hoisted to their shoulders. Dragging Conan's cloak behind them to erase their footprints, they climbed the farther slope and reëntered the woods.

Here along the Hyperborean border, the pines grew tall, thick, and dark. Wherever a break in the forest afforded a vista, the ridges could be seen to roll endlessly away, covered with snowcapped pines of a green as dark as sable. Wolves skulked along the nighted forest trails, their burning eyes lambent green coals, while above floated great white owls on silent wings.

The two well-armed hunters had no fear of the local creatures; save that, when a bear ambled across the path ahead, they gave it a respectfully wide berth. Like ghosts they glided through the darkened woods to join their fellow raiders, who lay encamped beneath the shoulder of a hill. Since both were woodsmen born and bred, they made no noise and left little trace of their swift passage. Even the scrubby bushes did not rustle as they slipped through them.

So well concealed was the Æsir camp that their first knowledge of its presence was the murmur of voices around a hidden fire; yet the watchful sentinels had seen their coming. An elderly Northman, whose locks had turned to silver, rose from the fireside to greet them silently. One of his eyes was bright and keen; the other was an empty socket concealed by a leather patch. He was Gorm, a bard of the Æsir, over whose bent shoulders slept a harp in a sack of deerskin.

"What word from Egil?" demanded the raider chief, lowering the pole from his shoulder and motioning to the cook to take it away.

"No word, Jarl," said the one-eyed man somberly. "I like it not." He moved uneasily, as does a beast at the scent of danger.

Njal exchanged a glance with the silent Conan. Two days before, an advance party had left the camp under cover of a moonless night to spy out the great castle of Haloga, which lay not far beyond the hills that ringed the horizon to the southeast.

Thirty warriors, seasoned and canny veterans all, led by Egil the huntsman, had gone to scout the way and to study the fortifications of the forbidding Hyperborean stronghold. Conan, unasked, had brashly spoken out against the imprudence of so drastically dividing their strength thus near the enemy, and Njal

Haloga Castle

had roughly bade the youth to hold his tongue. Later, regretting his harshness, the jarl had brought Conan with him in search of game as his rude way of making amends.

Egil's messengers should have returned many hours since. The fact that they had not stirred fear in the mind of Njal, and in the secret places of his heart, he wished that he had harkened to the young Cimmerian's warning.

Njal's shortness of temper and the urgency with which he had driven his men across the wilderness to the Hyperborean border were not without cause. Hyperborean slavers, a fortnight since—slavers with the red mark of Haloga on their black raiment—had carried off his only daughter, Rann.

Brooding over the fate of his beloved daughter and the whereabouts of his trusted scouts, the jarl repressed a shudder. The Witchmen of shadowy Hyperborea were feared far and wide for their uncanny mastery of the black arts; and Haloga's sadistic queen was feared like the Black Death.

Njal fought down the chill that clutched his heart and turned to Gorm the skald. "Tell the cook to broil the meat swiftly—and on charcoal, for we cannot risk the smoke of open fires. And bid the men eat fast. When night descends, we move."

2 • The Horror on the Parapet

All that night, like a band of wolves, the raiders from Asgard drifted in single file across the snowy hills into the clammy, swirling mists of Hyperborea. At first the night was star-decked only, but once they crossed the hills, cold mists blotted out even the wan and frosty glimmer of the stars. When at length the moon arose, the mists bedimmed it to a pearly blotch in the sky, like a moon reflected in wind-ruffled water. Despite the gloom that drenched this barren, bog-infested, scantily inhabited land, the raiders took advantage of every slightest bit of cover, every leafless bush and stunted tree and inky patch of shadow. For Haloga was a mighty fortress, and doubtless guarded well. Desperate and vengeful as he was, Njal well knew in the depths of his heart that his only hope of success lay in surprise.

The moon and mists had fled together before they reached Haloga. The castle stood on a low rise in the center of a shallow, bowl-shaped valley. Huge were its frowning walls of dark stone, and massive the masonry around the lone and ponderous gate. Above the main walls rose a castellated parapet. A few windows were set high in the towers; nothing else but arrow slits broke the clifflike surface of the megalithic walls.

It would, Njal knew, be difficult to storm this place. And where were the men whom he had sent ahead to scout the way? No sign of them had been discerned, even by his keen-eyed trackers; for the newly fallen snow had obliterated their footprints.

"Shall we essay the walls, Jarl?" asked a warrior— an outlaw fled hither from Vanaheim, if his red beard was any token.

"Nay, the dawn approaches, curse the luck!" growled the chief. "We must wait for night again, or pray the gods will let the white-haired devils grow careless and raise the portcullis. Tell the men to sleep where they are and to sprinkle snow over their furs so none can see them. Tell Thror Ironhand his squad has the first watch."

Njal lay down, wrapped his furs around him, and closed his eyes. But sleep came not soon; and when it came, dreams of shadowy, chuckling menace made it hideous.

Conan slept not at all. Possessed by uneasy foreboding, the youth still resented Njal's gruff dismissal of his argument against the scouting party. He was a stranger among the Æsir freebooters, driven from his homeland by a blood feud, and had with difficulty won a precarious place among these blond warriors. They approved his ability to endure privation and hardship without complaint, and the bullies among them had learned to respect his heavy fists; for despite his youth, he fought with the ferocity of a cornered wildcat and needs must be dragged bodily from a foe once he had felled him. But still, as youths will, the Cimmerian burned to win the applause of his elders by some feat of daring or heroism.

Conan had observed the windows of the keep, which were much too high to reach by climbing, were it humanly possible to scale such walls without a ladder. He had mastered many sheer cliffs in his homeland; but those had at least afforded a toe- and finger-hold. The stones of Haloga were fitted and trimmed to a glassy smoothness that defied the climbing efforts of any creature larger than an insect.

The arrow slits, however, were set lower in the walls and thus seemed more accessible. Those of the lowest tier were little more than thrice a man's height above the ground, to give the archers a fair shot at besiegers who might cluster about the base of the wall. Plainly too narrow for a full-grown man of the bulk of most Æsir, were they too narrow for the smaller, slenderer Conan?

When dawn broke, one raider was missing from the camp—the young Cimmerian outlaw, Conan. Njal had other things to think about and so had little time to ponder the fate of a surly, black-visaged young runaway, who seemed to lack the stomach for this raid.

The jarl had just discovered his missing scouts. They hung from the parapet, clearly visible as dawn lit the empty sky and dispelled the clammy fogs that shrouded the air of this accursed land. The men were still alive, dancing in their death throes at the ends of thirty ropes.

Njal stared, then cursed until his voice was hoarse, and he dug his nails into his hard palms. Although he felt sick to the roots of his soul, he could not tear his eyes away.

The eternally young queen of Haloga, Vammatar the Cruel, stood on the parapet fair as the morning, with long bright hair and full breasts, which curved sweetly beneath her heavy white robes. A lazy, languorous smile parted her full red lips. The men who attended her were true Hyperboreans, unearthly in their gaunt, long-legged stature, with pale eyes and skeins of colorless silken hair.

As the hidden Æsir, sick with rage and fury and helpless horror, watched, the men of Egil's party were slowly done to death with merciless hooks and wickedly curved knives. They squealed and flopped and wriggled, those gory, mangled things that had been stalwart warriors two days before. It took them hours to die.

Njal, his lips bitten through, aged much during that endless, terrible morn. And there was nothing at all he could do. A leader cannot throw a small band of men against high walls with only hand weapons. If he has a large, well-found army capable of keeping the field for months, he can batter down the walls with rams and catapults, or undermine them with tunnels, or roll siege towers up to them and swarm across, or surround the stronghold and starve it out. Lacking such over-mastering force, he needs at least scaling ladders as long as the wall is high, a force of archers or slingers to beat the defenders back from the ramparts, and above all surprise.

Surprise, the advantage on which Njal had counted, was now lost to him. However the Hyperboreans had captured Egil's scouting party, the mere fact of their capture had alerted the people of Haloga to the presence of Æsir in the vicinity. The Witchmen of this devil-haunted land must, by their weird arts, have known of the approach of the hostile force. The sinister legends about them were now proved true by the crimson evidence hanging against the red-stained stone of the parapet. Haloga had known that Æsir were out there all the time, and not even the cold-hearted and vengeance-loving gods of the Northlands could help them now.

Then it was that the first plume of jet black smoke drifted from the lofty windows of the keep, and the torturers broke, crying out in amazement, and scurried away with their black gowns flapping. The lazy, catlike smile vanished from the soft, curved lips of Haloga's queen. A feeble, flickering flame of hope leaped up within the breast of Njal of Asgard.

3 • Shadow of Vengeance

Scaling the wall had been neither easier nor harder than Conan had guessed. A rain spout, curved like the mouth of a vomiting dragon, caught and held the noose of his rope on the fifteenth or sixteenth try. The rope, knotted at intervals for better purchase, neither slipped nor broke beneath his weight.

When he had ascended to the level of the slit, Conan locked his legs about the rope and rocked back and forth, like a child on a swing. By throwing his weight from one side to the other, he increased the dimensions of the arc. It was slow going; but at last, at the end of a swing to the right, he came within reach of the slit.

The next time he swung, he shot out a hand and grasped the masonry. Still holding the rope in his free hand, he thrust a booted foot into the opening and followed it with the other. Slowly and carefully he shifted his weight until he was sitting on the sill of the arrow slit with his legs inside. He still grasped the rope with his left hand, for it occurred to him that, if he released it, his lifeline would fall away and hang out of reach when he would have need of it for a hasty departure.

The slit was too narrow for Conan to pass through in his present position. Already his lean hips were wedged into the opening, the sides of which were angled outward to give the defender a wider field of arrow shot. So, turning sideways, he wriggled his hips and midsection through the aperture. But when his arms and chest reached the narrow opening, his woolen tunic, bunched up beneath his armpits, arrested further progress. Would he not look an utter fool, he thought, if the Witchmen came upon him wedged in the arrow slit? He had visions of being caught forever in this stony vise. Even if undiscovered, he would perish of hunger and thirst and make good food for the ravens.

Gathering courage, he decided that by expelling all the breath from his lungs, he might just slip through. He took several deep breaths, as if preparing to swim under water, exhaled, and pushed ahead until his thrashing feet found a firm surface to stand on. Turning his head, he wormed it through the inner edges of the slit and collapsed on a rough wooden floor. In his excitement he had released the rope, which started to snake through the slit. He caught it just before it slipped away.

Conan found himself in a small circular chamber, an archer's roost that was unoccupied. As he peered around in the gloom, he sighted a rough stool, placed there for the comfort of the defender. He pulled the stool nearer and made the rope fast to it, so that the heavy wood might serve to anchor the rope during his escape. Then he stretched his cramped muscles. He must, he thought, have left a few square palms of skin on the stonework as he scraped through.

Across the room from the arrow slit, the masonry was interrupted by an arched doorway. Conan drew his long knife from its scabbard and stole through the aperture. Beyond the doorway a spiral stair led upward, and occasional torches set in wall brackets did little to dispel the almost palpable obscurity.

Moving a step at a time and flattening himself against the wall to listen, Conan slowly worked his way through many passages to the central keep, where prisoners of rank and worth might lodge. Day had dawned long since, although little light penetrated this massive pile of stone through the arrow slits and narrow windows. From the screams that filtered faintly through the thick walls, the Cimmerian youth had a grim notion of what occupied the Witchmen on the parapet.

In a corridor intermittently lit by torches set in brackets, Conan found his prey at last—two of them, in fact. They were guarding a cell and, from the look of them, he knew the old stories were true. He had seen Cimmerians and Gundermen and Aquilonians and Æsir and Vanir, but never before had he set eyes upon a Hyperborean at close quarters, and the sight chilled the blood in his veins.

Like devils from some lightless hell they seemed, long-jawed faces white as fungi, pale and soulless amber eyes, and hair of colorless flax. Their gaunt bodies were clad all in black, save that the red mark of Haloga was embroidered on their bony chests. It seemed to Conan's fancy that the marks were bloody tokens of hearts that had been torn from their breasts, leaving naught but a grisly stain behind. The superstitious youth almost believed the ancient legends that these men were mere cadavers, animated by demons from the depths of some black hell.

They did have hearts, however; and when cut, they bled. They could also be killed, as he found when he hurled himself upon them from the corridor. The first one squawked and went down, sprawling awkwardly under the thunderbolt impact of Conan's catlike leap, and died bubbling as the Cimmerian's knife pierced his breast.

The second guard, staring slack-jawed and blank-eyed, gaped for a heartbeat. Then he aimed a kick at the intruder and went for his sword. But Conan's knife, a serpent's tongue, flicked out and slashed the Hyperborean's throat, leaving a mirthless, red-rimmed smile below the guard's pale thin-lipped mouth.

When the two were dead, Conan stripped them of their weapons and, dragging the bodies to an empty cell, heaped upon them the straw that lay matted on the floor. Then he peered into the small compartment that they had guarded.

A tall, milk-skinned girl with clear blue eyes and long, smooth hair the color of sun-ripened wheat stood proudly in the center of the enclosure, awaiting a fate she knew not of. Although the maiden's high young breasts rose and fell in her agitation, there was no fear in her eyes.

"Who are you?" she asked.

"Conan, a Cimmerian, a member of your father's band," he said, speaking her tongue with an accent foreign to her. "If you are Njal's daughter, that is."

She lifted her chin. "I am indeed Rann Njalsdatter."

"Good," he grunted, thrusting into the lock a key snatched from the dead Witchmen. "I have come for you."

"Alone?" Her eyes widened, incredulously.

Conan nodded. Snatching her hand, he led the Æsir girl into the corridor and gave her one of the two swords of the slain Witchmen. With her behind him and his newfound weapon readied for action, he cautiously retraced his steps along the stone passageways through which he had come.

Down the long corridor he prowled, silent and wary as a jungle cat. Moving with every sense alert, his smoldering gaze swept the walls and the doors set in them. In the flickering torchlight, his eyes burned like those of some savage creature of the wild.

At any moment, Conan knew, the Witchmen might discover them, for surely not every denizen of the castle was on the parapet with the torturers. Deep in his primal heart, he breathed an unspoken prayer to Crom, the merciless god of his shadowy homeland, that he and the girl might, unobserved, attain the arrow slit whereby he had entered.

Like an insubstantial shadow, the young Cimmerian glided through the gloomy passageways, which now curved following the girdle of the curtain wall; and Rann, on little cat feet, followed after him. Torches smoldered and smoked in their brackets, but the dark intervals between the flickering lights were alive with evil.

They met no one; yet Conan was not satisfied. True, their luck had held thus far, but it might end at any moment. If two or three Witchmen fell upon them, they might still win through; for the women of the Æsir were not pampered playthings but skilled and daring swordswomen. Often in battle they stood shoulder to shoulder with their men; and when fight they must, they fought with the ferocity of tigresses.

But what if they were set upon by six or a dozen Witchmen? Young as he was, Conan knew no mortal man, however skillful with his sword, can face at once in all directions; and whilst they thrust and parried in these dark passages, the alarm would surely sound and rouse the castle.

A diversion was needed, and one of the torches they passed gave the youth an inspiration. The torches were soaked in tarry pitch to burn long and slowly, but they burned deep and were not easily extinguished. Conan glanced about. The walls of the castle were of stone, but the floor planks and the beams supporting them were wooden. Across his grim face flitted a small smile of satisfaction.

Conan needed to find a storeroom, and as he prowled the corridors, he peered into chambers whose doors were open. One was vacant. Another contained a pair of empty beds. A third appeared to be a storage place for broken or damaged weapons and other metallic objects awaiting repair.

The door to the next room stood ajar, leaving a narrow crack of darkness in the flickering torchlight. Conan pushed it, and the door swung open with a faint squeal of hinges. Then he started back and hastily shut out the sight of that dark chamber; for the room contained a bed, and on the bed lay a sleeping Witchman. Beside him on a stool were several phials, which Conan supposed held medications for a sick man. He left the fellow snoring.

The next chamber turned out to be the sought-for storeroom. As Conan surveyed it from the hall, the rising sound of footsteps and voices caused him to whirl about, lip lifted in a snarl. He gestured frantically to Rann.

"Inside!" he breathed.

The twain slipped into the storeroom, and Conan closed the door. Since the room had no window, they waited in complete darkness, listening to the clatter of the approaching Hyperboreans. Soon the party passed the door, speaking in their guttural tongue, and their footsteps died away.

When all was silent again, Conan drew a long breath. Holding high his Hyperborean sword, he opened the door a crack, then more widely as he viewed naught but the empty corridor. With the door ajar, the dim light of the torches pierced the gloom, and he could make out the contents of the chamber. Here were a pile of fresh torches, a barrel of pitch, and in one corner, a heap of straw to garnish the cell floors in lieu of carpets.

It was but the work of a moment for Conan to toss the pile of straw about the chamber, overturn the barrel of pitch upon it, and spread the viscous stuff around. Darting out into the passageway, he snatched a torch from the nearest bracket and heaved it into the combustible mass that covered the floor of the storeroom. Crackling lustily, the flames ate their way through the straw and belched black smoke along the corridor.

Hyperborean Sword

Tarred from face to boots and coughing from the acrid fumes, Conan caught Rann's hand, sprinted down the winding stairs, and regained the alcove through which he had gained entry. How long before the Witchmen would discover that their castle was ablaze, Conan knew not; but he trusted this diversion to occupy their full attention while the rescuer and rescued squirmed through the narrow slit and clambered down the rope to the safety of the frozen ground.

4 • That Which Pursued

Jarl Njal bellowed with joy and seized the laughing, weeping girl in his arms, crushing her against his burly chest. But even in his joy, the chieftain paused to look deep into Conan's eyes and clap the youth on the shoulder with a friendly buffet that would have knocked most striplings off their feet.

As they hastened to the Asgard camp beneath the cover of the snow-tipped pines, the youth, in terse words, described the day's adventure. But words were scarcely needed. Behind them a raven cloud of soot besmudged the afternoon sky, and the crash of collapsing timbers and fire-blackened masonry resounded like distant thunder in the hills. The Witchmen would doubtless save part of their fortress; although many of the lank, flaxen-haired devils must have already perished in the conflagration.

Wasting no time, Njal ordered his men to begin the long trek back to Asgard. Not until he and his band were deep in their own land could the chief of the Æsir count himself safe from Hyperborean vengeance. There would, no doubt, be pursuit; but for the moment the dwellers in Haloga had other matters to busy them.

The Æsir made haste to depart, and in their hurry they sacrificed concealment to speed. Since the face of the wan sun was still pillowed on the treetops, they could with effort put leagues between themselves and the castle before the early fall of the northern night.

From the parapet of Haloga, the agelessly beautiful Queen Vammatar watched them go, her jasper eyes cold with hate as she smiled a slow and evil smile.

There was little greenery in this flat land of bog and hillock, and what there was lay blanketed in snow. As the sun neared the horizon, clammy coils of choking fog rose from the stagnant meres and laid a chill upon men's hearts. The travelers saw few signs of life, save for a couple of Hyperborean serfs who fled from the band and lost themselves in the mist.

From time to time, one or another of the Æsir set an car to the ground, but no drumming of hooves could be heard. They hastened on, slipping and stumbling on the uncertain, frozen footing. But before day wrapped her icy cloak around her shoulders and departed, Conan glanced to the rear, and cried out: "Someone follows us!"

The Æsir halted and gazed in the direction that he indicated. At first they could see nothing but the endless, undulant plain, whose junction with the sky was hidden in the mists. Then a Northman with vision that transcended the sight of his fellows exclaimed:

"He is right. Men on foot pursue us, mayhap . . . mayhap a half a league behind."

"Come!" growled Njal. "We will not stop to camp this night. In these fogs, 'twere easy for a foe to creep upon us, no matter how many sentries we might post."

The band staggered on while the setting sun was swallowed by the voracious mists. After the Æsir had long trudged in darkness, a wan moon climbed above the mists that hemmed them in, and its light shone on a faint patch of rippling shade. It was the pursuing force, larger and nearer than ever.

Njal, a man of iron, strode forward with his exhausted daughter in his arms; nor would he entrust so precious a burden to another. Conan, full as he was with the vigor of youth, ached in every limb and sinew as he followed the giant jarl. The other raiders, uncomplaining, maintained the grueling pace. Yet their pursuers seemed to tire not at all. Indeed, the host from Haloga had not slowed, but was on the contrary gaining upon them. Njal cursed hoarsely and urged his men to greater speed. But however doggedly they struggled on, they were altogether played out. Soon they must turn and make a stand, albeit the jarl well knew that no seasoned warrior would choose to do battle on a strange terrain when overtaken by exhaustion. Still, their meager choice was plain: either fight or be cut down.

Each time they crested a low hill clad in winter's silvered garment, they could see the silent mass of moving men, twice their number, drawing nearer than before. There was something strange about these pursuers, but neither Njal nor Gorm nor any other of the company could quite tell what was wrong with them.

As the hunters drew closer, the hunted perceived that not all the members of the oncoming force were Witchmen, a race that tended to be taller and more slender than the Northmen. Many of the pursuing host had mighty shoulders and massive frames and wore the horned helmets of the Æsir and Vanir. Njal shivered, as from the icy touch of some uncanny premonition of despair.

The other strange thing about the pursuers was the way they walked. . . .

Ahead, Njal spied the loom of a hill, higher than most of the eminences of this flat land, and his weary eyes brightened. The crest of the hill would serve for a defensive position, although the chieftain wished it higher yet and steeper to force the enemy to charge uphill in the teeth of Æsir weapons. In any case, the foe was almost snapping at their heels, so stand they must, and soon.

Shouldering the girl, Njal turned to shout from a raw throat: "Men! Up yonder hill and speedily! There we shall make our stand."

The Æsir plodded up the misty slope, to assemble at the crest, well pleased to cease putting one road-weary foot before the other. And like true warriors everywhere, the prospect of a bloody battle brightened their flagging spirits.

Thror Ironhand and the other captains passed around leathern bottles of wine and water, albeit it little enough was left of either. The raiders rested, caught their breath, and limbered their bows. Long shields of wicker and hide, which had been slung upon their backs, were cast loose and fitted together to form a veritable wall of shields, encircling the crest of the hill. One-eyed Gorm uncovered his harp and began in a strong, melodious voice to chant an ancient battle song:

Our blades were forged in the flames that leap
From the burning heart of hell,
And were quenched in frozen rivers deep,
Where the icy bones of dead men sleep,
Who fought our sires and fell.

The respite was short. Shouldering through the fog, a swarm of sinister figures emerged from the murk, and with steady, rhythmic steps stalked up the slope, like men walking in their sleep or puppets worked by strings. The flight of javelins that met the shambling attackers slowed them not at all, as they hurled themselves against the ring of shields. Naked steel flashed darkly in the wan moonlight. The attackers swung high sword and axe and war hammer and brought them whistling down upon the living wall, cleaving flesh and shattering bone.

In the van Njal, bellowing an ancient Æsir war cry, hewed mightily. Then he paused, blinking, and the heart in his bosom faltered. For the man he was fighting was none other than his own captain, Egil the huntsman, who had died that morn on the end of a rope, suspended from the walls of Haloga. The light of the pallid moon shone plainly on that familiar face and turned Jarl Njal's bones to water.

5 • "Men Cannot Die Twice!"

The face that stared stonily into his own was surely that of Njal's old comrade; for the white scar athwart the brow betokened a slash that Egil, five summers before, had suffered in a raid against the Vanir. But the blue eyes of Egil knew not his jarl. Those eyes were as cold and empty as the skies above the starless, misty night.

Glancing again, Njal saw the mangled flesh of Egil's naked breast, whence hours before the living heart had been untimely torn. Revolted by the thing he saw, Njal perceived that however much he wounded his adversary's flesh, these wounds would never bleed. Neither would his old friend's corpse feel the bitter kiss of steel.

Behind the dead but battling Æsir, a half-charred Witchman stumbled up the slope, his face a grinning mask of horror. Here, thought Njal, was a denizen of Haloga who had perished in the fire set by the wily Conan.

"Forgive, brother," whispered Njal through stiffened lips, as with a backhand stroke, he hamstrung Egil's walking corpse. Like a puppet with severed strings, the dismembered body flopped backward down the hill; but instantly the cadaver of the grinning Witchman took its place.

The Æsir chieftain fought mechanically but without hope. For when your foe can summon forth the very dead from hell to fight you, what victory can ensue?

All along the line, men shouted in hoarse surprise and consternation as they found themselves fighting the walking corpses of their own dead comrades who

28

had perished under the cruel knives of the Hyperboreans. But the host that swarmed against them numbered others in their hideous ranks. Side by side with Witchmen crushed beneath collapsing walls or burned in the day's conflagration strode corpses long buried, from whose pale and tattered flesh grave worms wriggled or fell wetly to the ground. These hurled themselves, weaponless, upon the Æsir. The stench was sickening; and terror overwhelmed all but the hardiest.

Even old Gorm felt the icy clutch of fear at his heart. His war song faltered and died.

"May the gods help us all!" he muttered. "What hope have we when we pit our steel against the walking dead? Men cannot die twice!"

The Æsir line crumbled as wave after wave of walking corpses swept the warriors down, one by one, and crushed them into the viscid earth. These attackers bore no weapons but fought with naked hands, tearing living men asunder with their frigid grip.

The Cimmerian stood in the second rank. When the stout warrior before him fell, Conan, roaring with a voice as gusty as the north wind, leaped forward to fill the gap in the swaying line. With a sweep of the Hyperborean sword he bore, he severed the neck of a skeletal thing that was squeezing the life from the Northman at his feet. The skull-like head rolled grinning down the hill.

Then Conan's blood congealed with horror: for, headless or not, the long-dead cadaver rose and groped for him with its bony hands. With the nape of his neck tingling in primordial fear, Conan kicked out and stove in ribs that showed through the tattered flesh. The corpse staggered back, then came on again, talons clutching.

Gripping his sword hilt with both hands, Conan put all his young strength into a mighty slash. The sword bit through the lean and fleshless waist, severed the half-exposed spinal column, and sent the divided cadaver tumbling earthward. For the moment, he had no opponent. Breathing hard, he shook back his raven mane.

The Cimmerian glanced along the Æsir line. Njal had fallen, taking with him a dozen of the foe, hacked, like venison, into pieces. Howling like a wolf, old Gorm took his place in the wavering line, swinging a heavy axe with deadly skill. But now the line was breaking; the battle nearly done.

"Do not slay all!" a cold voice rang in the stillness, borne upon the icy wind. "Take such as you can for the slave pens."

Peering through the murk, Conan spied the speaker. On a tall black stallion sat Queen Vammatar in her flowing snow-white robes. Trembling in every limb, he knew the legions of the walking dead obeyed her least command.

Suddenly Rann appeared at Conan's side, her face wet with tears but blue eyes unafraid. She had seen Gorm and her father fall before the onslaught of the ghastly enemy and had pushed her way through the press to the young Cimmerian. She snatched up a discarded sword and prepared to die fighting. Then, like a gift from Crom, an idea shaped itself in Conan's despairing mind. The battle was already lost. He and the surviving Æsir were bound, as surely as day follows night, for the slave pens of Hyperborea. Something, however, might be saved from the wreck of all their hopes.

Whirling, Conan lifted the girl in his arms and tossed her over his shoulder. Then he kicked and hacked a path through the foe, down the corpse-littered slope to the foot of the hill, where the queen sat on her steed awaiting the end, an evil smile on her half-parted lips.

In the sable dark beneath the swirling coils of mist, the queen, eyes raised to watch the final struggle on the hilltop, failed to mark the noiseless approach of the Cimmerian. Nor did she see the girl he set upon the trampled snow. No premonition reached her senses until iron fingers closed about her forearm and thigh and hauled her, shrieking with dismay and fury, from her mount. With a mighty heave Conan hurled the queen from him, to fall with a splash into the chilly bosom of the bog. Then Conan lifted Rann and boosted her, protesting, into the vacant saddle.

Before he could vault up behind her on the prancing animal, several of the living corpses, obeying the furious commands of their mistress, seized Conan from behind and clung, leechlike, to his left arm.

With a superhuman effort, before he was dragged earthward by the putrid monsters, Conan struck the stallion's rump with the flat of his sword. "Ride, girl, ride!" he shouted. "To Asgard and safety!"

The black horse reared, neighing, and bolted across the foggy, snow-clad plain. Rann hugged the animal's neck, pressing her tear-stained cheek against its warm hide, and her long blond hair mingled with its flying mane.

As the steed swept around the base of the hill and off to the west, she cast one backward glance, just as the brave youth who twice had saved her life went down beneath a mound of fighting cadavers. Queen Vammatar, her white robes spattered with slime, stood in the frosty moonlight, smiling her evil smile. Then the loom of the hill and the rising fogs mercifully hid the scene of the carnage.

Across the plain, a score of Æsir survivors trudged eastward in the pallid moonlight, their wrists bound behind their backs with rawhide thongs. The walking dead—those who had not been cut to pieces in the fray—surrounded the captives. At the head of the weird procession marched two figures: Conan and Queen Vammatar.

With every step the queen, her handsome face twisted with fury, slashed at the Cimmerian youth with her riding whip. Red weals crisscrossed his face and body; but he walked with shoulders squared and head held high, although he knew that none returned from the slave pens of this accursed land. Easy it would have been to slay the queen when he threw her from her stallion, but in his natal land custom demanded chivalry toward women, and he could not forsake his childhood training.

As the eastern fogs paled with the approach of dawn, Rann Njalsdatter reached the borders of Asgard. Her heart was heavy, but she remembered the last stanza of the song that Gorm had chanted beneath the fog-dimmed moon:

> You can cut us down; we can bleed and die,
>> But men of the North are we:
> You can chain our flesh; you can blind our eye;
> You can break us under the iron sky,
>> But our hearts are proud and free!

The brave words of the song stiffened her back and lifted her spirits. With shoulders unbowed and bright head high, she rode home under the morning.

THE PEOPLE OF
THE SUMMIT

*After a year or two of felonious life as a thief in
Zamora, Corinthia, and Nemedia, Conan, who has just
about turned twenty, undertakes to earn a more or less
honest living as a mercenary soldier serving King
Yildiz of Turan. Following the events of the story
"The City of Skulls," the mighty Cimmerian, as a reward for his services to the king's daughter Zosara, is
given a noncommissioned rank corresponding to that
of sergeant. In this capacity he goes to the Khozgari
Hills as part of the military escort of an emissary sent
by the king to the restless tribesmen of that region, in
hope of dissuading them by bribes and threats from
raiding and plundering the Turanians of the lowlands.
But the Khozgarians are warlike barbarians who respect only immediate and overwhelming force. They
treacherously attack the detachment, killing the emissary and all but two of the soldiers. These two, Conan
and Jamal, escape.*

The lean Turanian, whose dusty crimson jerkin and
stained white breeches testified to the rigors of his
flight, reined in his mare at the signal. Turning quest-
ing black eyes upon his giant leader, he asked:
"Dare we tarry here?"
His companion, similarly garbed, save that the

33

flowing left sleeve of his woolen shirt bore the golden scimitar of a sergeant in the Turanian frontier cavalry, scowled. Blue eyes blazing beneath the crimson turban that bound his spired helmet, he tossed aside the flap of cloth that protected his face from the swirling dust and spat before he answered.

"The beasts must rest."

The heaving flanks of the two animals and their foam-flecked mouths made plain the need for a halt.

"But, Conan," protested the Turanian, "what if those Khozgari devils still follow us?" Uneasily he studied the curved scimitar thrust into his sash, and his grip tightened on the lance resting in its leathern pouch beside his right stirrup. He was comforted by the weight of the double-curved bow and the full quiver of arrows slung upon his back.

"Damn that stupid emissary!" growled the Cimmerian. "Jamal, thrice I warned him of the treacherous Khozgari tribesmen; but his head was so full of trade treaties and caravan routes that he would not listen. Now that thick-skulled head of his hangs in the smoke-room of a chief's hut, along with seven of our company. Damn him to Hell, and damn the lieutenant for permitting the palaver in the rock village!"

"Aye, Conan, but what could our lieutenant do? The emissary had full power to command. Our task was to protect him and obey him, only. Had he countered the emissary's orders, the captain would have snapped his scimitar before the regiment and reduced him to the ranks. You know the captain's temper."

"Better broken to the ranks than dead," growled Conan, scowling. "We two were lucky to escape when the devils rushed us! Listen!" He held up his hand. "What was that?"

Conan rose in his stirrups, blue eyes sweeping the gorges and crevices for the source of the faint sound he had heard. As his companion silently unslung his great bow and nocked an arrow, Conan's hand closed on the hilt of his scimitar.

Turanian Frontier Cavalry Uniform

A moment later, he flung himself from the saddle and, like a charging bull, rushed toward the nearby rock wall; for in that fleeting space of time, a youth had raced across the narrow gorge and scaled the steep cliff with the agility of a monkey.

Conan swept to the granite wall, found purchase for reaching hands and feet, and clambered upward with the assurance born of long experience. He heaved himself over the rim of the rock and cast himself aside just as a club descended on the spot where, a moment earlier, his head had been. Rolling to his knees, he rose and gripped the arms of his assailant before another blow could fall. Then he stared.

It was a girl he held, dirty and disheveled but nevertheless a girl, and her body would have graced the statues of a king's sculptor. Her face was pretty even through the grime, although she was sobbing now in impotent rage as she twisted her slim arms savagely against the fierce grip of her captor.

Conan's voice was rough with suspicion. "You are a spy! What tribe?"

The girl's emerald eyes flamed as she hurled back her defiance:

"I am Shanya, daughter of Shaf Karaz, chief of the Khozgari and ruler of the mountains! He will spit you on his lance and roast you over his council fire for daring to lay hands on me!"

"A likely story!" taunted the Cimmerian. "A chief's daughter without an armed following, here, alone?"

"No one dares lay violent hands on Shanya. The Theggir and the Ghoufags cower in their huts as Shanya, daughter of Shaf Karaz, rides abroad to hunt the mountain goat. Dog of a Turanian! Let me loose!"

She twisted angrily, but Conan held her slim body in the vise of his arms.

"Not so fast, my pretty one! You'll make a fine hostage for our safe passage back to Samara. You will ride before me on the saddle all the way; and you'd best

sit still, lest you make the journey bound and gagged."
He grinned in cold indifference to her hot temper.

"Dog!" she cried. "I do as you say for the present.
But have a care that you fall not into the hands of the
Khozgari in the future!"

"We were surrounded by your tribesmen a scant
two hours past," growled Conan. "But their bowmen
could not hit the wall of a canyon. Jamal here could
outshoot a dozen of them. Enough of this chatter! We
move, and move fast. Keep your pretty mouth shut
from now on; it is easy enough to gag."

The girl's lips curled with unspoken ire as the horses
picked their careful way between the rocks and
boulders.

"Which way do you plan to go, Conan?" Jamal's
voice was anxious.

"We cannot go back. I don't trust this hostage business too much in the heat of ambush. We will ride
straight south to the road of Garma and cross the
Misty Mountains through the Bhambar Pass. That
should put us within two days' journey of Samara."

The girl turned to stare at him, her face blanched
with sudden fright.

"You fool! Are you so careless of life as to try to cross
the Misty Mountains? They are the haunts of the
People of the Summit. No traveler has ever entered
their land and returned. The People emerged but once
out of the mists during the reign of Angharzeb of
Turan, and they defeated his whole army by magic
and monsters, as the king strove to recover the burial
grounds of the ancient Turanians. 'Tis a land of terror
and death! Do not go there!"

Conan's reply was indifferent. "Everywhere there
are old wives' tales of demons and monsters that no
one living has ever seen. This is the safest and shortest
way. If we make a detour, we shall have to spend a
week in the guardhouse for dallying along the road."
He urged his horse forward. The clatter of hooves on

37

stone alone broke the silence as they wove their way among the towering cliffs.

"This blasted fog is as thick as mare's milk!" exclaimed Jamal some time later.

The mist hung dank and impenetrable; the travelers could see a scant two yards ahead. The horses walked slowly, side by side, occasionally touching, feeling their way forward with careful steps. The thickness of the milky mist was inconstant; the whiteness wavered and billowed, and now and then the bleak walls of the mountain pass appeared for a fleeting moment.

Conan's senses were sharply tuned. One hand held the bared scimitar; the other clutched Shanya firmly. His eyes ranged the small field of vision, taking advantage of every opening to reconnoiter.

The girl's scream, ringing out with sudden shock, brought them to a halt. She pointed with a trembling finger, cowering in the saddle against Conan's massive chest.

"I saw something move! Just for a second! It was not human!"

Conan swept the scene with narrowed lids as a random billowing of the mist cleared the roadway in front for a moment. He stiffened in the saddle, then relaxed and urged the horses forward, saying:

"Naught for the daughter of a Khozgari chief to worry about!"

But the shape at the roadside was disturbing. A human skeleton danced from two poles, crossed slantwise. The bones were held together by some fluttering rags, bits of tendon, and shriveled skin. The skull lay on the ground, grinning, snapped from the neckbones and cracked open like a coconut.

A sound floated through the mists. It began as a demoniac laugh that rose and fell, changing into angry chattering, and ending in an ululating wail. The girl responded with keening. Stiff with terror, her lips moved dryly.

38

"The—the demons of the Summit are calling for
our flesh! Our bones will lie stripped in their stone
dwelling before evening. Oh, save me! I do not want
to die!"

Conan felt the hair rise on the nape of his neck; and
chills ran down his spine on little lizard feet. But he
shook off his fear of the unknown with a shrug of his
great shoulders.

"We are here, and we have to get through. Let that
howler come within reach of my blade, and he'll
scream in another key."

As his horse stepped forward, a heavy crash and a
groan caused Conan to glance back. At that moment,
he felt a tug upon his weeping captive. Before he
could grasp her more firmly, she rose screaming into
the mists on the end of a snakelike rope. Conan's horse
reared wildly, flinging him to the ground, and the
clatter of its hooves died away as he staggered to his
feet.

Nearby lay Jamal and his horse, both crushed beneath a giant boulder. The man's dead hand protruded
from under the gray stone, still clutching the war bow
and a quiver of arrows. These Conan scooped up in
one swift motion. He wasted no time in mourning the
death of his comrade; for here was deadly danger.
Snarling like an angry panther, he slung the bow over
his shoulder, stuck the arrows in his sash, and gripped
his bared scimitar.

The thick mist swirled around him as he felt a noose
drop over his head. Moving with the speed of light-
ning, he ducked, then seized the rope with his free
hand, gave a tug, and voiced a gurgling cry like that
of a strangling man. His eyes were slitted as he swung
upward, hauled by an immense power whose source
he knew not. The feel of the mist was wet in his
nostrils.

Heavy hands gripped him as he reached the edge of
the escarpment, but the figures he discerned in the
thinning mist were shadows only. He shrugged free

39

of the clutching fingers and drove in silent deadliness at the nearest shadow. Soft resistance and a shriek told him that his scimitar had entered living flesh. Then the shadows closed around him. Standing with his back to the edge of the abyss, he swung his great blade in devastating arcs.

Never had Conan battled in such eerie surroundings. His enemies disappeared into the misty whirls, only to return again and again, like insubstantial ghosts. Their blades flicked out like serpents' tongues, but he soon took the measure of their clumsy swordsmanship. With renewed self-confidence, he taunted his silent attackers.

"Time you learned something of the way of the sword, your jackals of the mist! Ambushing travelers does not make for skill with the scimitar. You need lessons. The undercut—like this! The overhand slash —there! The upward rip with the point into the throat—watch!"

His exclamations were accompanied by demonstrations that left many shadowy figures gurgling or shrieking on the rocks. The Cimmerian fought with cold and terrible control, and suddenly he carried the fight to his assailants in a swift and devastating charge. Two more figures fell to his vicious slashes, their crimson guts spilling out upon the moss. Suddenly the remaining foemen melted away in panicky flight.

Conan wiped the sweat off his forehead with the wide sleeve of his uniform. Then, bending down to stare at one of the corpses, he grunted in surprise. It was no human being that sprawled there with small, sightless eyes and flaring nostrils. The low forehead and receding jaw were those of an ape, but an ape unlike any he had seen in the forests on the shores of the Sea of Vilayet. This ape was hairless from head to toe, and its only accouterment was a heavy rope twisted around its bulging swagbelly.

Conan was puzzled. The great Vilayet apes never hunted in packs and lacked the intelligence to use arms and tools, save when trained for performances

Ape's Sword

before the royal court in Aghrapur. Nor was the
creature's sword of a crude design. Forged of the best
Turanian steel, its curved blade was honed to a razor's
edge. Conan noticed a penetrating, musky odor ema-
nating from the dead ape. His nostrils widened as he
inhaled the scent with care. He would smell out his
escaped prey and, following its trail, win a path
through the milky mist.

"I shall have to save that fool of a girl," he muttered
in an undertone. "She may be the daughter of an
enemy, but I will not leave a woman in the hands of
hairless apes." Like a hunting leopard, he moved forward on the scent.

As the mists began to thin, he trod more carefully. The spoor of the scent twisted and turned, as if panic had wrought havoc with his quarry's sense of direction. Conan smiled grimly. Better to be the hunter than the hunted.

Here and there beside the path small pyramids of spherical stones the size of a man's head rose above the low-lying mists. These, Conan knew, were ancient places of the dead, graves of the chiefs of the early Turanian tribes. Neither time nor the apes had managed to demolish them. The Cimmerian stepped carefully around each grave, not only to avoid a possible ambush, but also to show reverence for those who rested there.

Only torn shreds of mist remained as he reached the upper heights. Here the path became a narrow walkway atop a mountain wall, which bisected a dizzying abyss. At the end of the walkway, at the very summit of the mountain, an imposing keep of mottled serpentine loomed like an index finger of evil against the backdrop of bleak and distant mountain ranges. Conan hid behind one of the graves along the path to spy out the situation. But he saw no sign of life.

Shanya woke in odd surroundings. She lay upon a divan draped in a rough black cloth. No fetters bound her, but she had been deprived of all her clothing. She stretched her supple body upon this strange bed to look around and recoiled from what she saw.

In a wooden armchair, curiously carved, sat a man, but he was like no man that she had ever seen. His ashen face seemed made of chalk and strangely stiff; his eyes were black with no white showing around the iris; his head was bald. He wore a kaftan of coarse black cloth and hid his hands within the ebon sleeves.

"It has been many long years since a beautiful woman last came to the abode of Shangara," he said in a sibilant whisper. "No new blood has infused the race of the People of the Summit for twice a hundred years. You are a fit mate for me and for my son."

Horror ignited a bright flame of anger in the breast of the proud barbarian girl.

"Think you that a daughter of a hundred chiefs would mate with one of your abominable race? Rather would I fling myself into the nearest gorge than dwell within your house! Release me, or these walls will tremble to the thunder of a thousand Khozgari spears!"

A mocking smile parted the pale lips of the ancient, pallid face.

"You are a headstrong hussy! No spears reach through the Bhambar mists. No mortal lives who dares to cross these mountains. Come to your senses, girl! Should you persist in stubbornness, no easy leap from a cliff's edge will be your fate. Your body will, instead, be used to nourish the most ancient inhabitant of this forgotten land—one who is bound in serfdom to the People of the Summit.

"He it was who helped smite down the Turanian king who once endeavored to conquer our domain. Then we, ourselves, were strong and could do battle. Now we are few, our number dwindling through the centuries to a bare dozen who dwell here guarded by our cliff apes.

"Still we have no fear of enemies, for the ancient one lives, ready to come forth when peril threatens. You shall gaze upon his countenance. Then choose your fate!"

The aged man arose, shaking back the folds of kaftan, and clapped his clawlike hands. At the summons, two other white-faced, skull-eyed men entered the room, bowed, and grasped a pair of handles set into the stone wall. Two massive door halves rolled smoothly back, revealing a chamber filled with billowing mist. Like a scudding cloud, it swirled into the room, and as it thinned revealed the vague outline of a huge, unmoving shape.

43

As the mist roiled out, the girl perceived the *thing* inside. She screamed and fainted. Then the heavy doors were closed.

Conan, hidden behind a grave mound, fretted with impatience. During his long wait, no sign of life had appeared around the forbidding tower. Had he not scented the reek of musky ape, he would have deemed the tower to be deserted. Tensely he fondled the hilt of his scimitar and ran a hand along the curve of his bow.

At length a figure strode to the battlements and gazed out upon the crumpled brown terrain. Conan could not discern details at so great a distance, but the lean contours beneath the flowing robe revealed a human shape. Conan's mouth curved in a grim half-smile.

With a single motion, he drew and loosed an arrow; and the figure on the battlement flung up its arms and toppled, limp as a broken doll, over the crenellated wall into the depths below. He nocked another arrow and waited.

This time he had not long to wait. A pierced stone portal slowly opened, and a group of apes ran out, padding splayfooted along the narrow walkway. Conan loosed again and yet again, his marksmanship unerring. His merciless hail of arrows pitched them one after another into the shadowy gorge. But still the apes came on, with lolling tongues and slavering jaws.

Conan shot his last arrow and flung the bow aside. He rushed, sword raised, to meet the two that still defended the narrow, cliffside path. Ducking, he avoided the sword-thrust of the first and lunged, shearing through flesh and bone. The remaining ape proved quicker. Conan had scarcely time to wrench his reddened blade from the hairless corpse and parry a vicious swipe aimed at his head. He staggered at the impact of the great ape's blow and fell to his knees.

He saw with horror the dizzying depths of the preci-
pice that beckoned him to doom. The ape's dull mind
perceived the situation, and the creature rushed forward to sweep him into the bottomless abyss.

Still on his knees, Conan feinted swiftly and lashed
out with a disembowling thrust, too fast for the eye
to follow. His adversary, bellowing, pitched forward
and, trailing a receding cry, plummeted into the
shadowy depths.

Surefooted as a mountain goat, Conan dashed up
the unprotected walkway and reached the open portal.
Something hissed past his head as he threw himself
sidewise, and in swift retaliation, he thrust his scimitar at a black-clad figure lurking in the gloom of the
entrance. A muted gurgle was followed by the clatter
of a fallen weapon.

Conan bent down to peer at the corpse. A tall,
skeletal man with a curiously stiff face stared up at
him through sightless eyes. He saw that the face was
covered by a peculiar mask of some translucent substance. He snatched it off and studied it.

The Cimmerian had never seen anything remotely
like it nor like the material of which it was fashioned.
He tucked it into his sash and strode on into the silent
hall.

Conan moved more warily along a curving corridor
that he encountered further on. The stones were damp
when he laid a hand upon them, and the clammy air
reminded him of the chill of morning fog. Then suddenly the circular passageway widened into a great
chamber, where a strange assemblage confronted him.

Ten black-clad, corpselike people faced him, among
whom he saw two women whose stringy, colorless
hair framed chalky features. They stood like painted
ghosts, save that each held a murderous knife with a
sawtoothed edge.

Behind them on a black-draped catafalque, set in
the middle of the chamber, reclined the naked body
of a girl whom he recognized as Shanya. Motionless

45

Shangaran Sawtoothed Knife

she lay, her heavy-lidded eyes closed beneath long fringed lashes, save that her full breasts rose and fell with her even breathing. And Conan knew that she was either drugged or in a faint.

He gripped his sword more firmly as he studied the spectral group, whose coal-black eyes burned with the fire of commingled fear and hatred.

A tall, bald man began to speak. Although his voice was but a whisper borne upon the wind, it carried with bell-like clarity.

"What is your purpose here? You are no Hyrkanian, nor are you a mountain man, although you wear the garb of a Turanian."

"I am Conan, a Cimmerian. That girl is my hostage, and I have come to take her back that I may continue on my journey."

"Cimmeria—a tongue-twisting name for a land we know not of. Do you jest with us?" whispered the strange man.

"Had you voyaged to the frozen North, you would know I do not jest. We are a fighting people. With half my tribe at my elbow, I should be ruler of Turan!" growled Conan.

"You lie," hissed the old man. "The land of the north wind is the edge of the world and stretches beneath a starless, eternal night. The girl is ours by right of conquest. She shall give our race new strength, breeding strong men from her youthful womb. You, who have dared to intrude upon the People of the Summit, shall feed the maw of our defender, the ancient one."

"If I die, you will precede me into Hell," growled the Cimmerian, raising his sword.

In answer, the ghostly man struck a silver gong a single blow that reverberated from the rafters. Two men silently left the group and, moving together to the farther wall, grasped the iron handles and began to open the heavy doors. Like a great calla lily unfolding at dawn, a thick white vapor billowed from the opening and swirled toward the center of the room.

Moving in unison, the beady-eyed ancients passed their left hands across their faces. Before the thickening vapor blotted out his view, Conan saw that each had donned a curious transparent mask like that worn by his earlier assailant.

Impelled by an instinct as old as time, the barbarian reached into his sash, snatched up the mask, and managed to put it on before the cloying mists swirled and eddied around him, hiding his sable-clad enemies. To his surprise, the substance of the mask hugged the skin of his forehead, cheeks, and lids and lay like gossamer across his very eyes. Looking around the room, he was astounded to discover that he could see clearly, as if a puff of campfire smoke had vanished into the ambient darkness.

His adversaries had crept forward behind their misty shield, and now two were almost upon him. Moving on a thread of time, Conan's curved steel blade whistled through the damp air of the misty hall.

It was a massacre. The remnants of a once-powerful race stood little chance against the fury of the vengeful Cimmerian. Undulating knives glanced harmlessly off the whirling streak of his restless scimitar. Each time his blade licked out, a dark-robed figure sank dying to the floor. His rough code of chivalry tempted him to spare the white-haired crones; but when the women flung themselves upon him in unrelenting frenzy, he returned blow for blow.

At last Conan stood alone in the vaulted chamber, save for ten supine bodies and the still unconscious girl. Resting on his long, curved sword, he surveyed the scene with satisfaction. Then one of the bodies writhed and raised a gaunt, accusing hand. The head man, rekindling the last sparks of his departing life, glared and spoke through lips twisted with pain.

"Barbarian cur!" he hissed. "You have destroyed our race. But you shall not live to savor your victory. The ancient one will strip the meat from your foul bones and suck the marrow from their innards. Give me strength, O Ancient One . . ."

As Conan watched in fascination, the lean man with a hideous groan rose to his knees and exerted his last powers. He struggled, half crawling, to the scarcely opened doors, and with a clawlike hand tugged at one of the twin handles on the pair of heavy doors. With a roll of thunder, the door opened wide.

Conan's hair rose on his nape as he glimpsed the hulking form within the cavernous chamber. Huge and many-limbed was the body, and spiderlike, or like an egg with legs. Its stalked eyeballs and gaping jaw exuded an almost tangible power of evil, for it was a thing conceived in the dark eons before man ever walked the earth.

Mastering his horror, the Cimmerian flung himself forward and scooped up the body of Shanya, while a clawed and hairless limb fumbled at the other door to enlarge the opening. Bearing the limp body of the girl upon his shoulder, he sprinted down the long corridor leading to the outer portal. A wheezing snuffle followed him.

Conan had almost transversed the elongated walkway, balancing precariously in his great haste, when he ventured to look back. The monster, running agilely on its ten powerful legs, had reached the midpoint of the narrow path. Panting, Conan forced himself onward until he stood between two pyramidal grave mounds. Gently laying the unconscious girl at the foot of one mound, he turned to give battle.

Conan met the first onrush of the monster with a savage cut at one of the grasping limbs, but his blade splintered against the impenetrable horny hide of the creature. Although it fell back for a moment, it came on again with its weaving gait.

Desperate, Conan cast about for any weapon, and his eyes fastened upon the nearest mound of rounded stones. Flexing his great muscles, he lifted one of the spherical boulders above his head. And, straining his mighty thews, he hurled it at the terrible apparition that was almost upon him.

The forgotten spells chanted by unremembered Turanian sorcerers over the graves of long-dead chieftains had not lost their power against a monster that roamed the mountains before mankind was young. For, with a bloodcurdling shriek, the creature, half paralyzed, tugged at a limb crushed beneath insensate rock.

Conan snatched up a second boulder and flung it; pushed yet another, rolling it toward the thrashing monster; and hurled still another. Then the undermined pyramid of ponderous stones collapsed in a hurtling avalanche, which carried the many-limbed creature down into the abyss in a cloud of dust and shards.

Conan wiped his sweaty brow with a hand that trembled as much from revulsion as from exertion. He heard a stirring behind him and swung around. Shanya's eyes were open, and she gazed around her in bewilderment.

"Where am I? Where is the white-faced, evil man?" She shuddered. "He was going to feed me to . . ."

Conan's voice broke in roughly upon her. "I cleaned up that nest of mummified robbers. Their evil thing I returned to the abyss whence it came. Lucky for you that I arrived in time to save your pretty skin."

Shanya's emerald eyes flashed with haughty anger.

"I should have managed to outwit them. My father would have saved me."

Conan grunted. "Had he found his way hither, that monster would have made mincemeat of his warriors. Only by luck I discovered a weapon that could kill the overgrown cockroach. Now we must move fast. I have to be in Samara before week's end. And I still need you as a hostage. Come!"

Shanya stared at the rugged barbarian as he stood outlined against the indigo sky, one strong arm outstretched to help her rise. Her green eyes softened. For a moment her lids drooped, and she blushed, suddenly aware of her nakedness. Then she tossed her proud head, shrugged her bare shoulders, and said:

"I will come, Conan, not as your hostage, but as your guide to the border region. You saved my life, and you shall have safe conduct through Khozgari country as your reward."

Conan caught a new, warm undertone in her now-gentled voice, as she added with a ghost of a smile: "It will be interesting to learn something of the ways of a northern barbarian."

Shanya stretched her splendid body, rose-tinted by the setting sun, and reached for his outstretched hand.

Conan looked at her with appreciation. "By the bones of Crom! Perhaps dallying a few days along the way will be worth a week in the guardhouse!"

SHADOWS IN THE DARK

After mercenary service in various countries and a
spell of piracy with the black corsairs of the Kushite
coast, Conan adventures in the black kingdoms. Re-
turning north, he soldiers, first in Shem and then in
the small Hyborian kingdom of Khoraja. Following
the events of "Black Colossus," in which he defeats
the armies of the terrible Natohk, a long-dead sorcerer
revived by magic, Conan settles down as general of
the armies of Khoraja. He is now in his late twenties.
But complications arise. The princess-regent, Yasmela,
whose lover he had thought to be, is too preoccupied
with affairs of state to have time for him. Her brother,
King Khossus, has been treacherously seized and im-
prisoned by the hostile king of Ophir, leaving Khoraja
in perilous plight.

In the Street of Magicians in the Shemitish city of
Eruk, practitioners of the arcane arts put away their
paraphernalia and began to close their shops. The
scryers wrapped up their crystal balls in lambs' wool;
the pyromancers extinguished the flames in which
they saw their visions; and the sorcerers mopped
pentacles from the worn tiles of their floors.

Rhazes the astrologer was likewise busied with the
closing of his stall when an Eruki in kaftan and turban
approached him, saying:

"Do not close just yet, friend Rhazes! The king has bid me get a final word from you ere you set out for Khoraja."

Rhazes, a large, stout man, grunted his displeasure, then hid his feelings behind a suave smile. "Step in, step in, most eminent Dathan. What would His Majesty at this late hour?"

"He fain would know what the stars foretell about the fates of neighboring kings and kingdoms."

"You have brought my proper fee in silver?" asked the astrologer.

"Certainly, good sir. The king has found your prognostications worthy, and hence is loath to lose you."

"Were he so loath, why did he not do somewhat to abate the envy of my Eruki colleagues toward a foreigner and curb their harassments? But it is now too late for that; I'm off for Khoraja at dawn."

"Will naught persuade you otherwise?"

"Naught; for a greater prize awaits me there than this small city-state affords."

Dathan frowned. "Odd. Travelers say that Khoraja is much impoverished by the vanquishing of Natohk, may he fry in Hell."

Rhazes ignored this comment. "Now let's consult the stars. Pray, sit."

Dathan took a chair. Rhazes set before him a box-like brazen object with slip rings and dials upon its vertical faces. Through apertures along its sides, a multitude of brass gear wheels were plain for all to see.

The astrologer made adjustments, then slowly turned a silver knob affixed to the outer end of a protruding shaft. He watched the dials intently until they reached a setting of his choosing. At length he spoke:

"I see portentous changes. The star of Mitra will soon conjoin with the star of Nergal, which is in the ascendance. Aye, changes there shall be in Khoraja.

"I see three persons, all royal, either now, or formerly, or yet in times to come. One is a beautiful woman, caught in a web like unto a spider's. Another is a young man of high estate surrounded by walls of massive stone.

"The third is a mighty man, older than the other but still youthful, and of vast and sanguinary prowess. The woman urges him to join her in the web, but he destroys it utterly. Meanwhile the young man beats his fists in vain against the wall.

"Now strange shapes move upon the astral plane. Witches ride the clouds by the light of a gibbous moon, and the ghosts of drowned men bubble up from stagnant swamps. And the Great Worm tunnels beneath the earth to seek the graves of kings."

Rhazes shook his head as if emerging from a trance. "So tell your master that changes portend in Khoraja and in the land of Koth. Now pray excuse me; I must finish my preparations for the coming journey. Farewell, and may your stars prove auspicious!"

Through the halls of the royal palace of Khoraja, on marble floors beneath vaults and domes of lapis lazuli, strode Conan the Cimmerian. With a thud of boot heels and a jingle of spurs, he came to the private apartments of Yasmela, princess-regent of the kingdom of Khoraja.

"Vateesa!" he roared. "Where is your lady?"

A dark-eyed lady-in-waiting parted the draperies. "General Conan," she said. "The princess prepares to receive the envoy from Shumir and cannot give you audience now."

"To the devil with the envoy from Shumir! I haven't seen Princess Yasmela alone since the last new moon, and that she knows full well. If she can afford time for some smooth-talking horse-thief from one of these piddling city-states, she can afford the time for me."

"Is aught amiss with the army?"

"Nay, little one. Most of the troublemakers who resented serving under a barbarian general fell at Shamla. Now I hear naught but the usual peacetime grumbles over scanty pay and slow promotion. But I want to see your lady, and by Crom, I'll—"

53

"Vatessa!" called a gentle voice. "Permit him entry. The envoy can await me for a while."

Conan marched into the chamber where Princess Yasmela sat before her dressing table in the full splendor of her royal habiliments. Two tiring-women assisted in her preparations, one delicately tinting her soft lips, while another settled a glittering tiara on her night-black hair.

When she had dismissed her handmaidens, she rose and faced the giant Cimmerian. Conan held out his brawny arms, but Yasmela stepped back with a minatory gesture.

"Not now, my love!" she breathed. "You'd crumple my courtly rainment."

"Good gods, woman!" growled the Cimmerian. "When can I have you to myself? I like you better, anyhow, without that frippery about you."

"Conan dear, I say again that which I said before. Much as I love you, I belong to the people of Khoraja. My enemies wait like birds of prey to take advantage of my least misjudgment. 'Twas folly, what we did in that ruined temple. If I gave myself to you again and the word took wings, the throne would rock beneath me—and worse did I conceive a child by you. Besides, so busied am I with affairs of state that at the close of day I am too weary even for love."

"Then come with me before your high priest of Ishtar and let him make us one."

Yasmela sighed and shook her head. "That cannot be, my love, so long as I am regent. Were my brother free, something might be arranged, even though marriage with a foreigner is much against our customs."

"You mean if I can loose King Khossus from Moranthes' prison cell, he would take over all this mummery that uses up your life and keeps you from me?"

Yasmela raised her hands, palms upward. "Surely the king would resume his daily tasks. Whether he would permit our union, I do not know. Methinks I could persuade him."

"And the kingdom cannot pay the ransom demanded by Moranthes?" asked Conan.

"Nay. Before the war with Natohk, we raised a sum that he would have then accepted. But Ophir's price has risen, whilst our treasury is depleted. And now I fear Moranthes will sell my brother to the king of Koth. Would that we had a wizard to conjure poor Khossus out of his prison cell! Now I must go, my dear. Promptness was ever the courtesy of kings, and I must uphold the traditions of my house."

Yasmela rang a little silver bell, and the two servants returned to give the final touches to the princess's attire. Conan bowed his way out; then at the door he paused and said: "Princess, your words have given me a thought."

"What thought, my General?"

"I'll tell you when you have the time to listen. Farewell for now."

Taurus the chancellor brushed back the white hair above a face lined with the cares of many years. He looked intently at Conan, sitting across from him in his cabinet of state. He said:

"You ask what would befall if Khossus were slain? Why then, the council would choose his successor. As he has no legitimate heir, his sister is the likely choice, since the Princess Yasmela is popular and conscientious."

"If she declined the honor?" said Conan.

"The succession would pass to her next of kin, her uncle Bardes. If, good Conan, you think to grasp the crown yourself, dismiss the thought. We Khorajis are a clannish folk; none would accept a foreigner like you. I mean no offense; I do but utter facts."

Conan waved away Taurus' apology. "I like an honest man. But what if a ninny came to sit upon the throne?"

"Better one ninny on whom all agree, than two able princes wasting the land in a struggle for power. But

55

you came not to discuss the rule of kings but to advance some proposal, did you not?"

"I thought if I went secretly to Ophir and smuggled Khossus out, the kingdom would greatly profit, would it not?"

Experienced statesman though he was, Taurus' eyes widened. "Amazing that you voice this proposition! Only a few days since, a soothsayer broached a like suggestion. The stars foretold, he said, that Conan would embark on this adventure and carry it to success. Thinking naught of magic, I dismissed the matter. But perchance the undertaking might happily go forward."

"What mage was this?" asked Conan in surprise.

"Rhazes, a Corinthian, lately come from Eruk."

"I know him not," said Conan. "Something the princess said gave me the notion."

Taurus looked shrewdly at the barbarian general. He had heard rumors of the passion between Conan and Yasmela but thought it wiser not to mention the affair. The idea of a union between his adored princess and a rough barbarian mercenary made Taurus shudder. Still, despite his pride of class and ancestry, he tried to be fair-minded toward the savior of Khoraja. He said:

"'Tis but a forlorn hope, this rescue of the king, yet we must act upon it soon or not at all. Since we cannot pay Moranthes the ransom he demands, I fear he will deliver our young king to Strabonus of Koth, who offers Ophir an advantageous treaty. Once the Kothian gets Khossus in his clutches, he'll doubtless torture him until he signs an abdication in Strabonus' favor, making him ruler of our land. We'll fight, for certain; but a bitter end is foreordained."

"We beat Natohk's army," said Conan.

"Aye, thanks to you. But Strabonus commands in great numbers sound, well-disciplined troops, unlike Natohk's motley hordes."

"And if I free the king, what reward is mine?" asked Conan.

Taurus gave a wry smile. "You come straight to the point, do you not, General? Do you not hope to enjoy more of the princess's company, once her brother regains the throne?"

"What if I do?" growled Conan.

"No offense, no offense. But would not that reward suffice you?"

"It would not. If I am to win respect among your perfumed nobles, I shall need more than an officer's pay. I will accept half the sum you offered Moranthes for the king's return, ere he raised his price."

With another, Taurus would have bargained; but he judged Conan too shrewdly to think that he could gain by chaffering with him. The unpredictable Cimmerian might roar with laughter, or fly into a rage, storm out, and leave Khoraja just when the kingdom needed him.

"Very well," said Taurus. "At least, the money will stay within the kingdom. I'll send for this Rhazes, and we shall plan your expedition."

Conan strode in on Yasmela, Taurus, and another— a large, stout man of middle years, wearing a gauzy robe and a sleepy expression. At Conan's heels came a small and furtive man, skeletally thin, in ragged garments.

"Hail, Princess!" said Conan. "And hail, Chancellor. And good day to you, whoever you may be."

Taurus cleared his throat. "General Conan, I present Master Rhazes of Limnae, the eminent astrologer. And who is the gentleman who accompanies you?"

Conan gave a bark of laughter. "Know, friends, that this is no gentleman but Fronto, the most skillful thief in all your kingdom. I found him in a reeking dive last night when all you honest folk were sleeping."

Fronto bowed low, while Taurus seemed to be controlling his feelings of distaste.

"A thief?" said the chancellor. "What need have we for such an one in this enterprise?"

"Being one myself, once, I know something of thievish ways," said Conan quietly. "When I was in the trade, though, I never learned the art of picking locks. My fingers were too large and clumsy. But for our purposes now, we may need a lock-picker, and there is none more adroit at this than Fronto. I inquired among some other thieves I know."

"You have the most amazing acquaintance," said Taurus dryly. "But—but how can you rely upon persons of his character?"

Conan grinned. "Fronto has his reasons for helping us. Tell them, Fronto."

In a soft Ophirean accent, the thief spoke for the first time: "Know, good sirs and lady, that I have my own score to settle with King Moranthes of Ophir. I am, if not of noble blood, at least from a station in life higher than that wherein you see me. I am the only son of Hermion, in his time the foremost architect of Ophir.

"Some years ago, when Moranthes, then a stripling youth, came to the throne of Ophir, he chose to build a new and larger palace in Ianthe. For this task he hired my father. The king decreed that there should be a secret passage from the interior of the palace complex to a point outside the city walls, whereby he could escape a sudden uprising of the people or the destruction of his city by a foe.

"When the palace was complete, secret passage and all, the king ordered that the builders of the passageway be slain, so none should spread the secret. My father he did not slay. Deeming himself merciful, Moranthes merely had him blinded.

"The hideous injury broke my father's health. He died within the month. But ere he passed away, he revealed to me the secret of the passage, whereby I can lead the general into the palace. And since the passage opens into the dungeons and I can pick the lock of any door, we have a gambler's chance of rescuing the king."

"And what, good thief, are you asking for your services?" inquired Taurus.

"Besides revenge, I wish for a small pension—the kind Khoraja pays to her old soldiers."

"You shall have it," said the chancellor.

Conan shot a glance at the astrologer, asking: "What is your part in this, Master Rhazes?"

"I offer my services to your expedition, General. With my astronomical calculator," he said, pointing to the brass box fitted with dials and wheels that he set upon his palm, "I can seek out the most auspicious times for each step of your journey."

Rhazes held it forward and turned the silver knob. After frowning at the dials, he said: "A happy coincidence! The best time for departure for the next two months occurs upon the morrow. And while I am no sorcerer, I know a magical trick or two to aid you."

Conan growled: "I've managed not a few years without the aid of magical mummeries, and I see no reason to turn to them now."

"Furthermore," said Rhazes blandly, ignoring Conan's remark, "I know Koth well and speak the tongue without a trace of accent. Since we shall cross that vasty kingdom on our way to Ophir—"

"The devil with that!" said Conan. "Strabonus would love to get his hands on us. Nay, we shall skirt the borders of Koth, through Shem and Argos—"

"Rhazes has reason," Taurus broke in. "Time is of the essence, and the route you propose would add much to your journey."

Yasmela joined Taurus in the argument, until Conan with little grace agreed to take the shorter route and accepted the Corinthian as the third member of the party. Then the chancellor said:

"You will need personal guards and servants to do camp chores and care for your equipment—"

"No!" roared Conan, smiting the table in the audience room. "Every extra man is one more pair of eyes to see, ears to hear, and tongue to blab our secrets. I've camped out in many lands, in weather fair and foul, and Fronto also knows the rougher side of life.

If Master Rhazes does not wish to share these trifling hardships, let him remain in Khoraja."

Taurus clucked. "It is unheard-of for a man of your rank, General, to cross the country without even a varlet to clean his boots."

"I've done my own chores before, and it won't harm me to do them once again. On a journey of this kind, he travels the fastest who travels alone."

The fat astrologer sighed. "I will come alone, if I must. But ask me not to chop the firewood."

"Very well, then." Conan rose. "Chancellor, give Fronto a pass from the palace, lest some sentry assume the worst and clap him in irons." He flipped a coin to the thief, who caught it. "Fronto, buy yourself some clothes—decent but not gaudy—and meet me at the officers' quarters before the supper hour. Princess, permit me to escort you to your apartments."

When they neared Yasmela's rooms, Conan murmured: "May I come to you tonight?"

"I—I know not—the risk—"

"It may be our last time, you know."

"Oh, you wretched man to torment me so! Very well, I'll send my tiring women away before the changing of the guard."

Three riders and their pack mule trotted up the gentle slope that led toward the northern branch of the Kothian Escarpment. Now and again the travelers passed traffic on the road: a peddler afoot with his pack on his back, a farmer in a cart drawn by plodding oxen, a train of camels guided by Shemites in striped robes and headcloths, a Khorajan aristocrat whipping his chariot team ahead of his cantering knot of retainers.

At last the rampart of the escarpment towered above them. From below it seemed a solid wall of rock, but as they came closer, the wall was seen to be fractured into bluffs, parted by narrow gorges.

The road led into one of these defiles, and as they walked their horses up the winding path cut in the canyon, the wall of rock blotted out the setting sun. When the travelers mounted the highest rampart, the sun had set.

To the west, the rounded Kothian hills stood out against the skyline like breasts of recumbent giantesses. In the distance Conan could discern the peak of Mount Khrosha, its plume of smoke colored an angry red by the glow of the seething fires within the crater.

Ahead the ground rolled gently, and here a group of armed men, wearing the golden helmet of Koth embroidered on their surcoats, halted them. The travelers had reached the border. Rhazes said:

"General Conan, let me manage this."

With a grunt, the stout magician lowered himself from the saddle and approached the commander of the border guard. He took the officer by the elbow, led him aside, and spoke rapidly in fluent Kothic, now and then gesturing toward his companions. The officer's stern face broke into a smile. Then, uttering a guffaw and slapping his thigh, he turned to Conan and Fronto and jerked a thumb.

"On your way!" he said.

When the border post had shriveled in the distance, Conan asked: "What did you tell those knaves, Rhazes?"

The astrologer smiled blandly. "I said that we are on our way to Asgalun and we heard tales of war among the western states of Shem."

"Aye, but what made the fellow laugh?"

"Oh, I said that Fronto was my son, and we were going to offer prayers at the temple of Derketo to enable him to beget a son. I said he suffered from—ah —certain bodily weakness."

"You bastard!" roared Conan, doubling up with raucous mirth, while Fronto kept his eyes upon the road and scowled.

The moon swelled to full, then shrank to a slender scimitar as they plodded over the endless leagues of

Koth. They moved through a land of rolling prairie, where mounted neatherds tended longhorned cattle. They skirted the barrens of central Koth, where streams emptied into a lake so salt that the few plants marching along the marge were armed with spines and thorns. In time they reached more fertile country and stopped to rest.

Conan studied his companions. Fronto worried him. The little thief was a willing helper, active and adroit; but he muttered endlessly about his private woes and grudges.

"If the gods vouchsafe the chance," he said, "I'll slay that villain Moranthes, though afterwards they boil me in oil."

"I blame you not," said Conan. "Vengeance is sweet, and I, too, have enjoyed it. But one must survive to experience the pleasure of revenge.

"Remember that we come not to kill Moranthes, however much he may deserve it, but to get Khossus out of his confines. Later if you would fain go back to stalk the king, that's your affair."

But Fronto still muttered, chewing his lips and wringing his fingers in the intensity of his pent-up emotions.

Rhazes was different. The astrologer did no chores unless Conan bullied him, and he was so unhandy that he would have been but little help if willing. Always good-natured, he entertained the two with stories out of ancient myths and disquisitions on the arcane sciences.

Still, the astrologer had a way of evading answers to direct questions, slithering out from under them like a serpent wriggling away from a descending foot. Conan felt a vague distrust of the man; yet, however much he watched and listened, he could find nothing definite against him.

They were camped in a stretch of forest east of Khorshemish when Rhazes said: "I must cast our horoscope to ascertain if danger awaits us in the capital of Koth."

He took his calculating box from the large leathern sack, which contained his magical apparatus. He studied the stars overhead, peering through the branches of the surrounding trees, and turned the silver knob, watching the dials by the flickering firelight. At last he said:

"Indeed, peril awaits us in Khorshemish. We had best take the back roads around the city. I know the route." The astrologer frowned at his instrument, made small adjustments, and continued: "I am puzzled by an indication of another danger, close to hand."

"What sort?" said Conan.

"That I cannot tell, but we had best be on our guard." Rhazes carefully returned his machine to the sack, in which he fumbled and brought forth a length of rope. "I'll show you a trick of petty magic, which I learned from a sorcerer in Zamora. See you this? Catch it!"

He tossed the rope to Conan, who shot out a hand. Then Conan leaped up with a startled oath, hurling the object from him, for in midair it had turned into a writhing serpent. Falling to earth, the snake changed back to an inert piece of rope.

"Damn your hide, Rhazes!" snarled Conan, half drawing his sword. "Do you seek to murder me?"

The astrologer chuckled as he retrieved the rope. "Merely an illusion, my dear General. 'Twas never aught but a rope. Even if it had truly been a serpent, it was—as anyone could see—a snake of a harmless kind."

"To me, a snake is a snake," grunted Conan, resuming his seat. "Count yourself lucky your head still rides atop your shoulders."

Imperturbably, Rhazes returned the rope to his bag, saying: "I warn you not to pry into this pack. Some of the things therein are not so harmless. This casket, for example."

He drew out a small, ornately carved copper chest, larger than the calculating device, and soon returned it to the bag.

Fronto grinned an elfish grin. "So the mighty General Conan fears something after all!" he chortled.

"Indeed," growled Conan, "when we sight the towers of Ianthe, we shall see who fears—"

"Do not move!" said a harsh voice in Kothic. "You are covered by a dozen drawn bows."

Conan turned his eyes as a man stepped out of the shadows—a lean man in ragged finery, with a patch over one eye. A movement among the trees revealed the presence of his fellows.

"Who are you?" grated Conan.

"A distressed gentleman, collecting his fee for the use of his demesne, to wit: this greenwood," said the man, who called to his men, "Come closer, lads, and let them see the points of your shafts."

There were only seven archers in the robber band, but they were quite enough to keep three travelers covered.

Conan bent his knees beneath him, as if preparing to spring erect. Were he alone, he would have instantly attacked, trusting to the mail shirt beneath his tunic; but the fact that his comrades would surely perish if he did so made him hesitate.

"Ah!" said the leading robber, bending over Rhazes's leathern sack. "What have we here?" Thrusting in a hand, he brought out the copper casket. "Gold—not heavy enough. Jewels—mayhap. Let us see—"

"I warn you not to open it," said Rhazes.

The one-eyed man gave a small snort of laughter, fumbled with the catch, and raised the lid of the box. "Why," he exclaimed, "'tis empty—or full of smoke—"

The robber chief broke off with a shrill scream and hurled the box away. From it had issued what looked in the firelight like a cloud of sooty smoke. The cloud, like a living thing, swelled to man-size and wrapped itself around the one-eyed robber, who staggered about, thrashing his arms and beating his clothes as if to put out enveloping flames. As he danced, he continued screaming. Rhazes sat motionless, muttering to himself.

The box lay open where it had fallen, and from it poured another animated cloud and yet another. Shapeless, amorphous presences, they billowed through the air, like some shapeless creatures swimming through the depths of the ocean. One fastened on a second robber, who also began to leap about and yell.

The remaining robbers loosed their arrows at the inky clouds, which continued to roll out of the copper casket, but the shafts met no resistance. The robber chief and the archer ceased writhing and lay still. In a trice, the remaining archers vanished from the firelight, their pounding feet and shouts of terror receding into the silence of the forest.

Rhazes pushed himself erect and recovered his box. Holding it open, he raised his voice in a weird chant, and one by one the smoky clouds drifted toward him and poured into the casket. They seemed to have no trouble crowding back into their pen.

At last Rhazes snapped shut the lid and turned the catch. "He cannot say I did not warn him," said the astrologer with a smile. "Or, I should say, his ghost cannot so accuse me."

"You're more of a sorcerer than you care to own," growled Conan. "What were those spooks?"

"Elemental spirits, trapped by a powerful spell on this material plane. In darkness they obey me, but they cannot endure the light of day. I won the casket from a magician of Luxur in Stygia." He shrugged. "The stars foretold that I should win the game."

"Seems like cheating to me," said Conan.

"Ah, but he tried to cheat me, too, by enchanting the dice."

"Well," said Conan, "I've gambled away more gold and silver than most men see in a lifetime; but Mitra save me from being lured by a wizard into a game of chance!" Conan poked the fire thoughtfully. "Your man-eating clouds saved our gear and perhaps our necks as well. But had I not been listening to your chatter, I should have heard the men approach and not been surprised like a newborn lamb. Now stop the talk and go to sleep. I'll take the first watch."

Rhazes guided the party over little-traveled roads around Khorshemish, until they were again on the main road to Ophir.

As the leagues fell behind them, Conan grew more and more uneasy. It was not the prospect of breaking into King Moranthes' stronghold that daunted him; he had survived many such episodes. Nor was it fear of torture; and death had been his companion for so long that he paid it less attention than he would a fly.

He finally found the source of his unease: their journey so far had been too free of trouble. Whenever they were stopped by road patrols, Rhazes talked their way past them as handily as with the border guards. There had been no magical menace, no desperate combat, no wild pursuit. Conan smiled at the irony of it. He had become so hardened to peril that its absence made him uncomfortable.

At last they came in sight of Ianthe, straddling the Red River. A short, sharp rainstorm had swept the air clean, and the setting sun sparkled on the metal ornaments that crowned the city's domes and towers. Over the wall stared the red-tiled roofs of the taller houses. Fronto said:

"To cross the river by the floating bridge, one must enter the city—a questionable plan. Or we can ride half a league upstream to the nearest ford."

"Is the tunnel entrance on the northern side?" asked Conan.

"Aye, General."

"Then we'll go upstream to cross."

Rhazes looked sharply at Fronto. "Can we reach the tunnel by midnight?"

"I'm sure of it."

The astrologer nodded.

The moon, a thick crescent waxing toward the half, flitted palely through the trees as the three men dismounted in a grove on the northeast side of the city. A bowshot away, the crenellated city walls rose black against the star-strewn sky. Conan took from his saddle bags a bundle of torches—long pine sticks with one end wrapped in rags that had been soaked in lard.

"Stay with the horses, Rhazes," muttered Conan. "Fronto and I will enter the tunnel."

"Oh, no, General!" said the astrologer firmly. "I'll go with you. The tethered beasts will be quite safe. And you may need my bag of magic tricks ere you get Khossus out alive."

"He's right, General," said Fronto the thief.

"He's too old and fat for acrobatics," said Conan.

"I am more active than you think," replied Rhazes. "Further, the stars foretell that you will require my aid to bring off your enterprise."

"Very well," growled Conan. In spite of himself, Conan had been impressed by some of Rhazes' prognostications about such things as weather and accommodations at inns. "But if you lag behind and Ophireans seize you, do not expect me return to rescue you!"

"I am prepared to take my chances," said Rhazes.

"Then let's go!" hissed Fronto, fidgeting. "I cannot wait to flesh my dagger in one of Moranthes' villains!"

"No stabbing for mere pleasure!" growled Conan. "This is no pleasure hunt in the greenwood. Come on."

Muttering, the thief led his companions through the grove and into a clump of shrubs a few yards beyond the palace wall. Above them, the moonlight twinkled on the helmet and spear of a sentry pacing his rounds upon the parapet. All three froze, like hunted animals; and they held their positions, scarcely breathing, until the sentry passed out of sight.

In the center of the thicket, shielded on all sides from view by the circle of bushes, they found a patch of earth where the grass grew thin. Fronto scrabbled in this meager ground cover until he found a bronzen ring. Seizing it, he tugged upward, but nothing moved.

"General," he breathed, "you are stronger than I; try raising it."

Conan took a deep breath, stooped, grasped the ring, and heaved. Slowly, with a grating sound, the buried trapdoor rose. Conan peered down into fetid darkness. The moonlight outlined a flight of stairs.

"My father planned the thing aright," whispered Fronto. "Even so tall a man as you, Conan, can walk upright without butting the ceiling."

"Stay here to lower the trapdoor, after I light a torch," said Conan, feeling his way down the steps.

At the bottom, he went to work with flint and steel. After striking sparks for some time without result, he growled:

"Crom's devils! The rain has gotten into my tinder. Has anybody some that's dry?"

"I have that which will do in its stead," said Rhazes, leaning over Conan's shoulder. "Stand back, pray."

From his leather bag the astrologer produced a rod, which he pointed at the torch while muttering an incantation. The end of the rod glowed red, then yellow, then white. A beam of bright light speared the torch, which smoked, sputtered, and burst into flame. The rod's glow faded, and Rhazes returned the implement to his bag.

"Lower the trapdoor, Fronto!" said Conan. "Gently, you fool! Banging it down that way will alert the guards!"

Tinder Kit

"Sorry; my hand slipped," said Fronto, scuttling spiderlike down the stairs. "Give me the torch; I know the way."

In silence the three men plodded along the dark passage. It was lined with stone slabs on floor and sides and roofed with massive timbers. Moss and fungus splotched the crude stones and squelched noisomely underfoot. Rats squeaked and fled from their approach, red eyes glinting like accursed rubies in the blackness, claws scraping the damp stones as they fled.

Through the dripping darkness they proceeded, guided only by the flickering torch that Fronto held aloft. They said nothing. Was it out of inborn caution, or was it unwillingness to acknowledge the clammy breath of fear that followed them through the gloom and whispering darkness?

Conan looked about him, grimly. The flickering orange flames of the torch painted black shadows across the lichen-encrusted stones—shadows that swooped and billowed like enormous bats. The subterranean passage had for years been sealed away from the outside world; for now the air was vitiated and stifling, thick with the unwholesome odors of decay.

After a time Conan growled: "How much farther, Fronto? We must have walked clear across Ianthe and are beyond the city now."

"We are not halfway yet. The palace lies in the midst of the city, where once stood the citadel."

"What noise is that?" asked Rhazes when a rumble as of thunder reverberated overhead.

"Just an ox cart on Ishtar Street," said Fronto.

At last they reached the tunnel's end. Here a flight of steps led upward to a trapdoor like the other. Conan took the torch and examined the trap.

Conan asked softly: "Where in the dungeons does this passage lead?"

Fronto rubbed a reflective hand over a stubbled jaw. "To the far end of the south branch," he said.

"And King Khossus is held prisoner in the middle branch, parallel to this," murmured Rhazes from behind them. Conan, suddenly suspicious, shot him a glance.

"How do you come to know that?" he demanded sharply.

The plump seer spread both hands in a disarming gesture. "By my stars, General. How else?"

Conan muttered something that sounded like a curse.

The eager thief pushed up the trapdoor a finger's breadth at a time, pressing an attentive ear against the rough wood. At last he whispered: "There seem to be no guards in this part. Come."

Despite a faint squeal of hinges, he thrust the trap up all the way and beckoned to his companions.

Conan let his breath out with a sigh and set the torch down so that it leaned against the side of the tunnel and burned with a dim but welcome light. Then he followed Fronto to the dungeon. After him panted Rhazes.

They emerged into a corridor some twenty paces long and saw a row of untenanted cells on either side. The air was heavy with the prison stench of decay and mold and ordure. The only light came faintly from a torch mounted in a bracket on the wall of a transverse passage at the far end of their corridor, save that a roseate glow emanated from the torch Conan had set against the dank wall of the tunnel below them. To extinguish this telltale glow, Fronto began to lower the trap, but Conan hastily set a coin between the trap and the strut on which it rested, propping the door up ever so slightly; so that, by the slight irregularity of flooring, they could find it when they again had need of it.

Conan's sword whispered from its sheath as he turned and led his strange companions toward the distant torch. Under drawn brows, his blue eyes darted from side to side, scanning the cells. Most were empty, but in one a pile of bones gleamed whitely in the semidarkness. In another a living prisoner, ragged and filthy, his face all but invisible behind a tangled mass of grizzled hair, shuffled up to the bars and silently watched the invaders. So quietly did they move along the narrow hall that the very silence seemed to roar.

When they reached the corner of the corridor where the bracketed torch belched smoke, Fronto pointed to the right. Moving like a pride of hunting lionesses, they paced the cross-passage unseen, and turning left again, they reached another cell-lined passageway. As they proceeded noiselessly along it, Fronto jerked a thumb to draw Conan's attention.

This cell was twice the size of the others. In the dimness, Conan made out a chair, a small table, a washstand, and a bed. A man sitting on the bed rose as the three silent figures stopped outside the bars that held him. The man could not clearly be discerned, but from his stance and outline, Conan perceived that he was young and handsomely attired.

"Get to work, Fronto," whispered Conan.

The thief pulled from his boot a slender length of bent wire and inserted it into the keyhole, his feral eyes agleam in the flickering torchlight. After a momentary fumble, the lock clicked back and Conan shouldered in the door.

The prisoner recoiled as, sword in hand, Conan strode in. "Has Moranthes sent you here to murder me?" he whispered hoarsely.

"Nay, my lad; if you be Khossus of Khoraja, we've come to rescue you."

The young man stiffened. "You must not speak so to an annointed king! You should address me—"

"Lower your voice," snarled Conan. "Are you Khossus, or are you not?"

"I am he; but you should say 'Your Maj—'"

"We've no time for such courtesies. Will you come or stay?"

"I'll come," grumbled the youth. "But who are you?"

71

"I'm Conan, general of your army. Now come quickly and quietly."

"First lend me your sword, General."

"What for?" said Conan in astonishment.

"The captain of the guard here has used me with spite and contumely. He has insulted the honor of Khoraja, and I have sworn to fight him to the death. And I'll not leave until it's done!"

Khossus' voice rose as he spoke until it echoed in the narrow cell. Conan glanced at his companions, shook his touseled mane, and brought his huge fist up against Khossus' jaw. With a click, the king's teeth came together, and Khossus fell back against his cot.

An instant later, Conan with the king's unconscious body draped across one shoulder, led his companions from the cell. As they turned into the transverse passageway, they heard the tramp of booted feet and the clank of metal accouterments.

"Run for the tunnel. I'll stand off the guard," hissed Conan.

"Nay, you bear the king. You go ahead; I'll harry the lout," whispered Rhazes, fumbling in his bag.

"What goes on there?" rumbled an angry voice, as its owner, sword unsheathed, appeared around the third prong of the cell block.

As Conan and Fronto sprinted toward the passage in which the trapdoor lay, the astrologer, billowing robes etched by the feeble light of the single torch, drew from his leathern sack that which appeared to be a hempen noose. The prison warden checked his pace and threw up a hand to catch the flying rope. Then shrieking at the writhing thing within his grasp, he flung the serpent from him, turned abruptly, and still yelling like a madman, vanished down the farthest corridor.

Then Rhazes trotted to the open trapdoor, where Conan, still bearing the unconscious king upon his shoulder, reached up a brawny arm to steady his descent. As the astrologer reset his bag strap across his back, Fronto scampered up the steps and lowered the trapdoor carefully.

Conan muttered: "Is there no bolt to secure the trap?"

"I see none," said Fronto. "The fact that the door is masked by several flagstones makes it nigh invisible from the upper passageway."

"Then we must run," said Conan, and shifting the weight of the slender king, he followed Fronto, who darted ahead with upheld torch. Rhazes, like some merchant ship sailing before the wind, panted after them.

During their flight, Khossus revived. When his head cleared, and he realized his undignified position, he complained:

"Why do you carry me like a sack of tubers on the way to market? Put me down instanter! This is no way to treat your king!"

Conan, never slackening his pace, grunted. "When you can run as fast as I, I'll set you down. Unless, perchance you prefer to be overtaken by the prison warden and returned to your cell—or to a worse one. Well?"

"Oh, all right," said the young king sulkily. "But you seem to have no feel for royal dignity."

At the exit from the tunnel, Conan set the king upon his feet and, pushing past Fronto, scrambled up the stairs. With a grunt and a mighty heave, he pushed open the trapdoor. Fronto was at his heels.

"Put out that torch!" he snapped. Fronto obeyed.

Then Conan stepped out into the starlight. The moon had set, and Conan realized that the rescue had taken longer than expected.

With his companions crowding behind him, Conan worked his way through the circle of shrubbery around the open trapdoor and halted. A few paces ahead, standing in the thicket, was a score or more of armed men with crossbows cocked and trained on the fugitives. Behind them, in the grove, he saw the flames of a brisk campfire.

"What's this?" demanded Conan, sweeping out his sword.

"Pray, General," wheezed Rhazes behind him, "I can explain."

"Come out, Rhazes," said one of the dark figures in Kothic, "we should not wish to shoot you by mistake."

The astrologer pushed past Conan and turned. "Dear simple General, you'd best surrender quietly. These are soldiers of my native Koth, whose king I have the honor loyally to serve. Arrangements for this ambuscade were made on our way hither by our border guards. We avoided Khorshemish lest some acquaintance hail me and disclose my small imposture. You have helped me pluck King Khossus out of Moranthes' clutches; and now we'll take the pair of you to Koth. Thus shall we remove the last obstacle to reuniting Khoraja with her mother country."

Conan tensed, rocking forward on the balls of his feet, preparing for action. He trusted to his mailshirt to deflect the crossbow bolts; and if that failed—well, no man can live forever.

"Drop your sword, General Conan!" ordered the soldier who had already spoken.

"You'll have to kill me first!" shouted Conan, rushing forward to meet the Kothian officer.

Then Fronto moved. With a scream of rage, the little thief leaped forward, eyes gleaming in reflected firelight, and drove his dagger into Rhazes' paunch—once, twice, thrice. Two crossbows snapped, but the bolts whistled harmlessly into the dark, as the arbalesters feared hitting their own men.

Silently Rhazes sank down, his fluttering garments billowing like pale fog in the starlight. His leather bag fell open on the ground beside him. Like a jumping spider, Fronto leaped sidewise, snatched up the bag, and ran for the grove of trees. Then another crossbow twanged. Fronto strangled on a blood-flecked cough and dropped headfirst into the fire. The bag he bore likewise landed in the embers.

Conan, defending Khossus, traded blows with several Kothians. His blade whirled and clanged against his foes', as the cold stars glimmered on the steel. One Kothian gave back with a hoarse scream, gripping the stump of his sword arm with his remaining hand. Another fell, his belly ripped open, spilling out his guts. Bounding ahead, Khossus stooped and wrenched the sword from the severed hand in time to save the battling Cimmerian from a sword-thrust in the back.

Then, despite the noise and confusion, Conan perceived the faint jingle of mail, the crackling of broken branches, the tramp of booted feet as more men pushed through the thicket. Drawing Khossus with him, Conan faded into the bushes as a party of Ophirean prison guards poured from the tunnel on the trail of their liberated prisoner. Bursting through the thicket, they found themselves face to face with the men of Koth. Conan and his king, hidden in the shadows, heard the snap of a crossbow and shrieks of pain as the new battle was joined.

All was confusion. Kothians fought Ophireans. Men shouted contradictory orders.

"Khossus!" barked the Cimmerian. "Run for the grove—on the left—the horses tethered there."

They broke from their shelter and ran. Then the Ophirean prison warden recognized the slender king and shouted to his men: "To me! Here's the prisoner— and his rescuer! Seize them!"

"Faster!" said Conan, wheeling around to stem the tide of pursuers. He parried a slash from one scarcely seen antagonist and wounded another. He was about to strike down another, a Kothian, when an Ophirean attacked the man, and the fight swirled off into the darkness. In the confusion, Conan and Khossus plunged out of the melee, reached the grove, jumped over the embers of the fire, and raced for their tethered horses.

"Stop them! Stop them!" shouted a chorus of voices as the fugitives disappeared among the trees. Behind them Kothians joined with Ophireans, each intent on recapturing their human prize and his barbarian protector. One Kothian leaped the fire, and Conan, wheeling, struck him down just as a tremendous report shook the earth and showered the fugitives with embers and debris. Rhazes' bag, simmering on the fire, had at last exploded.

As two Ophireans plunged into the grove in hot pursuit, black, smoky clouds boiled up from the ruptured fire. In wave after wave the shadows rose, like huge amoeboids swimming in the deep. One swooped down upon the first oncomer and engulfed him. The man gave a wild shriek of terror and lay still. The other pursuer, whirling in his haste to get away, stumbled over a root and sprawled beneath another undulating cloud.

"Rhazes' shadows," muttered Conan, as another howl of horror from a dying man floated upward. "Untie the horses, fast. Ride one and lead the other!" With trembling fingers, Khossus obeyed.

The next instant Conan and the king flung themselves into their saddles and spurred out of the grove, faces close to the horses' necks to avoid the lashing branches. But even in their mad flight, Conan looked back to see the billowing shadows hovering like wings of death, impartially, above both the men of Ophir and their Kothian adversaries, whose fleeing cries of pain and terror melded into one indistinguishable shriek.

Conan and the king came out upon a road, and the ringing of their horses' hooves drowned out the clangor of the rout.

As the flying hooves cleaved the still night, Khossus called out in a shaky voice: "Conan! This is not the way to Khoraja! We're on the road to Argos and Zingara!"

"Which way do you think they'll go to look for us?" snarled Conan. "Come on, kick some speed out of that nag!" He galloped westward with the king of Khoraja close behind him.

Although the flying pair made exceptional speed by

frequent changes of mount, the following nightfall saw them still within the confines of Ophir. None challenged them, since their flight had outrun the news of their escape. They found a stretch of forest and made camp, eating dried fruits and biscuits from their saddlebags. Khossus, who had abandoned his efforts to make Conan address him in royal style, told how he came to be captured:

"Moranthes proposed an alliance against Strabonus of Koth, and that seemed logical to me. Like a fool, I went to parley with him with a small escort only, carefully bypassing Koth by traveling through the city-states of Shem. Taurus had warned me against Moranthes, but I was sure that no annointed king would sink to trickery. I know better now—for no sooner had I reached Ianthe than the scoundrel clapped me into prison.

"My lot was somewhat better than that of common prisoners. Now and then news of the outside world reached me. Thus I learned of your victory over Natohk at the Shamla Pass." The king peered narrowly at Conan. "I also heard that you had become my sister's lover. Be that true?"

Conan looked up from the fire with a slight suggestion of a smile. "If I had, it would be ungentle of me to admit it. Whilst no blushing virgin, I do not kiss and tell. But tell me, would you accept me as a brother-in-law?"

Khossus started. "Out of the question, my good General! You—a foreign barbarian and vulgar mercenary —nay, friend Conan, think not upon the matter. I appreciate your heroism and owe my life to you, but I could not admit you into the royal family. And now it is my royal wish to sleep, since I am weary to the bone."

"Very well, Your Majesty," grumbled Conan acidly. "Your royal will be done."

Long that night he sat beside the embers of the fire, his black brows drawn in night-dark thoughts.

Drinking Jack

The following day they crossed the Argossean border and put up at an inconspicuous inn. After supper, as they dawdled over jacks of ale, Khossus said:

"General, I have been thinking. You deserve well of me." He raised a hand as Conan opened his mouth for a reply. "Nay, deny it not, your rescue of your king from the Ophireans, the Kothians, and your treacherous friend Rhazes' elementals were feats worthy of an epic.

"A man like you should be well settled with a family, and I shall wish to keep you with us to direct our army. Since you cannot wed the princess Yasmela, I will find you an attractive maiden of the middle classes—some small landowner's daughter, perhaps—and unite the twain of you. And I shall likewise choose a royal marriage partner for my sister.

"However, while I wish you to direct our army, one of your lowly origins cannot continue to command Khoraja's knights and noblemen. You had trouble, did you not, with the unfortunate Count Thespides on that same score? So I shall choose a man of suitable rank to bear the name of general, yet he shall ever follow your advice. And I shall create some special, well-paid post, open to commoners, for your express benefit."

Conan looked at the king, his eyes inscrutable. "Your Majesty's generosity overwhelms me," he said.

Oblivious of the sarcasm, Khossus waved away a protest. "'Tis but your due, good sir. How would the title sergeant-general suit you?"

"Let us leave that till we return," said Conan.

Lying awake in the dark room of the inn, Conan pondered his future. He had ever been one to live for the moment and let the future take care of itself. Yet, it was obvious now that his career in Khoraja was headed for trouble. This haughty but well-meaning young ass believed every word he spoke about his royal rights and duties.

True, he could quietly kill the king and return to Khoraja with some cock-and-bull story about the idiot's end. But to risk so much to rescue him, only to murder the fool, would be ridiculous. Yasmela would never forgive him. Besides, he had given his word to save the king, and—this he noted with some small surprise—his passion for Yasmela had begun to cool.

At Messantia, Khossus found a port official who knew him, and who, on the strength of his position, lent him two hundred Argossean gold dolphins, borrowed from a moneylender. The king handed the bag containing this small fortune to Conan for safekeeping, saying:

"It becomes not the dignity of a monarch to carry filthy money."

They found a ship about to sail for Asgalun, whence they could make their way through Shem to Khoraja. As the sailors manned the ropes preparing to cast off, Conan dug into the bag of gold and brought out a fistful of coins.

"Here," he said, handing the money over to Khossus. "You'll need these to get home."

"But—but—what are you doing? I thought—"

"I've changed my mind," said Conan. As the vessel left the pier, he leaped from the ship's rail to the quay. Then he turned and added, "It's time I visited my homeland, and there's a craft sailing for Kordava tomorrow."

"But my gold!" cried the king from the receding deck.

"Call it the price of your life," shouted Conan across the widening stretch of water. "And say farewell to Princess Yasmela for me!"

Whistling an air, he walked away without another backward look.

THE STAR OF KHORALA

*Conan survives adventures as a leader among the
kozaki of the steppes east of Zamora and as a pirate
captain on the Sea of Vilayet. He saves Queen Taramis
of Khauran from a plot by her evil twin sister, rules
a desert band of Zuagir nomads, and gains a fortune
but quickly loses it in the stews and gambling houses
of Zamboula. He does, however, acquire, by a feat of
sleight-of-hand, a ring of supposedly fabulous magical
powers—the Star of Khorala.*

*Conan is now about thirty-one years old. After the
events of "Shadows in Zamboula," he rides westward
with the Star into the meadowlands of Shem and
across the vast stretches of Koth on his way to Ophir,
looking for a substantial reward from the queen of
Ophir for the return of her magical gem. He hopes, if
not for the rumored roomful of gold, at least for
enough to keep him in comfort for a while, with an
official post of good pay and power thrown in. Instead,
he finds neither the political situation in Ophir nor the
occult powers of the gem quite what he had expected.*

1 • The Road to Ianthe

The wanton river stretched lazily between the kingdoms of Koth and Ophir and smiled at the cloudless
sky, when a horse's hooves at the shallow ford shat-

tered the surface of the water into rainbows of spray. The flanks of the mare, sweat-darkened, heaved as she lowered her head to drink; but her rider, giving thought to her welfare, tightened the rein and guided her across to the farther bank. Later, when she had cooled, it would be time enough for her to drink the cold river water.

The rider's dusty face was streaked with runnels, and his attire, once black, was powdered mouse-gray from the dusts of the road. Still, the hilt of the service-able broadsword, which hung from his belt, bore the luster of meticulous care. For over a month Conan had been traveling the road from Zamboula, pushing through the deserts and steppes of eastern Shem and picking his way along highways and byways of turbu-lent Koth. He had perforce to keep his weapon ready for instant use.

In his pouch lay a comfortable weight—the Star of Khorala, a great gem set in a ring of gold, which had been stolen some time past from the young queen of Ophir and snatched in turn by Conan from the satrap of Zamboula.

The mighty Cimmerian, ever adventurous, was stirred by the thought of returning the stone to the beautiful Queen Marala. Such service to the ruler of so great a kingdom should earn him—if not the fabled roomful of gold—at least some hundreds of gold coins, riches enough for many years' comfort. The reward, so ran his thinking, would buy him land, or a commis-sion in a Hyborian army, or mayhap a title of nobility.

Conan despised the people of Ophir, whose king-dom had long been a cockpit of conflict among the feudal factions. The weakling ruler, Moranthes II, leaned for support on the strongest among his barons. It was said that, centuries before, a far-seeing count had sought to force the fractious nobles and their king to sign a charter. Many tales were told about this ancient effort to provide a stable government, but the present state of Ophir showed no lessening of its immemorial turmoil.

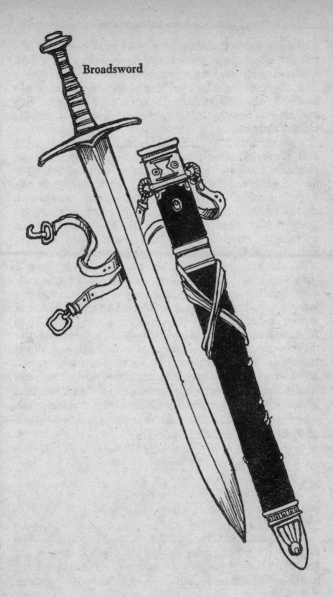

Broadsword

Conan chose the shortest route to Ianthe, the capital. His road wound through craggy borderland that huddled, lone and deserted, save for the ramshackle huts of peasants who eked out a bare living as goatherds. Then, little by little, the country grew fertile; and after seven days of journeying within the kingdom, Conan rode among golden fields of ripening grain.

The countryfolk here, as before, remained surly and silent. Although they permitted the traveler to purchase food and lodging at wayside hostelries, they answered his questioning with grunts and monosyllables or not at all. While Conan himself was not a garrulous man, this reticence irritated him; and to discover the cause of it, he asked the landlord of an inn outside the capital of Ophir to share a cup of wine with him. He asked:

"What ails the people hereabouts? Never have I seen a folk so sour and silent, as if the worm of death were feeding on their guts! I hear of no war, and the land is bursting with fruit and ripening grain. What is wrong in the kingdom of Ophir?"

"The folk are frightened these days," replied the taverner. "We know not what will happen. Word travels on forked tongues that the king has imprisoned his queen because, quoth he, she excelled in lewdness whilst he was busy with his councillors. But she is a gentle lady, always just and kind to the common folk when she travels in the land, and never the hot breath of scandal has scorched her before.

"Lately the barons have kept to their castles, laying up supplies and preparing for war. We know not how the king's mind runs."

Conan grunted. "You mean, you wonder if the king has lost his sanity. What faction now rules this weakling?"

"The king's cousin, Rigello, is said to be in favor again. Five years since, he burned ten villages of his fief when the rains came not and folk could not deliver to their liege their quota of crops. He was therefore banished from the court; but now, they say, he has returned. If true, this bodes ill for the rest of us."

The door of the tavern opened; a gust of air and the jingle of bells interrupted the talk. Conan beheld a grizzled warrior in helmet and mail, with a star-shaped emblem on his chest, who shortly doffed his casque and threw it clanging on the floor.

"Wine, damn you," he said hoarsely. "Wine to slake my thirst and deaden my conscience!"

A tavern maid hurried to fetch a pitcher and goblet. Conan asked: "Who is that man?"

The host lowered his voice and, leaning forward, murmured: "Captain Garus, an officer of Queen Marala's guard. The regiment is now disbanded. I do but hope he has the wherewithal to pay for his victuals."

Conan took a silver coin from his pouch. "This will pay for his eating and drinking, and mine, too. The balance will cause you to forget our talk."

The taverner opened his mouth as if to speak, but after a glance at the grim eyes of the black-browed Cimmerian, he merely answered with a nod and scuttled back to his wine taps. Picking up his own pitcher and goblet, Conan carried them to the old soldier's table and seated himself boldly.

"I offer you health, Captain!" he said.

The ex-officer's faded eyes fixed themselves on Conan's face with unexpected sharpness.

"Do you try to make a fool of me, stranger? By Mitra, do you mock me? I know full well that I should have laid down my life defending my queen and that I failed to do so. You need not tell me this!"

Conan curbed the curt reply that trembled on his lips when the tavern door slammed open and four men in ebon mail stamped in, hands on sword hilts. Their leader, a gaunt fellow with a white scar stitched from ear to mouth, pointed a mail-gloved finger. "Seize the traitor!"

The old captain lumbered to his feet, tugging at his sword, as the grasping hands of two soldiers seized and tried to disarm him. Conan leaped to the table top, and with a sweeping kick, sent one of the intruders tumbling into a corner. The other aimed a cut at Conan's legs; but the Cimmerian leaped high with folded knees, and the blade whistled harmlessly beneath his feet. Then his booted heels slammed into the chest of the attacker, and both men hit the straw-covered floor in a whirl of thrashing limbs. The man collapsed with a scream of anguish as his ribs cracked under the blows of the mighty Cimmerian.

Conan rolled to his feet and swept his sword out of its scabbard just in time to parry a slash from the scar-faced officer's weapon. Out of the corner of his eye, he saw his drinking companion trading blows with the remaining invader; swords flashed in the firelight. The other patrons of the inn scrambled out of the way—bursting out the door, pressing against the oaken walls, or ducking under the stout tables.

Thrusting, slicing, and parrying with the scar-faced officer, Conan roared: "Why the devil do you interrupt my drinking?"

"You will find out in Count Rigello's dungeons!" panted the other. "Your drinking days are done."

Scarface, Conan realized, was a seasoned and skillful fighter. During a brief pause, the officer drew a poniard from his belt, and after deflecting one of Conan's furious attacks, he threw himself into a body-to-body bind, stabbing at Conan with his free left arm.

Catching the man's wrist, Conan dropped his blade. With a speed no civilized man could match, he clapped a hand to the other's thigh, hoisted him high above his head, and hurled him to the floor with an earth-shaking crash. The officer's weapons clattered away, and he lay, barely breathing, blood gushing from his mouth.

Conan retrieved his sword and turned to see how Garus fared. The old soldier's opponent had lost his weapon and now stood with back to wall, nursing a bloodstained arm and murmuring pleas for quarter.

Poniard

"Have done with him!" shouted Conan. "Let us be off!"

Garus slapped the man's ear with a gusty blow to the side of his head, and the fellow, moaning, tumbled into the straw. The innkeeper and the bravest of the tavern's habitués clustered in the doorway, gaping at the carnage and the overturned tables; but Conan and Garus, ignoring their slack-jawed stares, sheathened their weapons and hastened out. Soon they were galloping toward Ianthe, hooves drumming on the clay roadbed, cloaks blown backward in the wind.

"Why did you, a stranger, save my hide?" grumbled Garus when they slackened their speed to a trot.

Conan's rude laugh floated back along the moonlit road. "I like not to be disturbed at my drinking. Besides, I have business with your queen, and I shall find your help of value to procure an audience."

He spurred his mount, and the horses plunged forward into the velvet night.

At dawn they thundered into the city, which straddled the Red River, a tributary of the Khorotas. The rising sun painted the windows of the tile-roofed buildings myriad shades of red, and the metallic ornaments on the domes and towers twinkled, jewel-like, in the clear morning light.

2 • "Fetch Me the Dragon's Feet"

Again a tavern, again a table, again a pitcher of wine. At the Wild Boar in Ianthe sat Conan and Garus, swathed in voluminous hooded robes, purchased with gold the Cimmerian had brought from Zamboula. The merchants of the city favored these garments because, Conan guessed, their sheer bulk aided many to cozen their customers. In this surmise, Conan was not altogether wrong; but the robes also lessened a man's chance of recognition by the minions of Lord Rigello, a useful aspect of the apparel.

The wine drinkers talked in low voices to a dark-skinned young woman in a servant's smock, of a quality that bespoke service in a wealthy household. The girl was red-eyed from weeping.

"I do so want to help my queen!" she said.

"Keep your voice down," growled Conan. "Where is she now?"

"In the West Tower of the royal palace. Ten of Count Rigello's men guard her door, and her chambermaid brings her food. The only person else allowed to visit her is her physician."

"What is his name?" said Conan, eyes glinting.

"The learned Doctor Khafrates, who dwells by the

Corner Gate. He is an old and wise friend to the queen."

"Fear not, little one," said Conan. "We shall meet with the good doctor to see if he can cure the queen's affliction. But first let's have a look at this West Tower."

The young evening wore a wreath of rosy clouds in honor of the coming night, and the streets of Ianthe rang with the shouts and laughter of the populace. Conan and Garus strolled among them and unnoticed reached the West Tower of the royal palace. The tower formed a corner bastion of the curtain wall encircling the palace grounds. Its cylinder of masonry rose abruptly from the side of one of the city's major avenues. There were no openings on the four lower stories of the tower, but above that level, windows pierced the massive structure, some illuminated from within.

"Which is the queen's chamber?" whispered Conan.

"Let me see," said the girl. "It is that one, the second row up, third window from the right end." She pointed.

"Don't point, lass; you'll draw attention." Conan walked to the base of the wall and examined the masonry.

"Nobody could climb that wall," said Garus.

"No? You have not seen what a Cimmerian hillman can do." Conan fingered the grouting between the ashlars of stone. "You're right in one way, Garus. The recesses between the stones lack depth for toe- and finger-holds. Had I the world of time, I could scale this wall by digging mortar from between the stones to make my own holds as I climbed. Well, let us now find Doctor Khafrates."

The good doctor was a portly man with a vast gray beard that lay, like melting snow, upon his expansive chest. Thoughtfully he answered Conan's questions.

"In accordance with my oath, I treat all who come

for healing, no matter on which side of the law they stand. So, in the course of timeless years, I have come to know the city's leading thieves. I would not reveal one name to any man, save for my queen. . . .

"I will accompany you to the lair of Torgrio the thief, who has but lately retired from his old profession. In his day he was a daring practitioner of his peculiar art. He was a burglar, apt at climbing lofty walls, who now lives on his ill-gotten gains, betimes selling stolen merchandise for younger colleagues. Come."

Torgrio's house, a small but well-kept structure, nestled between a magnate's mansion on one side and a pottery works on the other. It was a house to which a thrifty, hardworking tradesman might retire after a lifetime of scrimping; for it wore respectability like a garment. Torgrio was no man to make an ostentatious display of his felonious gains.

The man himself was of so spare a build as to remind Conan of a spider. When Khafrates introduced the newscomers and vouched for them, Torgrio smiled a snag-toothed grin.

"Like the good doctor, I have my principles," he said, "but this case admits of exceptions. What would you of me?"

"Means to climb the Western Tower," said Conan.

"Indeed?" said Torgrio, raising an eyebrow. "What means?"

"You know what I need," growled Conan. "There are such things in Ianthe. When I was in the business myself, I heard about them."

"I'll allow they do exist," said Torgrio.

"Then, will you show them to me?"

"Perhaps, for a consideration," said Torgrio with a shrug. He called across his shoulder, "Junia, fetch me the dragon's feet!"

Presently a middle-aged woman padded in, her arms full of steel devices. Torgrio took them and, fingering them, explained:

"This pair is clamped to your boots—if indeed they

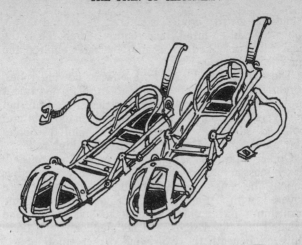

Climbing Spikes

will cover feet as large as yours—while this pair is for your hands. First, you adjust the clamps to the size of the courses of stone. Then you place a dragon's foot against one course and pull the handle down, so, clamping these claws into the upper and lower edges of a stone. To release the device, you push the handle up, so. Always retain your grip with one hand and foot while moving upward to another course of stone."

Garus shuddered. "If Mitra himself commanded me to crawl up a wall like a fly, I could not."

Conan's laughter was like thunder in the hills. "I got my head for heights on the cliffs of my native land. Sometimes it was either climb or lose your life. Let's practice somewhat on your garden wall, Torgrio."

3 • The Wall No Fly Could Climb

The captain of the guardsmen halted the stout Khafrates outside the chamber assigned to the queen.

Amid the guard's crude jests about his rotund figure, the physician endured their routine search. Then the heavy locks clanked open, and Khafrates entered the queen's apartment.

The dark-skinned slave girl, now in flowing robes, conducted him into the inner room. The apartment proved a luxurious prison. Tapestries from Iranistan and Vendhya adorned the walls; golden goblets and polished silver salvers gleamed on painted shelves above deep painted cupboards carved in high relief.

Queen Marala's shining hair poured a tousled, flaxen mass across her pillow as she lay weeping on her couch. The couch and cushions on which she lay were covered with Turanian cloth of gold, but the fine furnishings did nothing to assuage her sorrow. She exhaled in painful sighs, and her slender young body shivered beneath the whirlwind of her emotion.

The slave girl spoke softly but anxiously: "My Queen! The learned Doctor Khafrates is here. Will you receive him?"

Marala raised her head and wiped her eyes on a linen napkin. "Oh, yes! Come in, good Doctor! You are my only friend outside these walls; for you alone I trust. You may leave us, dear Rima."

Khafrates waddled in, briefly bent a knee, and grunted as he straightened it again. Marala motioned him to a settle near the pillows of her couch. As he sat down, she seized one of his hands in both of hers.

"It is so good to see you, Doctor Khafrates!" she said. "I grow desperate. I have now been here a month, friendless save for you and Rima.

"I have ever been loyal to Moranthes, but now his treatment of me has become too much to bear. Rima reports that Rigello's guards swagger about the palace and the city streets like conquerors, and my husband jumps when Rigello snaps his fingers.

"You must advise me, dear friend. You know my father persuaded me to wed King Moranthes to preserve the reigning blood line of this land. I cared not for the king, knowing him to be a weak and unstable vessel, but I did my patriotic duty. I think even Father had regrets before the nuptial feast, but he could not tell the king of them and hope to live.

"As it came to pass, Father's dreams of sturdy princelings for the throne of Ophir proved fruitless. Moranthes cares naught for women; his tastes run to . . . . in other directions. Then my troubles multiplied when, a year gone by, some worthless wight filched the Star of Khorala!"

Khafrates stroked his beard to collect his thoughts. Never had the queen addressed him with such candor. No courtier physician he, using his position for political gain, and for this reason he was still allowed to minister to the imprisoned queen. Yet now, he needs must risk that role and with it risk his very life.

He called to mind his recent conversation with the giant blue-eyed barbarian and the grizzled captain of the Queen's Guard who, in happier times, was wont to stride about his duties in the palace. His blood ran cold as he thought of the peril they had placed him in. Yet he loved the beautiful woman, hardly out of her girlhood, who now appealed to him for help. Suddenly he was glad that he had summoned up the courage to meet the would-be rescuers and abet their plot. He passed a soothing hand over the queen's forehead saying:

"Despair not, Your Majesty! Your heart is pinched by long confinement, lack of human contact, and ignorance of the world outside. Help may be closer than you think."

Queen Marala sat up and swept her hair back from her face, as her inborn courage strove to conquer her depression.

"You are kind, Khafrates. Yet you must realize that when I possessed the Star, Moranthes feared its power. Now he fears it no more and cares not what becomes of me."

Khafrates lifted bushy eyebrows. "What then was the power of the gem, my Queen?"

"Was and is, though vulgar legend misinterprets

it." She shrugged. "Moranthes imagined that the stone enabled me to enslave men as I wished. He so believed, and thus the people came, also, to believe it. But the legend is false."

She rose, drew herself up, and looked hard at the physician. "Think you that I need magic to persuade any man to my will—any normal, manly man, that is?"

Although Khafrates was old, he well knew the power to incite desire that lay within the queen's fine-chiseled lips and the sweet rondure of her lithe body—a body that her gown did little to conceal. He shook his head.

"I will tell you a story," said Marala, moving gracefully about the chamber, brows indrawn with thought. "Count Alarkar, my ancestor seven generations removed, first owned the Star of Khorala. A famous traveler of his time—and this was long before the present ruling house of Ophir ascended to the throne —he traveled in the East where no Ophirean had ere set foot. . . ."

Khafrates coughed an interruption. "Your Majesty, I have some urgent news. . . ."

Caught up in her recollections, the queen imperiously gestured him to silence. "When Alarkar traveled in the Vendhyan jungles, he came upon the ruined city of Khorala, inhabited only by a hermit. This hermit was nigh starved; for he had broken a leg and was unable to cultivate his garden patch.

"Alarkar nursed the injured man to health, while his retinue scoured the nearby forest aisles for food. In gratitude the lone old man disclosed a cache of treasure beneath the floor of a ruined temple thereabouts and told Alarkar to take whatever he wished. My ancestor chose a ring inset with a great gem stone of azure, and in the sapphire heart of the jewel pulsed an everlasting fire confined within the sphere, like a silver star. This he chose and nothing more."

"Why did he not take many jewels?" asked Khafrates in amazement.

The queen smiled. "Count Alarkar was not a greedy

man, nor was he without wide wealth at home. Besides, I suppose, he thought that if his retinue departed laden with the riches of the jungle city, they would run afoul of cutthroats and avaricious rulers. In any case, that single ring was all he asked.

"This proved a proper choice. The hermit was a wizard of ten score years and more. Had robbers entered his abode, he would have instantly destroyed them by supernatural means. But the mage discerned my ancestor's virtue and, in return for his assistance, granted him a favor. He cast a mighty spell upon the gem."

"The Star of Khorala?"

"Aye. When the wizard completed his spell, he said, 'This ring, in the possession of a good man, will cause other good men to rally round him to fight in a good cause.'" She paused, remembering.

"But—this gem—what does it signify to us today?"

Marala collected herself. "About two hundred years ago, the gem enabled Alarkar to rally the support of king and nobles for a charter to establish the rights and duties of all subjects of the kingdom. Because of treachery, his movement failed, and . . ."

The window of the apartment burst inward with a crash and the tinkle of broken panes. A black-clad giant with blue eyes blazing leaped into the room, his sword upraised.

In his free hand the man carried a pair of curious contraptions, huge bird claws cunningly wrought of steel. These he placed gently on the carpet, along with his weapon; then, sitting on a footstool, he removed a pair of similar devices from his feet. Rising, he glided to the door of the apartment to listen briefly. Alarming as this apparition was, Marala could not but admire the catlike way he moved.

The intruder turned to Khafrates and the queen, flashing white teeth in a wide grin. Khafrates had lurched to his feet, uncertainly fluttering his hands. At last the physician pulled himself together.

"Conan!" he said. "I have not yet had time to tell Her Majesty our plan! You burst in here like a bull in one of the legendary porcelain shops of Khitai!"

Conan ignored him. With eyes devouring Marala's splendid form, he said: "Your Majesty, you want your freedom from this prison, do you not?"

"Oh, yes—but how?"

"The same way that I entered—down the wall, with the use of these devices. You'll have to ride like a sack on my back."

"Whither would you take me, stranger?" The queen's eyes smoldered with excitement.

"First to a safe place where we can strike a bargain; and then wherever you choose."

"But what of me?" quavered Khafrates. "When the guards find Your Majesty gone, 'twill be the rack and boiling oil for me!"

Marala turned to Conan. "Can we not take him with us?"

The Cimmerian pondered. "Nay. These dragon's feet could not support the weight of more than two. But I shall give the good doctor an excuse for having failed to call the guard. We must hurry; Garus waits below with horses."

Marala's face betrayed her joy. "Is Garus still alive, then? I would entrust my life to him at any time!"

"Then let's be off, Lady! We have no time to lose."

Marala was unused to being addressed in a rough, peremptory manner, let alone by a foreigner with a barbarous accent. But she hastened to her dressing room and soon emerged in hunting dress to find Khafrates lying bound and gagged upon the carpet. The physician, who bore a purpling bruise about his jaw, knew neither where he was, nor what had befallen him.

Conan grinned as the queen approached him resolutely. "Your plan for Khafrates' safety was sound," she said. "I am ready."

The barbarian's ice-blue eyes warmed with admiration as much for her composure as for the lovely curves

scarcely shrouded by a velvet riding jacket and silken
pantaloons thrust into fine red-leather boots. Snatching
up a broidered coverlet, he said:

"I shall tie you to my back, lass, like a babe in its
mother's shawl. Put your arms around my neck and
press your knees against my waist. If heights make
you queasy, shut your eyes. Shift not your weight, and
these dragon's feet will serve for both of us."

Conan sat down to clamp the devices to his boots;
then enfolding the queen's slim body in the coverlet,
he tied two ends around his chest and two around his
hips. With Marala clinging to him, he backed carefully
out the window, feeling for joints in the masonry to
make fast his steel devices.

Conan moved slowly during the descent; for the
strain was great both on the dragon's feet and on his
gigantic frame. Moreover, his rude code of chivalry
compelled him to cherish any woman who entrusted
her safety to him.

Thus they descended foot by foot, while the city
slept under a moonless sky and no dogs barked.

4 • A Fire on the Mountain

"Stranger, tell me, pray," said Marala, "who are
you?"

After a long gallop away to the southwest, they were
walking their horses to breathe them. There had been
no surprises and no delays upon reaching the road
where Garus awaited them with three horses and
supplies for the journey. Nor had the thunder of
their horses' hooves disturbed the sleep of prince or
peasant as they rushed along the quiet streets of Ianthe
and the ghost-haunted country lanes.

"I am Conan, a Cimmerian by birth—and a wan-
derer," said the hulking barbarian. "I have fought in
more countries than most wise men know exist."

"And why did you rescue me?"

"I may have something you want, Lady, and I think
you will offer a fair price for it."

"Methinks I shall never be able to offer anyone a fair price, even for a loaf of bread. I am a queen without a throne. But tell me, what is this desirable thing?"

"We'll talk of such matters later, when we stop to rest. We must not tarry now."

When night drew curtains of darkness around the long day of their flight, they built a small campfire in the cleft of a rock where the glow was well hidden from the road. Their horses, unsaddled and tethered nearby, slaked their thirst in a bubbling mountain spring and cropped the sparse grass. In the markets of Ianthe, Conan had purchased bread, fruit, and dried meat, together with a skin of Kothian wine; and now they supped amid the cheerful crackle of burning logs.

His hunger satiated, Conan leaned back against his saddle and contemplated the beautiful woman beside him. This weary but courageous girl, then, was the Queen of Ophir, she who was reputed to enslave men with the great gem now hidden in his pouch. He had often imagined how he would come to Ophir, obtain an audience with the queen, bowing like a courtier, and hand her the ring in exchange for a thousand pieces of gold and, perhaps, a military post of consequence. He found himself, instead, stretched out upon the greensward, like a common laborer in a strife-torn land, beside a queen who was a penniless refugee. He spoke bluntly:

"Khafrates, I see, did not explain things to you, nor perhaps, to me. What of this gem they say you use to bend men to your will?"

The queen met his eyes with a level gaze. "Know, Conan, that Alarkar, my ancestor, received the jewel from a Vendhyan hermit long ago."

As she briefly repeated the story she had told to Khafrates, memories of ancient treachery made her voice heavy with unshed tears.

"Upon his return to Ophir, Count Alarkar, determined to strengthen the kingdom, called an assemblage of all the lords of the realm." She turned to Garus. "Captain, you have surely heard of the Battle of the Hundred and One Swords?"

Garus, half dozing, vanquished sleep, and his deep voice tolled:

"Aye, Your Majesty, I have heard of it, albeit as a legend, muddied by the passage of time. Count Alarkar called a meeting of these lords at his castle of Theringo, two hundred years agone. Each, with only his personal retinue, came to discuss the problems of the realm. They all met on the plain outside Theringo Castle but could agree on nothing. Then the count disappeared."

The queen broke in. "The remainder of the tale is known only to my family. I will tell it to you."

Conan sat still, intently listening. Marala went on:

"All the leading nobles gathered on the plain before the castle, but the conference proceeded at a snail's pace. Although my forbear feared the power of Koth and the growing might of Turan, he had no wish to command the magic ring save as a last resort."

Garus stirred the embers until they ignited a log fresh-laid upon the dying fire; and sparks, like fireflies, winged upward into the night. The queen took a swallow of wine before continuing:

"During the conference, the Count of Mecanta—from whom my kinsman Rigello descends—withdrew without a word. The Count of Frosol and the Barons of Terson and Lodier soon followed after him. All with their retainers saddled their mounts and sped away.

"A moment later, a rain of arbalest quarrels arcked from the nearby woods, where Mecanta's crossbowmen lay hidden along the ridge. There were a hundred nobles and their knights unarmed upon the plain that day, and most of them were slain. Alarkar rallied the remainder, who mounted their horses and pursued the traitors."

Marala's eyes filled with tears, and Conan pulled her to him, cradling her against his shoulder.

"What then befell?" asked Conan eagerly.

"Alarkar and his men had gone but a bowshot from the camp below the castle, when they met the army of Mecanta and his partisans, charging at full gallop. Alarkar stood to the attack, defending the family banner, until he fell, pierced by a crossbow bolt." Her voice became silent at the memory of ancient wrongs.

Conan's deep bass recalled her to herself. "So," he said, "the same as always. Nobles quarrel and stab each other in the back. What's new about that?" His tone was deliberately abrasive to spur Marala to further talk about the Star of Khorala. She resumed:

"All were buried when they fell, and there they all remain. The castle was laid in ruins. The countess and a few retainers escaped through the postern when they saw the outcome of the battle. The son she carried was my forebear."

"And what of the Star of Khorala?" rumbled Conan softly.

"Alarkar did not use its magic. He trusted in the power of reason because his cause was clearly in the right. The Star was carried away in the bosom of his wife—his widow, rather—who later married in another land. Her son, when grown, returned to Ophir to claim his fief and found my family line. And so the legend has been remembered and the jewel handed down the generations. Now it is lost forever."

"What would you do if it were returned to you?" asked Conan casually.

"I would try to work the magic in it. I would gather the good men of the kingdom to free my feckless husband from the clutch of Rigello and his ruthless kind. Do you question that I would oust Rigello and unite the kingdom if I could?"

The fierce courage of the slender girl who, sitting beside the embers of a campfire in the wilderness with but a retinue of two, still spoke of ousting tyrants and intriguers from a kingdom, struck a receptive chord in Conan's barbaric spirit. He cleared his throat, embarrassed at his surge of deep emotion.

"My Lady," he said, "mayhap I can help you on your way." He groped in his pouch and drew out the Star of Khorala. "Here is your ancestral bauble. You have better use for it than I."

The queen's lips parted in astonishment. "You—you *give* me this?"

"Aye. I'm no saintly character like your ancestor, but I . . . I sometimes like to help a brave woman beset by troubles."

Marala took the ring and gazed upon the gem, from whose oval, sapphire eye, firelit, burst the beauty of the star within.

"You put me under vast obligation, Conan. How can I repay you?"

Conan's burning gaze roved up and down Marala's sweetly curving body. With queenly dignity, she moved away from his embracing arm to signal disapproval of his unspoken suggestion.

Looking away, he said: "You owe me naught just now, my Lady. If you regain your throne and I attend your court, you might offer me a generalship."

Marala looked a question at Garus, who nodded. "He is the man for it, my Queen. Mercenary captain, chief of a band of wild nomads, guard commander— a clever strategist and skilled with sword and dirk. He saved my life and gained you your liberty."

"So be it," said Marala.

5 • "Fetch My Horse; We Ride at Once"

Count Rigello was clad in ebon mail. His sword and dirk rattled at his side; his black casque rested on an inlaid table. King Moranthes regarded him with anxious eyes, for he knew the power of this arrogant descendant of the house of Mecanta.

The king, betimes, considered ordering the black count done away with. But he feared that Rigello's kinsmen and followers would avenge their leader on the person of their king. Besides, with Rigello gone, might he not fall into the power of nobles even more ruthless, or be toppled from his throne by some reckless usurper, such as his rascally cousin Amalrus?

Intensity etched Rigello's coarse and swollen features as he leaned forward, like a dog straining at its leash. "The queen was abducted from the tower last night, Your Majesty," he said. "I have a hundred men ready to ride upon your command."

Rigello knew that the call to action would be his, but a show of obsequious fealty to the delicate young king amused him. He continued:

"This abduction, I am sure, occurred with her consent. Her trusted physician was found senseless, bound and gagged in her apartment; and the window was shattered."

"How could anyone enter and leave the chamber by way of the window?" asked the king in his high-pitched voice. "There is a sheer drop of fifteen or twenty paces!"

"Exactly so, Sire," said Rigello. "The queen doubtless lowered a rope or its like to her abductors, first making one end fast to the furniture. 'Tis plain she plots against Your Majesty, as I have oftimes warned you. It is but a matter of time before she foments a rebellion."

Biting his thumbnail, the king searched his gilded throne chamber, seeking advice from the speechless walls. But, save for the count, there was none to give him counsel other than the statuesque guards standing motionless in the doorway. Rigello persisted:

"Your Majesty, now is the time to end the strife among the noble families, once and for all."

"Yes, yes." The king wallowed in indecision. "What think you I should do?"

"Order immediate pursuit. The queen and her retinue—whoever they may be—cannot be far from Ianthe. Even with good animals, they needs must rest from time to time. Each of my riders leads an extra horse, so we shall soon catch up with them."

"How know you which way they went?" asked the king querulously.

"The queen would surely head southwest toward her ancestral lands of Theringo. There, if anywhere in Ophir, could she hope to rally supporters."

"But if she has regained the Star of Khorala, no man can compel her to do aught against her will, and none can stand against her. How will you overcome the power of the gem?"

"Sire, no one has seen the Star since it was filched a twelve-month past. Had she possessed it, she would not have fled the tower; for she could have commanded the obedience of the guards and so regained her freedom."

The king's weak face brightened. "I thank you, Rigello; you anticipate my wishes. Ride like the wind! Bring the queen to my torture chambers and spare not the men who have aided her!"

Rigello smiled as he left the throne chamber, drew on a mailed gauntlet, and hitched his sword belt more tightly around his hips. When he captured Queen Marala, he thought, he would use her popularity with the citizenry to foment a revolt against Moranthes, and overthrow and slay him. Then he, himself, would wed Marala and reign as king of Ophir.

With what the queen might say to this plan Rigello was not much concerned. Surely, she would prefer a virile man like him to that effeminate noodlehead now huddled on the throne. If she resisted, there were less pleasant methods of persuasion. He smiled again.

Rigello stood for an instant in the hallway, admiring his stalwart figure in a full-length mirror. Then drawing on his other gauntlet, he strode down the palace stairs to the courtyard.

"Barras! Fetch my horse. We ride at once!" he barked.

6 • "This Is Theringo Castle"

Conan left his horse with Garus below the crest of the hill and crept to the summit. He did not show his head above the bushes, but, instead, gently parted the foliage to study the land beyond.

Anxiously, Marala asked, "Why does he move so slowly? We are in haste to reach the Aquilonian border."

Garius replied: "He is the man who can bring you to safety if anyone can, my Lady. Although I take him to be little more than half my age, he has crowded into his youthful years a lifetime of battles and escapes. Trust him!"

Conan beckoned. When Marala and Garus reached the crest of the rise, they looked down upon a broad plain. In the middle distance, on a small hill, stood the ruins of a castle. Beyond, at the edge of the flatland, a distant river snaked its silvered way among the feet of the forested hills that rose against the skyline.

"I know now whose seat this was," whispered Marala.

Studying the countryside, Conan said, "Once we cross that plain and, after that, the river, we shall be close upon the border of Aquilonia. I believe the line is drawn along the crest of yonder mountain range. Your king's men would have trouble capturing us there; for the Aquilonians have no love of armed invaders."

Swiftly, they returned to their horses and, mounting, labored up the rise and cantered down the other side. As they reached the plain, Conan caught the faint sound of rhythmic thudding. He turned in his saddle, then cried:

"Spur your horses! As fast as you can! Ophirean cavalry!"

The three beasts broke into a furious gallop toward the ruined castle and the safety of the river beyond.

Yet the pursuing horsemen swiftly gained upon them. Instead of pounding down the road behind the fugitives, the pursuers spread out into a wide, crescent-shaped formation, with the horns of the crescent pointing forward.

"Damned Hyrkanian trick!" muttered Conan, driving his heels into his lathered beast.

The queen, a splendid horsewoman, rode hard between her escorts. Yet as they neared the ruined castle, the riders at the far ends of the pursuing crescent, traveling on light, fresh mounts, passed the structure and began to close a circle round about it.

Nearing the ruined castle, Conan roared: "Come, lass, here's a place we can defend! If this is to be our end, we'll take some of those bastards with us!"

They splashed through a small stream and pounded up the gentle slope. Dismounting, they led their winded animals through the rubble-clogged main gate. Within the crumbling curtain walls stood the keep, a massive cylinder of heavy masonry. The upper parts of the keep had fallen, leaving a talus of broken stone at its feet, but the walls of the lower stories still raised protecting masonry too high to scale without ladders. Although the guard towers that flanked the gate had fallen into ruin, spilling masonry into the space where the valves had been, man and beast could pick their way among the broken stones of the heaped remains.

"Mean you to make a stand here?" panted Marala, as they reached the inner courtyard.

"Nay; they'd climb the outer wall somehow and come at us from behind. The keep looks sound; that is our place to stand."

The wooden door had disappeared, but the arched doorway was narrow enough to insure the entrance of no more than one invader at a time. Slapping the rumps of the horses to send them around to the rear, Conan roughly pushed Marala into the doorway of the keep. He turned in time to parry the attack of two horsemen, who had forced their mounts over the broken stone at the main gate and now rode at them, gleaming swords upraised.

Conan leaped up to slash one rider's sword arm and felt a satisfying crunch of cloven flesh and bone. He wheeled to meet the second, but Garus had already dived beneath the attacker's horse and ripped open its belly with an upward thrust of his knife. The screams of the rider echoed those of the plunging beast when Conan lopped off the fellow's leg as he toppled from the dying horse.

The next Ophirean rider who rushed at them was hurled headlong as his mount stumbled on the detritus in the gateway, and he spilled out his brains against a jagged stone. As the thrashing, fallen animal blocked the entrance, Conan and Garus snatched up the weapons of the slain. Chief among them were a pair of crossbows with two quivers full of bolts.

"Inside!" cried Conan; and the two defenders scrambled through the doorway of the keep and turned to face the next attack. A few paces behind them, foot upon the winding stair, stood Marala, her lips curved in a happy smile, like one entranced. The Cimmerian turned and grasped her arm to waken her.

"What is it, lass?" His rough voice grew gentle.

"Know you where we are?" the queen replied.

"Close to Aquilonia. What of it? They'll attack at any time, and we can't flee."

She waved a hand to indicate the crumbling masonry. "Conan, this is Theringo Castle, where my ancestor Alarkar was betrayed."

Puzzled by her composure and the strange look in her amber eyes, Conan stepped back to the doorway to meet the next onslaught. Marala followed him, snatched up a crossbow, and said to Garus:

"Cock me both crossbows; I am not strong enough to do it."

When the weapons were readied, she carried them up the worn stone stair, which spiraled high inside the ruined tower. At the first turning, she discovered a small landing, dim-lit by a narrow window, scarce wider than an arrow slit.

Then the attack began.

7 • A Host on Horseback

Conan, Marala, and Garus leaned wearily upon the doorway of the keep. Twice they had beaten off attackers. In the second assault, they were almost overwhelmed by a mass of men pushing in with leveled spears. But so narrow was the opening that the crowded enemy could not wield their weapons, while Conan and Garus above them on the stairs grasped at spear points and hacked at heads and hands. Whereas Conan and Garus wore coats of stout chain mail, the soldiers of Ophir were armored in light leathern corselets to make possible a swift pursuit; and, unable to turn to flee the defenders' blows, many fell screaming in slippery pools of their own blood.

Marala, from the second-story window, picked off two attackers with her pair of crossbows. Although she was not a trained arbalester, the bolts she shot at the struggling mass of men near the doorway of the keep could not fail to find their mark. And after she discharged both weapons, she hurried down the stone stairs so that one or the other of her warriors could, in a moment of lull, recock them for her.

This steady attrition of their forces at last sent the surviving attackers streaming back through the main gate, leaving behind a tangled mass of maimed and dying men. Their broken bodies half blocked the doorway to the keep, and their shrieks and groans were horrible to hear. Conan pushed his way out, shoving dead and wounded aside, to retrieve their weapons.

Count Rigello, sitting his destrier on the slope below the ruin, received his officers impatiently. His black mail was dust-besmirched from the long ride, and his temper frayed by the ridiculous resistance of his quarry. A veteran captain, reining in his horse, saluted the count and said:

"Sir, the donjon is invincible. We have lost two-score men in the attempt to storm it. Others of our lads are like to bleed to death or to live crippled all their days. There is no way to bring our strength to bear."

"A hundred men against three, and one a woman?" sneered the count. "Pity your prospects when we return to Ianthe!"

"But, my Lord," said the captain earnestly, "this barbarian warrior is incredible. None can stand before his sword. And the woman in that window with her crossbows—if you would let our arbalesters pick off the woman . . ."

"Nay, she must be taken alive at any cost. But wait, how many arbalesters have we now?"

"Belike a score in condition to fight."

"Then hark. Order the lads to cock and load their weapons, then charge up the hill afoot. Let them enter the gate bent double to present a negligible target, and spread out before the keep, loosing their quarrels upon a single signal. If only one defender falls, our swordsmen can rush in and overpower the other. Fail not to kill the men, but take the woman captive."

Brows creased in doubt, the captain withdrew to order the attack. Rigello watched the preparations, stroking his mustache and imagining the silken cushions of the throne already at his back. Nothing, he thought, could stop him now.

The count's eyes suddenly grew wide. His men, dismounted, were advancing up the slope, when between them and the ruined castle walls appeared a host on horseback, clad in the armor of a fashion long gone by.

Rigello's men recoiled, amazed, as the newcomers started down the slope at a brisk trot, lances leveled and swords swinging. The arbalesters threw down their bows and, running for their horses, scrambled to their saddles and flogged their mounts into a mad retreat. The swordsmen held a moment longer, then joined the headlong flight.

"Mitra!" yelled Rigello, galloping against the ebbing tide of men. "What ails you? Stand and fight, you cowards! To me! To me!"

With courage born of desperation, Count Rigello spurred his palfrey up the slope, cutting a swath through the wrack of his army, and rode into the thick of the oncoming knights. Then a crossbow bolt split his skull.

8 • "Our Paths May Cross Some Day"

The three defenders stood, panting, at the ruined castle's gate, watching the rout of the Ophirean force.

"Good shot, girl!" cried Conan. Laughing, he added: "If you tire of playing queen, you can hire out as an arbalester in any army I command." Conan's mood changed and he frowned. "But I cannot understand this army that appeared from nowhere, chased away our foes, and vanished in a trice. Have you been working magic?"

Marala smiled serenely. "Aye, the magic of the Star of Khorala. The good men who fell here, two hundred years ago, were denied their chance to save their beloved kingdom. They waited till this day, when the Star and I—and you for giving it—released them to do their duty. Now Alarkar and his true men can rest at last."

"Those horsemen . . . were they solid flesh and blood or conjured phantoms, ghosts through which a man could pass like smoke?"

The queen raised her delicate hands, palms upward; and as she moved, the great jewel flashed its fire encased in azure ice.

"I know not, and I think none shall ever know. But you are hurt. Let me clean and bind your wounds—and Garus', too, as best I may."

She led the two, unarmored now and limping wearily, down the slope to the brook that gurgled merrily along the bottom before it disappeared into the distant river. She helped them wash their battle-sore bodies and bound their superficial wounds with strips of cloth torn from the garments of the dead.

Refreshed at last, Conan asked: "And what of you now, Lady? Rigello is dead, but others will scramble to control the king."

Marala tied the final bandage and stood back, biting her lower lip in thought.

"Mayhap the Star can rally the good men of the kingdom; but Ophir seems to lack good men—at least among the nobles of the realm. All the magnates whom I know are, like Rigello, greedy and unscrupulous. Of course, with the Star of Khorala . . ." She broke off, staring at her hand. "My ring! Where is it? It must have slipped off my finger whilst I dabbled in the chilly water!"

Until sundown the three sought the great jewel within the stream and along its banks; but the Star was not to be found. The rushing waters must have carried it downstream, or playfully buried it in the silver sand. When the search was ended, Marala burst into tears.

"Just when I had recovered it—to lose it again so soon!" Conan enfolded her in his strong arms to comfort her, saying: "There, there, lass. I never much liked magic anyway. You cannot trust the stuff."

"That settles it," said Marala, when at last her tears ran dry. "I had but feeble chance in Ophir when I possessed the Star; without it I should have no chance at all. Nor do I think that Mitra himself could make a man of Moranthes. I shall go to live in Aquilonia, where I have kin. Let the men of Ophir settle their feuds without me. And may Mitra help the people of my realm!"

"Have you money enough?" asked Conan with gruff concern.

"A moment, and I'll show you," said the queen with a flicker of a smile.

Turning away, she withdrew from her inner clothing a damask belt into which were sewn many pockets no larger than a fingernail. Tucked into these were sparkling jewels and coins of gold in dizzying profusion.

"You'll manage," growled Conan, "if some thief lightfingers not your wealth."

"For that, I shall rely on Garus." Turning to him prettily, she said: "You will go into exile with me, will you not?"

"My Lady," smiled the old soldier, "I would follow you into the very gates of Hell."

"I thank you, loyal friend," said Marala with a regal nod. "But what of you, Conan? I cannot offer you the promised generalship of Ophir's armies. Will you to Aquilonia with me?"

Conan shook a somber head. "I, too, have changed my plans. I'll head north, to see my native land once more."

The queen studied Conan's solemn mien. "You do not sound as if you liked the prospect. Do you fear to return?"

Conan's harsh laugh rang out like the clash of steel on steel. "Save for some sorcery and certain supernatural beings I have met, there's naught I fear. I may come home to trouble with an ancient feud or two—but that does not disturb me. It is just . . . well, Cimmeria is a dull country after the southerly kingdoms."

Taking both her hands in his, he surveyed her golden hair above her heartshaped face, her splendid bosom, and her proud and graceful carriage. His eyes burned with desire and his voice grew intimate.

"True it is that fair company shrinks the miles and warms the lonely heart."

Watching them, Garus tensed. Marala gently disengaged her hands and shook her lovely head.

"While Moranthes lives and I am yet his wife, I

111

will be faithful to my vows. But neither state will last forever." She smiled a trifle sadly. "Why go you to that bleak northland, if you enjoy it not? The Hyborian kingdoms offer many opportunities for a brave and generous man like you."

"I go to pay a visit."

"To whom? Some sweetheart of former days?"

Conan turned a cool glance on Queen Marala, but his blue eyes betrayed his painful disappointment. He replied: "Say that I go to visit an old woman. Who is she, is my affair. But where in Aquilonia will you settle? Our paths may cross again some day."

Marala smiled fondly at the brawny Cimmerian. "My Aquilonian kin dwell in the county of Albiona, near Tarantia. They are old and childless and look upon me as a daughter. They intend to leave me title to their ancestral lands. I am no longer Queen of Ophir, but one day men may call me 'Countess Albiona'!"

THE GEM IN THE TOWER

*After a visit to his northern homeland, Conan returns
to the kozaki. When the energetic new king of Turan,
Yezdigerd, scatters the outlaw bands, Conan serves as
a mercenary in Iranistan and wanders east to the
Himelian Mountains and the fabled land of Vendhya.
On his return to the West, he explores a phantom city
of living dead men and is briefly joint king of a black
empire in the desert south of Stygia.*

*Following the events narrated in "Drums of Tom-
balku," Conan makes his way across the southern
grasslands to the other black kingdoms. Here he is
known of old, and Amra the Lion has no difficulty in
reaching the coast, which he ravaged in his days with
Bêlit. But Bêlit is now only a fading memory on the
Black Coast. The ship that finally appears off the headland where Conan sits whetting his sword is manned
by pirates of the Barachan Isles, off the coasts of
Argos and Zingara. They, too, have heard of Conan
and welcome his sword and experience. He is in his
middle thirties when he joins the Barachan pirates,
with whom he remains for some time. This story tells
of one of his many adventures in this environment.*

1 • Death on the Wind

The first longboat beached on the yellow strand
near sundown, when all the West was a wild confla-

gration of crimson flame. As the boat attained the
shallows, the crew, splashing through the breakers,
dragged it up the beach so that the tide could not
float it out to sea again.

The men were a ruffianly lot, Argosseans for the
most part—stocky men with brown or tawny hair.
Several among them were sallow-skinned Zingarans,
with lean shanks and ebon locks; and not a few were
hook-nosed Shemites, swart and muscular, with ring-
leted blue-black beards. All were clad in rough sea
togs, but while some went barefoot, others wore high,
well-greased sea boots; and cutlasses, scimitars, or
dirks were thrust into the scarlet sashes wound about
their waists.

With them came a lone Stygian, a lean, dark-
skinned, thin-lipped man with a shaven pate and jet-
black eyes, wearing a short half-tunic and sandals.
This was Mena the conjuror, who despite his appearance and name was Stygian by courtesy only; for he
was a half-breed, begotten by a wandering Shemite
trader upon a woman of Khemi, the foremost city of
the sinister land of Stygia.

At their leader's command, the crew hauled their
boat into the shrubbery at the jungle's edge, where
like a forbidding wall, trees crept down to edge the
beach beyond the high-tide mark.

The man who gave the order was neither Zingarian
nor Argossean, but a Cimmerian from the frigid, fog-
bound hills to the north. He was a veritable giant in
a tunic of supple leather and baggy silken breeches,
with a cutlass on his hip and a poignard thrust into
his scarlet sash. Tall was he and deep-chested, with
powerful, sinewy arms and swelling thews. Unlike the
other pirates, he was clean-shaven, and his coarse
mane of straight raven hair was hacked off at the
nape. Grim was his mien, and beneath his dark brows
smoldered eyes with fires of volcanic blue. His name
was Conan.

Now a second longboat, with silent, rhythmic oars,
creased the azure waters of the little bay. Behind it,

outlined against the crimson tapestry of the West, the lean-hulled carrack *Hawk* rode at anchor. The longboat, beached, was manhandled over the sand to the verdant bushes wherein the first lay hidden. The leader of the second crew joined Conan as he watched his men drape palm fronds over the sterns of both to conceal them utterly.

Carrack

The newcomer was a true Zingaran, lean and elegant, with sallow features and an aquiline nose that seemed to reinforce his supercilious manner. Trim mustachios and a small beard framed his tight mouth and adorned his pointed chin. He was Gonzago, a freebooter of some repute among the Barachan pirates and captain of the *Hawk*. For the past month Conan had been his second mate.

"Get the men together and follow me." he said. The Cimmerian nodded and turned to wave the pirates on; but the conjuror touched his arm and halted him.

"What ails you?" demanded Conan gruffly. He did not like the Stygian's swarthy, vulpine features, shaven pate, and lackluster eyes. But then, he never had much use for wizards.

"Death," whispered the conjuror. "I smell death on the wind. . . ."

"Hush, you fool, before you panic the men!" growled Conan. He knew the Barachan corsairs for an unruly, quarrelsome, superstitious lot, and once again he wished that Captain Gonzago had heeded his advice not to enlist the Stygian magician for the expedition. But Gonzago was master here, not Conan.

"What holds you up?" snapped Gonzago, striding over to join them. "We have barely an hour of daylight left and must traverse this cursed jungle ere we can reach the tower. Every moment counts, so get the men moving."

Conan repeated the whispered warning, and the Zingaran looked at Mena the wizard.

"Can you not be more precise, man?" the captain grated. "What manner of death—and whose—and from what quarter?"

Mena shook his head, his eyes dull and haunted. "I cannot say," he replied. "But I regret that I have come to this dark isle with you. The Master Siptah is a high prince among magicians, and the spells of such an one are more powerful than any I command."

Gonzago spat a curse. Conan stood, arms folded on his mighty chest, and cast wary eyes about him. But innocent and normal seemed the yellow strand, the blue sea, and the red-streaked sky. Only the gloom-drenched forest, ominous with shadows, gave cause for hesitation. Its menace was merely of the unexplored, the wild, the savage—a matter of eyes gleaming with feral, hungry fires from the underbrush, or vipers gliding across the boles of fallen tree trunks, or quicksands and jungle fevers, or hostile natives and sudden storms.

Nothing in all these dangers was especially fearsome, for such were the ordinary hazards of the buccaneering trade. So far the weather had held fair; they had seen no sign of human habitation; and Conan's experience told him that, in general, small islands do not harbor dangerous animals.

Still, the wizard scented death upon the wind. And wizards sense things other men do not.

2 • Jewel of Wizardry

Before night drew her veil across the lingering light of day, the raiders gained the farther reaches of the island. A pair of pirates with bared blades plunged into the jungle ahead of their fellows, hacking away the lush vegetation and blazing the larger trees to mark a trail against their return. As one pair tired, another seized the task, and so the crew moved forward with little hesitation.

The trek proved neither difficult nor dangerous, and nothing occurred to fulfill Mena's dire prophecy. The men encountered no creature more fearsome than a sounder of small wild pigs, a few squawking parrots flaunting their vivid plumage, and a sluggish serpent, rope-coiled upon a root, which slithered away at the noisy approach of the pirates.

So easy was their progress that Conan felt a growing apprehension. He sensed a chilling air of unseen menace about the place, and like Mena began to wish that Gonzago had never undertaken the foray.

117

For longer than the memory of man, the tower that now loomed above the trees had stood upon the eastern coast of this small, nameless island off the shores of Stygia, south of Khemi. It was said to be inhabited by the Stygian sorcerer Siptah, and by him alone, save for divers uncanny creatures from other planes and ancient worlds that he might summon by his spells. The pirates of the Barachan Archipelago whispered that the sorcerer concealed within his slender spire a fabulous treasure, gleaned through the years from troubled souls who sought the seer's advice and supernatural aid. But it was not to win this treasure trove that Gonzago had decided to attack the tower.

Legends told of a mysterious gem recovered long ago by the Stygian mage from deep within a desert tomb. A huge and glittering crystal it was said to be, graven with magic sigils in a language unknown to any living man. Immense and uncanny were the reputed powers of that gem, for it was common gossip among the merchants and seamen of the ports of Shem and Zingara that, by secret spells locked within the massy jewel, Siptah could command the spirits of air, earth, fire, and water, and the less savory demons of the underworld.

Those seafarers who had purchased the favor of Siptah sailed serenely forth into harbors, safe and hospitable. No storm or flood could touch them; neither were their ships becalmed, nor fell they prey to hostile monsters of the deep. The merchant princes of those sea-lapped cities would offer fortunes to possess the crystal, for with it in their hands they could enjoy the safety of the seas without the ruinous tribute demanded by the sorcerer. Deprived of that great gem, Siptah would be powerless to do them harm, since the very touch of the enchanted crystal was the key to all his demon-raising spells.

Now there were those who whispered that Siptah of Stygia was dead; for many months had passed since the merchants of the seacoast cities had received demands for tribute, and even longer since the sorcerer had replied to their petitions. Indeed, if he were living, Siptah the Stygian would be of an enormous age— but wizards can transcend the mortality of common men, warding off senility and death with their uncanny powers.

At length, anxious to render the rapacious Stygian powerless and to arrogate to themselves his mastery over wind and wave, a consortium of merchants had approached the more daring of the Barachan pirate captains to commission such a venture. If in truth Siptah was dead, they urgently desired possession of the gem, to which the spirits of Stygia were bound by terrible oaths. If another wizard gained the gem in the tower, he might prove even more extortionate in his demands than Siptah.

This scheme appealed to the daring of Gonzago, and to his greed. The merchants' plan had roused in his breast a lust to seize the fabulous gem, even if he must wrest it from the withered arms of the ancient sorcerer. For if the maritime merchants would pay him well to secure the gem, another sorcerer, lusting for Siptah's power, might reward him far more handsomely.

Yet Gonzago was no fool. Wizards are dangerous, and men seldom live to enjoy the treasures stolen from practitioners of the black arts. Gonzago would be careful.

3 • Blood on the Sand

In a waterfront tavern at Messantia, the pirate captain first encountered Mena. A cunning thought inflamed his greed: how better to fight magic than with magic? He had bought the conjuror's services on the spot and bade his officers prepare the *Hawk* for a voyage to the lonely isle.

Now, as the pirates hacked a narrow path across the jungle and reached the eastern shore close to the tower, Gonzago knew his plans had been well laid. He had dropped anchor on the west side of the island lest the approaching carack and its ship's boats be seen from the sorcerer's stronghold. The raiders had transversed the jungle without loss of life and without discovery by the dreaded sorcerer—if in truth he still lived at all. Now that the blue-green of the sea shimmered through the trees, the men had but to rush the tower, batter their way in, and seize for themselves the gem and other treasures of the aged magician.

But Gonzago had not survived his hazardous trade thus long by acting rashly. So now he summoned the gaunt Stygian to his side.

"Can you cast a spell upon us, Master Mena, to ward off Siptah's magic?" he demanded.

Mena shrugged. "I can perchance becloud his vision so that he perceives not our approach until too late," he murmured.

Gonzago grinned, white teeth gleaming in his sallow, bearded face. "As you did in the tavern?" he suggested. For it had been this trick—a spell of seeming invisibility—that had inspired Gonzago to hire the conjuror to work his subtle arts against the Stygian mage. Mena nodded his shaven pate.

Without further words, the conjuror gathered dry twigs and built a little fire near the jungle's edge at a sheltered spot, where the trees ended and the sands ran out to meet the sea. As the curious pirates watched, Mena drew from his girdle small leathern bags and, with a tiny silver spoon, measured minute quantities of colored powders into a little copper pan. When the twigs had burned to a bed of glowing embers, he placed the pan upon the fire. A sharp and pungent vapor wafted seaward on the evening wind.

Conan sniffed and spat. He little liked such witcheries; his way would have simply been to charge the tower with naked steel, a band of fearless swordsmen at his back. But since Gonzago was master here, Conan held his tongue.

Mena sat crosslegged before the little mound of

coals, whereon the nameless melded powders seethed in the copper pan and wafted perfumed smokes upon the evening breeze. Arms folded on his bony breast, the conjúror chanted a sonorous spell in a sibilant tongue.

The crimson embers cast a weird, rosy light on the sorcerer's fleshless face, lending it the aspect of a living skull. Deep-sunken in their sockets, the magician's eyes gleamed like the ghosts of long-dead stars. He bent to peer into his bubbling melt, and his singsong wail sank to the faintest whisper.

Then Mena ceased his incantation and crooked a finger at Gonzago. When the pirate captain bent his head to listen, Mena hissed:

"You and the men must leave me. The last step in the cantrip requires a stringent solitude."

Gonzago nodded and herded his men back upon the trail along which they had come. When all were out of sight of the magician, they sat on fallen logs or rested elbows on the ground, idly swatting flies as they waited the Stygian's call.

Time passed. The light drained from the sky. Suddenly a hoarse scream rent the evening quiet.

With muttered exclamations, Gonzago and Conan dashed back to the small clearing where the magician plied his trade. Mena lay face-down beside his little fire.

Cursing sulphurously, Gonzago clutched the conjuror's bony shoulder and turned the body over. What he saw by the glow of the dying coals made him cry out to his forgotten boyhood gods. For Mena's throat had been cleanly cut, and his blood trickled out and soaked into the humus of the forest floor.

This meant, thought Conan, either that Siptah still lived to guard his treasure, or that the spirits bound to the terrible gem yet served his will though he himself were dead. Either way, the knowledge enkindled grim forebodings.

Gonzago stared down upon the ghastly figure as fresh gore welled from the gaping wound. The crew behind them muttered, the whites of their eyes gleaming redly in the gloom.

Gonzago squatted, brooding with thoughtful eyes. Conan, shivering in the warm air, said nothing. Mena had spoken but the truth when he said he scented death upon the wind.

4 • Where None May Enter

Few of the men were willing to return to their ship empty-handed, though all felt the cold breath of mysterious menace at their backs. Gonzago was determined to attack the tower, confident that bright steel would triumph over even the darkest wizardry. Therefore he led his party through the tangled vines that edged the jungle and out upon the beach where the first stars of evening gleamed above an oily, darkling sea.

Their spirits cowed by Mena's strange and unexpected death, the pirates plodded along the strand, hugging the jungle's edge and speaking in hoarse, furtive whispers.

Presently Conan parted a clump of tall dune grass that rose from a small headland and studied a smooth stretch of beach that lay as pale and untrodden as a silver stream beneath the wan glimmer of the far, uncaring stars. There were few sounds to break the hush of night—only the plash of little waves against the sands, the mournful cry of a distant gull, and the buzz and chirp of nocturnal insects.

A bowshot's distance along the deserted beach, a black shape like a pointing finger pierced the starry sky, now paling in the east. As Conan watched, a silver slice of moon, just past its full, manifested itself above the seascape. The moon moved slowly up the sky, turning the tower into an ink-sketched silhouette backed by the silvery light. It was a simple, slender cylinder surrounded at its tapered height by a narrow parapet; and above this prominence sharply rose the spire.

There was no sign of light or life within the tower. The tower seemed untenanted and forlorn; but where magic is concerned, looks can ever be deceiving. Besides, thought Conan grimly, someone or something had slain the conjuror. Now the pirates had no recourse but to attack the tower directly, sure that the Stygian wizard had perceived their presence. Since the advantage of surprise was lost, little could be gained by further secrecy.

So Gonzago set his men to felling a slender palm tree, cutting notches down its trunk, and tying thereto small lengths of branches. Then, beneath the risen moon, they carried this crude ladder across the virgin sand to the base of the black tower. But at the spire's foot they halted, staring at each other in wild-eyed disbelief.

For Siptah's tower had neither doors nor windows. Sleek walls of black basalt rose windowless from the rugged rocks of its foundation to the small parapet that crowned its castled height. Although they strained their eyes, they could discern no opening, crack, or crevice in the satin-textured fitted stones.

"Crom and Mitra," rumbled Conan, his nape-hair lifting and scalp a tingle, "has this sorcerer wings?"

"Only Set knows," mused Gonzago.

"Mayhap we could scale the height by means of a grappling hook," said Conan.

"Too tall," replied the captain heavily.

They explored the rocks around the base of Siptah's spire and found nothing that was useful in their predicament. The tower thrust skyward from a shelf of naked rock that jutted into the sea's edge as the tide came in. There was no possibility of entrance there.

Yet some way of entry must exist, however well concealed; for every dwelling—if this was a dwelling —must have a mode of entrance and egress. Gonzago stood silent for a moment, the sea breeze ruffling his black cloak as he chewed his lower lip.

"Back up the beach, bullies," he said at last. "We can do naught at night, without tools and a plan. We'll camp two bowshots from this accursed tower, lest one loose arrows from the parapet. Behind a jungle screen, we'll wait for dawn."

The raiders plodded dispiritedly back along the beach, subdued but seemingly relieved. None, Conan noted with wry amusement, had been too eager to beard the wizard in his lair, such gentry being as notoriously unlucky to disturb as hibernating bears.

The pirates set up camp in a sheltered spot where the tree line met the sand. Conan ordered some to gather brush to build a fire, while Gonzago dispatched a pair to the far shore whereon the longboats lay hidden under palm fronds. Then, rowing to the *Hawk*, they must inform Gonzago's first mate, the Argossean Borus, of all that had befallen on the island and gather sacks of axes, hammers, chisels, drills, and other tools to aid in their attack upon the spire. Food, too, and flasks of wine were needed to replenish their supplies.

Under the fitful glimmer of the inconstant moon, the others sat about the fire, broiling what meat they had and grumbling at the scarcity of water. Their grumbling was muted only, for their captain, not an easy man even in the best of times, was in the grip of icy fury. As the others fell asleep beside the dying fire, he sat apart, wrapped in his cloak, and brooded sulkily.

Conan set the watch and retired to the place that he had chosen for his rest. Thrusting his cutlass into the soil where it would be within reach of his hand, he leaned against a palm tree and prepared himself for slumber. But that night sleep did not come easily to the giant Cimmerian.

The playful waves ceased their chattering, and the jungle, like a crouching beast, silently watched and waited. Waited for *what*? Conan did not know, but he felt as tense as a coiled spring. With the fine-honed senses of the barbarian, he detected menace lurking in the uncanny silence of the night.

Something was out there, that he knew. And it was stalking them.

5 • Dreams in the Night

Toward midnight Conan slept at last, but through his troubled sleep flitted dark, chaotic dreams. An ominous foreboding hovered about him, and in the darkness of his dreaming he saw a beach whereon he and others slept with readied swords. The men around him were rough and villainous seafarers—not unlike his comrades—but their faces were unfamiliar to him.

One face among them was familiar. This man was lean and elegant, with aristocratic bearing, and the long jaw and icy, cunning eyes of Captain Gonzago.

In his dream it seemed to Conan that Gonzago, wrapped in his long cloak, sat huddled on a log brooding over the coals of a dying fire. And as the dreaming Cimmerian watched, another form materialized out of the gloom at the edge of the silent jungle. Like the seated man of Conan's dream, the stranger, too, was swathed in the folds of a long black cloak, which concealed his shape entirely.

Tall and lean was this dark figure, and strangely misshapen, although Conan could discern no obvious deformity. Perhaps it was his high, hunched shoulders that lent his figure a suggestion of abnormality, or the crooked, bony jaw and slitted yellow eyes that glared from the mask of his face like the feral orbs of a savage beast. But the shadow of nameless, misshapen evil clung as tightly about his motionless form as the dark cloak that shrouded him.

Although the dreaming Conan clearly saw both the brooding man and the tall stranger hovering behind him, Gonzago seemed entirely unaware of the masked and evil presence. Then within the barbarian's brain flared up the bright blue flame of apprehension. He struggled in the toils of his unseemly vision, trying to cry out to warn the seated man of the imminence of danger. But he could neither speak, nor move, nor otherwise attract the attention of Gonzago, who sat bemused beside the dying fire.

Then, with startling suddenness, the cloaked figure

sprang into motion. He hurled himself out of the jungle, amber eyes burning through the gloom. Straight for the back of the unknowing Gonzago the dark man launched himself, and coming, spread strange, slender arms with gaunt fingers hooked to rend and tear, like talons of some monstrous, predatory bird.

As the being spread his arms, Conan saw they were not arms at all and what he had perceived as the long folds of a dark cloak were the wings of an enormous bat.

And still Conan fought within the confines of his dream to rise, to shout to the oblivious figure of his captain, to warn him of the evil shape of darkness about to spring upon him with bared fangs and wicked claws extended.

Then a sudden scream ripped the unnatural stillness of the night, shattering the dream like tinkling shards of glass. For a timeless moment Conan lay propped against the palm tree, his heart thudding, not knowing whether he had waked or still lay trammeled within a nightmare's grasp.

That hoarse, despairing shriek aroused the other sleeping pirates with the same abruptness that wrenched Conan from his haunted slumbers. As the Cimmerian snatched up his cutlass and rolled to his feet, he sought the cause of the cry that had awakened him. His comrades likewise shambled from their earthen beds, fumbled with their weapons, and muttered confused questions.

The moon rode high in the sky, and in its opalescent light all eyes were drawn to the slumped figure of their captain. Silent and motionless, he sat upon his log before the gray-veiled embers, head bowed upon his knees. He alone had not been shocked awake by the scream that floated on the breeze. Deep indeed must be Gonzago's dreams if that terrible cry did not awaken him.

Conan's scalp prickled with a superstitious premonition as he strode to the captain and shook him by the shoulder. Gonzago sagged and tumbled forward as limp as a rag doll; and as he fell, his head flopped back upon one shoulder. Then Conan knew who had voiced that raw, despairing shriek, knew, too, that they were not alone on this small island. For Gonzago's throat, like Mena's, had been sliced across, as if by a hooked knife or by the talon of some monstrous bird of prey. Through the mask of blood that once had been a face, eyes stared forth sightlessly.

6 • Murder in the Moonlight

No raider slept for the remainder of that night. Not even the hardiest among them wanted again to risk the oblivion of slumber and an untimely end. So the men gathered more wood and built the fire again, piling the brush higher and higher still, until the flames licked the tops of the palms, and the rising smoke enveloped the unwinking and uncaring stars.

Conan had not spoken about his dreams, wherein he watched a hideous winged creature strike and slay from the dense shadows. Nor could the Cimmerian explain, even to himself, why he held his tongue in this matter. Perhaps it was simply that the men were frightened enough already by the weird demise of the conjuror and their captain; and it would be incautious of a commander to excite the primal superstitious fears of his unruly band. For were they to conceive the notion of a gaunt and murderous specter stalking the shadowy aisles of the jungle night, not even one such as the mighty Conan could hold them obedient to his orders.

With the death of Gonzago, command of the ill-starred expedition devolved upon Conan; for Borus, the first mate of the *Hawk*, was still aboard the pirate ship moored on the farther side of Siptah's isle. And even on his brawny shoulders the burden would rest uneasily.

Conan posted fresh sentries, twice as many as before, and sternly bade them to be vigilant. Gonzago's murder, he assured the men, had been the work of some strange jungle beast, which might still prowl abroad.

Conan was not entirely certain of the falsity of this explanation. A dream may be a dream and nothing more; yet the Cimmerian had never discredited the claims of those who read the future by means of a man's dreaming. And yet the slayer was more likely to be a little-known beast of prey brought by some unknown means from a distant coast of Stygia. Perhaps one of Gonzago's men, nursing a grudge against the captain, had stolen up behind him in the dark and cut his throat. Or, perhaps, again, the winged figure in his dream was some hybrid monstrosity, bred of an unholy experiment performed by the Stygian sorcerer. Who could say what creatures dwelt on such a nameless and unholy isle?

So meditated Conan, sitting among his sleepless men around the roaring fire. Then a strangled cry of horror ripped the velvet night.

Shuddering at the clammy touch of grisly premonition, Conan sprang, cursing, to his feet, his steel naked in the firelight. A running figure shouldered through the twisting jungle vines and, speechless, stopped before him.

It was no cloaked and amber-eyed thing with hunched and bony shoulders, but one of the posted sentries—a burly-chested, tawny-bearded Argossean named Fabio. The man's face was ghostly pale, and his hands shook as he pointed wordlessly into the jungle. Harshly bidding the others to remain, Conan followed the sentry back along the narrow path.

Up the jungle trail hacked out the previous day prowled the Cimmerian with catlike gait behind the trembling sentry. As he strode forward, his blue eyes penetrated the darkness, and he sniffed the air for telltale odors. Then Fabio halted, pointing.

Dappled moonlight filtering through the foliage revealed two men sprawled upon the ground. Conan bent and rolled the corpses over, grimly certain of the cause of death. The sailors earlier dispatched for tools and provisions had been returning, laden, when met by pitiless death. For bulging canvas bags were strewn beside the bodies, which lay with faces mangled almost beyond recognition.

Conan frowned and knelt, dabbling his fingers in the trickling gore. The blood was fresh and warm, and just beginning to scum over as it dried. Thus he knew the hapless men had perished within the quarter hour, and like the captain, died by the same hand—or claw.

7 • Winged Horror

Conan and Fabio hastened to the clearing wherein the huddled crew awaited them. Now there was no concealing from the crew the nature of the thing that had thrice struck from the shadows; for the sentry had seen the killer crouched before its prey. And he babbled the tale excitedly to all who listened.

"Like a tall man, he was—a winged man—and bald, with the yellow eyes of a cat and a long, crooked jaw. At first I thought he wore a black cloak; but as I watched, he spread his arms wide—so—and I saw the cloak was a pair of wings, black wings, like those of a bat. An enormous bat."

"How tall was he?" growled Conan.

Fabio shrugged. "Taller than you even."

"What did he then?" asked the Cimmerian.

"He slashed with talons affixed within his wings, cutting their throats. And then he—he sprang into the air and disappeared," said Fabio, wetting dry lips.

Conan was silent, scowling. The men looked fearfully at one another. Never had they heard of a man-sized bat that ripped out throats in the dark of the night. Unbelievable it was; yet there were three corpses to attest to the sentry's tale.

"Is it Siptah himself, think you, Conan?" a pirate asked.

Conan shook his raven mane. "From all that I have heard," he said, "Siptah is a Stygian sorcerer, naught more—a man like you or me, even though master of the blackest arts."

"What manner of beast, then?" asked another.

"I know not," growled the Cimmerian. "Maybe some demon Siptah has conjured out of the foulest pit of Hell to ward his tower against unwanted visitors. Or a survivor of some monstrous breed else vanished in the mists of long-forgotten ages. Whatever it is, it's made of solid flesh and blood, and so can die. Slay it we must, lest it destroy us one by one or force us to leave this misbegotten island empty-handed."

"How do we kill it, then?" demanded a hook-nosed Shemite named Abimael. "We know not where it lairs, and we must find it to attack it."

"Leave that to me," said Conan shortly. He studied the leaping flames of the roaring fire, and something in the seething fury of their crackling seemed to fascinate him. As he stared, an idea came to him.

"Surely, on all this isle the dwelling of the winged thing is in the tower of Siptah. For it occurs to me that a bird-man has no need of doors or windows."

"But the tower has a spire," said Abimael, "rising above yon parapet. How could it enter there?"

"In truth, I know not. But it seems the likeliest place. And the lair of every creature has an entrance, although we know not where," said Conan.

"If you be right, how can we reach the accursed thing?" asked Fabio. "*We* cannot fly, and the tower lacks doors or windows."

Conan nodded toward the fire and grinned. It was a mirthless thing, that smile: a wolfish baring of the teeth, white in a somber face suffused with fierce determination.

"We'll smoke the devil out."

8 • Death from Above

By dawn the men had finished their task, and weary but alert, they rested on the beach. Under the Cimmerian's direction, they had dragged piles of brush to join the driftwood on the beach. They felled trees and cut trunks apart to furnish logs and laid them in a ring around the tower's base. Frantically they labored, chopping and hauling, through the small hours of that terrible night.

When the east flamed with the approach of dawn, the makings of a tremendous bonfire circled the base of the black tower. Higher than a man the mass of logs and brush and leaves were heaped, and, Conan hoped, the coming conflagration would create such billowing smoke that no live thing within the tower could long endure the heat and choking fumes.

Surely the winged horror, if it nested in the tower, would emerge to fight or fly away; and then, in daylight, they could attack the demon-thing with man-made weaponry and hope to win. And to this end, Conan posted his finest archers so that they might command the tower's crest from every angle.

Dawn rose out of the sea in crimson and gold, as restless waves moaned against the strand and gulls circled the blue waters, uttering their harsh and lonesome cries. When the first rays of the rosy sun struck the tower's upper reaches, Conan shouted: "Fire!"

Men thrust torches into the high-piled brush, and flames leaped, like nimble dancers, from branch to branch. As the fire roared along the ebon stones, the tower shimmered before the gaze of the expectant watchers, who shielded their weary eyes against the glare of sun and flame. Clouds of pale-gray smoke swirled beneath the parapet and vanished within the tower or wafted into the azure sky.

"Pile on more logs," ordered the Cimmerian.

"Surely," said Abimael the Shemite, "nothing can long endure within the tower now."

"We shall see," growled Conan. "It takes time to

131

penetrate so vast a mass of stone. Pile on more fuel, buckos."

At last a bowman, shouting and waving to attract attention, pointed to the tower's upper reaches. Conan raised his eyes.

A dark, hunch-shouldered creature stood out against the morning sky, leaning like a gargoyle above the parapet to survey the beach with hate-filled yellow eyes. Conan heaved a gusty sigh of relief. Now it was all over but the killing!

"Ready with your bows," he roared.

A bowman yelled, as from the tower's crest the black-winged monster cast itself upon the ambient air. Colossal was the stretch of its batlike pinions; no earth-bred bird had ever soared the winds on wings so broad.

Tense bowstrings snapped, and swift arrows flicked about the soaring figure; but with the armor of enchantment around it, not one struck home. The creature wavered in a zigzag, batlike flight, so that no barbed shaft grazed its feathered flesh.

Conan stared skyward, eyes narrowed against the growing glare, and clearly saw the winged devil. The thing he saw was naked, with a pallid body, lean and fleshless. Its upper chest bulged forward to form a kind of keel; and on either side of its bird's breast bulged massive muscles. Its narrow, elongated skull was bald and shapen like that of some ancient, predatory reptile. Its translucent, leathern wings were supported by a structure that corresponded to a human wrist, whence were prolonged downward two free digits that ended in hooked and lethal claws.

Swooping like a striking hawk, the devil-thing approached the beach and slew a bowman as he nocked an arrow. The Cimmerian with a roar of rage rushed to meet it, his cutlass flashing in the morning sun. He aimed a blow that should have cloven the creature's skull in twain.

The blade snapped near the hilt, and only a small cut gaped in the creature's skin. Then Conan knew that he had struck no ordinary skull, but one of strange and sinister density.

Down came the taloned feet toward Conan's chest. With a mighty sweep of his left arm, he knocked aside the deadly claws and struck the devil's body with the brazen knuckle guard of his shattered sword. The grinning monster, ignoring Conan's hammerlike blows, closed in; and Conan fought for life against a relentless adversary. With superhuman strength, the wicked talons on feet and wings ripped the Cimmerian's leather jerkin, gashed his arms, and tore an opening in his scalp, streaking his face with crimson.

Beside him stood the Shemite Abimael, screaming curses as he slashed the winged form to no avail; and Conan realized with the clarity of the beleaguered that his life's span was measurable in minutes.

Half-blinded by his blood, Conan fought on, as other pirates, yelling and waving weapons, rushed toward him from all sides. And Conan knew, if he could but hold out a heartbeat more, the demon would be ringed with glittering steel, outnumbered, and cut down despite its unnatural vitality.

Suddenly, alerted to its peril, the otherworldly brute sprang away from Conan, turned, and spread its wings. But Conan, in a crimson fog of battle lust, refused to let it flap away, to attack again. With a howl of primal fury, he leaped upon its back and hooked an arm around its throat. He strove to break its neck or strangle it, but that lean neck was steel beneath its leathery skin.

The black wings spread, catching the shoreward breeze. Lean sinews writhed across the gaunt torso as the monster soared on laboring pinions with Conan on its back. A score of yards above the sea they rose, while Conan measured the languid, curling swells and wondered if he might survive a fall and swim ashore. And then he dug his iron fingers deeper into the gullet of his aerial steed. Behind them, pirates stared, eyes bulging in consternation, and none dared send an arrow after them, lest this seal Conan's doom.

The monster spiraled upward. Higher it rose with every turn, until at last it fanned the air adjacent to the parapet. The parapet, Conan saw, stood a mere foot above a flagstone walk. Over it, a cone-shaped roof, thrusting upward like a spire, was supported by four columns of black basalt. These strange supports were richly carved in high relief with creatures never before seen by mortal man. On one writhed squidlike beasts with reaching tentacles; another bore serpent bodies bedight with feathered pinions. A third showed horned beings with merciless eyes charging an unseen foe; and on the fourth were scribed narrow, manlike bodies with widespread batlike wings, which Conan recognized as like that which bore him now aloft.

Like some ungainly bird, the monster fluttered to the parapet and hopped upon the flagstoned walk. Conan slid free of its back. As the being whirled to face him, Conan snatched the poniard from his sash. It was a feeble weapon; but now that hope had fled, Conan prepared to sell his life as dearly as he might.

The thing came on, the claws of its bird-feet clicking on the flagstones, wings half-spread to reveal the knifelike digits on each wing joint. Conan crouched, his dirk held low, prepared for one last upward thrust.

Suddenly, with a cawing screech of pain, the monster lurched sidewise, one wing gone limp. The shaft of an arrow protruded from the fleshless shoulder, its point imbedded in a dorsal muscle. A cheer, wafting from the strand, did honor to this lucky shot by a Barachan archer. The winged devil was not so invulnerable as first appeared. If it could be hurt, it might be killed. Conan smiled grimly.

One wing outspread, the monster attacked again. It did not seem too discommoded by its wound. For a brief moment, Conan and the demon circled the stone pit that cut into the center of the flagstone pave. Then Conan, taking the offensive, ceased waiting for the creature to approach.

The Cimmerian, weary from the loss of blood and

the past night's vigil, summoned his last reserves of strength. Pouncing like a tiger, he leaped forward toward his foe and drove the poniard deep into its chest, hoping to pierce the heart.

The blade sank to the hilt in a deep flying muscle, and beneath the forceful blow the devil crumpled. Squawking furiously, the creature twisted its disabled body, wrenching the hilt-buried knife from Conan's hand, and then lay prone upon the flagstones. Conan, gasping painfully, wiped the blood from his eyes and looked for signs of life. He saw none.

The Cimmerian looked closely at the pit centered beneath the columned pavillion and saw that it housed a circular stair of stone that led down to a room below. He had indeed smoked the devil out, for even now the dwindling plumes of smoke from the surrounding bonfires swirled like a whirlpool beneath the conical roof of the pavillion and were sucked into the stairwell.

Not knowing what he should encounter there, he set his feet upon the narrow steps and clambered down. Within the tower the air was hot and stifling, and the smoke obscured parts of the circular chamber in which he found himself.

Here was luxury indeed. The polished wooden floor, inlaid with lighter woods in curious designs, was embellished with small silken rugs in which were woven pentacles and circles and other mystic patterns. The chamber's curved stone walls were hung with tapestries and rich brocades; and worked into the fabric Conan saw threads of gold and silver gleaming brilliantly in the slanting rays of sunlight that, by some strange arrangement of mirrors, lit the room as if the sun itself shone in upon it. To one side stood a lectern of carved and polished wood upon which rested an open book of ancient parchment leaves. Farther along the wall an idol leered, its wolfish mien a frozen mask of menace.

Conan moved quickly around the room, searching for a weapon; but he found nothing. The circumferential chamber had several curtained alcoves, that he ascertained; and choosing one at random, he flung the curtains back. And stared.

The center of the alcove was occupied by a high-backed chair of creamy marble, intricately carved into a labyrinthine tangle of serpent bodies and devil's heads; and seated on this throne was Siptah the sorcerer, his expressionless eyes returning Conan's stare.

9 • Slave of the Crystal

Conan, who had tensed, prepared to fight again, let his breath out with a sigh of satisfaction. Siptah was dead. His eyes were dull and shriveled, and the flesh had fallen in upon his visage, so that his face was but a skull over which dried skin was tightly stretched. Conan sniffed but could not, above the odor of the wood smoke, detect any taint of carrion. Siptah had sat for months upon his throne while his muscles and organs dried and shriveled.

The shrunken figure wore a gown of emerald cloth; and in the bony upturned hands resting in its lap was cradled a huge, unfaceted crystal, which glowed with topaz fire. This, Conan surmised, was the demon-dreaded gem whose quest had brought him and his comrades to this death-haunted isle.

Conan stepped forward to examine the crystal. To his untutored eyes it seemed but a glimmering sphere of glass lit by an inner glow. Yet so many men desired it that it must have value far beyond imagining. Demons were somehow bound to this pale sphere and could not be released from service save by this orb. But Conan knew not how. He did not understand such matters, and all that was clean and savage within him shrank from traffic with the powers of darkness.

The scrape of a clawed foot on flagstones roused the Cimmerian from his contemplation. He whirled.

The creature did not descend the stairs in human fashion, but on half-opened wings dropped down the well to the floor below. Amazed, Conan saw the arrow still transfixing its shoulder and his poniard still sunk into the muscles of its breast; and yet it showed no lessening of its preternatural vitality. A man, however strong, or a wild jungle beast would have been rendered helpless by such wounds; but not, it seemed, the guardian of Siptah's tower.

The creature raised a clawed forelimb and advanced upon him. Frantically, Conan leaped to the left and seized the lectern on which rested the ancient tome. The book crashed to the floor as the Cimmerian raised the heavy piece of furniture like an unwieldy club.

As the winged demon lurched toward him with taloned feet outstretched, Conan swung the clumsy weapon above his head and brought it down upon the monster's skull. The force of the blow sent the devil reeling back and smashed the lectern into a dozen shattered fragments.

Mewling and leaking blood from its crushed skull, the bat-man staggered slowly to its feet and once again advanced. Conan felt a momentary thrill of admiration for any being that sustained such crippling punishment and yet fought on. Still, his own plight was dire—a thing that would not die and Conan weaponless!

And then an idea, simple and audacious, exploded into consciousness; and Conan cursed himself for past stupidity. He turned and snatched the crystal from the mummy's lap, then hurled it at the oncoming monster.

Although Conan's aim was true, the wily creature ducked the missile; and it hurtled through the smoky air to land at last upon the lowest step of the stone staircase. And there, with a tinkling crash and a flash of amber light, the crystal shattered into a thousand pieces.

Then as Conan watched, slit-eyed and empty-handed, his adversary fell headlong to the floor. There was a puff of dust, an acrid odor. When the air cleared, he witnessed an amazing transformation: the monster's skin shriveled, curled up, and crumbled into powder. It was as if the process of decay were speeded up ten thousand times before his wondering eyes. He watched the membranes of the bat wings vanish and saw the bones disintegrate beneath the leathery hide. In a few minutes, nothing was left of the creature but an outline of its shape marked on the floor by little heaps and ridges of dust. And a spent arrow and Conan's dirk.

10 • Siptah's Treasure

The midday sun beat on the yellow sand when Conan's shaggy mane appeared above the parapet. A bloodstained bandage was wound around his head, and strips of sheeting staunched wounds on his arms and chest.

He waved to the cheering men below and, using a knotted strip of bedding for a rope, he lowered a small chest into their eager hands. Then grasping that self-same rope a trifle gingerly, he stiffly slid down into the ashes of the burned-out bonfire.

"Gods and devils, is there aught to drink in this accursed place?" he croaked.

"Here!" cried several corsairs, thrusting leathern wine skins toward him. Conan took a hearty swig, then greeted Borus, the first mate of the *Hawk*.

"While you were in the tower, the lads sent back for food and drink," explained the Argossean. "From what they told me, I thought it best to come ashore. What in the nine hells happened in the tower, Conan?"

"I'll tell you once I get these scratches cleaned and bandaged," growled the Cimmerian.

An hour later, Conan sat upon a stump, eating huge mouthfuls of brown bread and cheese and gulping red wine from the ship's stores.

"And so," he said, "the monster crumbled into dust in less time than it takes to tell of it. It must have been an ancient corpse kept living by Siptah's sorcery. The old he-witch laid some command upon it to drive all uninvited callers from the island; and under Siptah's spell, it followed the command long after its master's death."

"Is that the only treasure in the tower?" asked Abimael, pointing to the chest.

"Aye, all but the furnishings, and those we could not carry. I went through every alcove—where he cooked and worked his spells, where he stored supplies, even in his narrow bedchamber, but I found naught save this. 'Twill furnish all a good share-out—naught fabulous—and a good carouse in Port Tortage."

"Were there no secret doors?" said Fabio, when the men had ceased their shouts of laughter.

"None that I could find, and I hunted the place over. It stands to reason Siptah gained more gold than's in this little chest, but I saw no sign of it. Perhaps it's buried somewhere on this island, but without a map to guide us, we could dig a hundred years in vain." Conan took a gulp of wine and looked at Siptah's spire. "Methinks this tower was built centuries before the Stygian came with his black arts to conquer it."

"Whose was the tower, then?" asked Borus.

"My guess would be it was the winged man's, and others of his kind," said Conan somberly. "I think the devil was the last of a tribe that walked the earth—or flew the skies—before mankind appeared. Only winged men would build a tower with neither doors nor windows."

"And Siptah with his magic enslaved the bat-man?" asked Borus.

Conan shrugged. "That were my guess. The Stygian bound him to the magic crystal in some occult manner; and when the crystal broke, the spell was ended."

Abimael said: "Who knows? Mayhap the creature was not hostile after all, until the sorcerer compelled it to obey his cruel commands."

"To me a devil is a devil," said Conan, "but you may be right. That we shall never know. Let's get back to the *Hawk*, Borus, and trim sail for the Barachas. And once aboard, if any dog wakes me before I've slept my fill, I'll make him wish the bat-man had cut his throat instead!"

THE IVORY GODDESS

Among the Barachan pirates, Conan acquires more
enemies than even he can handle. Fleeing the isles, he
is picked up by a ship of the Zingaran buccaneers,
whose captaincy he usurps. He makes himself welcome
at the Zingaran court by rescuing the daughter of
King Ferdrugo from captivity among the Black Amazons; but other Zingarans, jealous of his rise, sink his
ship. Conan gets ashore, joins a band of condottieri
soldiering for Stygia, and finds an ancient city whose
people, divided into two factions, are waging a war of
mutual extermination. Escaping the final massacre,
Conan tries his luck in Keshan, a black kingdom
rumored to harbor a set of priceless jewels in the
ruined city of Alkmeenon. He wins the gems but loses
them in a matter of minutes.

After the events of "Jewels of Gwahlur," Conan
takes Muriela, the girl he picked up at Alkmeenon,
eastward to Punt. He means to use the actress to
swindle the Puntians out of some of their abundant
gold. He is disconcerted to find that his Stygian enemy
Thutmekri, like himself, has been compelled to flee
from Keshan and has already reached Kassali, the
capital of Punt. Thutmekri is deep in intrigues with
King Lalibeha, which fact calls for a sudden change in
Conan's plans.

Borne on winds from the west, the sound of drums beat against the temple tower, flamingo pink in the setting sun. On its sunlit wall the shadow of Zaramba, chief priest of Punt, stood transfixed, his attenuated form resembling a stork. The figure etched upon the wall was no darker than the black man whose shape it mimicked, although the outlined beak was but a pointed tuft of hair that decorated the front of his wooly pate.

Zaramba tossed back the cowl of his short purple robe and listened intently, straining to catch the message that pulsed out of the west. His drummer, clad only in a linen loin cloth, squatted beside two—now voiceless—hollow logs that served as temple drums, and marked each note as the distant roll of a great drum irregularly alternated wtih the clack of a lesser.

At length the drummer turned a somber face. "Bad news," he said.

"What says the message?" asked Zaramba.

"Keshan has been plagued by the intrigue of foreigners. The king has expelled all strangers. Priests of the shrine of Alkmeenon were massacred by demons, one priest alone escaping to tell the tale. The scoundrels who wrought this evil are on their way to Punt. Let the men of Punt beware!"

"I needs must tell the king," said Zaramba. "Send a message to our brother priests in Keshan to thank them for their warning."

The drummer raised his sticks and pounded the logs in a rattling code, as Zaramba hastened from the tower and bent his steps toward the royal palace of sun-dried mud, which raised its towers in the center of Kassali, the capital of Punt.

Days passed. The sun of late afternoon stood far down in the western sky, where long clouds lay athwart the deepening azure like red banners floating on the winds of war. From the grassy hill whereon the painted temple stood, the city stretched all around.

The low sun gleamed on the gold and crystal ornaments that topped the dun-brown palace in the middle
distance and lent sparkle to the temple on the hill.

Eastward, beyond the city, a stretch of forest en-
croached upon the uplands, and from the far side of
these clustered trees now issued two figures mounted
on wiry Stygian ponies.

In the lead rode a huge man, nearly naked, his
massive arms, broad shoulders, and deeply arched
chest burned to a bronzen hue. His only garments
were a pair of ragged silken breeks, a leathern baldric,
and sandals of rhinoceros hide. A belt of crocodile
skin, which upheld the breeches, also supported a dirk
in its sheath, and from the baldric hung a long,
straight sword in a lacquered wooden scabbard.

The man's thick mane of coarse, blue-black hair
was square-cut at the nape of his neck. Smoldering
eyes of volcanic blue stared out beneath thick, drawn
brows. The man scowled as a gust of wind dis-
ordered his sable mane. Not long before, he had worn
a circlet of beaten silver around his brows, denoting
him a general of the Keshani hosts. But the medal he
had sold in Kassali to a Shemitish trader for food and
other needfuls now carried in a sack, along with a
meager roll of possessions, on the back of the pack
horse he led.

Emerging from the forest cover, the man pulled up
his pony and rose in his stirrups to stare about. Satisfied that they were unobserved, he gestured to his
companion to follow.

This was a girl who slumped with exhaustion in her
saddle. She was nearly as nude as the man, for generous areas of smooth, soft flesh gleamed through the
rents in her scanty raiment of silken cloth. Her hair
was a foam of jet-black curls, and her oval features
framed eyes as lustrous as black opals.

As the weary girl caught up with him, the man
thumped his heels against the ribs of his mount and
trotted out upon the savanna. The westerly sun was

setting in a sea of flame as they crossed the grassy flatland and reached the somber hills.

Conan of Cimmeria, soldier, adventurer, pirate, rogue, and thief, had come to the land of Punt with his love of the moment, the Corinthian dancing girl Muriela, former slave to Zargheba. They came to search for treasure, having escaped a hideous death at the hands of the priests of Keshan.

There Zargheba, his slave girl Muriela, and his Stygian partner Thutmekri had concocted a plan to steal from the temple of Alkmeenon a chest of precious gems just when Conan, then a hireling general in Keshan, had set afoot a similar scheme. When all their plots were foiled and Zargheba fell victim to the supernatural guardians of the shrine, Conan and Muriela fled together from Keshan ahead of the vengeful Thutmekri and the furious, scandalized priests.

When Muriela's impersonation of the goddess Yelaya became known throughout the land, Thutmekri and his retinue narrowly escaped being thrown to the royal crocodiles. The Stygian claimed innocence in the blasphemous plot and strove to lay the blame on his enemy Conan. But the incensed priests refused to listen to his plaints, and he and his men departed hastily under cover of darkness and came to the land of Punt.

In Punt, the Stygian made his way to Kassali, the capital, where the mud-brick palace of King Lalibeha reared its towers, spangled with ornaments of glass and gold, into the blue tropical sky. Arguing that the Keshanis planned an invasion of Punt, the wily Thutmekri offered his services to the black ruler.

The king's advisers scoffed. The armies of Punt and Keshan, they said, were too evenly matched for either to attack the other with reasonable hope of success. The Stygian then claimed that the king of Keshan had formed a secret alliance with the twin monarchs of the southeasterly kingdom of Zembabwei to grind

Punt betwen them. He promised, if accorded gold and plunder, to train the black legions of Punt in the skills of civilized war and swore that he could lead the Puntish hosts to the destruction of Keshan.

Thutmekri was not alone in his search for wealth and power. The riches of Punt also drew Conan and Muriela; for there, it was said, people sieved golden nuggets the size of goose eggs in the sandy beds of sparkling mountain streams. There, too, the devout worshiped the goddess Nebethet, whose likeness was carved in ivory inlaid with diamonds, sapphires, and pearls from the farthest seas.

The flight from Alkmeenon had told upon the strength of Muriela, who had hoped to stop in Kassali long enough to recover; but when Conan learned that Thutmekri had preceded him thither, he abruptly changed his plans, bought a supply of food, and left the city. The Cimmerian now schemed to have the Corinthian girl, an accomplished actress, impersonate the goddess Nebethet, reasoning that the priests of Punt would not refuse to share their wealth when so instructed by their goddess. Conan would, in return, humbly obey the goddess's command to lead the Puntian army and defend the land against invasion.

Muriela doubted the wisdom of this plan. She pointed out that such a scheme had failed in the shrine of Alkmeenon and that their enemy, Thutmekri, had already arrived in Kassali and was closeted with King Lalibeha.

Conan growled: "Lucky that trader fellow, Nahor, warned us of Thutmekri's arrival before I sought an audience with the king. I could never match wits with that slippery devil. He would have denounced us to the king, and the fat would have been in the fire."

"Oh, Conan!" whimpered Muriela. "Give up this mad scheme! Nahor offered you a post in his caravan. . . ."

Conan snorted. "Take Nahor's piddling pay as a

caravan guard, when there's a fortune for the finding here in Punt? Not I!"

Before the first stars ventured forth upon the plain of evening, Conan and Muriela reached the hill they sought. Here in an uninhabited place stood the shrine-temple of the Puntish divinity, Nebethet. There was something about the place—the emptiness, the silence, the somber gloom draping the hills in velvet cloaks—that sent a chill of premonition into Muriela's heart.

Nor was the sight of the shrine reassuring when, having wound up the steep slope, they caught their first glimpse of it. It was a round, domed building of white marble, rare in this land of dun mud-brick walls and roofs of thatch. The barred portal resembled a mouth with bared fangs and was flanked on the second story by two square windows like empty eye sockets. A great silver skull, the edifice grinned down on them in the light of the gibbous moon, a lonely sentinel guarding a grim and silent land that stretched away on either side in barren desolation.

Muriela shuddered. "The gate is barred. Let us go, Conan; we cannot enter here."

"We stay," muttered Conan. "We will go in if I have to carve a way into this skull-shaped pile. Hold the horses."

Conan swung off his mount, handed his reins to the trembling girl, and examined the entrance. The portal was blocked by a huge portcullis of bronze, green with age. Conan heaved upon the structure; but, although the massive muscles of his arms and chest writhed like pythons, the portcullis would not budge.

"If one way does not serve, we'll try another," he grunted, returning to Muriela and the horses. From the sack strapped to the spare horse, he took a coil of rope, to which was attached a small grapnell. Then he disappeared around a curve of the building, leaving the fearful girl alone in the eerie place. As time passed, her fear turned into stark terror; and when a low voice called her name, she cried aloud.

"Here, wench, here!"

Startled, she looked up. At one of the dark windows above the portal, Conan waved at her.

"Tie the nags," he said. "And forget not to loosen their girths."

When she had tethered the beasts to one of the bars of the toothy portal, he added, "Grasp this and sit in the loop I have made."

The rope snaked down, and when she was seated in the bight, he hauled her up, hand over hand. The grazing horses and the grinning entrance wobbled and spun beneath her in the light of the rising moon. She bit her lip and closed her eyes; and her knuckles were alabaster as she clung to the rope. Soon Conan's strong arms closed about her. She felt the cold slickness of the marble sill against her bare thighs as he drew her slim weight in through the casement. When at last the flooring held firm beneath her feet, she breathed a sigh of relief, and her eyes fluttered open.

There was nothing in her new surroundings to give rise to superstitious fear. She stood in a small empty room, the stone walls of which were bare of ornament. Across the room she saw the outlines of a trapdoor, propped open by a stick of wood.

"This way," said Conan, grasping her arm to steady her uncertain steps. "Careful, now. The planks of this floor are old and rotten."

Below the trapdoor, a ladder descended into the gloom. Fighting her queasiness, she let her companion precede her downward. They found themselves in a spacious rotunda, ghostly in the semidarkness. A circle of marble columns surrounded them, supporting the dome overhead.

"The modern Puntians could not have built this temple," muttered Conan. "This marble must have traveled a long way."

"Who built it, then, think you?" asked Muriela.

Conan shrugged. "I know not. A Nemedian I met—one of those learned men—told me entire civilizations rise and fall, leaving but a few scattered ruins and monuments to mark their passing. I have seen such in my travels, and this may be another. Let us strike a light before the moon goes down and it grows too dark to see."

Six small copper lamps hung from long chains beneath the circle of the dome, and reaching up, Conan unhooked one from its hanging.

"There's oil in it and a wick," he said. "That means someone tends these lamps. I wonder who?"

Conan struck sparks from flint and steel into a pinch of tinder, and flame sputtered into being. He caught the flame on the end of the wick and held up the lamp, whence issued a warm yellow glow. The outlines of the chamber sprang into view.

On the perimeter opposite the great portal, backed by a fretted marble screen, they saw a dais set upon three marble steps. A figure stood erect upon the dais.

"Nebethet herself!" announced Conan, grinning recklessly at the life-sized idol.

Muriela shuddered. Revealed in the uncertain lamplight was a woman's beautiful naked body, well-rounded and seductive. But instead of a maiden's attractive features, the face of the statue was a fleshless skull. Muriela turned away in horror from the sight of that death's head, obscenely perched upon the voluptuous female form.

Conan, to whom death was an old acquaintance, was less affected. Nonetheless, the sight caused shivers to run along his spine. Raising the lamp, he saw with dismay that the statue was carved from a single piece of ivory. In his travels in Kush and Hyrkania, he had learned much of the elephant tribe; yet he could not imagine what sort of monster might have borne a tusk as thick as a small woman's body.

"Crom!" he grunted, staring at the grinning skull. "This means my scheme won't work. I planned to

spirit away the statue and put you in its place to
utter the auguries. But even a fool would never think
you that skull-faced abortion come to life."

"Let us fly, then, whilst we still live!" implored
Muriela, backing toward the ladder.

"Nonsense, girl! We'll find a way to persuade the
black king to oust Thutmekri and shower rewards on
us. Till then, we'll search out the rich offerings left
here by the faithful. In rooms behind the idol, maybe,
or in underground crypts. Let's explore. . . ."

"I cannot," said Muriela faintly. "I am fordone with
weariness."

"Then stay here whilst I look around. But wander
not away, and call to me if aught occurs!"

Lamp in hand, Conan slipped out of the room,
leaving Muriela in the enveloping silence. When the
dancer's eyes adjusted to the dark, she could see the
outlines of the statue with its sweetly curved woman's
body and its gaunt and ghoulish head. The idol was
faintly illuminated by the rays of the moon, down-
thrusting through an opening in the dome; and as
the tomblike silence seemed to take on a tangible
shape, so the statue in the moonlight seemed to sway
and waver. The beating of her heart became the tramp
of ghostly feet.

Resolutely, Muriela turned her back upon the
statue and sat, a small huddled shape, on the first step
of the dais. The things she felt and saw, she told herself, were illusions wrought by fatigue, lack of food,
and the weirdness of her surroundings. Still, her fear
blossomed until she could have sworn before the gods
of Corinthia that a dim, unholy phosphorescence
lifted the gloom of the columned hall and that she
heard the spectral shuffle of unseen presences.

Muriela felt a compelling need to turn and look
behind her; for she had an uncanny sensation that
something stood there, staring at her from the shadows. Time and again she resisted this temptation,
urging herself not to succumb to foolish fears.

A dirty, skeletal hand, like the claw of some huge bird of prey, closed on the flesh of her naked shoulder. She shrieked as she turned to find herself looking at a sunken face, with bony, withered jaws, topped by a mat of tangled hair that was barely visible in the palpable-seeming darkness. As she jerked away and began to rise, a lumbering monstrosity materialized on her other side. It picked her up like a doll and pressed her against its hairy, muscular chest. With a scream of sheer terror, Muriela fainted.

In the dusty apartments behind the marble rotunda, Conan whirled like a startled jungle cat as the echo of that shriek invaded his senses. With a coarse oath, he sprang from the cubicle he had been investigating and raced back along the corridor, retracing his steps. If something had befallen Muriela, he thought, he was to blame for abandoning her in this ghastly place. He should have kept her with him while exploring the ancient shrine; but, aware that she was near the end of her strength, he had taken pity on her weakness.

When he reëntered the central hall, sword in hand and lamp held high, there was nothing to be seen. The girl was no longer where he had left her, nor was she to be found behind one of the many moon-pale columns. Neither could his keen eyes discern any signs of a struggle. It was as if Muriela had evaporated into air.

A prickling of superstitious horror stirred the barbarian to the core. He paid little heed to the dogmas of priests or the oracular warnings of wizards. His Cimmerian gods did not much meddle in the affairs of mortals. But here in Punt, things might be different. Besides, he had survived enough encounters with presences from beyond earthly dimensions to have a healthy respect for their powers; and deep within him smoldered an atavistic fear of the supernatural.

Relighting his lamp, which had faltered and flickered out during his frantic survey of the great hall, he searched on, but with a sense of leaden futility.

Wherever the girl might be, she had indeed gone from the rotunda.

Muriela slowly came to her senses and found herself slumped against a wall of smooth stone. She was surrounded by darkness so impenetrable that never since the world began, it seemed to her dazed mind, had light plumbed this abyss of gloom.

Rising, she felt her way along the wall until she came to an angle. She set off in a new direction, brushing her fingertips against the rough stone for guidance. She turned another angle, and still another, until it occurred to the frightened and bewildered girl that she had completed the circuit of a small chamber in which she had not detected any door or opening, a featureless cube of stone. How, then, had she come hither? Had she been lowered through a trapdoor? Was she, perchance, in some dark well set deep into the living rock of the hill itself? Was this place her grave?

Muriela shrank into a huddle, staring into the featureless darkness trying to recall what had happened before her swooning. Suddenly, the gates of memory burst open, flooding her mind with living horror. She remembered the touch of the withered claw of the shriveled creature that had crept upon her in the hall of the idol. She felt again the grasp of the hulking monstrosity that had caught her up against its hairy breast.

As memory returned, she cried out again, sobbing Conan's name.

Faint as was that beseeching cry, Conan heard it. His catlike senses, honed through centuries of savage heritage, recognized the echo of Muriela's voice. He whipped about and sought down the corridor in the direction whence the cry had come. The orange flame of his guttering lamp grew feeble, as the gloom of night through which he strode drank up the flickering light.

Although the stony corridors and gloomy chambers

seemed untenanted, the Cimmerian was alert to the slightest sound. When he heard a faint rasp from the black mouth of a side passage, he stopped, wheeled, and thrust his lamp forward.

A wizened, shriveled thing, no taller than a child, leered, mummylike, from the lateral corridor. Ancient it seemed as the stones underfoot, and as dead, save for the fire in the bleary eyes set in cavernous sockets in the shrunken face. The thing cowered from the light of the lamp and threw up a skeletal hand as if to ward off a blow.

Then a second apparition took shape out of the darkness behind the first. The monstrous being pushed past the shriveled one and flung itself upon Conan, like a pouncing beast of prey. So swift was the assault that Conan had only a fleeting glimpse of a mountain of sable fur before the lamp was knocked from his hand, to go bouncing and clattering away. Conan found himself fighting for his life in absolute darkness.

Like a trapped leopard, his reaction was instinctive and violent. He tore himself loose from apelike arms, which tried to pinion him, and lashed out blindly with fists that thudded like triphammers. He was unable to discern the true nature of his assailant in the total darkness but assumed that it was some manner of two-legged beast. He felt the jolt of a solid hit travel up his arm and heard the satisfying crunch of a jaw-bone.

The unknown attacker came on again, swinging long arms. Conan sprang back, but not before the savage talons of the brute raked across his chest, laying his tanned hide open in long scarlet furrows. The cuts, stinging like fury, filled the Cimmerian with black barbaric rage. Needles of agony ripped away the veneer that civilization had placed upon his seething volcanic soul. Throwing back his tousled mane, he howled like a wolf and hurled himself upon his attacker, grappling breast to breast. Hot, fetid breath struck his face like the stinking fumes of a furnace. Sharp fangs slavered and snapped at his corded throat.

Hands like clamps closed about his wrists, holding him at bay.

Conan brought his booted foot up in a mighty kick at the enemy's crotch. With a scream of pain, the creature staggered back, loosening his grip on Conan's arms. Conan wrenched loose from the clutching paws and, with a bestial growl, hurled himself forward, groping for the monster's throat. As he locked his hands on the unseen windpipe, the beast tore loose and closed its fanged jaws on Conan's forearm. Lowering his head like a pain-maddened bull, the Cimmerian butted the staggering form in the belly.

His opponent was taller than he by inches, and heavier by far, but its breath erupted with a gasp of anguish and it went down with a crash. Snatching out his dagger, Conan seized a handful of coarse hair and stabbed frantically again and again, driving the weapon into the creature's belly, chest, and throat until he had buffetted the last spark of life from its battered hulk.

Conan rose unsteadily to his feet, gasping and nauseated with the pain of many bites and scratches. When he stopped retching and regained his breath, he wiped his blade on the monster's hairy leg and sheathed it. Then he groped for his lamp. Although the lamp had gone out, a tiny blue flame danced above a puddle of spilled oil. By the feeble light of this elfin fire, Conan found his lamp and lit it.

The dead thing at his feet was a curious hybrid, neither man nor beast. Manlike in shape, it was covered with black hair, like a bear or a gorilla. Yet it was clearly not an ape. Its body and limbs were too manlike in proportions, while its head resembled nothing that Conan had ever looked upon. It had the sloping forehead and protruding snout of a baboon or dog, and its inky, rubbery lips were parted to reveal gleaming canine fangs. And yet, it must have had some link to humankind, for its private parts were covered by a filthy breechclout.

Trembling with terror, Muriela listened to the shouts, snarls, and scuffle of the battle in the passageway above her prison. When it was over, she renewed her plaintive cries. Following the sound of her whimperings, Conan located a niche in the corridor, floored by a flagstone to which was fastened a ring of bronze. He hoisted the slab, bent down, and caught the arms that Muriela reached up to him.

The girl gasped and shrank away from the bloody apparition that supported her, but the sound of Conan's familiar voice reassured her as he helped her step across the battered, hairy corpse that blocked the passage.

Haltingly she described the withered ancient who had laid hands upon her in the rotunda and told how the monster had seized and borne her off. Conan grunted.

"The old hag must be the priestess or oracle of this shrine," he said. "Her voice is the voice of the ivory goddess. There is a closet behind the idol with a door hidden in the fretted marble wall. Hiding there, she can see and speak to those who come to seek her counsel."

"And the monster; what of him?" quavered the girl.

Conan shrugged. "Crom knows! Mayhap her servitor, or some deformed brute the savages of Punt considered touched by the gods and marked for temple duty. Anyway, the thing is dead and the priestess has taken flight. Now we have naught to do but hide in the small room behind the statue when someone comes to hear the oracle."

"We might wait months. Perhaps no one will ever come."

"Nay, our friend Nahor told us the chiefs of Punt consult the ivory wench before each grave decision. Methinks you will play the skull-faced goddess after all."

"Oh, Conan, I am sore afraid. We cannot stay here, even if we would, for we shall starve," said Muriela.

"Nonsense, girl! Our pack horse carries food enough

for many days, and this is as good a place to rest as any."

"But how about the priestess?" persisted the frightened girl.

"The old hag cannot harm us now that her monster is dead," said Conan cheerfully, adding, "If we use normal caution, that is. I would not accept a drink from her hand."

"So be it, then," said Muriela. A look of sadness crossed her beautiful face as she added, "In truth I am no oracle, but I foretell that this adventure will end badly for us both."

Conan put his arms around her to comfort her. And in the early morning light that stole through the opening of the dome, she saw the blood oozing from the razor cuts across his chest.

"My beloved, you are hurt and I knew it not! I must wash and bind your wounds."

"Just a few scratches," grumbled Conan. But he allowed her to lead him to the well in the little cloistered courtyard behind the skull-faced temple. There she washed the dried blood from his limbs and bandaged the beast's bites with strips of silk torn from her skirt. A half hour later, Conan and Muriela returned to the rotunda and rested behind a pillar out of sight of the ivory goddess. Keeping alternate watch, they slept all that day and the following night.

When Conan awoke, the golden rays of the rising sun were gilding the clouds of morning, and the East was ablaze with ruddy vapors. Muriela sat with her back to a pillar, cradling Conan's head in her arms.

He stretched. "I must go and get us some food," he said. "Here, take this dagger in case the old priestess returns."

Climbing the ladder to the small storeroom through whose window they had entered, he hooked the grapnell into the sill and prepared to descend the rope. Then he paused to peer westward, for he caught—or thought he caught—a glimpse of distant movement.

Beyond the hills that surrounded the temple-shrine lay a wide savanna, and at the far end of that grassy plain stood the city of Kassali, roof ornaments on temple and palace twinkling in the slanting sunlight. All seemed peaceful, the city asleep. Then Conan's keen eyes discerned a row of black dots moving across the plain. A faint plume of dust arose behind them.

"Our visitors are coming sooner than I thought," he growled. "I cannot leave the nags tethered here. The delegation would know at once that strangers occupied their temple."

He swung over the sill and let himself down swiftly. In a moment he had unhitched the horses. Tightening the girth on one, he vaulted into the saddle and departed at a gallop, leading the other two. A quarter hour later he returned, breathing hard from running up the long slope of the hill. He climbed the rope and drew it in, then made his way to the head of the ladder.

"Horsemen coming!" he gasped. "Tied the nags—in the woods—at the foot of the hill! Put on your goddess garb, and quickly." He tossed Muriela a bundle of female garments.

Returning to the window, he found that the line of dots had grown into a cavalcade, cantering toward the foot of the temple knoll. He raced to the ladder, clambered down, and said:

"Come; we have scarce time to hide ourselves in the oracle chamber. You remember your speech?"

"Y-yes; but I fear. It did not work when we tried it at Alkmeenon."

"There was a rascal then, and Bît-Yakin's accursed servants. This priestess lacks her monster, and I've seen no other temple denizens. This time, I'll stay beside you. Come!"

He took her hand and almost dragged her across the room. By the time the cavalcade reached the temple, Conan and Muriela were crowded into the small chamber behind the ivory goddess.

They heard the clop of hooves, the jingle of harness, and the mumble of distant voices as men dismounted. Presently Conan caught a slow mechanical rumble.

"That must be the portcullis," he whispered. "The priests must have some sort of key."

The voices grew louder, mingled with the tramp of many feet. Through the band of fretwork that ran across the door, Conan saw a procession file into the rotunda. First came a group of blacks in barbaric finery. In their midst paced a large, stout man with graying, wooly hair, on which rode an elaborate crown, made of sheets of gold hammered into the form of a hawk with outspread wings. This, Conan surmised, must be King Lalibeha. A very tall, lean man in a purple robe he took to be Zaramba, the high priest.

They were followed by a squad of Puntian spearmen with headdresses of ostrich plumes and rhinoceros-hide shields. Behind them strode Thutmekri the Stygian and a score of his personal retainers, among them Kushite spearmen and Shemitish archers armed with heavy double-curved bows.

Conan's neck hairs stiffened as he sighted his enemy.

Thutmekri the Stygian felt the morning breeze at his back. That same chill, or an echo of it, closed about his heart. Rogue and adventurer though he was, the tall Stygian cared little for this unexpected visit to the shrine of the ivory goddess. He remembered all too well the disaster that had befallen his partner in the temple of the goddess Yelaya at Alkmeenon.

Although Thutmekri had spoken plausibly about the possibility of war against Punt, King Lalibeha had remained doubtful and suspicious. Among the rulers of the northern tier of black countries, the old king was known as canny and cautious. To cap the king's doubts, his high priest Zaramba had received a drum message from his sacerdotal colleagues to westward, warning against certain pale-skinned troublemakers who were fleeing toward Punt. When the smooth-

157

talking Stygian persisted, Zaramba proposed a visit to the oracular shrine of Nebethet, to seek the advice of the goddess.

Thus king and high priest with their attendants had set out at dawn and traveled into the sunrise. It behooved Thutmekri to go with them, much as he disliked the notion. The Stygian thought little of these southern gods, but he feared their fanatical priests, who might turn upon him, denouncing him as a foreign interloper. His debacle in Keshan had honed a fine edge on his fears. And as they rode toward the skull-shaped temple on that distant hill, he wondered whether the whole expedition was a pretext by Lalibeha and his high priest to trap and destroy him.

So they had come to the shrine of the goddess Nebethet. Zaramba released the hidden catch that enabled his servants to raise the portcullis, and in they went. The king placed Thutmekri and his men in the center of the solemn procession, in order, the Stygian suspected, to give the royal escort the advantage should a fracas begin.

Eyes gleamed with holy awe; the priest and the courtiers knelt and bowed low to the ground. On the dais before the ivory, skull-faced goddess, the king placed a small, lacquered casket; and as he opened it, jeweled fire spilled out into the pale morning light of the secluded place.

Long black arms rose in homage to the ivory woman. Zaramba intoned an invocation, while youthful acolytes with shaven heads swung golden censers, spreading clouds of fragrant smoke.

Thutmekri's nerves were on edge. He fancied that he felt the pressure of unseen eyes. As the priest spoke in an archaic dialect of Puntic, which he could not understand, his restlessness grew. His Stygian ancestry whispered that something was about to happen.

In a bell-like voice, the skull-faced woman spoke: "Beware, O King, of the wiles of Stygia! Beware, O Lalibeha, of the plots of blasphemers from distant,

Censer

sinister lands! The man before you is no friend but a smooth-tongued traitor, come slinking out of Keshan to pave the road to your doom!"

Growling and lifting their feather-tufted spears, the Puntian warriors glared suspiciously at Thutmekri and his escort. The Stygian's men clustered together, the spearmen forming a circle of shields. Behind them, the Shemites reached back over their shoulders, ready to whip arrows from their quivers. In an instant, the hall might explode into a scene of scarlet carnage.

Thutmekri remained frozen. There was something familiar about that voice. He could have sworn that it was the voice of a much younger woman disguised to sound mature—a young woman whose voice, he was sure, he had heard before.

"Wait, O King!" he cried. "You are being cozened. . . ."

But the voice from the statue, continuing without pause, commanded the attention of all. "Choose, instead, as your general Conan the Cimmerian. He has fought from the snows of Vanaheim to the jungles of Kush; from the steppes of Hyrkania to the pirate isles of the Western Ocean. He is beloved of the gods, who have carried him victorious through all his battles. He alone can lead your legions to victory!"

As the voice ceased, Conan stepped out of the small chamber that opened on the rotunda. With a keen sense of the dramatic, he strode majestically forward, bowing formally to King Lalibeha and again to the high priest.

"The devil!" snarled Thutmekri. His face convulsed with rage, he told his archers: "Feather me yonder clown!"

As half a dozen Shemites pulled arrows from their quivers and nocked them, Conan's eye caught their action. He gathered his legs beneath him to spring behind the nearest pillar; for at that range, he would be an inevitable target for a volley of arrows. The king opened his mouth to shout a command.

At that moment the ivory statue of Nebethet creaked, groaned, and toppled forward, to crash down the steps of the dais. Where the statue had been now stood a woman on whom all eyes were fixed.

Staring with the rest, Conan saw that it was Muriela —yet it was not she. Nor was it merely the shimmering ankle-length gown or the few dabs of cosmetics. This woman seemed Muriela transfigured, taller, more majestic, even more beautiful. The air about her seemed to glow with a weird violet light, and the atmosphere of the rotunda was suddenly vibrant with life. The woman's voice was neither Muriela's light soprano nor her imitation of the ringing tones of the goddess she feigned to be. It was a deeper, more resonant voice—a voice which seemed to make the very floor vibrate like the plucked string of a lute.

"O King! Know that I am the true goddess Nebethet, albeit in the body of a mortal woman. Does any mortal contest this?"

Thutmekri, insensate with rage and frustration, growled to one of his Shemites, "Shoot her!"

As the man bent his bow, aiming over the head of the kneeling spearmen before him, the woman smiled slightly and pointed a finger. There was a flash and a sharp crack, and the Shemite fell dead among his comrades.

"Now do you believe?" she asked.

There was no reply. Every man in the chamber—king, priest, warriors, and the adventurers Conan and Thutmekri—sank to his knees and bowed his head. The goddess continued:

"Know, O King, that these two great rogues, Thutmekri and Conan, desire to gain whatever they can at your expense, as they sought and failed to cozen the priests in Keshan. The Stygian merits naught less than to be thrown to the crocodiles. The Cimmerian deserves no less a fate, but I would that he be leniently dealt with because he was kind to the woman whose body is my garment. Give him two days to leave the kingdom or become the reptiles' prey.

"I lay upon you one more command. My eidolon, cracked in its fall, was at best an ugly image. Set your artisans, O King, to carving me a new statue in the likeness of this woman whose form I now inhabit. I shall, in the interval, make my abode in her body. See that it be furnished with the best of food and drink. Forget not my commands. I grant you now permission to withdraw."

The purple light faded; the goddess stood motionless upon the dais. The men, bemused, rose silently to their feet and stood as men transfixed. Stealthily the Stygian and his retinue moved toward the open portal.

The king's command shattered the silence. "Take them!" he roared.

A long-bladed javelin soared from the hand of a

king's man, to bury itself in the black breast of one of Thutmekri's Kushites. The victim screamed, lurched drunkenly, and sank sprawling on the marble floor, blood gushing from mouth and nose.

The next instant, the hall was alive with yelling, struggling men. Javelins arced, bowstrings twanged, spears jabbed. Jagged-bladed throwing knives whirled through the air, and hardwood clubs thudded on rhinoceros-hide shields and woolly-pated heads. Again and again the men of Punt hurled themselves upon the compact knot of Thutmekri's men. As each wave receded, wounded or dying men clutched at spurting arteries or writhed in their own spilled viscera.

Thutmekri whipped out his glittering scimitar. Thundering oaths and calling on Set and Yig and all the other devil-gods of the Stygian pantheon, he hewed like a madman among his attackers. Shortly, he cleared a space before and around him, the nearest Puntians giving back before his deadly strokes. Through the thinning press, Thutmekri sighted Conan, standing with sword in hand beside the dais.

Eyes glaring, mouth twisted with hate, Thutmekri broke out of the crowd and rushed upon the man he blamed for the collapse of all his schemes.

"This for you, Cimmerian lout!" he screamed, aiming a decapitating slash at Conan's neck.

Conan parried, and the swords met with the clang of a bell. The blades sprang apart, circled, clashed, and ground. Sparks flew from the steel. Breathing heavily, the antagonists circled, thrusting and slashing in a frenzy of action.

After a quick feint, Conan struck home against Thutmekri's flank. With a groan, the Stygian doubled over, dropping his sword and clutching at his cloven side. Blood gushed across his fingers. A second blow sent his head leaping from his shoulders and rolling along the floor, while his body slumped into a swiftly widening pool of its own blood.

When their leader fell, Thutmekri's men—such as

were still standing—broke for the exit. In a mass, they crowded through the encircling Puntians, pushing some aside and trampling others. In a trice they were through the portal.

"After them!" shouted King Lalibeha. "Slay all!"

King, priests, and warriors streamed out after the fugitives. When Conan reached the portcullis, the grassy slope and the plain beyond were alive with men, some galloping on horseback and some running afoot like madmen. Some of the fugitives vanished into the forest that lapped the hill to southward.

Back in the shrine, Conan stepped over the silent dead and the groaning wounded to approach the dais. Muriela still stood motionless where once had stood the ivory statue. Conan said:

"Come, Muriela, we must be gone. How did you manage that purple glow?"

"Muriela?" said the woman, looking full upon his face. The violet radiance returned as she spoke. There was about her a chill remoteness of tone and manner far beyond the capacity of Muriela's not unskillful acting. "Do not presume, mortal, unless you wish the fate accorded that unfortunate Shemite."

Conan's skin crawled. Awe shone in the blue eyes he turned upon the goddess.

"You are truly Nebethet?"

"Aye, so some men call me."

"But—but what is to become of Muriela? I cannot just abandon her."

"Your concern does credit to you, Conan. But fear not for her. She shall be my garment as long as I wish. When I wish otherwise, I will see that she is well provided for. Now you had best be on your way, unless you prefer to end up in the bellies of Lalibeha's crocodiles."

Seldom in his turbulent life had Conan deferred to any human being, no matter how exalted. Now, for once, he became respectful, almost humble.

"On my way whither?" he said. "Your Divinity knows that I am out of money. I cannot return to Kassali to take up Nahor's offer, for my welcome either in Punt or in Keshan would be something less than hearty."

"Then bend your steps toward Zembabwei. Nahor of Asgalun has a nephew in the city of New Zembabwei, who may have a post for you as caravan guard. Now go, ere I bethink me of the blasphemies you plotted in my name!"

Conan bowed, backed away from the dais, turned, and strode out. As he walked beneath the raised portcullis, a shuffling sound behind made him whirl, hand on hilt.

From the darkness within, a withered, bent, and shrunken figure tottered into the light. It had once been a woman.

The aged priestess of the temple of Nebethet shook a bony fist at Conan. From her toothless jaws came a harsh, grating speech:

"My son! Ye have slain my son! The curse of the goddess upon thee! The curse of the child's father, the demon Jamankh, upon thee! I call upon Jamankh, the hyena-demon, to blast and rend this murderer, this blasphemer! May your eyeballs rot in your head! May your bowels be drawn from your belly, inch by inch! May ye be staked out over an anthill! Come, Jamankh! Avenge—"

A fit of coughing racked the aged frame. The crone pressed both bony hands to her chest, and her faded eyes widened in their cavernous sockets. Then she fell headlong upon the marble.

Conan stepped forward and touched the ancient body. Dead, he mused; she was so old that any shock would slay her. Perchance her demon lover, who begat the monstrosity on her, will come after me and perchance not. In any case, I must be on my way.

He closed the staring eyes of the corpse, strode out of the temple, and swung down the grassy slope to the place in the forest where he had left the horses.

164

MOON OF BLOOD

Failing to obtain his long-sought fortune in Punt, Conan travels north to Aquilonia and takes service as a scout on the western frontier, on the edge of the Pictish Wilderness. After the events of "Beyond the Black River," he rises rapidly in the Aquilonian service. As captain of regular troops, he is in the thick of the fighting that rages all over the province of Conajohara, from Velitrium to the Black River. These fights are skirmishes between the retreating Aquilonians and the oncoming Picts, reoccupying the territory they had enjoyed before the Aquilonians drove them out of it. Rumor says that the feuding Pictish clans have united and plan to attack Velitrium itself. So Conan and another captain are sent out with detachments to probe deep into the lost province and to find out what the Picts are up to.

1 • The Owl that Cried by Day

The forest was strangely silent. Wind whispered through the jade-green leaves of spring, but no sound came from the beasts and birds who dwelt within these verdant solitudes. It was as if the forest, with its thousand eyes and ears, sensed the presence of an intruder.

Then through the aisles of giant oaks came the

rustling of armed men on the move—the tramp of feet, the muted jingle of metal armament, the murmur of voices.

Suddenly the leaves parted and a burnished giant of a man entered a clearing. He was armed as if for war; a plain steel helm covered his mane of coarse black hair; and his deep chest and knotted arms were protected by a hauberk of chain mail. The dented helm framed a dark, scarred face bronzed by strange suns, wherein blazed eyes of smouldering volcanic blue.

He did not tramp along, but glided from bush to bush, now and again stopping to peer, to listen, and to sniff the air. He had about him the tense and wary look of one who expects an ambush. Soon a second man appeared behind the first—a well-built, blond young man of medium height, wearing the war harness

Helm and Hauberk

of a lieutenant in the Golden Lions, a regiment in the Frontier Guard of Numedides, King of Aquilonia.

The difference between the two was striking. The black-maned giant, obviously a Cimmerian from the savage wildernesses to the north, was vigilant but at ease; the younger officer, starting at every sound and swatting the myriad flies, appeared clumsy and nervous. He addressed the older man with deference:

"Captain Conan, Captain Arno asks if all is well forward of our position. He waits your signal to advance the troops."

Conan grunted, saying nothing. The lieutenant glanced uneasily about the glade. "It seems quiet enough to me," he added.

Conan shrugged. "Too quiet for my taste. These woods at midday should be alive with birdsong and the chattering of squirrels. But it's as silent hereabouts as any graveyard."

"Mayhap the presence of our troops has affrighted the forest creatures," suggested the Aquilonian.

"Or," said Conan, "mayhap the presence of a Pictish force, though as yet I have seen no certain sign. They may be here, or they may not. Tell me, Flavius, have any of our scouts returned?"

"Not yet, sir," said the young lieutenant. "But the scouts sent out by General Lucian report no Picts are in the forest."

Conan bared his fangs in a mirthless wolf's grin. "Aye, the General's scouts swear there's not a living Pict in all of Conajohara, that I know. They conclude the painted devils anticipate our strike in force and have withdrawn. But . . ."

"You distrust the scouts, Captain?"

Conan glanced briefly at the lieutenant. "I know them not. Nor whence Lucian brought them, nor how trustworthy their opinions may be. I'd trust the word of my own scouts—the men I had before Fort Tuscelan fell."

Flavius blinked, incredulous. "Do you suspect Viscount Lucian of wishing us ill?"

Conan's face became a mask as, slit-eyed, he studied his companion. "I've said naught to that effect. But I've seen enough of this world to trust few men. Go, tell Captain Arno. . . . Wait, here comes one of Lucian's vagabonds."

A lean man, with a brown skin seamed by a hundred small wrinkles, stepped from behind the trunk of a huge oak—an oak that was already old when the Picts ruled all the Westermarck. The man was clad in buckskin and bore a bow and hunting falchion.

"Well?" said Conan in lieu of other greeting.

"Not a sign of a Pict the whole length of South Creek," said the scout.

"Who is on our flanks?"

The scout repeated several names. "No Picts anywhere. There's the creek ahead of you," he said, pointing.

"That I know," said Conan, dryly.

As Flavius, peering through the massive tree trunks, discovered a glimmer of silver in the middle distance, the scout faded back into the forest.

The sounds of moving men grew louder as the head of the column appeared on the trail behind them. Of the hundred-odd Aquilonian soldiers, who traveled in ones and twos along the narrow trail, half were pikemen and half archers. The pikemen, mostly stocky, tawny-haired Gundermen, wore helmets and mail shirts. The archers, mainly Bossonians, walked unarmored save for hauberks of leather studded with bronzen rings or buttons, and here and there, a light steel cap. Arno, it seemed, had wearied of waiting.

A stocky, brown-haired officer hurried up to Conan, sweat running down his round, red face. The new arrival pushed back his helmet and said:

"Captain Conan, my pig-stickers begin to tire. They need a short rest."

"They find this a hard march? Ha! They need hardening, Arno, the way I've been hardening my archers. Let them rest for a moment. And go stop their loose tongues. If there's a Pict within a league, he'd know where and how many we are."

Captain Arno slapped at a fly on his neck. "Few men have legs as long as yours, Conan, or tongues as short." He returned to his soldiers, shaking his head.

"'Reconnaisance in force,' forsooth!" growled Conan to Flavius. "Under these conditions, it invites disaster."

"The general's orders were positive," said Flavius.

"Aye, but that makes them no less foolish. To war with Picts, you need news before the fight and numbers during it. So you scatter your scouts to seek the size and position of the foe, then concentrate your troops to hit them hard."

"That, sir, takes careful timing, does it not?"

"Aye, that it does. If you miscalculate, you're dead. Timing, lad, is half the art of war—what Numedides' gilded generals call strategy. But sending two half-companies thus along the creek, with no force to back us up in case of trouble, when the Picts can bring together thousands. . . ."

Conan's deepset blue eyes pierced the long aisles between the ancient trees, as if by staring hard he could penetrate the massive boles and see into the shadowy, hidden distances. He liked nothing about this expedition, which seemed to him foolhardy to the point of insanity. Soldiers long in the service of King Numedides never questioned their orders or the wisdom of their superiors. But Conan the Cimmerian was no common Aquilonian soldier, although for more than a year he had served as a mercenary here, fighting the country's wars for hire. He was beginning to regret his acceptance of a command in the Frontier Guard, although at the time it had seemed the wisest course. The sharing of command with Captain Arno partly accounted for his change of heart; but this blind expedition into an unknown and hostile wilderness irked him more. Every savage instinct in his primitive soul cried out in warning against so foolish a plan.

"Well, time to move on," he growled. "Flavius, return to Arno and have him get his pikemen on their feet."

Through the long morning, the troops with muted tread made their way over rocks and roots of trees along the trail to South Creek, the boundary of water that divided the province of Schohira from the lost Conajohara, now overrun by painted Picts.

Returning up the line of marching men, Flavius rejoined Conan at the front and delivered his message: "Captain Arno will hold the pace you set until you signal otherwise."

Conan nodded curtly, lips parted in a sour smile. "Praise be to Crom," he said.

"For what?" asked Flavius.

"For Arno's good sense to know that he knows not the frontier. So he takes my advice. In other circumstance, two commanders of one force would be an invitation to the gods of disaster."

"General Lucian insisted there be two of you."

"Still I like it not. Something stinks about this whole foray."

As the trail approached the creek, Conan turned to the soldiers in the van. "Fill your water jugs and skins, all of you. Pass the word along, but whisper it."

When the sun looked down from the center of the sky, the troop had covered another league along South Creek as it tumbled over its rocky bed in its haste to reach its junction with the Black River. Aside from the rippling of the water, the forest was as silent as a tomb.

Suddenly a sound broke the quiet. It was the hoot of an owl. Conan whirled and dashed back toward the disorderly column of marching men.

"Form square for attack!" he roared. "Archers, hold your shots till you see your targets plain."

Running after him, Flavius panted: "It was but an owl, Captain. There is no . . ."

"Whoever heard an owl at midday?" snarled Conan, as a chorus of yells from trees ahead half drowned his words.

2 • Death from the Trees

Arno, too, shouted orders, and the snakelike column dissolved into a shapeless mass of men. Then in accordance with the maneuvers that Conan had drilled into them, the mass shook itself out into a hollow square. The perimeter bristled with the low-held points of fifty-odd pikemen, and behind each stood an archer, bow in hand and arrow nocked. The pikemen knelt on the soft, leaf-covered forest floor, their pikes butt to the ground, shafts slanting forward, points waist high.

Pictish Hatchets and Spears

The wall of men had scarce been formed when a horde of painted savages erupted from the woods. Naked but for breech clouts and moccasins, and feathers in their tangled manes of knotted hair, the Picts charged the Aquilonians, shooting arrows as they came. Formidable they were, these swarthy, muscular men armed with copper-bladed hatchets and copper-headed spears. Some bore weapons of fine Aquilonian steel, stolen from the dead after the fall of Fort Tuscelan.

"Mitra! There must be thousands of them," breathed Flavius.

"Go to yonder corner of the square," said Conan as he positioned himself at the corner to the right. Arno and Arno's lieutenant occupied the remaining corners, facing outward toward the fast-surrounding hordes.

Several Picts fell before the withering rain of Bossonian arrows. Then the Picts were upon them. Some, in their warlike fury, impaled themselves on the points of the pikes. Others danced beyond the spears, yelling war cries and brandishing weapons. A few dropped to the ground and tried to roll beneath the jagged line of spears; but these were soon dispatched.

Defending his corner of the square, Conan whirled his heavy broadsword, lopping off a head here, an arm there. The archers, with the relentless rhythm of automatons, nocked arrows and loosed them into the surging mass. Pict after Pict fell screaming, trying to draw a shaft from his chest or writhing in his death throes. Blood flowed unchecked across last winter's leaves and soaked into the thick humus of the forest floor. The motionless air drank in the stench of blood and sweat and fear.

The screech of a bone whistle cut through the roar of battle. Pictish chiefs ran among the battle-crazed savages, pulling them back and shouting unintelligible commands. The frenzied tribesmen were not readily commanded; but at last they turned their backs on the foe. Trotting down the forest aisle, limping or hobbling away, or staggering beneath the weight of wounded comrades, they faded into the budding branches and were gone.

Around the armored square lay more than two-score dead and wounded Picts, some moaning, others feebly trying to crawl to safety. Conan wiped the blood and sweat from his face and turned to confront his soldiers, who stood expectantly beside the fallen members of the company.

"You! And you!" barked Conan, indicating two of the pikemen. "Fall out and dispatch me those dogs who still move. If it's a Pict, spear it; they are good at shamming dead. The rest of you, keep your places. Throw our dead out of the square. Tend our wounded."

Conan designated three archers to leave the square to gather up the spent arrows lying on the ground or sunk in Pictish flesh. Arno asked:

"Why have the savages quit when they outnumbered us ten to one?"

"Crom only knows. They've probably withdrawn to plan some other devilment. Don't break formation yet."

A gentle breeze carried the sound of a drum and a rattle shaken by a swarthy hand. The Aquilonians sighed in relief, wiped sweat from their faces, and drank deeply from their water jugs and skins. When some doffed helmets and mailshirts, Conan roared:

"Put back your harness, dolts! How think you we slew so many more than we, ourselves, have lost?"

In the airless afternoon, flies swarmed around the bodies of the fallen, forming black clusters on the bloody wounds; and the drumming and rattling of the savages droned on. The four officers gathered apart from the square of restless, weary men to confer in lowered voices. Conan said:

"I heard they have a new wizard, Sagayetha, nephew of old Zogar Zag. Methinks that racket means he's there among them directing the next attack."

"Beware, Conan!" hissed Arno. "If the men suspect there's sorcery afoot . . ."

"Anyone who wars with Picts fights sorcery," said Conan. "'Tis the natural condition of the frontier. They cannot stand against good Aquilonian steel, the steel that plucked the Westermarck out of Pictish hands. So they turn to their black devil-magic to even up the odds."

"What mean you, 'plucked'?" said Arno with indignation. "The land was bought from them, piece by piece, by legal treaties bearing royal seals."

Conan snorted: "I know those treaties, signed by some Pictish drunken ne'er-do-well who knew not what he placed his mark upon. I love not Picts, but I can understand the fury that drives them now. We'd best march back in column of fours, pikes without and archers within. Should they again attack, we can re-form our hedgehog."

The officers returned to their posts, but before the column had proceeded a hundred paces, the rattling and drumming ceased abruptly. The marchers paused, disquieted by the sudden silence.

A piercing scream ripped through the garment of uncanny silence. A man staggered out of ranks and fell writhing among the twisted roots. Another likewise fell; and suddenly the line vibrated with fearful cries of horror.

Snakes—Pictish vipers, some as long as a man, with wedge-shaped heads and diamond patterns down their thick, scaly bodies—dropped from the trees among the Aquilonians. On the forest floor they coiled, heads swaying, and lunged at the nearest soldier. Then slithering to their next victim, they coiled and struck again.

"Swords!" shouted Conan. "Kill them! Keep your ranks, but kill them!"

Conan's blade divided a six-foot serpent into writhing halves; but there seemed no end to the rain of snakes. An archer, shrieking in mindless terror, dropped his bow and broke into a run.

"Back in the ranks, you!" roared Conan.

The flat of his sword felled the fleeing Aquilonian. But it was too late; panic had taken hold. Arno, snake-bitten, lay writhing on the ground.

The Frontier Guards dissolved into a stream of fugitives, casting aside armor and weapons in their head-long flight. The Picts swarmed out of the forest cover and rushed after them, hacking, stabbing, and cudgeling those they overtook.

Conan's whirling broadsword struck down two Picts. "Flavius!" he cried. "This way!"

The young lieutenant fought through the press to join Conan, as the Cimmerian strode away from the fleeing Aquilonians.

"Are you mad?" panted Flavius, catching a Pictish hatchet blow on his buckler and missing a swipe at the wielder.

"See for yourself," growled Conan, running another Pict through the body. "If you'd leave this place alive, follow me."

The two hastened northwestward. Suddenly, there were no more Picts ahead, the nearest having given a wide berth to the two mailed warriors with bloody blades. Conan and Flavius ran down the trail and were soon out of sight of the battlefield.

The savages sprinted after the bulk of the Aquilonians, fleeing back toward Velitrium. But the Picts avoided the area where the Aquilonians had formed their square, for there lay bodies heaped and serpents still slithered and coiled and struck.

3 • Blood Money

In time the creek spread itself voluptuously beneath the blue sky, which it caught in reflected splendor. As Conan and Flavius pushed through the lush greenery cradling its shores, a sharp clap shattered the stillness. A splash roiled the placid surface of the pond, and drops of water leaped up the slanting rays of the afternoon sun, glittering like topaz.

"Fish?" whispered Flavius.

"Beaver. They splash with tails like broadswords to warn the others when danger approaches. See you their dam downstream of the pond? That's their abode."

"Mean you they live beneath the water?"

"Nay, in dry nests of twigs above the surface within the confines of the dam. Can you see that opening beyond the dam?"

On the right bank of South Creek, below the beaver dam, Flavius saw a clearing. Once neglected and overgrown, it had been lately cleared again. Through the trees that crowned this promontory, Flavius glimpsed the steel-blue water of the Black River.

In the midst of the clearing rose a granite statue twice the height of a man. Little more than a large upright boulder, it was roughly trimmed to suggest a human shape. In front of this rude eidolon, a smaller flat-topped boulder appeared above the long grass.

"The Council Rocks," muttered Conan. "The Picts were wont to meet here before the Aquilonians drove them out of Conajohara. Now they've cleared the place again and use it for their gatherings. We'll hide behind the beaver house to watch and listen. They'll hold a council, now that our forces are in disarray."

"But they'll spy us, Conan, and take us prisoner or worse!"

"I think not." Conan pulled ferns and water plants from the margin of the pond and fastened them about his helmet. "Tie plants about your helm, like mine."

"This hides our heads full well," said Flavius. "But what about mail-clad bodies?"

"All is invisible in blackish water, son."

"Mean you we must lurk within this pond, in all our harness, like some scaly creatures of the deep?"

"That's it. Better wet than dead."

Flavius sighed. "I suppose you are right."

"The day I'm wrong, they'll hang my head in one of their altar huts. Come on!"

Conan stepped into water no deeper than his waist and led his young companion across the pond to the beaver house, a wide mound of sticks two feet above the water. As they approached, a turtle, sunning itself on the wattled dam, slipped off into the water and vanished.

As they crouched until the water reached their chins, only their heads, all but undetectable under the leafy disguises, showed above the surface.

"I'd rather pray to Mitra in a temple than kneel on this dank leaf mold," said Flavius with a wry little smile.

"Be still; our lives depend upon it. Can you hold this pose for hours if need be?"

"I'll try," said the lieutenant gamely.

Conan grunted approvingly, and like a crouching leopard, ceased to move.

Insects hummed around them, and the frogs, which had fallen silent when the men appeared, resumed their croaking chorus. A red sun hung low above the fan of greenery that dabbled its feet in the roseate water. Slowly the woods darkened.

Flavius whispered desperately, "Something is biting me."

"Bloodsucker," said Conan. "Fear not; it will not steal enough of your blood to weaken you."

With a shudder, Flavius pinched the writhing leech and cast it from him.

"Hist! They come," murmured Conan.

Flavius quieted, hardly daring to breathe, as Picts in ones and twos flitted among the darkening trees, whooping with laughter. Flavius was surprised. From what he had seen of Picts, he deemed them a dour and silent folk. Evidently these savages could rejoice as well as other men.

The clearing filled as Picts, in clan regalia, squatted in rows and passed around skins of weak native beer, amid chatter and boasting.

"I see Wolves, Hawks, Turtles, Wildcats, and Ravens," whispered Flavius, "all in seeming amity."

"They are learning to put aside their clannish feuds," muttered Conan. "If ever the tribes unite at once, let Aquilonia beware. Ha! Look at those twain!"

Two figures, distinct from the throng of nearly naked savages, stepped into the clearing. One was a Pictish shaman, wearing a harness of leather in which was set a score of tinted ostrich feathers. These plumes, Flavius knew, must have been borne for nearly a thousand leagues over trade routes that wound like ribbons through the deserts and savannas of the south.

The other man was a lean, weatherbeaten Aquilonian in buckskins. Conan whispered:

"Sagayetha, and—by Crom—that's Edric, the scout whom Lucian foisted on us!"

Cutting a path through the squatting warriors, who swayed like fields of grain to let them pass, the shaman and the scout came through the throng and climbed the smaller boulder. The Aquilonian spoke in his native language to the Picts, pausing betimes for Sagayetha to translate.

"You have seen, my children," began Edric, "that your great and loyal friend, General Viscount Lucian, is not one whose words are straw. He said he would betray a company of Aquilonians into your hands, and did he not? Even so, when he promises you all of Schohira, he will not fail you.

"Now the time has come for the reckoning. In return for aiding you to recover the land that was stolen from you but a few decades ago, he now asks payment of the promised treasure."

Sagayetha translated the last phrase and ripped out a short speech of his own.

"What says he?" whispered Flavius.

"He told them to fetch the money. Now hush."

Four Picts appeared, staggering under a stout chest slung from a pole, which the Picts carried on their shoulders. As they lowered the chest to the ground, Sagayetha and Edric jumped down from the boulder and raised the lid. From their watery lurking place,

Conan and Flavius could not see the contents; but Edric dipped a hand in, brought up a fistful of the gleaming coins, and let them trickle back into the container. Flavius could hear the metallic clatter.

"Where would the Picts get so much gold and silver?" he whispered. "They use not coins, save now and then for trading with the Aquilonians."

"Valannus' pay chest," muttered Conan. "A full one had arrived at Fort Tuscelan just before it fell, and the Picts got their hands on it before it could be paid out to the soldiers."

"Why in the name of all the gods would Lucian betray his own folk and sell their land to savages?"

"I know not, albeit I have some ideas."

"I will slay those villains or die trying. One quick rush might reach them ere they struck me down—"

"Try it and I'll throttle you," growled Conan. "This news we hear is more important than aught that you could do. If we live not, it will never reach Velitrium. Now keep your head low and stay your tongue."

The two men in the beaver pond watched in silence as the four Picts hoisted the pole, from which hung the chest, and set off with Edric into the forest. Sagayetha mounted the boulder again and launched into an oration, telling the Picts of their past heroism and future glories. His gaudy plumage swayed and flapped with his fiery gestures.

Before Sagayetha finished, the sun had set, leaving overhead a scattering of scarlet clouds in a sapphire sky. In the gathering dark, the Picts began a victory dance, hopping, shuffling, and stamping in long lines, while others applied themselves to the beerskins.

By the time a few stars appeared through the canopy of leaves, the dance had become a savage thing of leaping, shadowy figures. Maddened by the liquor of their victory, the Picts cast off restraint, reverting to the beast that sleeps within all men. As the roistering became obscene, Conan grunted in disgust.

The moon was high when the forest grew still, save

for the croaking of frogs and the hum of mosquitoes. Fireflies flashed their elfin lights as they soared above the recumbent Picts. Conan said:

"They're all asleep. We go."

Across the beaver pond they waded, bent low to shield their passage from the sight of any waking Pict. As they emerged dripping and sought the shelter of the trees, Flavius shivered in the chilly evening air. He suppressed a groan as he stretched his stiffened muscles and fought down an urge to sneeze.

Conan struck out along the trail that had led them to the beaver pond. The Cimmerian seemed to possess the ability to see in darkness as well as by day, and moved through the trees with catlike ease. So little moonlight penetrated the dense cover that Flavius had much ado to keep from straying off the path or blundering into clumps of brush or trunks of trees. The best way to travel, Flavius found, was to follow Conan closely and trust blindly in his barbarian instincts.

The forest was alive with the chirp and buzz and twitter of nocturnal insects, as they passed the site of the past day's battle, where rotting corpses had already begun to exude a fetid stench. Flavius started at the sound of some unseen beast crashing through the darkness.

When Flavius began to gasp at the stiff pace set by Conan's long legs, the Cimmerian halted to rest his young companion. When his breath returned, Flavius said:

"Why did Lucian turn traitor to his country? You said you knew."

"'Tis plain enough," said Conan, drawing his sword to cleanse it of the water of the pond. "After the fall of Tuscelan, Lucian became the temporary governor of Conajohara and commander of what troops remain in this rump province."

"True," said Flavius. "It's nothing but a strip along

Thunder River, joining Conawaga and Schohira with Oriskonie . . . and the city of Velitrium."

"Aye. And this rump province will not keep its independence long, for Thasperas of Schohira and Brocas of Conawaga have gone to Tarantia to press before the king their claims to this poor remnant.

"Lucian well knows that his governorship will end when King Numedides bestows the land on one or the other or, perchance, gives parts to each of them. It's said that Thasperas and Lucian hate each other, so he gains both fortune and revenge by betraying Schohira to the Picts. That pay chest held a half-year's pay for nigh a thousand men—a tidy sum indeed. Lucian is said to be a gambler and, belike, is to his jowls in debt."

"But, Conan, what fate will overtake the common folk of Schohira?"

"Lucian cares not a fig for them. He works for General Viscount Lucian first and last, as do most feudal lordlings."

"Baron Thasperas would do no thing so foul, I know," said Flavius.

"At least Thasperas did not recall the companies he sent us as reinforcements after Tuscelan, and that cannot be said of Brocas. Still, I trust none of them. Besides, Lucian's plot is no less fair than that whereby you Aquilonians took the Westermarck—at least, so think the savages."

Anger tore at Flavius' devotion to his captain. "If you so despise us Aquilonians, why do you risk your neck, fighting for us against the Picts?"

Conan shrugged, there in the moonless forest. "I do not despise you, Flavius, or any of the other good men I have met among your people. But good men are hard to find in any land. The quarrels of lords and kings mean nothing to me, for I am a mercenary. I sell my sword to the highest bidder. So long as he pays me, I give him fair value in strength and strokes. Now, get up, young sir. We cannot stay here babbling all night."

4 • Moonlight on Gold

In the officers' quarters in the barracks at Velitrium, the fortress-headquarters of the Golden Lion regiment, four men sat in the yellow light of a brazen oil lamp, which swung from the sooty ceiling. Two were Conan and Flavius, both red-speckled from the myriad bites of mosquitoes. Conan, little affected by the grueling day and night that he had survived in the wilderness, spoke forcefully. Flavius fought the tides of sleep that threatened to engulf him. Each time he jerked himself awake, he forced his attention back to the two men, who stared at him with searching eyes. Then his eyelids would droop, his body slump, and his head nod until he jerked himself awake again.

The other two men wore parts of the uniform of Aquilonian officers. Neither was fully dressed, since both had been aroused from bed. One was a heavy-set man with a grizzled beard and a battle-scarred face. The other was younger, tall and handsome in a patrician way, with wavy blond hair that hung to his shoulders. The blond man spoke:

" 'Tis incredible, Captain Conan, what you tell us! That one of gentle blood, like General Lucian, should so foully betray his trust and his own soldiers! I cannot believe it. Were you to make such accusation publicly, I should feel obliged to denounce *you* as a traitor."

Conan snorted. "Believe what you like, Laodamas; but Flavius and I saw what we saw."

Laodamas appealed to the older officer. "Good Glyco, tell me, am I hearing treason, or have they both gone mad?"

Glyco took his time about replying. "It is a serious charge, surely. On the other hand, Flavius is one of our better junior officers, and our Cimmerian friend here showed his loyalty in the fighting last autumn. This Lucian I know not, save in the way of duty since he came here to command us. I say naught against him without evidence, but naught for him, either."

"But Lucian is a *nobleman*!" persisted Laodamas.

"So?" growled Conan. "Laodamas, if you believe a title renders a man above ordinary temptation, you have much to learn about your fellow beings."

"Well, if this fantastic tale be true, . . . wait!" said Laodamas as Conan's blue eyes flashed menace and a deep growl arose in his throat. "I gave not the lie to your story, Captain. I only said *if*. Now if it be true, what would you propose? We cannot go to our commander and say: 'Traitor, dismiss yourself from command and reside in the guardhouse pending trial.'"

Conan uttered a short bark of laughter. "I won't hazard anyone's neck without evidence. That pay chest should come across yon Thunder River soon, to be delivered unseen to the general. Flavius and I walked half the night to arrive ahead of it, reckoning the weight would delay those who bore it. If you two will finish dressing, we can intercept it ere it reaches the shore."

Muffled in cloaks against the chill and talking in low tones, the four officers stood about the narrow pier that jutted out from the Velitrium waterfront. Several small boats, tied to the pier, bobbed gently on the sinuous tide of the river. The moon, nearly full, hung a misshapen disk of luminous silver in the west. Overhead, white stars wheeled slowly, while from the surface of the river, a ghostly mist was rising. Above the mist could be seen the shaggy silhouettes of trees on the farther bank.

There was little sound save the lapping of water against the piles of the pier and the faint scrape of the small boats as they nudged each other in the current. The cry of a loon came from afar. The other three looked a question at Conan, who shook his head.

"That's a real call," he said, "not a Pictish signal."

"Flavius!" said Laodamas sharply. The lieutenant had slumped down with his back against a post.

"Let the lad have his nap," said Conan. "He has earned it thrice over."

Soon Flavius was snoring gently. Laodamas looked toward the east and asked: "The sky has paled a little. Is it dawn so soon?"

Conan shook his head. "That's the false dawn, as they call it. The real won't come for yet another hour."

Silence fell again, and the waiting officers paced noiselessly back and forth. As he paused to make a turn in his pacing, Conan came up short.

"Listen!"

After a moment, he said: "Oars! Take your posts."

He nudged Flavius awake with the toe of his boot, and the four retreated to the base of the pier, crouching behind such cover as they could find.

"Quiet, now!" said Conan.

Again there was silence. The moon had set, and without its competition, the stars blazed brightly. Then they dimmed again as the eastern sky paled with the approach of day.

A faint rhythmic splashing and creaking became audible, and a black shape took form out of the mist and resolved itself into a rowboat. As it came closer, the heads of five men could be discerned, rising from the indeterminate mass.

As the boat pulled up to the end of the pier, a man leaped out and made the painter fast to a cleat. With few words and much grunting, the oarsmen manhandled a heavy, bulky object out of the craft.

Four men, manning a carrying pole, hoisted the load to their shoulders. The fifth led them shoreward along the neck of the pier. In the waxing light, a keen eye could discern that the five wore the buckskin garb of Aquilonian scouts. At some time in the portage, thought Flavius, the Picts must have transferred their burden to these men.

As the five neared the base of the pier, Conan leaped out in front of them, drawing his sword.

"Stand or you're dead men!" he grated sharply.

The three other officers closed in with bared blades. For a heartbeat, there was silence.

The bearers dropped the chest with a crash. As a

single being, they raced back to the end of the pier and leaped into their boat, rocking it perilously. One cut the painter with a knife; others snatched up oars and shoved off.

The leader also leaped back before the apparition of the giant Cimmerian, but he collided with the chest and toppled backward over it. In a flash, Conan was upon him, catching his scrawny neck in an iron grip and pointing the blade of his sword against the fellow's throat.

"One word and you'll never speak another," said Conan, eyes blazing through the shredded mists of dawn.

The other officers pushed past Conan and his hostage and reached the end of the pier. But the waterborne scouts were already rowing away, soon to be lost in the fog.

"Let the dogs go," growled Conan. "This one is Edric, the traitor who steered us into yesterday's trap. He'll tell us what we want to know, eh, Edric?"

When the scout remained silent, Conan said, "Never mind. I'll have him talking soon enough."

"What now, Conan?" asked Glyco.

"Back to barracks. We'll use your room."

Flavius said: "Conan, how can we get both man and chest back to barracks? It takes four to carry the chest, leaving no guard for our prisoner."

"Flavius, take this dog's knife away and bind his hands behind his back. His belt will serve. Now you take charge of him."

Releasing his grip on the traitorous scout, Conan straightened his great back and heaved on the chest. "Glyco and Laodamas, hoist this thing up so I can get my shoulder under it."

The two officers put their shoulders under the ends of the pole and, grunting, straightened up. Conan crouched, set his shoulder beneath the chest and, with taut muscles cracking, rose.

"By the gods!" said Laodamas, "I never thought mortal man could bear such weight."

"Help Flavius bring the prisoner to the barracks. I cannot hold this thing till the sun comes up."

In the pallid light, they set out along the muddy streets. First came the scout, with Glyco and Laodamas on either side while Flavius walked behind, sword point goading the man's unwilling steps. Conan followed, weaving and staggering, but holding the chest fast upon his shoulder with arms like knotted ropes.

They reached the barracks as the first bird songs greeted the dawn. The sentry stared but, recognizing officers, saluted without comment.

5 • The General Is Shaved

Minutes later, the five men sat in Glyco's quarters. The chest, lid raised to show its glittering contents, stood in the center of the small room. Edric sat on the rough boards with his wrists and ankles lashed together.

"There's your evidence," said Conan, still breathing deeply. He turned to Edric. "Now, fellow, will you talk, or must I try some Pictish persuasion?"

The sullen prisoner remained silent.

"Very well," said Conan. "Flavius, give me yon fellow's knife."

Flavius drew the scout's knife from his boot top and handed it to the Cimmerian, who thumbed it purposefully.

"I mislike to use my own blade," he mused, "because heating it to red takes the temper out of steel. Now, set the brazier here."

"I'll talk," whined the prisoner. "A devil like you could wring a confession from a dead man." Edric drew a deep breath. "We of Oriskonie," he said, "live far from the rest of the Westermarck and care little about the other provinces. Besides, the general promised to make us rich after we had delivered Schohira to the Picts. What have we had from our baron, or

186

from the rest of you lordlings for that matter, but robbery and abuse?"

"It is your place to obey your natural lords . . ." began Laodamas, but Conan cut him off with a sharp gesture.

"Go on, Edric," said Conan. "Never mind the rights and wrongs of it."

Edric explained how General Lucian had put him and other scouts to work guiding the Aquilonians at Velitrium into Pictish traps.

"We set the trap at South Creek so that the general could show good faith to his Pictish allies and get the pay chest from them."

"How can a man like you betray your own countrymen for gold?" demanded Laodamas hotly.

Conan, brows knit, turned to the officer. "Quiet, Laodamas. Edric, what was this trap the general set?"

"The wizard, Sagayetha, can master serpents from afar. His people say he puts his soul into the body of a serpent, but I . . . I do not understand such matters of vile witchery."

"Nor I, nor any man," said Conan. "Think you Lucian would in truth deliver Schohira to the Picts?"

Edric shrugged. "I know not. I had not thought so far ahead."

"Is it not likely that he would have betrayed you, too? Have you and your comrades slain, lest any bear tales of his treachery to the throne of Aquilonia?"

"Mitra! I never thought of that!" gasped Edric, turning his head to hide his frightened eyes.

"Perhaps this wretch lies, and Lucian is a loyal Aquilonian after all," said Laodamas. "Then we need not. . ."

"Fool!" exploded Conan. "A loyal Aquilonian, to sacrifice a company of good men merely to. bait a trap? Glyco, how many survived the rout?"

"Two score straggled back ere nightfall," said Glyco. "We hope a few more may . . ."

"But—" began Laodamas.

Conan smote his palm with a clenched fist.

"They were my men!" he snarled. "I had trained them, and I knew each one. Arno was a good man and my friend. Heads will pay for this treachery, whatever scheme the general may have had in mind. Glyco and Laodamas, go to your companies and choose a dozen men you can trust. Tell them it's a perilous action against treachery in high places, and if they want revenge for South Creek, they must follow orders. Meet me on the drill ground in half an hour. Flavius, take our prisoner to the lockup and then join me."

"Conan," said Laodamas, "whilst I concede your plan is sound, it is I should command the venture. I am of noble blood and stand above you on the promotion list. This is irregular . . ."

"And I stand above you, young man," snapped Glyco. "If you make an issue of rank, I'll take command. Lead on, Conan; you seem to know what you're about."

"If he does not," said Laodamas, sulkily, "we shall all hang for mutiny. Suppose the general cries to the men: 'Seize me those traitors!' Whom will they obey?"

"That," said Conan, "is a question time will answer. Come!"

On the drill ground, the three officers and their lieutenants lined up their two-score soldiers. Briefly, Conan explained the Pictish trap and who had planned the massacre. He told four men to carry the chest and said:

"Follow me."

The sun had mounted the tops of the rolling Bossonian hills when Conan's group arrived at the generous dwelling wherein lived the commander of the Frontier Guard of Conajohara. Built on a slope, the house fronted on a high terrace, reached by a dozen steps from street level. At the officers' approach, two sentries on the terrace snapped to attention.

Conan stamped up the steps. "Fetch the general!" he barked.

"But, sir, the general has not yet arisen," said a sentry.

"Fetch him anyway. This matter brooks no delay."

After a searching look at the grim faces of the officers, the sentry turned and entered the house. A groom appeared in the muddy street, leading one of the general's chargers.

"Why the beast?" asked Conan of the remaining sentry.

"His Lordship oft goes cantering before his morning meal," replied the sentry.

"A magnificent animal," said Conan.

The first sentry reappeared and said, "The general is being shaved, sir. He begs you wait . . ."

"To hell with him! If he comes not forth to treat with us, then we shall go to him. Go, tell his Lordship that!"

With a small sigh, the sentry reëntered the house. Presently, General Viscount Lucian appeared with a towel around his neck. Although he wore breeches and boots, his upper torso was bare. He was a short, stocky man of middle age, whose well-developed muscles were growing flabby; and his black mustache, usually a pair of waxed points, looked—without the morning's pomade—frayed and drooping.

"Well, gentlemen," said Lucian haughtily, "to what emergency do I owe this untimely visit?" To a sentry he said, "Fetch a stool. Hermius can finish my shave whilst I listen to my early visitors. Captain Conan, if I remember aright. You seem the leader here. What is it you would say to me?"

"Few words, indeed, my lord Viscount," growled Conan. "But we have something to show you."

He gestured savagely, and the soldiers waiting in the street below moved briskly up the steps and deposited the chest on the mosaic floor of the terrace. Then they stepped back.

Glyco and Laodamas studied the general's face like scribes deciphering an ancient parchment. At the first glimpse of the chest, Lucian started, his face went pale, and he bit his underlip. But he stared at the bulky object, saying naught. There was no doubt in the hearts of those who watched him that the general recognized the chest, for the wine-red leather whereof it was fashioned and the gilt-tipped design of dragons incised upon it were unmistakable.

Then Conan lashed out with his booted foot, kicking the lid back upon its creaking hinges. The sentries blinked and Lucian flinched as the golden coins glittered in the sunlight.

"The time for lies is past, Viscount," said Conan grimly, his steel-blue eyes boring into those of his superior. "The evidence of your crime is here before you. I doubt me not that King Numedides will call it treason; I have other word for it: foul treachery. Foulest treachery to betray into a death trap your own soldiers who fought for you valiantly and blindly, trusting in you!"

Lucian made no move, save that he wet his lips with the tip of his tongue, as delicately as a cat. His eyes were bright and unwinking.

Conan's eyes narrowed to slits through which burned naked hate.

"We saw the Picts give yonder pay chest to your man Edric, and we have a full confession from him. You are under arrest . . ."

Holding the bowl of scalding water under the general's chin, the barber lifted his razor to make a stroke. Like a striking serpent, Lucian moved. He snatched the bowl from the astonished barber and hurled it into Conan's face.

With amazing speed, Lucian rose and, placing both hands upon the chest, gave it a mighty shove. It toppled off the terrace, lid flapping; and turning over in it descent, it spewed forth a golden shower of coins, a veritable rain of flashing precious disks.

A collective gasp of sheer delight came from the soldiers who had followed Conan and his fellow mutineers. As the chest crashed to earth, sending more coins bouncing and rolling along the street, the soldiers broke ranks to scramble for the money.

Lucian brushed past Conan, who stood half blinded by the scalding, soapy water, took the steps two at a time, rushed through the scattered soldiers, and flung himself into the saddle of his stallion. By the time that Conan could see again, the horse was disappearing down the street at a mad gallop, clods of mud flying from its hooves.

Laodamas shouted to his dismounted cavalrymen to run to the barracks, mount, and pursue the fugitive.

"You'll never catch him," said Conan. "That's the best horse in all the Westermarck. Not that it matters greatly; when our sworn statements reach Tarantia, we shall at least be free of Lucian here. Whether the king chops off his head or inflicts him on some other province—that is his affair.

"Right now we have to stop the Picts from ravishing all of Schohira and drenching it in blood." To the waiting men below the terrace, he said:

"Gather up this money as best you may, ere it is lost in the mire. Then back to barracks to await my orders. Who comes with me to save the land for Mitra and Numedides?"

6 • Massacre Meadow

"Snakes do not terrify me, but I'll not vouch for my pikemen if those vile things begin to fall on them. All the troops now know about this Pictish magic from yesterday's survivors," said Glyco.

Laodamas shuddered. "In battle I am no worse a coward than most, but serpents . . . 'Tis no knightly way of war. Let's lure the Picts into open land where there are no trees for serpents to fall from and where my horsemen could cut the savages to bits."

"I see not how," grunted Conan. "Their next thrust is like to be across South Creek into Schohira, since that's the province Lucian sold to them; and for many leagues southwest that land is naught but forests. The Aquilonians have yet to clear and settle it."

"Then," persisted Laodamas, "why not muster our forces at Schondara, where the open land invites the use of cavalry?"

"We cannot force the Picts to seek us out on ground of our own choosing," said Conan. "The settlements of Schohira are scattered, and the Picts could swallow up the rest of the province while we sat like statues awaiting their attack. They flow through woods as water flows through gravel, while our men must be mustered and marched in battle array."

"What is your plan, then?" asked Glyco.

"I have picked from my archers scouts with forest experience. When they report back, I'll seek the place where the enemy plans to cross the creek and strike them there."

"But the serpents . . ." began Laodamas.

"Devils swallow the serpents! Whoever told you that soldiering was a safe trade? The snakes will cease to plague us when Sagayetha is dead. If I can slay him, that I will do. Meanwhile, we must do what we can with what we have. Crom and Mitra grant that we have enough."

Along the trail above the Council Rocks, South Creek ran through a patch of level ground, swampy on both sides of its serpentine bed. Since the creek was broad and shallow and easy to cross at this point, several trails converged there. The boggy flatland supported grasses and brush, but trees were rare. Still, Massacre Meadow, as it was known, was more open than most of the great Pictish wilderness.

Back from the open space, where dense forest began, Conan posted his army. Pikemen and archers were arrayed in a crescent beneath the trees, while Laodamas' horse were positioned on Conan's right flank. The riders sat on the ground, throwing dice, and the tethered animals stamped and switched their tails to discourage the tormenting flies.

Conan walked up and down his line, inspecting equipment, encouraging the fearful with rude jokes, and issuing orders.

"Glyco," he called. "Have you told off the men who are to make torches of their pikes?"

"They are preparing them now," said Glyco, pointing toward the dozen Aquilonians who were binding brushwood to the heads of their spears.

"Good. Light not the fire until the Picts are in sight, least we reveal ourselves without need."

Conan strolled on. "Laodamas! If I'm not here to give the command, order your charge when the Picts are halfway across the creek."

"That would be taking unfair advantage," said Laodamas. "'Twere not chivalrous."

"Crom and Mitra, man, this is no tournament! You have your orders."

Back among the infantry, he sighted Flavius and said: "Captain Flavius, are your men ready?"

Flavius beamed at hearing the title of his temporary rank. "Aye, sir; the extra quivers are laid out."

"Good. Whether an army is in more peril from having in command an honest idiot like Laodamas or a clever jackal like Lucian, I know not. You I can count upon." Flavius smiled broadly.

The afternoon wore on amid buzzing flies and grumbling men. Water jugs passed from hand to hand. Conan, sitting on a fallen log, made marks upon a sheet of bark as scouts came to him, reporting the position of the Pictish force. At length he had a rude sketch map from which to plan the coming fray.

As the sun was setting, the first Picts appeared across Massacre Meadow, yelling defiance and brandishing their weapons. More and more poured out of the forest until the low ground beyond South Creek was thronged with naked, painted men.

Flavius murmured to Conan: "We are outnumbered here as much as at the battle of the serpents."

Conan shrugged and rose. Commands rang up and down the Aquilonian line. The pikemen designated as snake destroyers kindled a fire from which to light their improvised torches, while archers drew arrows from their quivers and thrust them into the ground before them.

A drum began to beat like a throbbing heart. Yelping war cries, the Picts splashed across the creek, trotted across the boggy land on the southwest side of the meadow, and closed with the Aquilonians. Amid the savage whoops and the shouts of command, arrows whistled across the meadow, like specters of the damned.

Knots of painted Picts dashed themselves against the lines of pikemen. When one savage was transfixed by a pike and his weight dragged the weapon down, others pushed in through the gap thus created, thrusting with spears and slashing with hatchets. Pikemen of the second line, sweating and cursing, thrust them back. About the meadow, the wounded crawled, twitched, shrieked, or lay still.

Conan himself held the center of the line, towering like a giant above the stockier Gundermen and Aquilonians. Armed with a steel-shafted axe, he reaped a gory harvest of the foe. They came at him like yelping hounds seeking to drag down a boar. But the dreadful axe which he wielded as tirelessly as if it were a willow wand, split skulls, crushed ribs, and lopped off heads and arms with merciless precision. Roaring a tuneless song, he fought, and the mounds of dead grew around him like grain after the scything.

Before long the Picts began to avoid the center where he stood unconquerable above the heaped corpses. Ferocious, blood-mad fighters though they were, it seeped into their wild consciousness that the giant figure sheathed in iron and splattered from head to foot with gore was not to be overcome by such as they.

The fighting ebbed for a moment, in one of those lulls that sometimes come in the midst of battle. As Conan leaned upon his ax to catch his breath, his new-made captain hurried over to him.

Axe

"Conan," called Flavius, "we are sore beset! When will the horse charge?"

"Not yet, Flavius. Look yonder, on the distant meadow. Not a quarter of the painted ones have yet crossed the stream. This is but a skirmish to probe for our weakness. They'll draw off presently."

Soon whistles sounded. The Picts trotted back across the meadow and swam the creek, pursued by Aquilonian arrows.

"Archers!" shouted Conan. "Two men from each squad harvest arrows."

The archers hastened to push through the pikemen and pull spent shafts from the ground or from the blood-soaked bodies of the fallen, while the remainder cleansed their equipment or drank deeply from the waterskins.

"Whew!" said Flavius, doffing his helmet to wipe his blood-spattered face. "If that be but a skirmish, I hate to contemplate the onslaught. How knew you when the fiends would fall back?"

"When savages find a plan that works, they often repeat it blindly," replied the Cimmerian. "Sagayetha's earlier attack destroyed us, so belike he follows the same scheme now. Some civilized officers do likewise."

"Then will the next assault be one of serpents?"

"No doubt. Hark!"

From the deep woods came the distant sound of a drum and a rattle pounded in the same rhythm as that which preceded the magical assault of the previous battle.

"'Twill soon be full dark," said Flavius, fearfully. "We shall not see the Picts to shoot nor the snakes to burn."

"You can do your best," growled Conan. "I'm going after that devil Sagayetha. Pass the word to the other officers."

Conan strode swiftly down the line to the glade wherein Glyco stood. To this seasoned veteran, Conan repeated his intention.

"But, Conan . . ."

"Seek not to dissuade me, man! I, alone, may hope to discover the lair of this hyena. The rest of you have orders; to you I give command till I return."

"*If* you return," muttered Glyco, but he found himself addressing empty air. Conan had vanished.

7 • Serpent Magic

The night air throbbed with the songs of insects. Skirting the lines of Aquilonians, Conan picked up the trail to Velitrium and jogged along it until he was well away from combatants. When the trail wandered close to South Creek, he left it and forded the stream, cursing beneath his breath as he stepped into a hole and went in up to his neck. Wading and swimming, he gained the other side and pushed through heavy undergrowth along the waterway until he reached the open aisles of the virgin forest beyond.

The moon, grown to a great silver disk since the defeat on South Creek, rode high in the sky. Guiding his steps by her light, Conan followed a circular course, calculated to bring him around to the rear of the Pictish army. He walked softly, pausing from time to time to listen and taste the air. Although afire with impatience to confront the wizard, he was enough of a seasoned warrior to know that haste would gain him only a swift demise.

Presently he picked up the sound of the drum and rattle, and stood, holding his breath and cocking his head to locate the direction whence it came. Then he set forth once more.

The rumble of the Pictish army reached his ears, as the bulk of the savages continued to gather on the northeast side of Massacre Meadow, across the creek from the Aquilonian force. Conan moved with more care than before, lest Pictish sentries discover him.

He met no Picts until the drumming and rattling became loud enough to locate the precise source of the clatter. Conan felt sure that in daylight he could have seen the wizard's tent from afar. But he was almost upon it before he found it, standing in the deepest gloom between two giant oaks in a glade feebly lit by a few dots of moonlight. Conan's nerves tingled in the presence of magic, like those of a jungle beast at the throat of unknown danger.

Then his keen eyes spied a Pict, leaning against a tree and staring in the direction of the massing savages. With exquisite care, Conan approached the fellow from the rear. The savage heard a twig snap behind him and whirled just in time to receive Conan's axe full in his war-painted face. The savage fell, twitching, his head split open like a melon.

Conan froze, fearing the sound of the blow and the fall might have alerted Sagayetha. There was, however, no immediate letup in the rhythmic pounding.

Conan approached the tent, but as he raised his hand to lift the flap, the ear-splitting sounds died away. At the former battle of the serpents, this silence presaged the serpentine attack from the trees.

Conan lifted the tent flap and stepped in, his nostrils quivering from the reptilian stench. The dim red glow from the coals of a small fire in the center of the tent provided the only illumination, and beyond the fire, vaguely visible in the roseate dimness, sat a hunched figure.

As Conan stepped around the fire, preparing a swift blow that should end this menace once and for all, the silent figure remained motionless. He saw that it was indeed Sagayetha, in breech clout and moccasins, sitting upright with his eyes closed. He must, thought Conan, be in a trance, sending his spirit out to control the snakes. So much the better! Conan took another step.

Something moved on the floor of the tent. As Conan bent to see more closely, he felt a sharp sting on his left arm below the short sleeve of his mailshirt.

Conan jerked back. A huge viper, he saw, had its fangs imbedded in his forearm. This must be king of all Pictish vipers; the creature was longer by a foot than the giant Cimmerian was tall. As he jerked back, he dragged the serpent half clear of the earthen floor.

With a gasp of revulsion. Conan struck with his axe. Although ragged and notched from the day's fighting, the blade sheared through the reptile's neck a foot below its head. With a violent shake of his injured arm, he sent the head and neck flying, while the serpent's severed body squirmed and coiled upon the earthen flooring. In its writhings, it threw itself into the fire, scattering coals; and the smell of roasting flesh filled the confined space.

Conan stared at his forearm, cold sweat beading his brow. Two red spots appeared where the fangs had pierced his naked flesh, and a drop of blood oozed from each puncture. The skin around the punctures was darkening fast, and a fierce pain spread to his shoulder.

He dropped the axe so that the spike on its head buried itself in the dirt. Then he drew his knife to incise the skin at the site of the wounds. Before he could do so, the seated figure stirred. Sagayetha's eyes opened, cold and deadly as the eyes of serpents.

"Cimmerian!" said the shaman. The word sounded like the hiss of a monstrous snake. "You have slain that into which I sent my soul, but I shall . . ."

Conan hurled his knife. The wizard swayed to one side, so that the implement struck the skin of the tent and stuck there. Sagayetha rose and pointed a skinny arm.

Before the wizard could utter a curse, Conan snatched up his axe and reached him with a single bound. A whistling blow ended in a meaty thud. Sagayetha's head flew off, rolled toward the embers, and came to rest on the hard-packed dirt. Blood poured from the collapsing body, soaking into the earth and hissing as it flooded over the hot coals in the center of the tent. Sinister vapors rose in the dim rosy light.

Conan recovered his knife and slashed at his bitten arm. He sucked blood from the wound and spat it out, sucked and spat, again and again. The dark discoloration had spread over most of his forearm, and the pain was agonizing. He took but an instant to strip the corpse of the belt that supported its loin cloth and made of it a crude tourniquet, which he placed on his upper arm.

As he continued to suck the venom from the wound, the rising roar of battle came to him from afar. Evidently the Picts, impatient at the delay of their serpentine allies, had launched their own attack. Conan fretted to be gone, to join in the slaughter. But he knew that for a man freshly bitten by a venomous snake to set out at a run would mean immediate death. With a mighty effort of will, he forced himself to continue sucking and spitting.

At last the purplish stain seemed to spread no further. When it receded a little, he bandaged the arm with cloth found among the wizard's effects. Carrying his axe in his good hand and swinging Sagayetha's head by its hair in the other, he left the tent.

8 • Blood on the Moon

Under the high-riding, heartless moon, an endless stream of Picts crossed South Creek to assail the embattled Aquilonians. Bodies of Aquilonians joined those of Picts in heaps on Massacre Meadow.

"Laodamas!" said a deep, harsh voice in the shadows. Sitting his horse, the cavalry commander turned in his saddle.

"Mitra save us!" he cried. "Conan!"

"Whom did you expect?" growled Conan.

As the full moon, now near its zenith, fell on Conan's upturned face, Laodamas saw that Conan staggered as he approached. In that face, he saw signs of exhaustion, as if Conan had pushed himself beyond the limits of endurance. Perhaps it was a trick of the silvery light, he thought, but Conan's mien was deathly pale.

"Why in Hell haven't you charged?" continued Conan. "More than half the Picts have crossed the creek."

"I will not!" said Laodamas. "To take such advantage of the foe while he is thus divided, were unknightly conduct. 'Tis clean against the rules of chivalry."

"Ass!" shouted Conan. "Then we must do it another way!"

Setting down his grisly burden and his weapons, he grasped Laodamas' ankle, jerked it out of the stirrup, and heaved it up.

"What . . ." cried Laodamas. Then he was tossed out of the saddle, to fall with a crash of armor into the soft soil on the far side of his horse.

An instant later, Conan swung into the empty saddle. He raised his axe on the spike of which he had impaled Sagayetha's head.

"Here's your Pictish wizard!" he roared. "Come on, my friends, by squads, advance!"

The trumpeter winded his horn. Aquilonian horsemen, chafing at Laodamas' long delay, spurred their mounts with a clatter of armor and a creaking of harness. Conan bellowed:

"Cry 'Sagayetha is dead!' Sound the charge, trumpeter!"

Conan held his gruesome banner high as the troop poured out of the forest, yelling at the footmen to get out of the way. They scrambled off, and the cavalry thundered through the gap.

The squads of mailed horsemen plowed through the loose knots of Picts, like an armored thunderbolt. At their fore rode Conan, his gory axe held in the crook of his left arm, so that the wizard's severed head thrust up above his shoulder, a ghastly standard. With his good right hand, he held the reins and guided the charger he had commandeered.

At his swift heels hurtled the iron-sheathed cavalry, thrusting and smiting to right and left. As they smote the reeling ranks of the foe, they chanted hoarsely the battle-song, "Sagayetha is dead! Sagayetha is dead!" Although the Picts knew not their words, the moonlight silvered the grisly visage of the dead shaman affixed to the shaft of Conan's axe, and they understood the meaning.

Now the infantry took up the chant in a deep, resonant cry. Stout Gunderman and sturdy Aquilonian yeomen armed with pikes splashed across the ford behind the horsemen. Yammering at one another, the savages pointed to the hideous head atop the shaft of Conan's axe; and, wailing in dismay, they broke away on every side, ignoring the shouting of their chiefs. The battle turned into a rout. The lines of painted, howling savages disintegrated into fleeing forms, glimpsed through the shafts of moonlight among the distant trees.

In a single broad front, the troop pounded through the marsh and meadow, riding down the masses of fleeing Picts. The Aquilonian pikemen and archers advanced behind the horse, spearing and stabbing, like avenging angels; and the Pictish army dissolved into a panicky mob. The face of the moon, reflected in the surface of the creek, was red with the blood of the dead and dying.

At length, Conan drew his horsemen up and shouted orders to the trumpeter. On signal, the riders wheeled into column of squads and cantered toward the sheltered field whence they had come. Conan knew that at night in dense forest, horsemen would be useless.

"Press on, Glyco!" he shouted. "Give them no chance to rally!"

Glyco waved acknowledgement as he and his men charged into the woods after the fleeing Picts. Conan spurred his borrowed mount to overtake the head of the column. Then the world dissolved in whirling blackness. He had pressed himself too far—beyond the limits of his fading vigor.

Glyco and Flavius sat in Conan's bedroom in the barracks at Velitrium. Propped up in bed, Conan with ill grace accepted the ministrations of the army's physician. Old Sura fussed about his patient, changing dressings on Conan's left arm, which bore from wrist to shoulder a rainbow pattern of red, blue, and purple discolorations.

"The wonder is to me," said Glyco, "how you managed to support that axe with the wizard's head upon it, with such an arm as this."

Conan spat. "I did what I had need to do." Then, turning to the doctor, he asked: "How long will you keep me here, swaddled like an infant, good Sura? I have things to do."

"A few days of care will see you restored to duty, General," said the gray-haired doctor. "If you overdo before then, you risk a relapse."

Conan growled a barbaric oath. "What was the final tale of the battle?"

Glyco replied: "After you swooned and fell from your horse—Laodamas' horse, I should say—we harried the painted devils till the last of them vanished, like smoke, into the forest depths. While we lost not a few good men, we slaughtered many more."

"I must be getting old," said Conan, "to faint from a mere snakebite and a bit of action. Who was it called me 'general'?"

Flavius spoke: "Whilst you lay here unconscious, we sent a messenger to the king bearing a report of our successes in the province of Schohira, and a memorial praying him to confirm you as our new commanding officer. Our choice was unanimous—albeit we put no small pressure on Laodamas to make him sign it. He was much angered with you for usurping his horse and his authority and talked of challenging you to a duel."

Conan laughed enormously—a laugh that spread and resonated like the sound of trumpets blown at dawn. "I'd have been sorry to carve up the young ninnyhammer. The lad means well, but he lacks sense."

A knock preceded the opening of the door, and a lean man in the tight leather garments of a royal messenger entered.

"General Conan?" he asked.

"Aye. What is it?"

"I have the honor to deliver this missive from His Majesty." The messenger handed over a scroll with a deferential bow.

Conan broke the seal, unrolled the scroll, and peered at the writing thereon.

"Bring that candle nearer, Sura," he said. "This light is poor for reading." His friends watched with eager interest as he sat in silence, moving his lips.

"Well," he drawled at last, "the king confirms my appointment. What's more, he bids me to Tarantia for an official investiture and a royal feast."

Conan grinned and stretched his great body beneath the bedclothes.

"After a year of dodging Picts through trackless forests and unmasking traitorous commanders, the fleshpots of Tarantia sound tempting. Whatever Numedides' shortcomings, 'tis said his cooks are superb. And I could use some fine wine and a bouncing, high-bred damsel in place of the bellywash we get here and our slatternly camp followers!"

"My patient must rest now, sirs," said the doctor.

Glyco and Flavius rose. The old soldier said: "Till later, then, Conan. But have a care. At court, they say, there's a scorpion under every silken cushion."

"I'll take care, fear not. But if neither Zogar Sag nor Sagayetha, for all their uncanny powers, could slay me, I think the hero of Velitrium will be in little peril at the court of Aquilonia's king!"

HYBORIAN NAMES

In choosing names for the people and places in his stories of the Hyborian Age, Robert E. Howard revealed a number of facts about his sources, his reading, and the writers who had influenced him. Concerning these names, H. P. Lovecraft once remarked (in a letter to Donald A. Wollheim about Howard's essay "The Hyborian Age," reprinted in *The Coming of Conan*): "The only flaw in this stuff is R. E. H.'s incurable tendency to devise names too closely resembling actual names of ancient history— names which, for us, have a very different set of associations. In many cases he does this designedly—on the theory that familiar names descend from the fabulous realms he describes—but such a design is invalidated by the fact that we clearly know the etymology of many of the historic terms, hence cannot accept the pedigree he suggests."

Many of the personal names used by Howard in his Conan stories are ordinary Latin personal names (Publius, Constantius, Valeria) or Greek names (Dion, Pelias, Tiberias) or modern Italian versions of these (Publio, Tito, Demetrio). Others are modern Asiatic or Arabic names, sometimes modified (Aram Baksh, Yar Afzal, Jungir Khan, Bhunda Chand, Shah Amurath) while still others are apparently made up (Thak, Thaug, Thog, Yara, Yog, Yogah, Zang, Zogar Sag). In RN occur a number of Aztec or pseudo-Aztec names; in BR, TT, and BB, pseudo-Iroquois names.

Perhaps Lovecraft had especially in mind the Asiatic names that originated in the conquests of Alexander the Great in −IV, or in those of the Muslim Arabs in +VII. It is interesting to note that the three made-up names above, beginning with "Th," are all names of monsters.

Despite Lovecraft's criticism, there was much to be said for Howard's use of real ancient names and names derived from these, because his purely made-up names show a disagreeable sameness (Ka, Kaa-u, Ka-nu, Kaanuub; Thak, Thaug, Thog, etc.). The reason for this is probably a lack of linguistic sophistication on Howard's part. When he graduated from the Kull stories to the Conan stories, he seems to have sworn off made-up names in favor of real names from history and geography, sometimes slightly modified. These borrowed names are usually well-chosen and euphonious. They convey the glamor of antiquity by their near-familiarity without being too difficult for the modern reader, who, having been taught to read by sight-reading methods, is apt to boggle at any name more exotic than "Smith."

Moreover, Lovecraft sometimes borrowed real ancient names (Menes, Kranon, Sarnath) in exactly the manner which he chided Howard for doing.

Howard's geographical names come mainly from the more accessible bodies of myth: Classical (e.g., Stygia), Norse (Asgard), or biblical (Kush); and from the kind of geographical lore to be had from an atlas. Besides the names of obvious derivation, there are many whose origin is more complex, showing wide reading by Howard.

Anybody who made a practice of reading *Adventure Magazine* during the 1920s will recognize, in Howard's Hyborian stories, the influence of the historical adventure stories by Harold Lamb and Talbot Mundy, published in this magazine at this time. Lamb's tales were usually set in an Asiatic locale, dealing with such events as the Crusades, the Mongol and Turkish conquests, and the rise of the Russian state. Howard's stories of Conan and the *kozaki* are closely derived from Lamb's yarns of sixteenth- and seventeenth-century Cossacks.

Mundy's stories were usually laid in modern India, Afghanistan, Tibet, or Egypt. Mundy's picture of these countries is highly romanticized, full of assumptions of ancient sorceries and occult wisdom. Howard's Stygia and Vendhya are essentially Mundy's Egypt and India, respectively, with the names changed. There may also have been some Kipling influence on Howard.

Besides Lamb and Mundy, Howard must have read many other stories in *Adventure*. A search reveals derivations from other leading adventure-story writers of the time, such as Frederick Faust, A. D. Howden Smith, and Sax Rohmer. The stories "Beyond the Black River," "The Treasure of Tranicos," and "Wolves Beyond the Border" are derived from the Indian-fighting novels of Robert W. Chambers, which were often laid in upstate New York in late +XVIII, and possibly also from the novels of J. Fenimore Cooper.

Other fictional influences on Howard were Jack London (whom he much admired), Howard Pyle, and Edgar Rice Burroughs. He also read travel books, such as those of Sir Richard Burton and (possibly) Rosita Forbes. And he read a lot of history. His knowledge of the medieval Muslim world was not negligible, as was shown by the original manuscript of "Hawks over Shem" (entitled, before I rewrote it as a Conan story, "Hawks over Egypt"). This story dealt with the reign and disappearance of the mad eleventh-century Caliph Hakim.

The fantastic side of Howard's stories seems to have been derived largely from Lovecraft and from Clark Ashton Smith, as is shown by several of Howard's names (Crom, Valusia, Commoria, etc.). There is some slight, inconclusive evidence that Howard had read Eddison's *The Worm Ouroboros*: the Iron Tower of Tarantia and the Iron Tower of King Gorice of Carcë; Eddison's Gallandus and Howard's Gallanus; and the mention of Hyperboreans by both. He had also read some of Lord Dunsany's stories.

Here follows a glossary of personal and place names in the fifty Conan stories professionally published so far. Besides the names devised by Howard for his original Conan stories, I have also included (a) names adopted by the living Conan authors for their stories, including stories written in posthumous collaboration with Howard, and (b) names discarded by Howard in the course of his writing. The living authors have tried to follow the same system in choosing names that Howard did. Howard often changed the names of places and persons between his first and his final draft; Glenn Lord, working from Howard's rough drafts, has furnished a list of these discarded names. When an entry is followed by another name in boldface, in parentheses and preceded by =, the first name was discarded in favor of the second before the story reached final form.

As far as possible, supposed derivations are given for all names. Where no derivation is given, either the source of the name is not known, or it has been forgotten by the author responsible for it, or it is thought that the name is a purely made-up one. Stories are referred to by code letters, as shown below. Stories are listed in the chronological order in which they occur in Conan's life. The lower-case letters in parentheses following each title refer to authorship, thus: *c* for Carter, *d* for de Camp, *h* for Howard, and *n* for Nyberg. Here are the stories:

LD—Legions of the Dead (cd)
TC—The Thing in the Crypt (cd)
TE—The Tower of the Elephant (h)
HD—The Hall of the Dead (dh)
GB—The God in the Bowl (h)
RH—Rogues in the House (h)
HN—The Hand of Nergal (ch)
PP—The People of the Summit (dn)
CS—The City of Skulls (cd)
CM—The Curse of the Monolith (cd)
BG—The Bloodstained God (dh)
FD—The Frost Giant's Daughter (h)
LW—The Lair of the Ice Worm (cd)

QC—Queen of the Black Coast (h)
VW—The Vale of Lost Women (h)
CT—The Castle of Terror (cd)
SD—The Snout in the Dark (cdh)
HS—Hawks Over Shem (dh)
BC—Black Colossus (h)
SI—Shadows in the Dark (cd)
SM—Shadows in the Moonlight (h)
RE—The Road of the Eagles (dh)
WB—A Witch Shall be Born (h)
BT—Black Tears (cd)
SZ—Shadows in Zamboula (h)
SK—The Star of Khorala (dn)
DI—The Devil in Iron (h)
FK—The Flame Knife (dh)
PC—The People of the Black Circle (h)
SS—The Slithering Shadow (h)
DT—Drums of Tombalku (dh)
GT—The Gem in The Tower (cd)
PO—The Pool of the Black One (h)
CB—Conan the Buccaneer (cd)
RN—Red Nails (h)
JG—Jewels of Gwahlur (h)
IG—The Ivory Goddess (cd)
BR—Beyond the Black River (h)
MB—Moon of Blood (cd)
TT—The Treasure of Tranicos (ex-The Black
      Stranger) (dh)
BB—Wolves Beyond the Border (dh)
PS—The Phoenix on the Sword (h)
SC—The Scarlet Citadel (h)
CC—Conan the Conqueror (ex-The Hour of the
      Dragon) (h)
CA—Conan the Avenger (ex-The Return of
      Conan) (dn)
WM—The Witch of the Mists (cd)
BS—Black Sphinx of Nebthu (cd)
RZ—Red Moon of Zembabwei (cd)
SH—Shadows in the Skull (cd)
CI—Conan of the Isles (cd)

Dates are indicated thus: Arabic numerals mean years; Roman numerals, centuries; Arabic numerals followed by M, millennia. The signs + and − mean A.D. and B.C. respectively, although + is omitted for years after +1000. Hence −65 means 65 B.C.; +III denotes the third century of the Christian Era; −2M means the second millennium B.C.

Abdashtarth In HS, the high priest of Pteor in Asgalun. A Phoenician name.

Abimael In GT, a Shemitish sailor in the crew of the *Hawk*. A biblical name (Gen. 10:28).

Abombi In SC, a town on the Black Coast sacked by Conan and Bêlit. From Abomey, West Africa.

Acheron In CC, an empire that fell 3,000 years before Conan's time, sometimes called the "northern Stygian kingdom." In Greek mythology, one of the four rivers of Hades; also the name of several rivers in ancient Greece, the largest (modern Gourla) being in Thesprotia.

Adonis In QC, a Shemitish god. In HS, Asgalun has a "Square of Adonis." The Greek name for a Semitic god of vegetation and agriculture, called Adonai ("Lord"), Tammuz, or (in Babylonia) Dumuzi.

Æsir In FD, QC, PS, &c., the blond folk of the northern country of Asgard. In Norse myth, the chief gods (singular, As): Odin, Thor, &c.

Afari In SD, a henchman of the Kushite nobleman Tuthmes. From the Afar, a Hamitic or Erythriotic tribe of Abyssinia (Ethiopia) and Somaliland; their name may be connected with ancient Ophir (q.v.).

Afghuli In PC, CA, one of the people of Afghulistan (q.v.).

Afghulistan In PC, a region of the Himelias. A mixture of Ghulistan (q.v.) and Afghanistan. The Afghuli tribe, of which Conan becomes chief, dwells here.

Ageera In SD, a Kushite witch-smeller.

Agha This title occurs in the names of Agha Shu-

pras (BC) and Jehungir Agha (DI). From *ağâ*, a
Turkish title of respect.

Aghrapur, Agrapur   In HN, SZ, DI, &c., the capital
of Turan. After Agrâ, India, the site of the Taj Mahal,
+ the Hindustani *pur*, "town."

Ahriman   In CC, BN, RZ, the Heart of Ahriman is
a magical jewel. The evil god of Mazdaism or Zoroastrianism (Old Persian, *angra mainyu*, "evil spirit").

Ahrunga (=Gwarunga)   In the first draft of JG;
discarded.

Aja   In VW, the chief of the Bakalah. Possibly from
Jaja, an enterprising king of the Ibo or Igbo of Nigeria
in the 1870s.

Ajaga   In SC, a Kushite king. Possibly from the
same source as Jaja or Ajonga (q.v.).

Ajonga   In CC, a Negro galley slave. Possibly from
Wajanga, a place in southern Libya mentioned by
Rosita Forbes; or from *ajoga* (or *ajonga*) meaning
"wizard" in the speech of the Lango of Uganda.

Ajujo   In DT, the god of the black tribesmen of
Tombalku. Possibly from "juju," a West African fetish,
which comes from the French *joujou*, toy.

Akbatana, Akbitana   In BC and JG, a Shemitish
city. From Agbatana or Ecbatana, the Greco-Roman
names for Hagmatana or Hangmatana (mod. Hama-
dan), the capital of ancient Media.

Akeb Man   In CA, a Turanian officer. A pseudo-
Arabic name.

Akhirom   In HS, the mad king of Pelishtia. A
Phoenician name, Hiram in Hebrew.

Akhlat   In BT, a Shemitish town in the Zuagir
deserts.

Akif   In SZ, CA, a Turanian city. A Turkish proper
name; e.g., 'Akif Pasha, a Turkish poet of +XIX.

Akivasha   In CC, an evil immortal princess. From
the Egyptian name (Ekwesh or Akkaiwasha) for the
Achaioi or Achaeans (in archaic Greek, Achaiwoi).

Akkharia, Akkharim   In HS, WB, BT, a Shemitish
city-state and its people. Possibly from Akkad (Agade)
in ancient Iraq.

Akkutho   In SC, a former king of Koth. Possibly from the same source as Akkharia (q.v.).

Akrel   In PC, an oasis in the desert near Khauran.

Akrim   In RE, a river entering the Vilayet Sea from the southeast.

Alafdhal, Yar Afzal   Respectively a Turanian guardsman in SZ and a Wazuli chief in PC. From al-Afḍal (literally, "the most generous"), an Arabic name.

Alarkar   In SK, a count, ancestor to Queen Marala.

Albiona   In SK, CC, an Aquilonian countess, formerly Queen Marala of Ophir. From Albion, an old name for Britain, which in turn comes from the Albiones, the name given the Britons by several ancient geographers, such as Pytheas of Massilia (paraphrased by the late-Roman poet Avienus).

Alcemides   In WB, TT, a Nemedian philosopher. From various Greek names like Alkides (Herakles), Alkimenes (Bellerophon's brother), Alkman (a poet of −VII), &c.

Alimane   In CC, BS, a river between Aquilonia and Zingara, a tributary of the Khorotas. Probably from Allemagne, French for "Germany."

Alkmeenon   In JG, IG, a deserted place in Keshan, once the capital of white rulers of the country. From one or more of the Greek names Alkman, Alkmaion, or Alkmenê.

Almuric   In SS and CC, a prince of Koth. The name was used in Howard's posthumously published interplanetary novel, *Almuric*, as the name of the distant planet to which the hero is transported.

Altaku   In BC, a well in the Oasis of Aphaka. From Altaqu or Eltekeh, a place in ancient Judah, about 12 miles northwest of Jerusalem, where Sennacherib's Assyrians defeated the Egyptians in −700.

Altaro   In CC, a Nemedian priest, subordinate to Orastes. Possibly from Altare, Italy.

Alvaro   In CI, a Zingaran pirate of the Barachas. A Spanish given name.

Amalric   In BC, a Nemedian soldier of fortune; in

CC, the Nemedian baron of Tor—perhaps intended as the same man, although the stories do not clearly so state; also, in DT, a young Aquilonian mercenary soldier. An old Germanic name (Gothic *Amalreiks*, French *Amaury*, English *Emery*, *Emory*, *Amory*), common in the Middle Ages; e.g., the name of two Christian kings of Jerusalem. Howard probably took the name from these last, since he wrote a historical novelette, "Gates of Empire" (*Golden Fleece* for Jan. 1939) wherein one of these Kings Amalric of Jerusalem appears.

Amalrus   In SK, SC, a noble and later king of Ophir. Probably from Amalric (q.v.).

Amazons   In CB and mentioned in "The Hyborian Age," a southern Negro nation ruled by women. In Classical legend, nations of warrior women in Asia Minor and North Africa. The legend may be based upon the Sarmatians, a nomadic Iranic tribe of the Kuban, whose women were required to slay an enemy before they might marry.

Amboola   In SD, an officer of the black spearmen of the kingdom of Kush. Probably from *bamboula*, a drum used in West African and Voodoo ceremonies and the dance performed to it. Cf. Bambula.

Amerus (=Posthumo)   In the first draft of GB, discarded; from the same source as Amalric (q.v.).

Amilio (=Tiberias)   In first draft of BR, discarded; from the same source as Amilius (q.v.).

Amilius   A barony in Aquilonia mentioned in CC. From Æmilia (mod. Emilia), a province in northern Italy, and Æmilius, the corresponding Roman gentile name.

Amir   In PC, the Amir Jehun pass is in Ghulistan. Arabic for "commander."

Amra   In CC, the name, meaning "lion," by which Conan was known when he sailed with the black corsairs. Howard had used the name before, as Am-ra, a young Atlantean in the Kull story "Exile of Atlantis," and again as the hero of the story "Gods of the North," rewritten from a Conan story, "The Frost Giant's

Daughter," but when it was rejected published in a fan magazine with the title and the hero's name changed. Several possible derivations have been suggested. Amra is the name of a small place in Kâthiâvâr, western India. In Arabic, *'umara* or *'amara* means "princes." *Amra* ("strange") is the title of a poem in praise of St. Columba, allegedly by the Irish bard Dallán Forgaill (+VI), although the poem is by some scholars considered a pseudographic work of later date. None of these derivations seems completely satisfactory.

Amric   In BN, a Kothian soldier in Conan's guard. From Amalric (q.v.) and Alric, a +VIII king of Kent, England.

Amurath   In SM, Shah Amurath is a Turanian noble. A Turkish proper name, also rendered as Murad.

Anakia, Anakim   In HS, WB, CA, a Shemitish city-state and its people. A race of tall mountaineers in southern Palestine before its conquest by Joshua, mentioned in Deut. 1:28; 9:2; Josh. 11:21f.

Andarra   In SS, a dream place mentioned by a man of Xuthal. From Andorra, a small Pyrenean principality.

Angharzeb   In PS, a onetime king of Turan. From Aurangzeb Almagir, a +XVII Mughal emperor of India.

Angkhor   In WM, RZ, the capital of Kambuja. From Angkor Wat, the ancient capital of Cambodia.

Anshan   In FK, the capital of Iranistan. A city in ancient Elam.

Antar   In FK, a Zuagir. From Antara, a legendary Arab hero.

Antillia   In CI, an archipelago between the former site of Atlantis and the American coast. The name given a suppositious land in the western Atlantic by pre-Columbian geographers; the name (Italian, Antigla; Portuguese, Antilha; all pronounced the same way) means "counter-island."

Anu   In RH, a Hyborian god. The Babylonian sky god.

Aphaka In BC, an oasis in the Shemitish desert. Probably from the Lebanese village known to the Classical Greeks as Aphaka, mod. 'Afqa, near al-Munteira. It was destroyed by a landslide in 1911.

Aphaki In DT, the former ruling caste of Tombalku, of mixed Shemite-Negroid ancestry. Probably from the same source as Aphaka (q.v.).

Aquilonia In TE, QC, RN, &c., the leading Hyborian kingdom, of which Conan eventually becomes king. The name of an ancient city in southern Italy, between modern Venosa and Benevento; ultimately from Latin *aquilo, -onis*, "north wind."

Arallu In FK, a hell referred to by Antar. The Babylonian hell.

Aram In SZ, Aram Baksh is a villainous innkeeper of Zamboula. An Armenian proper name, going back to a king of Urartu in −IX. Also the Hebrew name for Syria, whence "Aramaic."

Aratus In SM, a Brythunian pirate. From the Greek proper name Aratos, borne by a statesman of −III among others.

Arbanus In SC, the general of King Strabonus of Koth. From Artabanus, the Latin form of Artabanush (later Artaban, Artavan), borne by various Persian and Armenian notables including four Parthian kings.

Ardashir In CS, a Turanian officer. An Iranian name, originally Artaxerxes or Artakhshathra. In CA, another Turanian officer.

Arenjun In TC, HD, BG, &c., the "thief-city" of Zamora. From Erzincan, Turkey (the Turks use *c* for the sound of English *j*).

Argos In QC, WB, PO, &c., a maritime Hyborian nation. A Peloponnesian city in classical Greece, reputedly the oldest city in Greece, at the head of the Gulf of Argolis near modern Nafplion. Howard calls the people of his Argos "Argosseans," whereas the folk of the historical Argos were called "Argives."

Argus In QC, an Argossean ship. From Argos, a Greek name borne by a mythical hundred-eyed giant, Odysseus' dog, and others. Cf. Argos.

Arideus   In CC, the squire of Tarascus. Possibly from Philip Arrhidaeus (Arridaios), a half-brother of Alexander the Great.

Ariostro   In BN, CI, the young king of Argos, successor to Milo. From Lodovico Ariosto, the Italian poet of +XV and +XVI, author of *Orlando Furioso*.

Arno   In MB, an Aquilonian officer. A North European given name; also a river in Italy.

Arpello   In SC, an Aquilonian noble. Possibly from Rapallo, Italy, or Apelles, a Greek painter of −IV, or a combination of the two.

Arshak   In BG, a Turanian prince; in FK, the successor to Kobad Shah as king of Iranistan. An Iranian name (also Arshaka or Arsaces) borne by the founder of the Parthian dynasty among others.

Artaban   In RE, a Turanian general. From the same source as Arbanus (q.v.).

Artanes   In CI, a Zamorian pirate in Conan's crew. A Persian name (later Arten) borne by various Achaemenid and Armenian notables.

Artus   In CA, a Vilayet pirate. A form of "Arthur."

Arus   In "The Hyborian Age," a Nemedian priest of Mitra, missionary to the Picts. In GB, a Nemedian watchman. In CA, a name taken by Conan on his way to Khanyria. Possibly from Arûs, a medieval sultan of Wadai (q.v.), Africa.

Aryan, Aryas   In the prolegomenon to CC (see the introduction to the Ace Books edition of *Conan*), Howard speaks of the Hyborian Age as the time "between the years when the oceans drank Atlantis and the gleaming cities, and the years of the rise of the Sons of Aryas." I do not know whether "Aryas" is an individual or an error for "sons of *the* Aryas." In "The Hyborian Age," Howard speaks of the Aryans as the people of mixed Vanir, Æsir, and Cimmerian descent who conquered lands in Europe and Asia after the Picts and the Hyrkanians had overthrown the Hyborian nations and a convulsion of nature sank much of the Hyborian land beneath the Atlantic Ocean and the North and Mediterranean seas.

The true history of the term "Aryan" is complex.
Ârya is a Sanskrit word meaning "noble." Between
−1500 and −1000, nomadic, cattle-raising barbarians
calling themselves Ârya, "noble ones," overran Iran
and northern India. About the same time other nomads,
speaking similar tongues, conquered most of Europe
and parts of the Near East. They ruled the natives,
imposed their languages upon them, and finally mixed
with them. On linguistic evidence, these nomads probably radiated out originally, perhaps before −2000,
from what are now Poland and the Ukraine. They
were enabled to conquer their neighbors and their
neighbors' neighbors by having been the first people
to tame the horse.

In +XIX, scholars discovered the relation of the
speech of Iran and northern India on one hand and
of Europe on the other, and also came upon this word
Ârya. They called this family of languages Indo-
European or, sometimes, "Aryan." Since then, "Aryan"
has been used in several senses: (a) the Indo-European
family of languages; (b) the Indo-Iranian or eastern
branch of this family; (c) the original Indo-European-
speaking, horse-taming nomads; (d) the descendants
of these nomads; or (e), loosely, anybody of the
Caucasoid or white race speaking an Indo-European
language. Strictly speaking, the term has no racial
meaning and is avoided by most scientists because of
its equivocality.

In addition, in the late +XIX and early +XX,
"Aryan" was used by a number of writers, cultists,
demagogues, and politicians (notably Gobineau,
Chamberlain, and Hitler) who built up a pseudo-
scientific cult about the supposedly pure, superior
Aryan race. They used the term as a vague equivalent
of "Nordic," which describes the tall, blond, long-
headed type of the Caucasoid race found most commonly in northern Europe. Actually, there is no reason
to think that the original horsemen were Nordics.
Since the Alpine type predominates in their land of
origin, it is most likely that they were Alpines. And,

whatever their racial type, it soon disappeared by intermixture with those whom they conquered.

Although, like other pulp writers of his time, Howard was given to national and racial stereotypes, he was as far as I can tell no crackpot Aryanist. In his introduction to "The Hyborian Age," he was careful to state that the essay was a mere fictional background for his stories and not to be taken as a serious theory of prehistory. And some of the most vigorous peoples in his pseudohistory are racially mixed.

Ascalante   In PS, BN, an Aquilonian outlaw, formerly count of Thune; in the Kull story "Exile of Atlantis," a minor character alluded to—an Atlantean once enslaved in Valusia. From Escalante, a town in Spain near Santander. Howard probably took the name from Father Silvestre Vélez de Escalante, a missionary of +XVIII who explored the country that became the southwestern United States and whose name is borne by several places (towns, a river, a mountain range) in Colorado and Utah.

Asgalun, Askalon   In QC, HS, JG, the capital of Pelishtia, a Shemitish city-state. From Ascalon or Ashkelon, an ancient city of Palestine.

Asgard   In LD, FD, PS, &c., a northern land (cf. Æsir). From Ásgarð, in Norse mythology the home of the Æsir or principal gods.

Ashkhaurian Dynasty   In WB, the ruling family of Khauran (q.v.).

Ashtoreth   In QC, a Shemitish deity. (*See* Ishtar.)

Askia   In DT, a black wizard, servant of King Sakumbe. From Askia Muḥammad or Askia the Great, king of the Songhoi Negroes, who ruled the Songhoi Empire from Timbuktu, 1492–1529.

Asshuri   In BC, RE, WB, Shemitish mercenary soldiers. From Asshur (Assur, Ashur, Ašsur), the original name of Assyria, of one of its capital cities, and of its patron gods.

Astreas   In WB, a Nemedian philosopher. Possibly from the Greek name Asterios, borne by the mythical Minotaur among others.

Asura   In PC, CC, a god of an eastern religion flourishing secretly in Aquilonia. In Indian mythology, a term for a god, spirit, or demon, cognate with the Persian *ahura.*

Atali   In FD, the daughter of Ymir. Possibly from Attila the Hun, who appears in the *Völsungá Saga* as Atli.

Atalis   In HN, a philosopher of Yaralet in Turan. Probably from the Greek name Attalos or the Hunnish Attila.

Athicus   In RH, a prison guard. From Æthicus, a Byzantine geographer.

Atlaia, Atlaians   In DT and "The Hyborian Age," a Negro nation far to the south. Possibly from Atlas (cf. Atlantis).

Atlantis   An imaginary sunken continent in the Atlantic Ocean, conceived by Plato for his dialogues *Timaios* and *Kritias* and named for the demigod Atlas; used by Howard (along with many fantasy writers, geographical speculators, and cultists) as part of the background for his King Kull stories and mentioned in TE, PC, the prolegomenon to CC, &c.

Attalus   In PS, CC, an Aquilonian barony. From Attalos, a common Macedonian personal name, borne in Roman times by three kings of Pergamon in Asia Minor.

Attelius   In BB, a baron of the Westermarck. Possibly from Attila, or Attalus, or both.

Auzakia   In CS, one of the seven sacred cities of Meru.

Ayodhya   In FK, PC, CA, the capital of Vendhya. From Ayuthya, the former capital of Thailand, and Ayodha, the legendary capital of India in the Golden Age of King Rama.

Aztrias Petanius   In GB, a Nemedian noble. "Aztrias" is probably from the same source as Astreas (q.v.); "Petanius" may be from any of several Classical names like Petines and Prytanis.

Azweri   In CS, a people of Meru.

Baal   In CC, a minion of Xaltotun; (also =Baal-Pteor, discarded). From *ba'al*, Hebrew-Phoenician for "lord." Cf. Bel, Baal-Pteor.

Baal-Pteor   In SZ, a Kosalan strangler. From Baal-Peor, a place in Moab (Num. 25). Cf. Pteor. In Howard's preliminary drafts, this character was called Baal or Bel.

Badb   In PS, a Cimmerian deity. An Irish goddess, more exactly Badhbh (pronounced BAHV, BAHDHV).

Bajujh   In VW, the Negro king of Bakalah. There was a piratical tribe of Borneo, the Bajau, but the derivation is dubious.

Bakalah   In VW, a Negro village and tribe of Kush. From a Central African tribe, the Bakalai or Bakalei.

Bakhariot, Bakhauriot   In WB, PC, CA, an adjective describing a kind of broad belt. From Bokhara, Turkestan.

Bakhr   In BN, a Stygian river, an affluent of the Styx. From the Arabic *bahr*, "river."

Bakra   In HN, a Turanian general.

Baksh   See Aram. Probably from *bakshi, bakshish*, used in the Near East and India for "giver" and "gratuity" respectively (from the Persian *bakhshi, bakhshish*, or the Arabic *baqshish*).

Balardus   In BN, the king of Koth, successor to Strabonus. A pseudo-Latin name.

Balash   In RK, chief of the Kushafi tribe in the Ilbars Mts. A Persian name (Balas, Valash, Valagash, &c.) of Parthian and Sassanid times.

Balthus   In BR, a young Tauranian settler in Conajohara. Possibly from Baltia, a Latin name for Scandinavia (whence the Baltic Sea).

Bamula   In VW, CT, a Kushite tribe. Possibly from Bambuba, an existing Negro tribe near Lake Edward; or from Bambara, a tribe on the upper Niger; or from *bamboula*, for which see Amboola.

Baraccus   In CA, an exiled Aquilonian nobleman. From Galaccus, in TT.

Baracha   In PO, GT, JG, &c., an archipelago in the

Western Ocean, used as a pirate base. From Barataria, Louisiana, used as a base by Jean Lafitte, a pirate of the early +XIX.

Bardiya   In FK, an official of Kobad Shah's court. An ancient Persian name (Greek, Smerdis).

Barras   In SK, a henchman of Count Rigello. A French place name; the Comte de Barras was a French Revolutionary and Napoleonic politician.

Bel   In TE, QC, BC, &c., the Shemitish god of thieves. An Assyro-Babylonian word meaning "lord" (cognate with the Hebrew-Phoenician *ba'al*) applied originally to En-lil, an old Babylonian earth god, and later to Marduk, the Babylonian Zeus. A discarded name for Baal-Pteor (q.v.) in the first draft of SZ.

Belesa, Beloso   Respectively, the Zingaran heroine of TT and a Zingaran man-at-arms in CC. Origin uncertain; remote possibilities are Belesis, a Babylonian priest of −VII mentioned by Ktesias; a Belesa River in Ethiopia; and Berosos (or Berossus, &c.), a Hellenized Babylonian priest and writer of early −III.

Bêlit   In QC, CI, a Shemitish woman pirate. Assyro-Babylonian for "goddess."

Belverus   In CC, the capital of Nemedia. Possibly from Belverde, Italy.

Bhalkhana   In PC, an adjective describing a breed of horse. Probably from the Balkans or from Balkh, a city in Afghanistan.

Bhambar Pass   In PS, a pass in Hyrkania.

Bhunda   In PC, Bhunda Chand is king of Vendhya. From various Indian names: Bundelkhand, Bhândârkar, &c.

Bigharma   In DT, Howard's manuscript spoke of "the Baghirmi, the Mandingo, and the Bornu" as peoples of the Tombalku Empire. All are modern: the Baghirmi, a Negro tribe near Lake Chad; the Mandingo, a Sudanic people widely spread about West Africa; Bornu, a province of northern Nigeria, once an independent sultanate. I changed the sentence to "the Bigharma, the Mindanga, and the Borni," thinking that the use of so many well-known, modern tribal and geographical names, unmodified, would put too great a strain on the reader's sense of illusion.

Bît-Yakin   In JG, a Pelishti wizard. In Assyrian times, the capital of Chaldea (Kaldi) or, sometimes, Chaldea (modern southern Iraq) itself.

Black River   In BR, BB, a river on the western Aquilonian frontier. Probably from the Black River in upstate New York, mentioned in the frontier stories of Robert W. Chambers.

Bombaata   In HS, a Kushite captain in Asgalun. A pseudo-Bantu name.

Bori   In "The Hyborian Age," the deified eponymous ancestor of the Hyboreans or Hybori; from Hyperborea (qq.v.).

Borni   In DT, a people of the Tombalku Empire. *See* Bigharma.

Borus   In GT, the first mate of Captain Gonzago's *Hawk*. From Boros, an uncommon Greek name.

Bossonian Marches   In GB and all the stories from BR to CC, the western frontier province of Aquilonia. Possibly from Bossiney, a former Parliamentary borough in Cornwall, England, which included Tintagel Castle, connected with the Arthurian legends.

Bragi   In FD, a chief of the Vanir. The Norse god of poetry.

Bragoras   In DT, a former Nemedian king.

Brant   In BB, Brant Drago's son is the elected governor of Thandara. "Brant" is probably from Joseph Brant, the English name of Theyendanegea, a Mohawk chief of American Revolutionary times.

Brocas   In MB, BB, the baron of Torh, lord of Conawaga. Possibly from the Roman cognomen Brocchus, borne by several relatively obscure Romans of the Senatorial class.

Brythunia   In TE, SM, DI, &c., an easterly Hyborian land. From the Welsh Brython, "Briton," derived from the same root as the Latin Brito, Britannia.

Bubastes   In BN, the Styx is crossed at the Ford

of Bubastes. From Bubastis (ancient Egyptian, Per-baste), a city in ancient Egypt, near modern Zagazig.

Bwatu   In CB, a man of Juma's tribe. A pseudo-Bantu name.

Byatis   In RZ, a deity of the serpent-men of Valusia. From "serpent-bearded Byatis," an entity in Robert Bloch's Cthulhuvian tales.

Caranthes   In GB, a priest of Ibis. *See* Kalanthes.

Castria   In RZ, an Aquilonian barony. From various European places named Castra (ancient Roman), Castries (French), and Kastri (Greek).

Catlaxoc   In CI, a harlot of Ptahuacan. A pseudo-Mayan name.

Cenwulf   In BN, a captain of Bossonian archers. From the Anglo-Saxon names Cenric and Ceolwulf.

Cernunnos   In BN, a god invoked by Diviatix. A stag-horned Gaulish god.

Chabela   In CB, BN, the daughter of King Ferdrugo of Zingara. The common Spanish nickname for Isabel. Since Isabel is Spanish for Elizabeth, Chabela is the exact equivalent of Betty.

Chaga   In SD, one of the ruling caste of the Kushite capital of Jumballa, of mixed Stygian-Negroid ancestry. From the Chaga or Chagga, an advanced, progressive Negro tribe of Tanzania.

Chakan   In BB, one of the race of Pithecanthropoid sub-men dwelling in the Pictish wilderness. Possibly from the same source as Chaga (q.v.) or from Chaka or Tshaka, the Zulu emperor, 1783–1828.

Chand   *See* Bhunda. An Indian proper name, also spelled Cand, Chund.

Chelkus   In VW, the Ophirean family to which Livia belongs. Possibly from Chelkias, a Judaean mercenary soldier and a favorite of Queen Kleopatra III of Egypt at the end of −II.

Chengir Khan   In CA, a Vendhyan nobleman. From Chiang Kai-shek (or from Jengis, Genghis, or Chingiz) + Khan (q.v.).

Cherkees   In WB, an adjective designating a broad, curved knife. From Cherkess, a name for the Circassians or Adighe of the Caucasus.

Chicmec   In RN, a man of Xuchotl. From the Chichimecs, a tribe of Mexican Indians.

Chiron   In CC, a minion of Xaltotun. A wise centaur (Cheiron) of Greek myth. Howard may also have been thinking of Charon, in Greek mythology the supernatural boatman who ferried souls across the Styx.

Chunder   In PC, Chunder Shan is the governor of Peshkauri. A common Indian proper name, also spelled Chandra or Candra.

Cimmeria, Cimmerians   In all the Conan stories, a land and people north of the Hyborian nations, from whom the Gaels or Celts are descended. Historically, the Gimirai or Cimmerians were a nomadic people who invaded Asia Minor in −VII; the modern Armenian language descends from theirs. In Homer, a people (the Kimmerioi) living in a foggy western land. Howard may have had in mind a once proposed but now discredited connection between the Kimmerioi and the Cymry or Welsh.

Codrus   In FK, a lieutenant of Conan. From Kodros, a legendary king of Athens.

Colchian Mts.   In CA, a range south of the Vilayet Sea. From Colchis, a Caucasian land of Classical times (modern Georgia).

Commoria   In TE, a kingdom of Atlantean times. From Commorion, the capital of Hyperborea in Clark Ashton Smith's stories "The Testament of Athammaus," "The Seven Geases," &c.; or from the probable source of these, Comoria or Comorin, the cape at the southern tip of India.

Conajohara   In BR, BB, MB, a province on the Aquilonian frontier between the Black and Thunder Rivers. From Canajoharie, a town on the Mohawk River, New York State. Upstate New York also has a Black River, and Howard probably derived both town and river from Robert W. Chambers's stories.

Conan   The hero of the Conan stories, a gigantic

Cimmerian adventurer. A common Celtic name (e.g.,
A. Conan Doyle and the Dukes Conan of medieval
Brittany), from Conann, a king of the Fomorians
(Fomór, pron. "fuh-WORE" or Fomhóraigh) in Irish
mythology, in which Conann was killed in battle with
the Nemedians (q.v.). Howard also wrote stores of
medieval Ireland, unconnected with the Hyborian Age
series, with heroes named Conan or Conn (q.v.).

Conawaga In BB, MB, a province of the Westermarck, the borderland between the Pictish Wilderness
and Bossonia. From Caughnawaga (or less probably,
Conewago), New York.

Conn In the stories from WM to CI, the nickname
of Conan's elder son, later King Conan II. A legendary
ancient king of Tara, Ireland, claimed as ancestor by
various Irish and Scottish dynasties.

Constantius In WB, a Kothic adventurer. The
name of three Roman emperors of +IV.

Corinthia In JG, IG, a southeasterly Hyborian
nation. From Corinth (Korinthos), a rich city in Classical Greece. Possibly suggested to Howard by the
Biblical book of Corinthians.

Couthen In CA, CI, a county of Aquilonia.

Coyoga In BB, a province of the Westermarck, the
borderland between Pictland and Bossonia. From Lake
Cayuga, New York.

Crassides In CA, captain of the guard at the gate
of Khanyria. From Crassus, a common Roman cognomen, + the Greek patronymic suffix *-ides*.

Cratos In CB, a physician of Kordava. From Kratos,
a Greek mythological figure.

Crom In all the Conan stories, the chief Cimmerian
god and Conan's favorite oath. Usually translated from
the Irish as "bent," as in Crom Cruaich, "the bloody
bent one," a famous Irish pagan idol. An alternative
translation of Crom Cruaich is "lord of the mound."

Ctesphon In TT, PS, the king of Stygia. From
Ctesiphon, an ancient ruined city in Iraq, near Bagh-
dad, which flourished in Parthian and Sassanid times.

Cush *See* Kush.

Dagon, Dagonia   In DI, Dagonia is an ancient kingdom on the Vilayet Sea, and Dagon, its ruined capital on the isle of Xapur. In JG, Dagon is a god of Zembabwei. Dagon was a fish-god of the Philistines and Phoenicians.

Dagoth   In SC, a hill in Koth. Probably from Dagon (q.v.) + Koth (q.v.).

Dagozai   In PC, a Himelian or Ghulistani tribe. Probably from Dagon (q.v.) + the Pakhtun (Pashtun, Pathan) tribal ending -*zai* (from *zoe*, "son") as such modern Pakhtun tribes as the Ghilzai and Yusufzai.

Damballah   In WM, RZ, another name for Set. The serpent god of Haitian Voodoo, of Dahomean (West African) origin.

Danu   In BN, a deity invoked by Diviatix. A Celtic mother goddess, also Dana.

Darfar   In SZ, RN, a land of Negro cannibals. Howard derived this name from the region of Darfur in north-central Africa. Darfur is an Arabic name, meaning "abode (*dâr*) of the Fur," the dominant Negroid people of the area. In changing the name to Darfar, Howard unwittingly changed the Arabic meaning to "abode of mice"! The original Darfur is now the westernmost part of the Sudanese Republic.

Dathan   In SD, an official of the king of Eruk. A biblical name (Num. 16:1).

Dayuki   In RE, a Hyrkanian chief. From Dayaukku or Deioces, a Median ruler of −VIII.

Dekanawatha   In BN, RZ, a Pictish chief. From the historical Iroquois leaders Hiawatha and Dekanawida.

Demetrio   In GB, a Nemedian magistrate; in CC, an Argossean sea captain. Italian for Demetrios, a common Greek name, from Demeter, goddess of agriculture.

Derketa   In RN, a Kushite goddess. From Derketo (q.v.).

Derketo   In QC, BC, SS, &c., a Shemitish and Stygian goddess, also worshiped in Zembabwei. A Greek name for the Syrian fertility goddess 'Atar'ata. (Cf. Ishtar.)

Devi   In PC, CA, the title of the sister of the king of Vendhya. Hindi for "goddess."

Dexitheus   In TT, CI, a priest of Mitra. From Greek names like Dexippos and Dorotheus.

Diana   In SD, a Nemedian slave girl in Jumballa. Originally an Italian goddess of light, mountains, and woods, early identified or merged with the Greek Artemis.

Dion   In PS, an Aquilonian noble. A common Greek name, borne by, among others, a tyrant of Syracuse in −IV.

Dionus   In GB, a Nemedian prefect of police. From Dion (q.v.) and possibly also Dianus, an old spelling of the Roman god Janus.

Dirk   In BB, Dirk Strom's son is the commandant of Fort Kwanyara. "Dirk" is the Dutch and Danish form of the old Gothic name Theodoric or Theiudareiks (German Dietrich, English Derek, French Thierry).

Diviatix   In BN, RZ, a Ligurean Druid. From the Gaulish chieftains in Caesar's army, Diviciacus and Dumnorix.

Dongola   In DT, a Negro tribe mentioned in the synopsis but not in the unfinished rough draft. From a town and province of that name in the Sudan, on the Nile. The people are the Dongolavi.

Drago   See Brant.

Drujistan   In FK, a place in the Ilbars Mountains. Persian for "land of demons."

Duali   In CA, a Zuagir tribe. Possibly from Dooala, a place somewhere in Africa.

Edric   In MB, an Aquilonian scout. A Saxon king of Kent in +VII.

Egil   In LD, an As. A common Nordic name, e.g., of a Swedish king of the legendary Yngling dynasty, before +VI, and of Egil Skallagrimsson, an Icelandic poet of +IX.

Eiglophian Mts.   In LW, a range south of Asgard. From Clark Ashton Smith's story, "The Seven Geases."

Emilius   In CC, Emilius Scavonus is an Aquilonian

noble. From Æmilius, a Roman gentile name (cf. Amilius, Scavonus).

Enaro, Enaros In GB, a Nemedian charioteer; in the King Kull story "By this Axe I Rule!" (later rewritten as PS), Enaros is the commander of the Black Legion. Both probably from Inaros, the Greek name for a Libyan rebel against Persian rule in Egypt, −V, mentioned by Herodotus; the original Egyptian name was probably An-ha-heru-ra-u.

Enosh In BT, the chief of Akhlat. A Biblical name, a variant of Enos (Gen. 5:9).

Epemitreus In PS, CI, a long-dead sage. From Epimetheus, in Greek legend Pandora's husband.

Epeus In DT, a former king of Aquilonia. Probably from Epeius or Epeios, in Greek legend the builder of the Trojan horse.

Epona In BN, a deity invoked by Diviatix. The Gaulish goddess of horses.

Erlik In SZ, CA, a Turanian god. The name of a god of the underworld of the Altai Tatars. Howard possibly got his Erlik from Robert W. Chambers's novel *The Slayer of Souls*, which exploits this deity. Howard also brought "priests of Erlik" into a fantasy with a modern setting, "Black Hound of Death" (*Weird Tales*, Nov. 1936).

Erlikites In FK, worshipers of Erlik (q.v.).

Eruk In QC, SD, a Shemitish city-state. From ancient Uruk, Erech, or Orchoê in Babylonia (modern Warka, Iraq).

Escelan In RN, a man of Xuchotl. Probably from the same source as Ascalante (q.v.).

Fabio In GT, an Argossean sailor in the crew of the *Hawk*. An Italian name, from the Roman gentile name Fabius.

Farouz In HS, a name assumed by Mazdak. From the common Persian name Peroch, Peroz, Firuz, &c.

Femesh Valley In CA, site of a battle fought by Conan in Vendhya.

Feng   In CM, a duke of Kusan. A common Chinese surname, rhyming with "hung."

Ferdrugo   In CS, CB, BN, the king of Zingara. From Federigo, Spanish for Frederick.

Flavius   In MB, an Aquilonian officer. A Roman gentile name.

Fronto   In SD, an Ophirean thief. A common Roman cognomen.

Frosol   In SK, a feudal county in Ophir.

Fulk   In WM, an Aquilonian. A name borne by several medieval French notables (French, Foulques).

Galacus   In TT, a Kothic pirate. Latin for "Galician."

Galannus   *See* Servius. Probably from either the Roman emperor Galienus or Gallandus, a Carcean pirate in E. R. Eddison's *The Worm Ouroboros*.

Galbro   In TT, a Zingaran seneschal. Possibly from Gabriello, Italian for "Gabriel."

Gallah   In SD, the lower, Negroid caste of Jumballa. From the Galla, an Erythriotic-Negroid people of Abyssinia (Ethiopia) and Kenya.

Galparan, Galporan   In CC, a place in western Aquilonia. The former spelling is Howard's; the latter appears only on Kyle's end-paper maps in the Gnome Press editions of the Conan stories.

Galter   *See* Jon. An English occupational surname, meaning "clay-digger."

Galzai   In PC, CA, a Himelian or Ghulistani tribe. From the Ghilzai, a modern Afghan-Pakhtun tribe.

Gamburu   In CB, the capital of the Amazons. From various African place names, e.g., Gambaga (Ghana) and Omaruru (Namibia).

Garma   In PS, a road.

Garogh (=Teyanoga)   In first draft of BB; discarded. Probably from Caroga (also Lake and Creek), Fulton County, New York.

Garus   In SK, an adherent of Queen Marala of Ophir.

Gath (=Aphaka)   In first draft of BC; discarded. A town in western Judea.

Gault   In BB, Gault Hagar's son is the narrator. "Gault" is an old English word for stiff clay, also used in the form "Galt" as a surname.

Gazal   In DT, a city in the desert of northern Darfar. From the Bahr al-Ghazâl (Arabic for "the gazelle river"), an eastward-flowing river, which joins the White Nile at Lake No.

Gebal   *See* Djebal. Possibly either from the Arabic *jabal*, "mountain," or from the town of Gebal (Jebeil or Jubayl), Lebanon—Classical Byblos, Phoenician Gubla.

Gebellez   In TT, a Zingaran. The name was Gebbrelo in the original manuscript (probably from the same source as Galbro ,q.v.), but I changed it because it was too much like Galbro, another character in the same story.

Ghanara, Ghanata   In SZ, CB, CC, adjectives designating a desert south of Stygia and its people. From Ghana, a medieval empire in the western Sudan. The name has been revived for the Dominion of the Commonwealth formerly called the Gold Coast.

Ghandar Chen   In CA, a spy of King Yezdigerd of Turan in Tarantia. From the Swedish name Gunder (that of a Swedish world champion runner in the 1940s) + "Chen" from "Shan" or "Shah" (qq.v.).

Gharat   In CA, a ruined temple in the Zuagir desert. From "carat," the unit of weight.

Ghaznavi   In DI, a Turanian councillor. From Ghaznavid, an adjective designating the dynasty founded by the +XI Afghan conqueror Mahmud of Ghazna, which in turn is the city called Gazaka in ancient times.

Ghemur   In CA, a Vendhyan conspirator. From "lemur," a member of the Lemuroidea, a suborder of primitive primates (bush-baby, galago, loris, &c.).

Ghor   In PC, a place in Afghulistan. From Ghor or Ghur, a medieval Afghan kingdom. (Ghor is also the name of the Dead Sea Valley in Palestine, but Howard probably got the name from the other source.)

Ghorbal   In first draft of CC, the demesne of a Nemedian lord at the execution of Albiona; discarded. Probably from the same sources as Ghor and Khorbul (qq.v.).

Ghori   In DI, a fort near Khawarizm. A subprovince of modern Afghanistan. The adjective "Ghorid" designates the medieval dynasties of Ghor (q.v.).

Ghoufags   In PS, a Hyrkanian mountain tribe.

Ghulistan   In PC, CA, a region of the Himelian Mts. A combination of Arabic *ghûl*, "ghoul," + Persian *istân, estân*, "country"; hence "land of ghouls." (In Persian, Ghulistan would mean "land of roses," but I do not think that is what Howard had in mind.)

Ghurran (=Tauran)   In first draft of BR; discarded. Probably from Ghurian, Afghanistan.

Gilzan   In DI, a Shemitish torturer. Probably from the same source as Galzai (q.v.).

Gitara   In PC, Yasmina's maid. From *gitana*, Spanish for "Gypsy woman." Like "Gypsy," the word is a corruption of that for "Egyptian," although the real Gypsies originally came from India. (Cf. Zingara.)

Gleg   In RE, a Zaporoskan robber lord. An old Russian name.

Glyco   In MB, an Aquilonian officer. From Glykon, the name of several Greek writers.

Gobir   In DT, a Ghanata brigand. The name of a medieval Negro kingdom in the western Sudan.

Godrigo   In CB, a Zingaran philosopher. From the Spanish name Rodrigo.

Golamira   In PS, CI, a magical mountain.

Gomani   In CB, a Kushite slave. A minor +XIX African king and his kingdom, on the border of Tanzania and Mozambique.

Gonzago   In GT, captain of the *Hawk*, a Barachan pirate ship. From Gonzaga, an Italian princely family, lords and eventually dukes of Milan, +XIII to +XVIII.

Gonzalvio   In CI, Trocero's son. From the Spanish name Gonsalvo, e.g. Gonzalo or Gonsalvo de Córdoba, a Spanish general of +XV.

Goralian Hills   In CC, a region in western Aquilonia. Possibly from the Goralians or Gorales, mountaineers of southern Poland.

Goram Singh   In CI, a Vendhyan pirate in the Barachas. An Indian name; Singh (Hindi for "lion") is regularly used as a surname by adherents of the Sikh religion.

Gorm   In FD, an As (see Æsir); in LD, a bard of the Æsir; in BB, Otho Gorm's son is a forest ranger of Schohira (see Strom); in "The Hyborian Age," a Pictish chief after Conan's time. The first king of Denmark, in +X.

Gorthangpo   In CS, a Meruvian. A pseudo-Tibetan name.

Gorulga   In JG, a Keshian priest. Possibly from the Goruol River, a tributary of the Niger.

Gotarza   In FK, the captain of Kobad Shah's royal guard. An ancient Persian name (also Gotarzes, Godarz, Guderz, &c.).

Graaskal Mts.   In CA, a range on the borders of Hyperborea. Possibly from the Norwegian grå skål, "gray bowl."

Gromel   In PS, a Bossonian commanding Conan's Black Legion.

Grondar   In FK and the Kull stories, a pre-Catastrophic kingdom, coeval with Valusia.

Guarralid   In BN, a Zingaran dukedom. From Spanish place names like Guadarrema and Valladolid.

Guilaime   In WM, CI, an Aquilonian baron. From Guillaume, French for William.

Gullah   In FK, BR, the Pictish gorilla-god. One of a group of American Negroes living along the coast of Georgia and speaking a distinctive Afro-American dialect.

Gunderland, Gundermen   In TE, GB, RH, &c., the northernmost province of Aquilonia and its people. Probably from Gunther (Gundicar) or Gunderic, +V kings of the Burgundians.

Gurasha   In PC, a valley in Afghulistan.

Gwahlur   In JG, IG, the Teeth of Gwahlur are the treasure of Alkmeenon. From Gwalior, India.

Gwarunga   In JG, a Keshian priest. Possibly from Garua, West Africa.

Gwawela   In BR, a Pictish village. Gwalia is an old name for Wales, and there is a Gwala, Egypt, but such derivations seem unlikely.

Hadrathus   In CC, a priest of Asura. Possibly from the Roman name Hadrianus, an emperor of +II.

Hagar   *See* Gault. A Germanic personal name, also Hager.

Hakhamani   In FK, an informer for Kobad Shah. The original Persian for Achaemenes, legendary founder of the Achaemenid dynasty.

Hakon   In BB, Hakon Strom's son is a commander of rangers in Schohira. "Hakon" is from the Norse name, Haakon or Hákon; e.g., Hakon the Dane in the *Völsungá Saga.* For "Strom," *see* Dirk, Strom.

Haloga   In LD, the stronghold of Queen Vammatar in Hyperborea. From Halogaland, in the *Heimskringla,* a place in Lapland.

Hamar Kur   In CA, a Turanian officer. From the Norwegian city Hamar, and "Kur" from Kurdistan.

Han   In RZ, a deity of the serpent-men of Valusia.

Hanuman   In SZ, FK, a monkey-god of Zamboula. The Indian monkey-god.

Hanumar   In GB, a Nemedian city. Probably from Hanuman (q.v.).

Hatupep   In CI, a merchant of Ptahuacan. A synthetic Egypto-Mayan name.

Hattusas   In FK, a Zamorian serving under Conan. The capital of the Hittite kingdom, near modern Boğazköi (renamed Boğazkale).

Heimdul   In FD, a Van or Vanaheimer. From Heimdall, in Norse myth, the guardian of the gates of Valhalla.

Hildico   In HN, a Brythunian slave girl in Yaralet. From Hilda or Ildico, the last of the many wives of Attila the Hun.

Himelian Mts.   In PC, CA, a range north or northwest of Vendhya. From the Himalayas or Himalayan Mountains.

Hormaz   In CS, a Turanian officer. From Hormazd or Ahura Mazda, the good god of the dualistic Zoroastrian universe.

Horsa   In FD, an As (*see Æsir*). A half-legendary Saxon chief who, with his brother Hengist or Hengest, led the Saxon invasion of Britain in the middle of +V.

Hotep   In HS, a Stygian servant of Zeriti; in CA, a name assumed by Conan in Fort Wakla. An old Egyptian name meaning "contented."

Hsia   In CM, a former king of Kusan. A semi-legendary early dynasty of China.

Hyborian, Hyborean, Hybori   In RN, BR, TT, &c., the race that overthrew the empire of Acheron and set up in its place the kingdoms of Nemedia, Aquilonia, Brythunia, Argos, and the Border Kingdom. From Hyperborea (q.v.). *See* Bori.

Hyperborea   In TE and GB, a northeasterly land, east of Asgard. In Greek legend, a happy land in the Far North; the name means "beyond the North Wind."

Hyrkania, Hyrcania   In TE, QC, BC, &c., the land east of the Vilayet Sea. The Turanians, dwelling west of that sea, are also of Hyrkanian origin and are commonly called Hyrkanians. In Classical geography, a region southeast of the Caspian or Hyrcanian Sea corresponding to modern Iranian Mazanderan + Asterabad. The name is Greek for the Old Persian Varkana, one of the Achaemenid satrapies, and survives in the name of the river Gurgan. The original meaning may have been "wolfland." Hyrkania was briefly an independent kingdom in +I. In Iranian legend, Hyrkania was remarkable for its wizards and demons.

Ianthe   In SK, KD, the capital of Ophir. In Greek myth, an oceanid or marine nymph.

Ibis   In GB, a god. Any of several species of heron-like birds, one of which, *Threskiornis aethiopica*, was held sacred in ancient Egypt.

Ilbars In SM, a Turanian river; in FK, a range of mountains south of the Vilayet Sea. From the Elburz Mountains, Iran.

Ilga In LW, a Virunian girl. A combination of the Norse names Inga and Helga.

Imbalayo In HS, the commander of the Kushite troops in Pelishtia. A pseudo-Zulu name.

Imirus In CA, WM, CI, a barony of Aquilonia.

Irakzai In PC, a Himelian tribe. From the Orakzai, Pakhtum tribe mentioned in Lowell Thomas's *Beyond Khyber Pass*, which Howard read.

Iranistan In BG, RE, PC, &c., an eastern land corresponding to modern Iran. From Iran + the Persian *istân, estân*, "country."

Irem In SM, Shah Amurath's horse. From "ancient Irem, the City of Pillars," mentioned by H. P. Lovecraft in "The Nameless City," and possibly ultimately from Iram, in Arabian legend a deserted city in Yaman. *See* "The City of Many-Columned Iram and Abdullah Son of Abi Kilabah" in Burton's translation of the *Arabian Nights*, v. IV, pp. 113ff.

Ishbak In HS, a name assumed by Conan in Asgalun. A Phoenician name.

Ishtar In QC, BC, SM, &c., a Shemitish goddess also worshiped in the Hyborian nations. The Assyro-Babylonian goddess of love (Hebrew Ashtoreth, Phoenician 'Atar'ata, Syrian Atargatis, Greek Astartê).

Issedon In CS, one of the seven sacred cities of Meru.

Itzra In CI, an Antillian chief. A synthetic Egypto-Mayan name.

Ivanos In SM, RE, a Corinthian pirate. From Ivan, Russian for "John," + the Greek masculine nominative ending *-os*.

Ivga In WB, Valerius' sweetheart. Possibly from Inga, a Norwegian female given name.

Jaga In CM, a head-hunting tribe of the hill region between Kusan and Hyrkania. A Bantu tribe of southern Zaïre.

Jalung Thongpa   In CS, the god-king of Meru. A pseudo-Tibetan name.

Jamal   In PS, a Turanian soldier. From the Arabic *jamal*, "camel," often used as a personal name.

Jamankh   In IG, a hyena-demon. From Jajamankh or Zazamankh, a legendary Egyptian magician.

Jehun   *See* Amir. From Shah Jahan or Jehan, a Mughal emperor of +XVII, the builder of the Taj Mahal.

Jehungir, Jungir   Jehungir is a Turanian lord in DI, while Jungir Khan is another in SZ. From Jahangir ("world-conqueror"), Shah Jahan's predecessor as Mughal emperor, +XVII.

Jelal   In DI, Jelal Khan is a Turanian noble. From the Arabic proper name Jalal.

Jerida   In CB, a place in Zingara. From the Spanish place names Jérez, Mérida.

Jhebbal   *See* Djebal.

Jhelai   In PC, a place in Vendhya. From the Jhelam or Jhelum River, a tributary of the Indus.

Jhil   A supernatural being mentioned in BR. Possibly from Chil, the kite in Kipling's *Second Jungle Book*; there is also a Jhal, India, and a Hindi word *jhil*, "swamp."

Jhumda   In PC, a river in Vendhya. From the river Jamna, Jumna, or Yamuna in India, and the river Jhelam in Pakistan.

Jihiji   In VW, a village in Kush. Possibly from Jijiga, Abyssinia (Ethiopia).

Jhilites   In FK, a cult of followers of Jhil (q.v.).

Jillad   In BG, a pseudonym of Zyras. This name was used in Howard's original non-Conan story, "The Trail of the Blood-Stained God."

Joka   In RH, a servant of Nabonidus. Possibly from the Djukas, tribal Negroes of Surinam, South America, descendants of escaped slaves. (Cf. Ajonga.)

Jon   In BB, Jon Galter's son is a dead friend of the narrator. From "John"; *see* Galter.

Jugra   In PC, a Wazuli village. A name for the Magyars or Hungarians.

Julio   In CB, a Zingaran goldsmith. A Spanish given name, from the Roman gentile name Julius.

Juma   In CS, CM, a Kushite serving in the Turanian army; later, in CB, he becomes the chief of a tribe in Kush. A common East African given name.

Jumballa   In SD, the capital of Kush. Howard spelled it "Shumballa" (possibly from Shambalai, a hill region in Tanzania) but I changed the name because Carter and I needed the similar name "Shamballa" (q.v.) for CS.

Junia   In SK, the wife of Torgrio the thief. From Junius, a common Roman gentile name, e.g., Decimus Junius Brutus Albinus, one of Caesar's assassins.

Kaa-Yazoth   In CI, a ruler of the Atlantean Age.

Kalanthes (=Caranthes)   In GB, discarded. Kalanthes was Howard's original form, but I changed it to Caranthes because I thought it too much like Kallian (q.v.), the name of another character in the same story.

Kallian   In GB, Kallian Publico is an art dealer. From the common Greek name Kallias.

Kambuja   In WM, a land east of Vendhya. The original name of Cambodia, now Kampuchea.

Kamula   In CB, a long-vanished city of Atlantean times.

Kamelia   In TE, a kingdom of Atlantean times. Possibly from the camellia, a shrub of the tea family bearing large white flowers. The Knights of the White Camelia, formed in 1867, was one of a number of white-supremacist secret societies, of which the Ku Klux Klan is the best known, active in the former Confederate states at that time. Possibly also from Camelot, King Arthur's legendary capital.

Karaban   In PS, an Aquilonian county. Possibly from Karaman, Turkey.

Kang Hsiu   In CA, a Khitan. Common Chinese names.

Kang Lou-Dze   In CA, a Khitan girl. Common Chinese names.

Kapellez   In CB, the captain of the Zingaran royal yacht. A pseudo-Spanish name.

Karlus   In BB, an Aquilonian ranger at Fort Kwanyara. From the common German name Karl (Latin, Carolus).

Karnath   In the first draft of CC, a Stygian city (discarded). Possibly from Lovecraft's Sarnath, in "The Doom That Came to Sarnath." Lovecraft invented the name and was then surprised to learn that it was the name of a real city near Banaras, India.

Kassali   In IG, the capital of Punt. From Kassala, a town in the Sudan.

Kchaka   In RZ, the ancestors of the dominant tribe of Zembabwei. From Chaga, an East African tribe, or from Chaka, the Zulu emperor, for which *see* Chagan.

Keluka   In HS, a Kushite soldier in Asgalun. A pseudo-Swahili name.

Kemosh   In CA, a Zuagir god. From Chemosh, a Canaanite god (Num. 21:29).

Keraspa   In BG, a Kezankian chieftain. From Keresaspa, a legendary Persian hero.

Kerim   In PC, Kerim Shah is a Turanian spy in Vendhya. From the Arabic *karîm*, "generous," used as a proper name in Muslim countries.

Keshan, Keshia   In JG, IG, RZ, a black kingdom and its capital respectively. Probably from Kesh or Kash, an ancient Egyptian name for Nubia, whence Hebrew (and Howard's) Kush.

Kezankian Mts.   In BG, a range separating Turan from Zamora. Suggested by the Russian geographical names Kazan and Kazak.

Khafra   In HS, a Stygian servant of Zeriti. The Fourth Dynasty king of Egypt who built the Sphinx (Greek, Chephren).

Khahabul (=Khorbul, q.v.)   In first draft of PC, discarded.

Khajar   In CB, BN, an oasis in western Stygia, where Thoth-Amon lived. From Kajar or Qajar, an Iranian tribe and a Persian dynasty, 1794–1925.

Khan   See Chengir, Jehungir, Khosru. A Turko-Tatar word meaning "lord" or "prince."

Khannon   In HS, a Pelishti wine-seller. A Phoenician name.

Khanyria   In CA, a city in Khoraja. From Khan + Graeco-Roman names like Syria, Illyria, &c.

Kharamun   In SZ, a southeastern desert. Possibly from the same source as Karaban (q.v.).

Kharoya   In CA, a Zuagir tribe.

Khauran   In WB, CA, a small southeastern Hyborian kingdom. Probably from Mt. Hauran, Syria.

Khawarizm, Khawarism   In DI, a Turanian city near the southern end of the Sea of Vilayet. From Khwarasm of Chorasmia, a medieval Muslim kingdom in Turkestan; modern Khurasan or Khorassan, Iran. The name comes from the Old Persian Huvarazmish, a satrapy of the Achaemenid Empire. (Cf. Khorusun.)

Khaza   In FK, a Stygian. An Egyptian king of the Fourteenth Dynasty, c. −1700.

Khel   See Khosatral Khel. Probably from *khel*, a Pakhtu word for family or sept; e.g., "Mal Khel Mahsud," a man of the Mal family of the Mahsud tribe.

Khemi   In QC, SZ, TT, &c., the main seaport and administrative capital of Stygia. From Kamt, Kam, Chêm, or Chêmia, ancient names for Egypt, probably connected with *qam*, "black," of "Khem," an Egyptian god of fertility.

Khemsa   In PC, a wizard serving the Black Circle. From Khamseh, a tribe of Arabian origin in southern Iran.

Kherdpur   In CA, a Turanian city. From the Kurds of Kurdistan.

Kheshatta   In VW, a city of magicians in Stygia. Probably from Peshitta, the name of an old Syriac version of the Bible.

Khirgulis   In CA, a Himelian tribe. From Kirgiz, a Turko-Tatar people, now a republic of the Soviet Union, bordering Sinkiang.

Khitai, Khitans   In TE, RH, WB, &c., a far-eastern

land and its inhabitants. From "Khitan," a medieval Tatar word for China, whence the English word "Cathay."

Khor In first draft of CC, a valley in Aquilonia (discarded). Probably from the same sources as Ghor and Khorbul (q.v.).

Khoraf In CA, a Vilayet port favored by slavers.

Khoraja, Khorala Respectively, a small southern Hyborian city-state in BC and a place in Vendhya, whence came the jewel "Star of Khorala," in SZ, SK. The first syllable is probably from the Arabic *hor*, "lake" or "marsh," which occurs in many place names. Khôr was also an ancient Egyptian name for the Khurri or Hurrians.

Khoraspa (=Khoraja, q.v.) In the first draft of BC (discarded).

Khorbul In PC, a city in the Himelias. From *hor* (*see* Khoraja, above) + Kabul, Afghanistan.

Khorosun, Khorusun, Khurusun In DI, PC, CA, a Turanian city. From Khurasan, Iran (cf. Khawarizm).

Khorotas In CC, the Aquilonian river on which Tarantia stands. Probably from *hor* (*see* Khoraja) + Eurotas, the Greek river on which Sparta stands (modern Iri or Evrotos).

Khorshemish In SC, KD, the capital of Koth. From *hor* (*see* Khoraja) + Carchemish, an ancient Syrian city later called Europus.

Khosala *See* Kosala.

Khosatral Khel In DI, a demon who once ruled Dagonia. "Khosatral" is possibly a combination of Khushal Khan, a Pakhtun poet and leader of +XVII, + Chitral, a Pakhtun tribe. (*See also* Khel.)

Khosru In PC, Khosrun Khan is the governor of Secunderam; in CA, a Turanian fisherman. The name of several Iranian kings, also spelled Khusru, Khosrau, or Chosroês.

Khossus A king of Khoraja in BC, SD, and of Koth in SC. From Knossos or Cnossus, the capital of Minoan Crete.

Khotan In BC, Thugra Khotan is the original name

of Natohk, the veiled prophet. A river and a town in Sinkiang or Chinese Turkestan. (Cf. Thugra, Natohk.) "Natohk" is an obvious anagram of "Khotan."

Khozgari   In PS, a Turanian mountain tribe. Probably from Kashgar, a city in western Sinkiang or Chinese Turkestan.

Khrosha   A volcanic region in Koth alluded to in SM, SD, CC. Possibly from Khorshid, Iran, or from Kosha, Nubia. Kosha, like its neighbor Akasha, probably gets its name from Kash, ancient Egyptian for Nubia (cf. Keshan, Kush).

Khumbanigash   In WB, the general of Constantius' Shemitish mercenaries. A king of Elam (modern Khuzistan) in –VIII.

Khurakzai   In PC, a Himelian tribe. From Khuram, Afghanistan, + -zai (cf. Dagozai, Khurum).

Khurum   In PC, a Wazuli village and a legendary Amir. From Khuram, Afghanistan (cf. Khurakzai).

Khurusun   See Khorusun.

Khushia   In RE, the chief wife of King Yildiz.

Khusro   In CM, a Turanian soldier. A variant of Khosru (q.v.).

Kidessa   In DT, an oasis in the southern deserts, near Tombalku.

Kobad Shah   In FK, the king of Iranistan. A Persian name (also Kavata, Qobadh, &c.; Greek, Kobades) borne by various Iranian notables.

Kordava, Kordafan   In the original manuscript and outline of SD, Howard mentioned a black country as "Kordafan" and a wizard from there as "a Kordafan." The name comes from Kordofan, a province of the Sudan. To bring the noun and the adjective into proper relationship, I changed the name of the country to "Kordafa."

Kordava   In PO, CB, TT, &c., the capital and main seaport of Zingara. From Cordova (Spanish Córdoba), Spain.

Kordofo   In DT, Conan's predecessor as general of the cavalry of Tombalku. From the same source as Kordafa (q.v.).

Kormon In BB, Lord Thasperas of Kormon is patron of Schohira. There is a French surname, "Cormon," but any connection is doubtful.

Korunga (=Gwarunga, q.v.) In one non-final draft of JG, discarded. See Ahrunga.

Korveka A place mentioned in WB. Cf. Korvela.

Korvela In TT, a bay on the Pictish coast, so named by Zingaran settlers. Possibly a combination of Cordova + *caravela* ("caravel"), Portuguese for a small, lateen-rigged ship.

Korzetta In TT, a county of Zingara. Possibly suggested by Khorbetta (Hurbeit, Bilbeis, ancient Pharbaëthos), Egypt.

Kosala, Khosala An eastern nation alluded to in SZ, PC, RN. From Kosala or Koshala, a kingdom in northern India in the time of the Buddha (−563 to −483).

Kosha See Yag-Kosha, Khroṣha.

Koth In TE, QC, SM, &c., a southern Hyborian kingdom. Probably from the "Sign of Koth" in H. P. Lovecraft's "The Dream-Quest of Unknown Kadath." There is a town of Koth in Gujarât, India, but the connection is doubtful. Howard used the same name in his interplanetary novel *Almuric*.

Kozak In SM, WB, DI, &c., one of a brotherhood of outlaws in Turan and Hyrkania. Russian for "Cossack," ultimately from the Turkish *quzak*, "adventurer."

Krallides In WB, a Khauranian councilor. Cf. Trallibes.

Kshatriyas In PC, CA, the Vendhyans or their ruling caste. The warrior caste of ancient India.

Kuigars In CS, CM, a nomadic people of Hyrkania. From the Uigurs, a Turkish people of Mongolia and Turkestan.

Kujala In FK, a Yezmite. From Kujula (q.v.).

Kujula In CS, CM, the khan of the Kuigars. A king of the Yüe-Chi, +I.

Kulalo In CB, Juma's capital. From the Kololo, a Tswana people who ruled an empire in Zambia and Rhodesia in the 1830s and 40s.

Kull   In TC, CT, SH, and the Kull stories, an At-
lantean who becomes king of Valusia.
Kurush Khan   In RE, a Hyrkanian chief. Kûrush is
the original Persian form of the name of Cyrus the
Great (cf. Kyros).
Kusan   In CM, SH, a small kingdom in western
Khitai. A pseudo-Chinese name.
Kushaf   In FK, a region in the Ilbars Mountains.
Kutamun   In BC, a Stygian prince. Possibly from
Kutama, a medieval Berber tribe of Algeria.
Kuth   In SS, a dream place, probably from the same
source as Koth (q.v.).
Kuthchemes   In BC, FK, a ruined city in the
Shemitish desert. Possibly from the Hindustani *kut*,
"fort," + Chemmis (ancient Khemmis, Shmin, Apu, or
Panopolis; modern Akhmîm), Egypt.
Kwanyara   In BB, a fort on the borders of Schohira.
A pseudo-Iroquois name.
Kwarada   In BB, the Witch of Skandaga, Valerian's
mistress. A pseudo-Iroquois name.
Kyros   A wine-growing region mentioned in HS,
CB, CC. The Greek spelling of Cyrus (Old Persian,
Kûrush; cf. Kurush Khan).

Lalibeha   In IG, the king of Punt. From Lalibela,
a Zangwe king in Abyssinia (Ethiopia) in +XII.
Laodamas   In MB, an Aquilonian officer. The name
of several Greek mythological heroes.
Laranga   In CC, a Negro galley slave. A pseudo-
Bantu name.
Larsha   In HD, a ruined city near Shadizar. From
Larsa, a city of ancient Babylonia.
Lazbekri   In CA, the Mirror of Lazbekri enables
Conan and Pelias to spy on the sorcerer Yah Chieng.
Lemuria   In TE, an eastern archipelago of At-
lantean times. A hypothetical land bridge from India
to South Africa, invented by scientists in the late +XIX
to explain the distribution of lemurs and the similarity
of some geological formations in India and South

Africa; later, in Theosophical and other occult doctrines, a sunken continent in the Indian or the Pacific Ocean, contemporary with or preceding Atlantis (q.v.). Lemuria as a scientific hypothesis has been discredited by the advances of +XX geology.

Leng Chi   In CA, a Khitan; common Chinese names.

Libnun Hills   In HS, a range near Asgalun. From Libnân, Arabic for Lebanon, the mountain and the republic. In Howard's original non-Conan story, "Hawks Over Egypt," these hills were the Mokattam (Arabic, Muqattam) Hills near Cairo.

Ligureans   In BB, BN, a race of light-skinned savages dwelling in small clans in the Pictish Wilderness, culturally similar to the Picts but racially distinct from them. From the Ligurians, a pre-Roman people of northwestern Italy and southern France, who mixed with the invading Celts and were conquered by the Romans.

Lilit   In SH, the ruler of Yanyoga. In Semitic mythology, Lilith or Lilitu is a nocturnal female demon.

Lir   In SS, a god by whom Conan swears. The Irish sea god. (Lir is the genetive; the nominative is properly Lér.) The character also appears as the Welsh god Llyr and as the "King Lear" of Geoffrey of Monmouth (*Historia Regum Britanniae*, II, 11–14) and Shakespeare.

Lissa   In DT, a girl of the desert city of Gazal. From Elissa, the name of the Tyrian princess (better known by her nickname of "Dido") who is traditionally believed to have fled from Tyre during a dynastic struggle and founded Carthage, −XIX or −VIII. Howard used another name from the same source, Nalissa, in the King Kull story, "Swords of the Purple Kingdom."

Livia   In VW, an Ophirean girl of noble family, carried off by Kushites to Bakalah. The feminine form of Livius, a Roman gentile name. Before the Christianization of the Roman Empire, Roman women had no personal names. They were known by the feminine form of their father's gentile (clan) or middle name only; hence, for instance, Gaius Julius Caesar's daughter was automatically called Julia. If a man had more than one daughter, the later ones were given numbers (Secunda, &c.) or diminuitives (Livilla, &c.) to tell them apart.

Lodier   In SK, a barony in Ophir.

Lor   In CA, a barony of Aquilonia.

Lotus   In TE, the powder of the black lotus of Khitai is a deadly poison. In TE, CA, the "fumes" and the pollen of the yellow lotus of Khitai are narcotics. In CC, the smoke of the burning pollen of the black lotus is a powerful drug. In RH, the dust of the gray lotus, which grows beyond Khitai, is a deadly poison. In SC, the juice of the purple lotus of Stygia paralyzes. In SM, the juice of the golden lotus restores sanity. In Homer (*Odyssey*, IX) the fruit of the lotus (probably the jujube, the shrub *Zizyphus* and its relatives) reduces people to a dreamy, lethargic, forgetful state. In modern botany, any of several Old World water lillies of the genera *Nelumbo* and *Nymphaea*.

Louhi   In WM, the witch-mistress of Pohiola. The mistress of Pohjola in the *Kalevala*.

Loulan   In FK, a region of eastern Hyrkania. A pseudo-Chinese name.

Lubemba   In RZ, the king of Zembabwei who first tamed the wyverns. The country of the Bemba, in modern Zambia.

Lucian   In MB, an Aquilonian general. From the Greek Loukianos (Latin, Lucianus), a common name borne by, among others, the Syrio-Greek satirical writer Lucian of Samosata, +II.

Ludovic   In BN, the king of Ophir, successor to Amalrus. A common North European name, also Hlodovic, Ludwig, Clovis, Louis, Lodovico, Luigi, Luís, &c.

Luxur   In FK, TT, CC, &c., the capital of Stygia. From Luxor, Egypt (from Arabic al-Aqsur or al-Uqsur, "the castles," in ancient times called Wesi, Opet, No-Amun, or Thebes).

Lyco   In CA, a Kothian captive in Paikang. From Lykon, a common Classical Greek name.

Macha   In PS, a Cimmerian deity. From Emain Macha (pronounced approximately EV-in MAH-khah), Cúchulainn's home in Irish myth.

Mannanan   In SS, a god by whom Conan swears. From Manannán (pronounced mah-nah-NYAWN), in Irish mythology a sea god, the son of Lér.

Manara   In CA, a county of Aquilonia.

Marala   In SK, the queen of King Moranthes II of Ophir; later the Countess Albiona.

Marco   In CI, a Barachan pirate in Conan's crew. An Italian given name, from the Latin praenomen Marcus.

Marinus   In CA, a hireling of King Yezdigerd in Tarantia. From the Greek Marinos, a common name borne by, among others, a noted +II Tyrian geographer.

Matamba   In CB, a Kushite tribe. A pseudo-Bantu name.

Mattenbaal   In HS, a priest of Pteor. A Phoenician name.

Maul   In TE, HD, the thieves' quarter in a Zamorian city.

Mayapan   In CI, the American coast adjacent to Antillia. The Mayas' own name for their country.

Maypur   In CA, a Turanian city. Probably from the Mayan Indians.

Mazdak   In HS, a Hyrkanian mercenary in the Pelishti army. A Persian name, notably that of the founder of a communistic religion in +V.

Mbega   In RZ, SH, one of the twin kings of Zembabwei. A legendary conquering East African chieftain, c. +1700, in the present Tanzania.

Mbonani   In CB, a Ghanata slaver. A +XIX East African chieftain.

Mecanta   In SK, a county in Ophir.

Mena   In GT, a Shemitish conjuror in Captain Gonzago's crew. The more or less legendary founder of the First Dynasty of Egypt, c. −3100.

Menkara   In CB, a priest of Set. The name of a Fourth Dynasty king of Egypt, also Menkaura, Menkure, or Mycerinus.

Meru   In CS, CM, SH, a tropical valley between the Talakma and Himelian mountain ranges. In Hindu mythology, the mountain on which the gods dwell.

Mesmerism   An obsolete name for hypnotism, after its discoverer Franz Anton Mesmer (1733–1815), an Austrian physician; used in this sense by Howard in SZ, PC.

Messantia   In PO, CC, CI, the main seaport of Argos. Probably from Messina, Italy.

Metemphoc   In CI, the chief of the thieves of Ptahuacan. A synthetic Egypto-Mayan name.

Milo   In CS, BM, the king of Argos; in CI, Conan's boatswain. From the Greek Milon, a legendary athlete of Crotona; also a Roman cognomen.

Mindanga   In DT, a people of the Tombalku Empire. *See* Bigharma.

Mithridates   In CA, a king of Zamora. The Greek version of the Persian Mithradata, borne by various Achaemenid Persian notables and by several kings of Pontus, especially Mithridates VI, the Great, c. −100.

Mitra   In GB, RH, QC, &c., a Hyborian god. In Indian mythology, a sun god, cognate with the Persian Mithra or Mithras.

Mkwana   In SH, a Zembabwan officer. A pseudo-Bantu name.

Monargo   In CI, the count of Couthen. From Monaco.

Moranthes   In SD, SK, the king of Ophir and the second of that name, Amalrus' predecessor. Possibly suggested by Orontes, a Persian name (Aurwand, Alwand) borne by a character in Molière's *The Misanthrope*. Also a river in Syria (modern Nahr al-'Asi).

Morrigan   In PS, a Cimmerian deity. An Irish goddess, who appears in Arthurian legend in the guise of

247

Morgan le Fay (Malory's English for the French Morgain la fée).

Mulai   In CM, a Turanian soldier. A Turkish name.

Munthassem Khan   In HN, a Turanian governor.

Muriela   In JG, IG, a Corinthian dancing girl. From the feminine proper name Muriel.

Murilo   In RH, HN, a noble of a small city-state west of Zamora. Probably from Murillo, a —XVII Spanish painter.

Murzio   In RZ, a Zingaran serving with Conan. From the Italian name Muzio, which comes from the Roman gentile names Mucius and Mutius.

Nabonidus   In RH, a priest in a small, unnamed city-state west of Zamora. Latin for Nabu-naid, the last Babylonian king.

Nafertari   In DI, the mistress of the satrap Jungir Khan. From Nefertari, the name of several Egyptian queens.

Nahor   In IG, a Shemitish merchant in Punt. A biblical name (Gen. 11:23).

Namedides   *See* Numedides.

Nanaia   In FK, a woman of Kobad Shah's harem. From Nana, an ancient oriental name.

Natala   In SS, a Brythunian girl. Presumably from the feminine proper name Natalie or Natalia.

Natohk   In BC, SD, the name used by Thugrá Khotan; "Khotan" (q.v.) backward.

Nebethet   In IG, the dominant goddess of Punt. From Nebthet or Nephthys, an Egyptian goddess.

Nebthu   In BN, RZ, SH, a ruined city in northern Stygia. From the Egyptian goddess Nebthet or Nephthys.

Nemain   In PS, a Cimmerian deity. An Irish goddess, pronounced approximately NEV-in.

Nemedia, Nemedians   In TE, GB, QC, &c., a powerful Hyborian kingdom and its people. In Irish mythology, the Nemedians, descendants of the Scythian chief Nemed, were among the first invaders of Ireland. Cf. Conan; also *Lebor Gabála Érenn*, V, 237–56.

Nenaunir   In WM, RZ, SH, one of the twin kings of Zembabwei, also priest of Damballah. A Sudanese name.

Nergal   In HN, the Hand of Nergal is a powerful talisman. Nergal or Nerigal was the Babylonian war god.

Nestor   In HD, a Gunderman officer of Zamorian troops. In Homer's *Iliad*, a wise old king of Pylos with the Achaean host.

N'Gora   In QC, a subchief of the black corsairs. A pseudo-Bantu name.

Nezvaya   In HN, a river in Turan. Possibly suggested by the Russian rivers Nyeva and Velikaya, or similar names.

Nilas (=Styx)   In the first draft of BC, the Nemedian name for the river (discarded); from Nilus, Neilos, or Nile, also mentioned as "Nilus" in "The Hyborian Age."

Nimed   In CC, the king of Nemedia (q.v.). From Nemed, in Irish mythology a Scythian chief whose descendants invaded Ireland.

Ninus   In HD, the Fountain of Ninus is west of Shadizar; in CB, RZ, a priest of Mitra. In Greek legend (Ninos), the founder of Nineveh.

Niord   In FD, an As (*see* Æsir). From Njorth or Njörð, one of the Vanir (q.v.) of Norse mythology.

Nippr   In BC, a Shemitish city-state. From Nippur, an ancient Babylonian city.

Njal   In LD, a chief or *jarl* of the Æsir, raiding into Hyperborea. From Njal (pronounced NYAHL) Thorgeirsson, hero of one of the most famous Icelandic sagas, *Njal's Saga* or *The Saga of Burnt Njal.*

Nordheim   In QC, the land of the Æsir and the Vanir. A medieval German place name, meaning "north home."

Nuadens   In BN, a god invoked by Diviatix. A Celtic god, also Nuada or Nodens.

Nuadwyddon   In BN, a sacred grove of the Ligurean Druids. A pseudo-Welsh name.

Numa In PS, a king of Nemedia. A legendary king of early Rome.

Numalia In GB, a Nemedian city. From Numa (q.v.).

Numedides, Namedides In DT, MB, TT, &c., a king of Aquilonia slain and superseded by Conan. From Numa and Nimed (q.v.) + the Greek gentile suffix *-ides*. Howard used both spellings, but in current editions of the stories the former is used exclusively.

N'Yaga In QC, a black corsair. A pseudo-Bantu name.

Nzinga In CB, RZ, the queen of the Amazons; in RZ, also, her daughter of the same name. A black warrior queen who fought the Portuguese in Angola in +XVII.

Octavia In DJ, a Nemedian girl. The feminine form of the Roman gentile name Octavius (cf. Livia).

Ogaha In BB, a creek between the provinces of Conawaga and Schohira. A pseudo-Iroquois name, probably suggested by upstate New York place names like Oquaga, Otego, &c.

Olgerd In WB, FK, Olgerd Vladislav is a Zaporoskan chief of the Zuagirs. From Olgierd, a grand duke of Lithuania in +XIV (*see* Vladislav).

Olivero In BN, the husband of Princess Chabela. A Spanish name.

Olivia In SM, an Ophirean princess. An Italian and English feminine proper name.

Ollam-Onga In DT, the god of Gazal.

Olmec In RN, a chief of Xuchotl. From the Olmecs or Olmeca, a tribe of Mexican Indians.

Onagrul In CA, a pirate settlement on the eastern shore of the Vilayet Sea. From "onager," the Asiatic wild ass.

Onyaga In BB, the Hawk Clan of the Picts. A pseudo-Iroquois name.

Ophir In TE, QC, SM, &c., a Hyborian kingdom. A goldmining region in the Old Testament, possibly on the shores of the Red or Arabian seas (e.g., western

Arabia) or the country of the Afar, in Eritrea on the opposite side of the Red Sea.

Orastes In CC, a former priest of Mitra. From Orestes, in Greek myth the son of Agamemnon; also regent of Italy in +V for his son Romulus Augustulus, the last West Roman Emperor; executed by order of Odovakar in +476.

Oriskonie In MB, BB, a province of the Westermarck. From Oriskany (now Oriskany Falls), New York, site of a battle in the Revolutionary War.

Orklaga (=Ogaha) In first draft of BB; discarded. A pseudo-Iroquois name.

Ortho A pirate alluded to in RN. Possibly from Otho, a Roman cognomen or family name.

Ostorio In BG, a Nemedian. From Ostorius, a Roman gentile name.

Othbaal An Anaki intriguer. From Ithobaal or Ethbaal, king of Sidon in −IX.

Otho See Ortho, Strom.

Paikang In WB, CA, a city in Khitai. From Peiking, China.

Palian Way In GB, a street in Numalia. Probably from the Mappalian Way, a street in Carthage alluded to in Flaubert's *Salammbô*; possibly also from the river Pallia, a tributary of the Tiber.

Pallantides In PS, CC, CA, &c., an Aquilonian general. In Greek mythology, a collective name for the fifty sons of Pallas, uncle of Theseus, who slew all the Pallantides in a struggle for the throne of Athens. Howard may, however, have derived the name from a combination of Palamedes, a Trojan hero, and Pallancia (modern Palencia), Spain.

Pantho In BN, a Zingaran, the duke of Guarralid. From Sancho Panza (Castillian z = English th).

Pelias In SC, CA, a Kothian wizard. In Greek myth, a king of Iolkos and Jason's wicked uncle.

Pelishtim In WB, CI, JG, a Shemitish nation. Hebrew for the Philistines, whence "Palestine" is also derived. Howard used "Pelishtim" in the singular, whereas the Hebrew singular would be "Pelishti," which form I have substituted where appropriate in the current editions.

Pellia   In SC, CC, a principality in Aquilonia. Probably from Pella, the ancient capital of Macedonia.

Peshkauri   In PC, a city in northwestern Vendhya. From Peshawar (or Peshâvar), Pakistan.

Petanius   See Aztreas.

Petreus   In RH, a conspirator against Nabonidus. From Petrus, the Latin form of Peter (Greek, Petros).

Picts   In TE, GB, BR, &c., the primitive inhabitants of the Pictish Wilderness, along the west coast of the main continent. The primitive pre-Celtic inhabitants of Britain, who were finally absorbed by the invading Scots from Ireland. The affinities of their language are much disputed, some holding them to have spoken a Celtic tongue, some a non-Celtic Indo-European, and some a non-Indo-European one. In the Conan stories, Howard made the Picts a swarthy folk with an Iroquois-like culture; in other stories, he assumed they were dwarfish and Neanderthaloid. From anthropological considerations, it seems most likely that they were physically much the same as the present people of Scotland.

Pohiola   In WM, BN, RZ, a sorcerous Hyperborean stronghold. From Pohjola, in the *Kalevala* the "North Country," corresponding to Lapland or a suppositious land even farther north.

Poitain   In TT to BN, the southernmost province of Aquilonia, at times independent of that kingdom. From Poitou, a French province on the west coast. Howard spelled the corresponding adjective "Poitanian."

Posthumo   In GB, a Numalian policeman. From the Roman cognomen Posthumus, which originally meant "born after his father's death."

Pra-Eun   In WM, RZ, a Kambujan wizard. In Cambodian mythology, the king of the angels.

Promero   In GB, a Nemedian clerk.

Prospero   In PS, CC, CA, &c., a Poitanian supporter

of Conan. The magician in Shakespeare's *The Tempest*; ultimately possibly from Prosper Aquitanicus, a Roman theologian of +V.

Ptahuacan   In CI, the capital of Antillia. A synthetic Egypto-Mayan name.

Pteion   In CA, a demon-haunted Stygian ruined city.

Pteor   In JG, the god of the Pelishtim. From Baal-Pteor, for which *see* Baal-Pteor.

Publico   *See* Kallian, Publius. From the Roman names Publicius, Publicola.

Publio   In CC, an Argossean merchant. Italian for Publius (q.v.).

Publius   In TT to CI, the chancellor of Aquilonia under Conan. A Roman praenomen or personal name.

Punt   In RN, JG, IG, &c., a Negro kingdom. A place with which the ancient Egyptians traded, probably Somaliland.

Purasati   In FK, a Vendhyan girl in Yanaidar. A Hindi feminine name.

Python   In FK, CB, CC, the capital of the fallen empire of Acheron. In Greek mythology, a great snake slain by Apollo at Delphi; hence, in modern zoology, a genus of constrictor snakes found in Africa, Asia, and Australia, including the largest existing snakes; also a Greek personal name.

Qirlata   In CA, a Zuagir tribe.

Radegund   In BN, Conan's elder daughter. From Radegund or Radegunda, daughter of King Berthar of Thuringia in +VI.

Rakhamon   In CA, a Stygian sorcerer of former times. From the Egyptian gods Ra and Amon.

Rakhsha   In PC, a kind of oriental wizard. From *râkshasa*, a class of demons in Hindu mythology.

Raman   In CA, a county in Aquilonia. From the Indian bull Rama in Kipling's *Jungle Books*.

Ramiro   In CB, the founder of King Ferdrugo's Zingaran dynasty. A Spanish given name.

Rammon   A wizard or priest alluded to in PS. From Rimmon or Ramman, a Semitic storm god.

Rann   In LD, Njal's daughter. A Norse sea goddess.

Rhamdan   In CA, a port on the Vilayet Sea. From *Ramaḍân*, the Muslim Lent.

Rhazes   In KD, a Kothian astrologer. The Latinized form of the name of ar-Razi, an Arabic physician of +IX.

Rigello   In SK, a powerful nobleman, cousin to the king. Suggested by Lake Regillus in Italy, site of a battle in the Second Punic War.

Rima   In SK, a slave girl.

Rimush   In RZ, SH, a Shemitish astrologer. A king of Assyria, c. −2000.

Rinaldo   In PS, SC, a mad Aquilonian poet. An Italian proper name, cognate with Ronald; one of the heroes of Ariosto's *Orlando Furioso*. In his King Kull story, "By This Axe I Rule!", which Howard rewrote as PS, he called the corresponding character "Ridondo."

Rolf   In CA, an As at the court of King Yezdigerd. A common Scandinavian name (Old Norse, Hrolf, cognate with English Ralph), e.g., Hrolf Ganger, the Norse conqueror of Normandy.

Roxana   In RE, the Zamorian mistress of Prince Teyaspa. The Greek form of the name of several Persian women of Achaemenid times, e.g., one of the wives of Alexander the Great (Old Persian, Rushanek).

Rufia   In HS, the mistress of Mazdak. From the Roman cognomens Rufus, Rufinus.

Ruo-Gen   In CA, a Khitan kingdom. A pseudo-Chinese name.

Rustum   In BG, a Kezankian tribesman. From Rustam, the legendary Iranian hero.

Sabatea   A sinister Shemitish city in HS, CC. From the ancient Arabian kingdoms of Sabaea (Sheba) and Nabataea, or the Arabian city of Sabata (modern Sawa), or a combination of these.

Sabina (=Zenobia)   In first draft of CC, discarded. The feminine form of Sabinus, a Roman cognomen, which comes from Sabini, a people of central Italy who received Roman citizenship in −III.

Sabral   In CB, a taverner in Kordava. From the Portuguese surname Cabral.

Sagayetha   In MB, a Pictish shaman. A pseudo-Iroquois name.

Sagoyaga   In RZ, a chief of the Picts. A pseudo-Iroquois name.

Saidu   In DT, a Ghanata brigand. After King Mallam Saidu of Nupe, Nigeria, *reg.* 1926–34.

Sakumbe   In DT, one of the joint kings of Tombalku. Possibly from Sakpe, Nigeria.

Salome   In WB, the wicked twin sister of Taramis (q.v.). In Matthew 14, the daughter of Herodias.

Samara   In PE, a Turanian outpost. From Samarra, a city in Iraq, once briefly the capital of the Caliphate.

Sancha   In PO, a Zingaran girl, the daughter of the duke of Kordava. A Spanish and Provençal proper name.

Sareeta (=Livia)   In first draft of VW; discarded. Possibly from the feminine given name Serena.

Sarpedon (=Tuscelan)   In first draft of BR; discarded. A Lycian prince in the *Iliad*, slain at Troy by Patroklos.

Sassan   In BG, an Iranistani treasure-hunter. Sasan or Sassan was the legendary founder of the Sassanid dynasty (+III to +VII) in Iran.

Satha   In SC, a giant snake. From Sathanas, a Greek form of Satan.

Sathus (=Set)   In first draft of CC; discarded. From the same source as Satha (q.v.).

Scavonus   *See* Emilius. Possibly from Savona, Italy, or from such Roman names as Scaevinus, Scaevola.

Schohira   In BB, MB, a province of the Westermarck. From Schoharie Creek or County, New York.

Schondara   In BB, the principal town of Schohira. Possibly a combination of Sconodoa and Thendara, New York.

Sebro (=Gebellez)   In first draft of TT; discarded.

Secunderam   In PC, CA, a city between Turan and

Vendhya, under Turanian rule. From Secunderabad (Sikandarâbâd, "Alexander's place"), India, named for Sikander Lodi of Jaunpur (f. 1500), whose name in turn may come from that of Alexander the Great, + the common -*am* ending found in many southern Indian cities, e.g., Vizagapatam.

Sergius   In SM, a Kothic pirate captain. A Roman gentile name.

Servio   In CC, a Messantian innkeeper. Italian for Servius (q.v.).

Servius   In CC, a Servius Galannus is an Aquilonian noble. A Roman gentile name.

Set   In GB, QC, BC, &c., the Stygian serpent-god. In ancient Egypt, the jackal-headed god of war or, later, a god of evil, called Sêth or Typhon by the Greeks.

Shadizar   In TC, HD, PO, &c., the capital of Zamora. Possibly from Shanidar, Iraq. Cf. Shalizah.

Shaf Karaz   In PS, a chief of the Khozgari tribesmen of Hyrkania.

Shah   *See* Amurath, Kerim. Persian for "king."

Shahpur   In DI, CA, a Turanian city. The name of several cities in Iran and India, meaning "king's town."

Shalizah   In SC, a pass in Ghulistan. Possibly from the Shalamar Gardens, Lahore, India.

Shamar   In SC, a southern Aquilonian city. Probably from the Jabal Shammar, a range in Arabia.

Shamballah   In CS, SH, the capital of Meru. A Siberian city in Tibetan legend.

Shamla   In BC, a pass in Khoraja. From any of various Asian places like Shamil, Iran; Simla, India; or Shamlegh, a village on the Indo-Tibetan border mentioned in Kipling's *Kim*.

Shamu   In SC, a plain in Ophir. Probably from Shamo, a Chinese name for the Gobi Desert.

Shan   *See* Chunder Shan. Probably a combination of "khan" and "shah" (q.v.), although it is also the Chinese word for "mountain."

Shan-e-Sorkh   In BT, the Red Waste in the Zuagir Desert. Modern Farsi (Persian) for "red sand."

Shangara   In PS, the abode of the People of the Summit.

Shanya   In PS, the daughter of a chief of the Khozgari.

Shapur   In CA, a Turanian soldier. A common Persian name (Greek, Sapor) borne by several Sassanid kings.

Shaulun   In CA, a village in Khitai near Paikang.

Shem   In TE, QC, BC, &c., a land south of the Hyborian nations, divided into city-states and bordering Stygia. In the Bible, Noah's eldest son, the ancestor of the Hebrews, Arabs, and Assyrians; hence the modern "Semite" and "Semitic" (via Greek Sêm), used properly to designate the family of languages spoken by these peoples.

Shevatas   In BC, a Zamorian thief. Possibly from Thevatata, a figure in Indian mythology, or Thevatat, a sorcerer-king of Atlantis in Theosophical pseudo-history, which is also derived from Indian myth.

Shirakma   In CA, a wine-growing region of Vendhya. A pseudo-Hindi name.

Shirki   In CC, a river in western Aquilonia. Possible sources are Sirki, the original Assyrian name for a town at the confluence of the Euphrates and Khabur rivers, later called Phaliga, Circesium, and Buseira or Bessireh; and *shikari*, an Indo-Iranian word for "hunter."

Shondakor   In CS, one of the seven sacred cities of Meru. From the title of Leigh Brackett's story "The Last Days of Shandakor," in *Startling Stories* for April 1952.

Shu   In CM, SH, the king of Kusan. One of the Three Kingdoms of China in +II.

Shubba   In SD, a servant of Tuthmes. Possibly from *jubbah*, the long, loose Arabian gown.

Shu-Chen   In CA, a Khitan kingdom.

Shukeli   In SC, a eunuch. Possibly from Shukriya, a Sudanese tribe.

Shumir   In QC, BC, KD, a Shemitish city-state.

From Shumer or Sumer, the land of the Sumerians, the pre-Semitic inhabitants of ancient southern Iraq.

Shupras   In BC, the Agha Shupras is a Khorajan councilor. Possibly from Shuqra, Arabia. (Cf. Agha.)

Shushan   In BC, a Shemitish river: in DI, a Shemitish city. One of the names of ancient Shusha, Sousa, Shush, or Sus, Iran; the capital of ancient Elam, Elymais, Hûja, Uvja, Goution, or Sousiana (modern Khuzistan).

Sigtona   In LW, WM, a stronghold in southwestern Hyperborea. A town of early medieval Sweden.

Sigurd   In CB, CI, a Van sailor. From Sigurð or Siegfried, the great North European mythical dragon-slaying hero.

Simura   In HS, a city gate of Asgalun. From Simurgh, in Persian myth a gigantic bird, mentioned in the *Shah Nameh* as dwelling on Mt. Qaf.

Siojina-Kisua   In CB, the former name for the Nameless Isle. From Swahili *si-jina kisiwa*, "no-name island."

Siptah   In GT, a Stygian magician, living in a tower on a nameless island. An Egyptian king of the Nineteenth Dynasty, c. −1200.

Skandaga, Scandaga   In BB, Kwarada (q.v.) is called the Witch of Skandaga; Howard in "Notes on Various Peoples" describes it (under the alternative spelling) as the largest town of Conawaga. From the Sacandaga River or Vlaie (Swamp), New York.

Skelos   In BC, DI, PC, &c., an ancient author of magical books. Probably from "skeleton," which means "dried up" in Greek. The Greek word *skelos* means "leg."

Skuthus   In first draft of CC, a necromancer; discarded.

Socandaga (=Ligurean)   In first draft of BB; discarded. From the same source as Skandaga (q.v.).

Sogdia   In RE, a region in Hyrkania. From Sogdiana, the northernmost province of the Achaemenid Empire; later part of the Seleucid and Bactrian Empires, now the Uzbek Socialist Soviet Republic.

Soractus In BR, an Aquilonian woodsman. Probably from Mt. Soracte, Italy.

Sraosha In CB, a deity of the Mitran pantheon. In Zoroastrianism, the personification of the divine word.

Strabo In CI, an Argossean bully. From Strabon (Latin, Strabo), a common Greek name, borne by the noted geographer Strabon of Amasia, −I and +I.

Strabonus In SD, SC, the king of Koth. From the same source as Strabo (q.v.).

Strom, Strombanni In BB, Hakon Strom's son is an Aquilonian ranger, while his brother Dirk Strom's son is commander of Fort Kwanyara. In the original manuscript of TT, Strom was an Argossean pirate captain; but, since all his other Argossean names are Italianate, I changed it to "Strombanni." In BB, Howard had characters named Strom, Storm, and Gorm; believing that this would confuse readers, I changed "Storm" to "Otho." A rare English and Scandinavian surname.

Stygus (=Styx, q.v.) In first draft of BC, the Kothian name for the same river; discarded.

Styx, Stygia In TE, OC, WB, &c., respectively a river and a kingdom south of Shem, from whose people the Egyptians are descended. In Greek mythology, the Styx was the largest of the four rivers of Hades. The name was also applied to a real river in Arcadia and means "horror" or "hateful thing." "Stygia" comes from the English adjective "stygian," which in turn comes from the Latin *stygius* (Greek, *stygios*) meaning "Stygian," "infernal," "hellish."

Subas In DT, the original tribe of Sakumbe, on the Black Coast.

Sukhmet In RN, a southern frontier city in Stygia. From Sekhmet (Sekhet or Skhemit), a lion-headed Egyptian goddess.

Sultanapur In DI, CA, a Turanian city. From Sultanpur ("sultan's town"), India.

Sumeru Tso In CS, the inland sea of Meru. From Sumer (cf. Shumir) + Tso, Tibetan for "lake."

Sumuabi　　In HS, a king of Akkharia. From Sumu-abu, founder of the First Dynasty of Babylon, −3M.

Sura　　In MB, an Aquilonian physician. A common Roman cognomen.

Swamp Snake (=Zogar Sag)　　In first draft of BR; discarded.

Tachic　　In RN, a man of Xuchotl. Possibly from Tactic, Guatemala.

Talakma Mts.　　In CS, CA, a range in Hyrkania north of the Himelias, corresponding to the modern Tien Shan. From the Takla Makan, a desert in Sinkiang.

Tamar　　In SC, in Howard's original manuscript, the capital of Aquilonia, elsewhere called Tarantia (q.v.). Probably from the city of Tamar ("palm tree") mentioned in I Kings 9:18; this in turn is probably an error for Tadmor (Palmyra), Syria. In current editions, I changed this name to Tarantia for consistency.

Tameris (=Bêlit)　　In first draft of QC; discarded. From the same source as Taramis (q.v.).

Tammuz　　In HN, the Heart of Tammuz is a powerful amulet. Another name for Adonis (q.v.).

Tananda　　In SD, the sister of the king of Kush.

Tanasul　　In CC, WM, a place in western Aquilonia.

Tanzong Tengri　　In CS, the chief wizard of Meru. A pseudo-Tibetan name.

Taramis　　In WB, the queen of Khauran. From the Russian feminine name Tamira; or Tamara, a medieval queen of Georgia; ultimately from Tomyris, a Scythian queen in battle with whom Cyrus the Great is said by Herodotus to have been killed.

Tarantia　　In MB, TT, CC, &c., the capital of Aquilonia. Probably from Taranto (ancient Tarentum, Taras), Italy. (Cf. Tamar.)

Tarascus　　In CC, CA, the brother of the king of Nemedia. Possibly from Tarascon, France, or from the Tarascan Indians of Mexico.

Tarim　　In DI, PC, a Turanian divinity. A river in Sinkiang.

Tartur   In CA, a Wigur shaman. From Tartar, a medieval European corruption of the Persian Tâtâr, originally meaning a member of one of the tribes of Siberian Mongoloid nomads, of Turkic or Tungusic stock, but later applied to all Central Asian Mongoloid nomadic peoples, who periodically invaded the civilized lands to the east, west, and south.

Tashudang   In CS, a Meruvian. A pseudo-Tibetan name.

Tauran   In BR, TT, a northwestern province of Aquilonia. Probably from the Taurini, an ancient Ligurian people for whom Turin (Italian Torino, ancient Augusta Taurinorum) is named.

Taurus   In TE, a Nemedian thief; in BC, SD, chancellor of Khoraja; in BN, Conan's younger son. Latin for "bull"; the Greek cognate *tauros* was also used as a personal name.

Techotl   In RN, a man of Xuchotl. From Techotlala, an Aztec chief of +XIV.

Tecuhltli   In RN, one of the feuding clans of Xuchotl. From *tecuhtli*, Aztec (=Nahuatl) for "grandfather" or "councilor."

Terson   In SK, a barony in Ophir.

Teyanoga   In BB, a Pictish shaman. A pseudo-Iroquois name.

Teyaspa   In RE, a Turanian prince. From the Persian name Tiyasp and other names ending in *-asp* or *-aspa*.

Tezcoti   In RN, a chamber in Xuchotl. Possibly from Tezcoco or Texcoco, Mexico.

Thabit   In CA, a Zuagir. An Arabic name, e.g., of Thâbit ibn-Qurra, a +IX Arab scientist.

Thak   In RN, a man-ape. Possibly from the Hindi *thag*, "thug." Cf. Zembabwei.

Than   In HN, a nobleman of Yaralet.

Thanara   In CA, a woman spy for King Yezdigerd. From the Saxon word *thane* or *thegn*, "chief," "nobleman."

Thandara   In BB, the southernmost province of the Westermarck. From Thendara, a place alluded to in Robert W. Chambers's novel *The Little Red Foot*, set in New York State in Revolutionary times; now the name of a town in Herkimer County, New York, formerly Fulton Chain.

Thasperas   In MB, BB, Lord Thasperas of Kormon is the patron of Schohira. Possibly from Tharypas, a king of the Molossians in −V.

Thaug   In WB, a toad-demon. Possibly from the same source as Thak (q.v.).

Theggir   In PS, a Hyrkanian mountain tribe.

Thenitea   In BB, the location of a Schohiran army arrayed against the Numedidean forces of Brocas. Probably a coinage from New York State place names like Thendara and Caneadea.

Theringo   In SK, a feudal demesne in Ophir.

Thespides. Thespius   Respectively in BC, SD, a Khorajan councilor and in CC a renegade Aquilonian count. From Thespis, a Greek poet of −VI.

Thespius (=Thasperas)   In first draft of BB; discarded. From the same source as Thespides (q.v.).

Theteles   In VW, Livia's brother, slain by the Bakalah. Probably from Classical names like Thestius.

Thog   In SS, the demon-god of Xuthal. Also (=Jhebbal Sag) in first draft of BR; discarded. Probably invented, but cf. Thak.

Thogara   In CS, one of the seven sacred cities of Meru.

Thorus   In BN, a Gunderman serving with Conan's army. From the Norse Thor (þór) + a Latin ending.

Thoth-Amon   In GB, TT, PS, &c., a Stygian sorcerer-priest. A compound of the Greek names for two Egyptian gods, Thoth (Thout, Tehuti, Dhuti) and Amon (Ammon, Amun). Howard also used Thoth-Amon's copper ring and its attendant baboon-demon in a story with a modern setting, "The Haunter of the Ring" (*Weird Tales*, June 1934).

Thothmekri   In CC, a dead priest of Set. From Thoth (*see* Thoth-Amon) + Mekri (Mikerê, Mery-kara), a Tenth Dynasty king of Egypt.

Thrallos In CC, a fountain outside Belverus. Cf.
Trallibes.

Throana In CS, one of the seven sacred cities of
Meru.

Thror In LD, a subchief of the Æsir. In the Prose
Edda, a dwarf; also one of the names of Oðin.

Thugra In BC, Thugra Khotan is an ancient Sty-
gian wizard brought back to life under the name
Natohk. Possibly from the Thugra Gorge near Petra,
Jordan. (*See* Khotan, Natohk.)

Thule In HN, a northern kingdom of pre-Cataclys-
mic (Atlantean) times. From Thule or Thoulê, a
northern land reported by the −IV Greek explorer
Pytheas of Massilia, identified variously with the Ork-
ney and Shetland Islands, the Faeroes, Norway, and
Iceland.

Thune In PS, a county of Aquilonia; also part of
the name of the wizard in the Kull story, "The Mirrors
of Tuzun Thune." Possibly from the same source as
Thule (q.v.).

Thuria In "The Hyborian Age" and CI, the main
(Eurasian) continent of Atlantean times. In Burroughs's
Martian tales, the Martian name of Phobos, the nearer
of the two Martian satellites. Also a town, Thouria, in
the ancient Peloponnesos, but any connection thereof
with Howard or Burroughs is doubtful.

Thutmekri In JG, IG, a Stygian adventurer. From
the same sources as Thothmekri (q.v.).

Thutothmes In CC, a Stygian priest. From Tho-
thmes (Thoutmosis, Teḥuti-mesu), the name of several
Eighteenth Dynasty kings of Egypt.

Tiberias In BR, an Aquilonian trader; in CC, an
Aquilonian noble. An ancient town in Palestine, modern Tabariya.

Tiberio In CC, Publio's secretary. Italian for Ti-
berius, a Roman praenomen or personal name.

Tibu In DT, a desert tribe of Kush, subject to
Tombalku. From the Tibbu or Tibu, a Saharan tribe
living around the Tibesti Mountains.

Tilutan   In DT, a Ghanata brigand.

Tina   In TT, a young Ophirean girl. Diminutive of feminine names like Albertina, Christina, &c.

Tito   In QC, an Argossean sea captain. Italian for Titus, a Roman praenomen or personal name.

Tlazitlan   In RN, the race that built Xuchotl. Possibly from Tizatlan, Mexico; or a combination of Tlascala or Tlaxcala, Mexico, and Zatlan, a place in Aztec mythology.

Tolkamec   In RN, a wizard of Xuchotl. Possibly a combination of Toltec and Chichimec, two dynasties or dominant tribes from pre-Conquest Mexican history.

Tombalku   In DT, a city on the southern edge of the desert south of Stygia. From Timbuktu or Timbouctou, in the République du Soudan, the capital of a succession of Negro empires in medieval times.

Topal   In RN, a man of Xuchotl. Possibly from copal, a resinous gum collected from various tropical American trees and used as incense.

Tor   In CC, a Nemedian barony. The word means "hill" or "peak" in English.

Toragis   In first draft of RN, the place near which Conan's ship was sunk; discarded. Possibly from the same source as Tortage (q.v.).

Torgrio   In SK, a thief of Ianthe.

Torh   See Brocas. Probably from the same source as Tor (q.v.).

Tortage   In PO, a pirate town in the Barachas. From Tortuga (Spanish for "turtle"), the name of two Caribbean islands with a piratical history.

Tothmekri   In TT, a Stygian prince. From the same sources as Thothmekri (q.v.).

Tothra   In SS, a dream place. Possibly a combination of the names of the Egyptian gods Thoth and Ra.

Totrasmek   In SZ, a priest of Hanuman.

Tovarro   In CB, the brother of King Ferdrugo. From the Spanish surnames Tovar and Navarro.

Trallibes   In TT, a place on the coast of the Western Ocean. Possibly from Tralles in Roman Asia Minor.

Tranicos   In TT, CI, a pirate admiral. Possibly from the Portuguese name Trancoso.

Trocero   In TT to CI, the count of Poitain. Possibly from the Trocadéro Palace, a museum in Paris whose name has been appropriated by many American movie and burlesque theaters.

Tsathoggua   In CB, CA, a toad-shaped idol on the Nameless Isle. A god mentioned in Clark Ashton Smith's story "The Ice Demon" (*Weird Tales*, April 1933).

Tsotha-Lanti   In SC, a Kothian wizard. Possibly suggested by Thoth + Atlantis.

Tubal   In FK, a Shemite serving under Conan. A Biblical name (Gen. 4:22).

Turan   In WB, DI, QC, &c., the kingdom set up west of the Vilayet Sea by Hyrkanian invaders. The Old Persian name for Turkestan. In Firdausi's *Shah Nameh*, the main repository of ancient Persian legend, Feridun (Old Persian, Traetaona) divided the world among his three sons, giving Rum (Europe) to Silim, Turan to Tur, and Iran to Irij. Much of the *Shah Nameh* is taken up with the efforts of King Afrasiyab (Frangrasiyan) of Turan to conquer Iran, and his successive defeats by the Persian hero Rustam under various Iranian kings.

Tuscelan   In BR, MB, an Aquilonian fort on the Pictish frontier. From ancient Tusculum, Italy.

Tuthamon   In FK, CC, a former king of Stygia, the father of Akivasha. From the same sources as Thoth-Amon (q.v.).

Tuthmes   In SD, a nobleman of the kingdom of Kush. From the same sources as Thutothmes (q.v.).

Tybor   In SC, a river in southeastern Aquilonia. From the Tiber River, Italy.

Upas   In TE, PS, a poisonous tree. A Javanese tree, *Antigris toxicaria*, yielding a poisonous sap; formerly reputed to destroy any living thing near it.

Ura   In FK, a legendary king of Yanaidar.

Uriaz   In HS, a former king of Pelishtia. From the Hebrew name Uriah (Greco-Latin Urias).
Uthghiz   In CA, a Turanian admiral. From Utgård or Útgarðar, the land of giants in Norse mythology.
Uttara Kuru   In CA, a region east of Vendhya. A legendary land in Hindu mythology.

Valadelad   In first draft of RN, a town burned by Conan just before the sinking of his ship by the Zingarans; discarded. From Valladolid, Spain.
Valannus   In BR, MB, an Aquilonian officer commanding Fort Tuscelan; in CC, another Aquilonian officer. Probably from the Roman names Valens, Valentius.
Valbroso   In CC, a Zingaran robber-count. From Vallombroso ("shady valley"), Italy.
Valenso   In TT, a Zingaran count. Probably from Valencia (ancient Valentia), Spain.
Valeria   In RN, an Aquilonian woman pirate. The feminine form of Valerius (q.v.). Cf. Livia.
Valerian   In BB, a nobleman of Schohira. From Valerianus, a common Roman cognomen, borne by one emperor. It is the adoptive form of the Roman gentile name Valerius, indicating that the bearer has been adopted into the Valerian gens.
Valerio   In CB, a Zingaran fencing master. From Valerius (q.v.).
Valerius   In WB, a young Khaurani soldier; in CC, an Aquilonian noble. A Roman gentile name.
Valkia   In CC, a river and its valley in eastern Aquilonia. Possibly from Valkyrie (Old Norse *valkyrja*), in Norse mythology one of Oðin's maidens. Valka, a god mentioned in the Kull stories, is probably from the same source.
Valusia   In TE, CB, RZ, and the Kull stories, a kingdom of Atlantean times. The place name Volusia (possibly connected with the Volusci or Volsci of ancient Italy) occurs in New York State and Florida.
Vammatar   In LD, the queen of Haloga. In the *Kalevala,* the daughter of evil.

Vanaheim   In FD, TT, PS, &c., a northern land, west of Asgard. In Norse mythology, the home of the Vanir (q.v.).

Vancho   In CB, the first officer of Zarono's *Petrel*. From the Spanish name Sancho.

Vanir   In FD, QC, TC, &c., the people of Vanaheim (q.v.). In Norse mythology, a class of deities (singular Vanr or Van) originally of fertility and later of weather, agriculture, and commerce.

Varanna (=Velitrium)   In first draft of BR; discarded. Probably from the same source as Valannus (q.v.).

Vardan   In CA, a Turanian soldier. A common Persian name (Greek Ouardanes, Latin Vardanes), borne by various Parthian and Armenian kings.

Vardanes   In BT, a Zamorian adventurer. From the same source as Vardan (q.v.).

Varuna   In BN, a god invoked by Conan. The creator-god of ancient Brahmanism.

Vateesa   In BC, SD, a Khorajan lady. Probably from Vanessa, a name constructed by Dean Swift from that of his sweetheart Esther Vanhomrigh.

Vathathas .   In first draft of BC, a legendary king of thieves; discarded. Possibly from the same source as Vathelos (q.v.).

Vathelos, Vezek   Respectively the blind author of magical books in BC and a Turanian outpost in WB. Possibly from Vathek, William Beckford's spelling of the name of the Caliph Wathiq (+IX), in Beckford's Gothic novel of that name (1786).

Velitrium   In BR, MB, a frontier city on the western borders of Aquilonia. From Velitrae (modern Vellitri), Italy.

Venara (=Venarium, q.v.)   In first draft of BR; discarded.

Venarium   A frontier fort in Gunderland referred to in BR; probably from Virunum, capital of Roman Noricum, near modern Klagenfurt, Austria.

Vendhya   In WB, PC, TT, &c., a land to the far southeast, corresponding to modern India. From the

Vindhya Mountains, India. The name means "rent" or "ragged," i.e., having many passes.

Ventrium (=Thenitea)   In first draft of BB; discarded. From the same source as Venarium (q.v.).

Verulia   A kingdom of Atlantean times, mentioned in "The Hyborian Age." Probably from Verulamium, a Romano-British town, later Verulam; near modern St. Albans.

Veziz Shah   In CA, a Turanian city governor. From Vezir, the Arabic ministerial title, and Shah (q.v.).

Vilayet   In SM, DI, BR, &c., an inland sea east of Turan, corresponding to the modern Caspian (also in former times called the Hyrcanian Sea and the Sea of Ghel). Turkish for "province."

Vilerus   In DT, a former king of Aquilonia. Probably from Valerius (q.v.).

Villagro   In CB, the duke of Kordava. A pseudo-Spanish name.

Vinashko   In RE, a chief of the Yuetshi. From Kanishka, a Yüe-Chi or Kushana king in India, c. +100.

Virata   In FK, a Kosalan magus of Yanaidar. The king of Matsya in the *Mahâbhârata*.

Virunians   In LW, a people of Hyperborean descent dwelling in the Border Kingdom. From Virunum (*see* Venarium).

Vladislav   *See* Olgerd. A Russian proper name.

Voivode   In WB, the title of the mercenary captain Constantius. A title of medieval Slavic generals and governors and of Romanian princes.

Volmana   In PS, an Aquilonian noble. Possibly from the Vomano River, Italy.

Wadai   In SZ, a Negro country. A part of the Republic of Chad, Africa; formerly, a powerful black kingdom in that area, conquered by the French in 1908–12.

Wakla   In CA, a Turanian fort in the Zuagir desert. Originally "Whagra," from the verb "wager."

Wamadzi   In CA, a Himelian tribe.

Wazuli   In PC, a Himelian tribe. From the Wazirs,

a Pakhtun tribe of Pakistan. Burroughs used Waziri as the name of an African tribe.

Westermarck   In BB, MB, the borderland between Bossonia and Pictland. From "western" and "mark," an old variant of "march" in the sense of "border."

Wigurs   In CA, a tribe of Hyrkanian nomads. From the Uigurs, for which *see* Kuigars.

Wodan   In WB, Conan's horse. From the North European creator-god, Oðin, Odin, or Wotan.

Wuhuan   In CA, a desert west of Khitai. A pseudo-Chinese name.

Wulfhere   In FD, an Æsir chief. An old Saxon name, meaning "wolf army," borne by a pious +VII king of Mercia. Also a character in the stories of Howard's Dark Age hero, Cormac Mac Art.

Xag   In first draft of DI, the Yuetshi fisherman; discarded.

Xaltotun   In CC, CA, BN, an Acheronian wizard. Probably from Xulun, Mexico.

Xapur   In TE, an island in the Sea of Vilayet. Probably from Shahpur (q.v.).

Xatmec   In RN, a man of Xuchotl. A pseudo-Aztec name.

Xotalanc   In RN, one of the feuding clans of Xuchotl. Probably from Xicalanco, Mexico.

Xotli   In CI, the devil-god of Antillia. A pseudo-Aztec name.

Xuthal, Xuthol   In SS, a city south of the kingdom of Kush. The former spelling is Howard's; the latter appears only on Kyle's end-paper maps for the Gnome Press editions of the Conan stories.

Yag   In TE, SC, a distant planet; also a place (spelled "Yagg") in Howard's novel *Almuric*.

Yagkoolan   An expletive in SM, SC. Possibly from Yaxchilan, Guatemala, a city of the so-called Mayan Old Empire on the Usumacinta River.

Yag-Kosha or Yogah   In TE, an elephant-headed native of the planet Yag (q.v.). *See* Khrosha.

Yah Chieng In CA, a Khitan magician. A pseudo-Chinese name. From the names of the Chinese leaders Sun Yat-sen and Chiang Kai-shek.

Yajur In SZ, FK, a god of Kosala. From Yajur-Veda, a section of the Vedas (Hindu scriptures) dealing with ritual.

Yakov In CI, a Zaporoskan pirate in the Barachas. A Russian name, cognate with "Jacob."

Yama In CS, the Meruvian creator-god. In Hindu myth, the god of the underworld.

Yamad Al-Aphta In CA, a name of Conan among the Zuagirs. From the villain Jamal in the movie *Sinbad the Sailor* (with Douglas Fairbanks, Jr.) and the Arabic definite article *al*, and "Aphta" from "naptha."

Yanaidar In FK, a sinister city in the Ilbars Mts. From Janaidar, a legendary city in Central Asia.

Yanak In CA, a Vilayet pirate. From *Kanaka*, Polynesian for a native man.

Yanyoga In SH, the stronghold of the Valusian serpent-folk south of Kush.

Yar *See* Alafdal. A Pakhtun name.

Yar Allal In CA, a Zuagir.

Yaralet In HN, a city in Turan. Probably from Tokalet, an abandoned Berber city in the western Sahara.

Yasala In RN, a woman of Xuchotl.

Yasmela, Yasmina Respectively the queen regent of Khoraja in BC, KD, and the Devi of Vendhya in PC, CA. From the Arabic *yasmin*, "jasmine," whence the feminine names.

Yasunga In CC, a Negro galley slave; in CI, a black Barachan pirate.

Yateli In DI, a Dagonian girl.

Yelaya In JG, IG, the long-dead princess of Alkmeenon. Possibly from the Spanish surname Zelaya, e.g., José Santos Zelaya, dictator of Nicaragua, 1893–1909.

Yelba River In CA, a stream in southwestern Turan. From the German *gelb*, "yellow."

Yezdigerd   In DI, PC, CA, &c., the king of Turan. From Yazdegerd or Yezdjird, the name of three Sassanid kings of Persia, +IV to +VII.

Yezm   In FK, the eponym of a cult of assassins in the Ilbars Mts.

Yezud   In HD, TC, PC, a city in Zamora where a spider-god is worshiped. Possibly from the Yezidis or "devil-worshipers," a Mazdean sect among the Kurds of Armenia and the Caucasus.

Yig   In RZ, a god of the serpent-men of Valusia. From H. P. Lovecraft's story "The Curse of Yig" (with Zealia Bishop).

Yildiz   In SM, HN, CM, &c., the king of Turan, the predecessor of Yezdigerd. From *yildiz*, Turkish for "star," used in Turkey as a woman's name (but never as a man's), and also commercially: Yildiz Construction Co. &c. Howard probably got the name from the Yıldız Palace in Istanbul. (The Turkish letter ı stands for a vowel between those of "pit" and "put.")

Yimsha   In PC, CA, the mountain stronghold of the Black Circle. Possibly from Yashma, in Soviet Azerbaijan.

Yin Allal   In CA, a Zuagir chief. A pseudo-Arabic name, suggested by "Allah."

Yizil   In PC, a god or demon. Probably from the Turkish *kizil*, "red," which appears in many geographical names.

Ymir   In FD, PS, SC, a supernatural giant. In Norse mythology, a primeval giant.

Yo La-Gu   In CA, a Khitan soldier. A pseudo-Chinese name.

Yog   In DI, a Zamboulan god.

Yogah   *See* Yag-Kosha. In Howard's novel *Almuric*, Yogh is the name of a river.

Yota-Pong   In JG, a place in Kosala referred to.

Yothga   In SC, a magical plant.

Yuetshi   In DI, RE, a primitive tribe living around the southern end of the Sea of Vilayet. From the Yüe-Chi or Kushana, a Turko-Tatar people that conquered an Indian empire in +I.

Yukkub   In CA, a Turanian city. Possibly from *kub*, Swedish for "cube."

Yun   In TE, a Khitan god.

Zabhela   A coastal place mentioned in RN. Possibly from the same source as Zargheba (q.v.).

Zahak   In FK, a Hyrkanian captain in Yanaidar. A demon in Persian mythology, also Zohak and Dahaka.

Zaheemi   In BC, a clan living near the Pass of Shamla.

Zal   In BG, a Zamorian. In Persian legend, Rustam's father.

Zamboula   In SZ, SK, TT, a city in the southeastern deserts. From Stamboul, a French spelling of Istanbul, the former Constantinople or Byzantium.

Zamora   In TE, QC, SM, &c., an ancient kingdom east of the Hyborian lands. A town and a province in Spain, also used as a Spanish surname.

Zang   In WB, a priest.

Zapayo Da Kova   In DT, the commander of the mercenary force that invades Stygia. "Zapayo" is pseudo-Spanish; "Da Kova" is possibly from Reginald De Koven, an American composer (*Robin Hood*, 1900).

Zaporavo, Zaporoska   Respectively a Zingaran pirate captain in PO and a Hyrkanian river in WB, CA. From "Zaporogian," which comes from the Russian *zaporozhets*, "beyond the rapids," used in +XVI and +XVII to designate the Dniepr Cossacks.

Zarallo   In RN, the chief of a band of mercenaries in Stygian service. Possibly from the Spanish surname Zorilla.

Zaramba   In IG, the chief priest of Punt.

Zargheba, Zarkheba   Respectively a Shemitish adventurer in JG, IG, and a southern river in QC. Possibly from Zariba, Arabia.

Zarono   In CB, TT, CI, a Zingaran buccaneer captain. A pseudo-Spanish name.

Zebah   In CA, a name assumed by the leader of a band of Zuagir raiders. From Sheba or Sabaea in southern Arabia.

Zelata   In CC, an Aquilonian wise woman. Possibly from the Spanish surname Zelaya (cf. Yelaya).

Zeltran   In CB, the first officer of Conan's *Wastrel*. From the Franco-Spanish surname Beltran.

Zelvar Af   In CA, a Himelian hunter. From Halvar, a common Scandinavian name, and Af, a made-up syllable.

Zembabwei, Zimbabwe   In JG, WM, RZ, &c., a black kingdom. (The first spelling is used in JG; the second in "The Hyborian Age.") From Zimbabwe, a ruined fortified town in Rhodesia, first built about 1,300 years ago and used in +XVIII and early +XIX as the capital of the Monomotapa Empire. The name was used again by Howard in the form "Zambabwei" in a story, "The Grisly Horror," in *Weird Tales* for Feb. 1935. Although this tale was laid in the United States, it alluded to Zambabwei as a place in Africa where people were sacrificed to a man-eating ape.

Zenobia   In CC, WM, BN, &c., a Nemedian girl wedded by Conan. The Greek version of the name of Septimia Bath-Zabbai or Bat-Sabdai, queen of Palmyra in +III.

Zeriti   In HS, the witch-mistress of King Akhîrom. A pseudo-Egyptian name.

Zhaibar   In PC, CA, a pass northwest of Vendhya into the Himelian Mts. From the Khaibar (Khyber) Pass in Pakistan. Howard's description closely follows Talbot Mundy's account of the Khyber Pass in *King of the Khyber Rifles*.

Zhemri   In "The Hyborian Age," HD, a people surviving from Atlantean times to become the Zamorians.

Zhurazi Archipelago   In CA, a group of islands in the Vilayet Sea.

Zikamba River   In CB, a stream in Kush. A pseudo-Bantu name.

Zillah   In BT, the daughter of Enosh of Akhlat. A biblical name (Gen. 4:19).

Zingara   In QC, WB, BR, &c., a southwestern maritime kingdom. Italian for "Gypsy." (Cf. Gitara.) The name is probably also connected with Zalgara, a hill region mentioned in the Kull stories.

Zingelito   In TT, a Zingaran. A pseudo-Spanish name.

Zingg   In "The Hyborian Age," the valley in which the nation of Zingara (q.v.) arose. A remote possibility is a connection with the Zing or Zinj, a Sudanese people mentioned by the medieval Muslim writer Mas'ûdi.

Zlanath   In RN, a man of Xuchotl.

Zogar Sag   In BR, MB, a Pictish wizard.

Zorathus   In CC, a Kothic merchant. Probably from Zaratas, a Greek form of Zoroaster (Old Persian Zarathushtra, modern Zardusht).

Zosara   In CS, CM, the daughter of King Yildiz of Turan. The Greek spelling of Zeresh, wife of Haman in the Book of Esther.

Zuagirs   In WB, SZ, RN, &c., Shemitish nomads dwelling in the eastern deserts. Probably from the Shagia (Shaigiya, Shaikiyeh), a tribe of Egyptian Arabs, and the Zouia or Zuia, a tribe of Libyan Arabs.

Zuagros   In first draft of SZ, Conan's destination at the end of the story; discarded. From the same source as Zuagirs (q.v.) + the Zagros Mts. of western Iran.

Zugites   In BC, an ancient and degraded Stygian cult.

Zuru   In CB, a Ghanata slaver. A chief of the Ngoni of East Africa in +XIX.

Zurvan   In CB, a deity of the Mitran pantheon. From Zarvan or Zarwan, in Zoroastrianism a personification of time.

Zyras   In BG, a Corinthian. A pseudo-Greek name.

ABOUT THE AUTHORS

L. SPRAGUE DE CAMP is well known for his fantasies, science popularizations and historical novels as well as his work in the science fiction world. His work appeared in many of the science fiction magazines of the 1930s, including *Astounding* and *The Magazine of Fantasy and Science Fiction*. De Camp has also worked on unfinished manuscripts of Robert E. Howard and, with Lin Carter, created new Conan stories. He is the author of *The Science Fiction Handbook*, a guide for writers on how to plot, write and sell science fiction.

LIN CARTER is a writer and editor of fantasy. Born in 1930, he became a regular contributor to the fan magazines before taking up writing as a career. He completed a number of Howard's unfinished drafts and has collaborated with L. Sprague de Camp in producing new *Conan* stories. He has compiled several fantasy anthologies and is the creator of the *Thongor* series.

BJÖRN NYBERG is a business executive who lives in France. He began collaborating with L. Sprague de Camp on *Conan* stories in the mid-1950s.

CONAN
CONTINUES!

CONAN THE SWORDSMAN is just the first of at least six new, authentic Conan action adventure books to be published by Bantam. These authorized editions from the Robert E. Howard estate are being written by L. Sprague de Camp, Lin Carter and Björn Nyberg; and Karl Edward Wagner. Every one of them will contain maps and illustrations of weapons and artifacts created by the famous Tim Kirk.

LOOK FOR CONAN #2

THE ROAD OF KINGS by Karl Edward Wagner. While in his early twenties, Conan comes to Kordava, capital of the Hyborian Kingdom of Zingara. The capital city, ruled by the aging despot King Rimanendo, is seething with conspiracies and plots. Yet young Conan enlists in Zingara's mercenary army. After a bloody fight to the death with an evil officer, he is thrown in jail and sentenced to die. However, just as he is about to be executed, he is rescued by a small, hardy band of revolutionaries. Conan joins with Mordermi and a renegade Stygian sorcerer to help the band overthrow the King. After many furious battles they are successful, and Mordermi is crowned King. But it is only a matter of time before Conan realizes that Mordermi is just as evil as the former King . . . and he plots a daring revenge.

COMING IN 1979

Watch for CONAN THE LIBERATOR #3 in 1979 followed by three more originals.

All Conan books will be available in Bantam editions, wherever paperbacks are sold.

Bantam Book Catalog

Here's your up-to-the-minute listing of every book currently available from Bantam.

This easy-to-use catalog is divided into categories and contains over 1400 titles by your favorite authors.

So don't delay—take advantage of this special opportunity to increase your reading pleasure.

Just send us your name and address and 25¢ (to help defray postage and handling costs).